PRAISE FOR THE NOVELS OF GREGORY HARRIS!

THE DALWICH DESECRATION

"One of my favorite Victorian mystery authors. The author's research into the era is impeccable."

—*Historical Novels Review*

THE BELLINGHAM BLOODBATH

"A terrific story . . . both storylines come together in perfect symmetry, making for an incredibly pleasing mystery. The author nails it yet again!"

—*Suspense Magazine*

THE ARNIFOUR AFFAIR

"Colin has Holmes's arrogance, but is dimpled and charming, while Ethan is a darker Watson. . . . [T]he relationship between the leads is discreetly intriguing."

—*Kirkus Reviews*

"Pendragon matches Sherlock Holmes in his arrogance. . . . [H]e is redeemed, in part, by his brains and his gentle treatment of Pruitt."

—*Publishers Weekly*

"The mystery is extremely well done, the characters carefully drawn, and the story moves quickly to a satisfying conclusion."

—*Washington Independent Review of Books*

Books by Gregory Harris

THE ARNIFOUR AFFAIR

THE BELLINGHAM BLOODBATH

THE CONNICLE CURSE

THE DALWICH DESECRATION

THE ENDICOTT EVIL

Published by Kensington Publishing Corporation

THE ENDICOTT EVIL

A Colin Pendragon Mystery

GREGORY HARRIS

KENSINGTON BOOKS

www.kensingtonbooks.com

KENSINGTON BOOKS are published by

Kensington Publishing Corp.
119 West 40th Street
New York, NY 10018

All Kensington titles, imprints, and distributed lines are available at special quantity discounts for bulk purchases for sales promotion, premiums, fund-raising, educational, or institutional use.

Special book excerpts or customized printings can also be created to fit specific needs. For details, write or phone the office of the Kensington Sales Manager: Kensington Publishing Corp., 119 West 40th Street, New York, NY 10018. Attn. Sales Department. Phone: 1-800-221-2647.

Kensington and the K logo Reg. U.S. Pat. & TM Off.

eISBN-13: 978-1-61773-890-6
eISBN-10: 1-61773-890-5
First Kensington Electronic Edition: April 2017

ISBN-13: 978-1-61773-889-0
ISBN-10: 1-61773-889-1
First Kensington Trade Paperback Printing: April 2017

10 9 8 7 6 5 4 3 2 1

Printed in the United States of America

For Karen Clemens

and

Melissa Gelineau

*Two tireless champions to whom
I owe a deep debt of gratitude*

CHAPTER 1

Eugenia Endicott was diminutive of height, stout of figure, and furious of face. Her thinning, silvery-white hair was pulled tight in a small roll at the back of her head that attested to the fineness of what hair she had left. Her austere black dress was wholly unadorned just as one would suspect for a woman in mourning, though she was not wearing the expression of one overcome by the burden of grief and horror at the sudden murder of her elder sister, Adelaide. That she was the only person who currently believed her sister murdered certainly explained some of the rage coloring her face—the Yard had as much as told her that an old woman tumbling out an upper-story window was hardly a concern of theirs—but it was the implication that Miss Adelaide could have done such a thing willfully that left Eugenia Endicott looking ready to claw Colin and me to shreds with her bare hands.

"Your insinuation is offensive, Mr. Pendragon," she was stating from her position in the doorway to her sister's room, her lips curled back as though she had come upon something rotting and foul, and I supposed she felt that she had. "The Endicott family has faultlessly served the Crown and Commonwealth for hundreds of years without the slightest whisper of scandal, and yet here you are, ferreting about in my poor sister's private quarters on a mission to decree whether or not she might have purposefully contributed to the end of her own life. It is unconscionable."

Colin turned toward Miss Eugenia from the casement window he had been carefully inspecting, the window Miss Adelaide's personal footman, Freddie Nettle, had been the sole witness to her falling from three nights prior. It was that event that had brought him to our door, begging us to prove his innocence in the face of Miss Eugenia's immediate allegations against him. "You do me a great injustice," Colin said quite simply. "I have not come to prove anyone's theory. Your Mr. Nettle may have retained my services, but you may rest assured that I am here only to uncover the truth, wherever that may lead. It is what I do."

"He is not my Mr. Nettle," she fired back. "He served my sister at her request, not mine. I never liked the man. What kind of name is *Nettle* anyway?"

Colin's left eyebrow arced toward the ceiling. "Tell me"—he continued to speak with uncharacteristic patience—"is there some reason you believe he would have taken your sister's life?"

"How the devil would I know that?! I am sure there is no explaining the mind of a deviant. Surely you would understand that better than any of us, Mr. Pendragon, given your unseemly line of work."

Colin allowed a thin smile to fleet across his lips. "I have found the reasons that compel those who commit terrible crimes to be as complex and fundamental as that which drives the rest of us. It can be a razor's edge. . . ."

"Spare me." She bit out the words with the wave of a hand. "My sister was infirm, Mr. Pendragon. She could not walk. Mr. Nettle's sole function was to either push her about in her wheeled chair or carry her, as the circumstances necessitated. He brought her down every morning and took her up every night, doing as she bid on all but her most intimate needs. Adelaide had two nurses who shared duties in attending to such chores for her. But it was Mr. Nettle who slept in my sister's anteroom, not the nurse, though I was never settled with that arrangement," she added with noticeable distaste. "So how do you suppose Adelaide made it all the way from her bed to that . . . *window. . . .*" She said the word as though it were something indecent. "Mr. Nettle's claim that she did so on her own is preposterous and meant to cast doubt on his own disreputable character."

"Could she not support herself on her feet at all?" Colin pressed. "Is it not possible that she might have been able to hold on to the wall and make her way forward?"

Miss Eugenia's expression disintegrated even further. "I will not quibble with you about the state of my sister's ability to move."

"Of course not," Colin answered, his patience beginning to show signs of fracturing. "But Mr. Nettle states that he was woken in the middle of the night by your sister's screams, and when he rushed into her room it was to find her already by the window. Is it truly not possible—" But he got no further before Miss Eugenia blasted over him.

"I *know* what he claims. He *claims* that she unlatched the window and threw herself to the cobbles below before he could even attempt to reach her. She was eighty-three years old, Mr. Pendragon. Mr. Nettle is barely out of his twenties. Do you really believe such a story merits so much as a whisper of consideration?" She spoke in a tone that was harsh and acerbic, leaving no doubt as to precisely how she felt.

"I will not deny that his tale would seem to stretch the boundaries of credulity and sense, yet I can assure you that I have come upon equally implausible events over the years. And I have very often found that such events are not only explicable, but many times will lead to the very heart of the case itself."

She curled her heavily lined face into a most disapproving pucker. "This is not a *case*, Mr. Pendragon." Once again she was able to say a word as though it were foul and untoward. "It is the murder of my sister at the hands of a malevolent rogue. And you may be certain that I take great umbrage at your willingness to come here and root about my sister's room, giving credence to what that man has said against her."

"Miss Endicott—" Colin started to say, his own voice edging toward a tightness that concerned me, before being interrupted again as though he had not even taken a breath.

"I have known your family since long before you were born. Your mother . . . God rest her soul . . . was an outspoken and headstrong woman, but she would be scandalized to find her son here on such a devil's errand. As will your father when I inform him."

The muscles in Colin's jaw clenched as his eyes went dark and steely, and I knew he was about to say something regrettable. "Miss Endicott . . ." I blurted before Colin could have a chance to say anything. "It would seem that Mr. Pendragon and I have been unforgivably insensitive." I nearly choked on the lie as I forced it past my lips, but was determined to avoid a surly visit from Colin's father demanding to know why we had so agitated a genteel spinster in the midst of her grieving; a spinster whose younger brother just happened to be a senior member of the House of Lords. "It is not our intention to suggest that your sister inflicted any sort of injury upon herself," I insisted, keeping my voice low and steady as I locked my gaze on hers and hoped that Colin would remain silent. "We would never presume to sully either your sister's memory or the reputation of the Endicott family itself. We mean only to ensure that the facts are appropriately gathered so that the scoundrel responsible is made to pay for his actions as he should, whether that might be Mr. Nettle or another."

She stared back at me and I could tell she was trying to gauge the depth of my sincerity as she did so. It took a long moment, but she finally relented, though in a notably begrudging way. "I suppose you have something of a point," she said, flipping her hand glibly as if I were just another domestic to be dismissed. "Scotland Yard *has* been woefully inadequate in responding to my insistence that they charge Mr. Nettle. It is appalling that everyone seems so content to believe that a righteous, God-fearing woman would harm herself." She shook her head and her expression soured. "It is really most unsavory."

"I'm afraid the Yard has its hands full with countless other cases," I pointed out, "so when a death occurs that would seem to be as straightforward as that of your sister . . ."

"*Straightforward?!*" she barked.

"I meant only in its cause," I hastily added, desperate not to lose her dollop of goodwill. "Mr. Nettle appears to have told them a tale that they feel both sound and believable, which allows them to close one file without any undue fuss. They don't have the wherewithal to realize that there might indeed be a great deal more at hand here. That perhaps there is some reason why Mr. Nettle would wish to harm your sister." I continued to watch her to see if my supposition had struck a note, but her face remained unreadable behind its discontent.

"Well, of course there would be reasons," she sallied back after another moment, but did not elaborate.

"It is also possible"—Colin spoke up, and I could tell by the evenness in his tone that he had settled himself again—"that Mr. Nettle is mistaken about what he believes he saw. After all, he admits to having been awakened from a sound sleep. Without so much as a candle in hand, how can he be certain of anything that happened? For all we know, Miss Adelaide herself was disoriented and simply lost her balance. . . ." He let his voice trail off.

"Oh . . ." Miss Eugenia caught her breath, one hand flying up to her mouth, and I realized that, like me, this was a possibility she had not conceived of. "Oh . . ." she repeated as she came into the room and nearly fell into one of the chairs just inside. "But could you ever prove such a thing?" And for the first time since our arrival she sounded almost contrite and dismayed.

"The truth can often be elusive, but it is never fickle." Colin flashed the barest of grins. "I believe it can be found whenever one seeks it with an open mind."

Miss Eugenia exhaled in a slow, arduous way, as though it had come from deep within. "Yes," she finally said. "I can see that I owe my sister better than the possible folly of my indignation over the perceived cause of her death. While I have never held

Mr. Nettle in any esteem, neither do I wish to see him castigated for no greater reason than one moment's foolish misperception."

"There you are then." Colin gave a slight nod. "We are all intent on the same resolution."

"You have a most peculiar way of saying things," Miss Eugenia noted as her spine stiffened and her eyes once more assumed a stern cast. "I do believe I prefer the finer considerations of your point of view, Mr. . . ." She turned to me and her face went blank, and I knew she had no memory of my name. And so it ever was.

"Pruitt . . ." I said with a smile, "Ethan Pruitt."

"Pruitt . . ." she repeated in a vague sort of way. "Why does that name sound familiar? Did your family come from Coventry?"

"No. We were from Leeds. Sheep farmers before my grandfather began working in the printing trade. My father was the first from his family to settle in London. He eventually became the Deputy Minister of Education," I heard myself brag before realizing what a dangerous wire I was walking.

"Oh . . ." Miss Eugenia sucked in a startled breath as she leaned away from me, her ramrod posture accentuating what was clearly a desire to put space between the two of us. "Are you referring to John Pruitt? Was John Pruitt your father?"

I cursed myself for having said too much. "He was," I answered stiffly, knowing what would come next.

"How . . . unfortunate," she said, her eyes darting away from me even as her face pinched with distaste. "Such a sordid end and all of it trundled out in the *Times*. It's a wonder you didn't move to the Continent. I can see why you understand how unacceptable it would be for the Endicott name to suffer any such similar stain."

"We seem to have traveled quite far afield from the topic at hand." Colin spoke up before I could even fathom how to respond. "Do we have your consent to continue our investigation into your sister's death?"

"You have better than that," she replied as she pushed herself back to her feet. "I shall hire you myself for just that purpose. And should you come to discover that my dear Adelaide did indeed suffer a terrible accident"—she let out a stilted breath—"then it shall be thus. But if you uncover the specter of malfeasance, then I will insist you persevere with Scotland Yard until they fulfill their rightful obligation by arresting that duplicitous Mr. Nettle." She nearly spit the man's name as if it were caustic or barbed in her throat.

I was so surprised by this sudden turn of events that I found myself quite at a loss for words and so it was Colin who responded first. "Yes," he managed to say quite effortlessly. "It is likely to be one or the other." Colin flashed her a mirthless smile that Miss Eugenia seemed quite content to accept as she started for the door.

"I hope you will join me for some tea in the drawing room once you have finished here," she said, turning back in the doorway and giving us a smile as forced and fleeting as Colin's had been. She did not wait for our answer before turning and leaving the room.

"I believe that is the first time I have ever heard your mother's memory exploited in order to get you to do something. . . ." I remarked as soon as I knew Miss Eugenia was well gone. "Does she really imagine you to be so difficult?"

Colin gave a sly shrug. "Well, she has known me all of my life." He released a soft chuckle before abruptly waving a hand through the air as if to dismiss her as nothing more than a pestering insect buzzing about our ears, which is precisely what I knew he meant. "I told you before there was good reason she has always been a spinster." He turned back to the window and shoved both sides of it wide open, and then leaned out and began running his fingers along the wood casement. "I always found Adelaide a gentle soul if slightly potty in her thinking," he continued as he sat down on the sill, his broad shoulders not quite fitting between the mullion and the jamb so that he had to turn slightly sideways before he could stretch farther out and slide his hands along the smooth stones of the building itself. "But Eugenia was always just this side of intolerable."

"And Lord Endicott?" I could not stop myself from asking. "Which of his sisters is he most like?"

Colin swung back inside and quickly turned onto his belly,

leaning back out in such a precarious way that I felt compelled to go over and grab his waistband for safety. "This is hardly the time to become spirited," he smirked over his shoulder.

"You're not funny. I only thought it best not to lose two people out this window."

He pushed himself back inside. "If I tumbled out that window, the only thing I think you would have saved was my trousers." He stood up and brushed himself off, nodding toward the gaping window. "Have a feel of the jamb along the outside. See if you notice anything."

I thought perhaps he was jesting at first, intending to get me dangling three floors above the ground just to rattle me, but there was earnestness in his expression and I realized that he was being perfectly serious. So, like the dutiful pupil, I did as he requested, finding myself leaning outside and struggling to keep my eyes from focusing on the cobbles three floors below. With my heart in my throat I reached down and ran my fingers along the bottom of the jamb. It took a moment, but I began to realize that there was a fairly regular pattern of pitting all along the jamb and up the vertical mullion that divided the window. I did not feel it nearly as distinctly on the window's head or sill, but it was quite distinct in the other areas. "What are those little nicks?" I asked as I gratefully ducked back inside. "It feels like a woodpecker has been searching for a meal up here."

"That's a rather fitting way of describing it," he muttered as he took my place leaning out the window before reaching around to shove the other side shut and quickly running his fingers along its outside jamb and rail. "It is something of a curiosity, wouldn't you say?" He hopped off the sill and reversed his position, pushing open the closed window and tugging the other one shut. Once again he slid his fingers along the jamb and rails of the closed window before popping up and stepping away. "A woodpecker . . ." he chuckled under his breath and I suddenly felt unaccountably foolish.

"What is it? What are you thinking?" I pressed.

He tossed me a rogue's grin and headed for the door. "We

shall have a look around downstairs and then we will know for sure. Come now, we mustn't keep Miss Eugenia waiting. In case you hadn't noticed, she hasn't the temperament for it." He wagged a finger and snickered before disappearing out into the hallway.

Had he not made such a hasty retreat he would have seen the rolling of my eyes. I was certain he did not need to poke about downstairs to discern the reason for the pitting around the window, which left me vastly more annoyed that I too was not able to ascertain the reason for it. Twelve years trundling along in his wake and I could still feel ever the laggard.

I headed back down to the foyer and was met at the bottom of the main staircase by a tall, elegant footman with sandy hair and a short, bushy mustache, who tipped a subtle nod to me without deigning to make eye contact. "Right this way, please," he said in a brusquely formal tone, and I realized he had been set there for no other purpose than to escort me to Miss Eugenia's drawing room. I wondered if someone had been posted for Colin as well and discovered that to be the case as another footman crossed our path heading the opposite direction just as I was bidden into a large, sunny room near the back of the home.

"Thank you . . ." I started to say, but the man had already moved off.

I entered the room to find Miss Eugenia on one settee with Colin seated across from her, a pretty, young woman in a pristine maid's uniform dispensing items onto the table between the two of them from a delicate rolling tea cart. She set out several platters covered with finger sandwiches and a three-tiered pastry tray brimming with a decadent assortment of cakes, tartlets, and biscuits. I had not seen such an enticing display since our work for Lady Nesbitt-Normand.

The young maid moved with exceptional grace as she swiftly poured the tea and handed it out with exceeding crispness before preparing a small plate with a mixture of triangular sandwiches for each of us. "Will there be anything else, mum?" she asked.

"No," Miss Eugenia answered indifferently, and then seemed

to think better of it by the time the young woman reached the doorway. "Emily," she called to her. "Send Mr. Galloway in, will you? And do tell him we have visitors."

"Yes, mum," the young woman replied and was gone.

"Mr. Galloway is my house steward," she explained. "He knows everything that goes on here and is likely to save you a good deal of time and effort. All the better," she enunciated sharply, "to get this business behind us and Mr. Nettle a proper rope cravat."

Colin sucked in a tight breath. "I really am curious as to why you are so certain that Mr. Nettle would have harmed your sister. Was there an issue between them? Does he perhaps stand to inherit something of value?"

Miss Eugenia looked quite horrified at the suggestion. "Certainly not. How terribly improper."

"Nevertheless, it does happen," he needled, and I feared he was simply trying to agitate her again.

"I am quite certain all manner of indecencies happen on a regular basis," she shot back, "but that hardly makes them acceptable. Really, Mr. Pendragon, you seem quite determined to vex me."

Colin's eyebrows rose in unison and all I could see was mock innocence. "Oh my," he managed to say with earnestness. "Then I owe you an apology, for I do not mean to do any such thing. My only intent is to implore you to consider two critical questions as we seek the truth of what happened to your sister. If Mr. Nettle is truly the villain you believe him to be, then what did he have to gain by murdering your sister? And why would he then come to hire me to prove his innocence? Surely he could not imagine himself clever enough to deceive me?!" He gave a slight chuckle. "After all, I am not known for being easily misled."

"Any man who believes himself beyond the capacity to be fooled has already revealed himself to *be* a fool," she snapped back. "And do you not suppose that a man who means to deceive might not purposefully seek you out for the express purpose of making his innocence seem that much more apparent?" She sniffed resolutely as she took a sip of tea. "That, Mr. Pendragon, is something I would implore *you* to consider."

I was so stunned by her response that I momentarily found myself speechless. Only after I realized that Colin's reply was not apt to be pleasant was I finally able to tear my eyes from Miss Eugenia's face to check on the state of his imminent reaction. To my amazement, I found a slow smile creeping onto his face as he too sipped his tea. "You are a clever woman, Miss Endicott," he said at length, "and I pity the man who tries to get the better of you."

"Such a man would deserve no pity from you or any other. Now . . ." She set her cup down with great purpose and settled back, eyeing us closely, clearly well pleased at having made her point. "How exactly are you going to carry out your investigation? And how long is it likely to take? I shall see justice done and will not take the chance that Mr. Nettle might vanish while you fiddle about trying to gauge his guilt or innocence."

"I can assure you that our investigation has already begun," Colin answered, his tone having taken on an abruptly sober note. "And should we determine someone guilty of foul play, you may be certain that person will be made to pay for the crime. Mr. Pruitt and I are not in the habit of allowing criminals to simply evaporate," he added emphatically, and I knew he was referring to his own continuing outrage at Charlotte Hutton having accomplished precisely that at the end of the Connicle case. She had disappeared just as Colin made the first arrest for that string of murders, at the very moment when her complicity was on the verge of being revealed. He blamed the Yard for the blunder—and they *were* supposed to have been watching her—but he took the stain against his own reputation nonetheless. She remained the only person he had failed to bring to justice in the whole of his career.

"Very well," Miss Eugenia finally allowed with an irritable sniff. "See that you succeed or I shall bring the whole of Victoria's empire down upon your brow, your good father be damned."

I watched Colin's eyes narrow with fury and knew the boundaries of his goodwill had finally been breached.

"Madam . . . ?"

A male voice thankfully interrupted the conversation as I swung my gaze to the doorway and found a tall, dark-haired, middle-aged man with a raven's nose and doughy features standing at attention as though he were a member of the Queen's Guard. This, I knew at once, had to be the aforementioned Mr. Galloway, as he was dressed in formal attire topped by a dove-gray morning coat. I could not have been happier to see him even if he had come to confess tossing Miss Adelaide to her death. For there was no doubt in my mind that his sudden presence was the only thing that was keeping Colin and Eugenia Endicott from tipping into a most disagreeable abyss.

"Do come in, Mr. Galloway," Miss Eugenia commanded as she freshened our tea. "Mr. Pendragon . . . Mr. Pruitt . . . this is Mr. Galloway, to whom I must give credit for keeping my house and my life in impeccable order at all times. If he does not know about something, then you may be certain it did not happen." She handed him the tiered pastry tray and he dutifully passed it between Colin and me without paying the slightest heed to the delicacies upon it. "These two men," she addressed Mr. Galloway, "are now working for me to determine whether it might be possible that my dear Adelaide could have suffered some sort of tragic accident rather than been a victim of that vile murderer Mr. Nettle."

If Mr. Galloway was surprised by her statement he did not show it in the least, merely nodding once and answering, "Very good, madam."

"Feel free to ask him anything at all, Mr. Pendragon," Miss Eugenia said, leveling her gaze on Colin in what felt more like a challenge than an invitation.

Colin flashed the barest hint of a smile as he locked eyes with her. "While there is a great deal I wish to know, I would much prefer to speak with Mr. Galloway, as well as the rest of your staff, individually and on their own whenever that can be arranged."

"Whatever for?"

"They need to be able to speak with the utmost frankness," I quickly answered before Colin could fling a more acerbic retort her direction. "There is always the concern that they could feel pressured or compelled to give a response that might not otherwise reflect their absolute truest opinion."

Miss Eugenia pinched her lips as she turned to me. "My staff has no reason to feel that way."

"Nevertheless . . ." I returned a warm smile and left the word to sit there on its own.

She heaved a sigh that sounded far more annoyed than tired before abruptly flicking a dismissive hand at her houseman. "Very well, then," was all she said.

"There is one question I should like to ask without delay." Colin spoke up before Mr. Galloway could evaporate. "Was the window open or closed when Miss Adelaide fell?"

"It was open, sir."

"Then she did not fall through the glass."

"No, sir."

"And yet I noticed that the pane of glass on the left side has been replaced recently." He turned and looked toward Miss Eugenia. "The putty around it is new and freshly painted."

"Yes, sir," Mr. Galloway answered in his flat, stoic way. "A bird struck that window about a fortnight ago. Sent a web of cracks through it. I had it replaced the following morning."

"Ah . . ." Colin said, giving the first genuine smile I had seen from him almost since our arrival. "Thank you. Till we speak again, Mr. Fitzroy. . . ."

Before I could correct Colin's error, Mr. Galloway had already given a quick nod and disappeared.

"How clever of you to have noticed that glass was recently replaced," Miss Eugenia said with a grudging trace of respect in her voice.

"It is part of what you have hired me to do," Colin replied as he stood up and slid his empty teacup back onto the tray. "And now I believe Mr. Pruitt and I have imposed upon you enough today. We shall begin our investigation in earnest tomorrow and will be sure to conclude it with all due haste."

"That would be most welcome, Mr. Pendragon. I cannot abide the fact that Mr. Nettle is allowed to roam freely."

"You are assuming that he will be proven guilty," Colin reminded her as he headed for the door with me close on his heels. "You must remain tolerant of all possibilities until we have concluded our examination of the events."

"Well, of course I will," she snapped back. "But I should hardly expect this inquiry of yours to take longer than a day or two. Honestly, Mr. Pendragon, I shall not sit for such a thing. My *brother* will not sit for such a thing."

Colin grimaced at her mention of Lord Endicott yet again, recognizing it for the veiled threat that it was. However, what made it worse, and what I knew lay at the crux of his reaction, was that in mentioning her brother she was also alluding to his lifelong relationship with Colin's father, Sir Atherton. And there was nothing that infuriated Colin quicker than such a coarse attempt at intimidation.

"We shall see you tomorrow then," I replied as smoothly as I could, pressing a hand into the small of Colin's back to keep him moving through the doorway. The same sandy-headed footman who'd delivered me here was still waiting out in the hall, and without a word escorted us back to the foyer.

"Would you like me to ring a cab?" he asked.

"Ring a cab?" I parroted without understanding what he was referring to.

"Madam has recently had a telephone installed," the man replied in the most perfunctory way. "I can call the livery and request to have someone drive round and pick you up. It does not always work. . . ." he added, and I was certain I caught a modicum of embarrassment in his tone.

"You needn't trouble yourself," Colin answered as he headed

outside and across the colonnaded porch that stretched the length of the massive house.

"Very well, then," the man muttered as Colin disappeared around the far corner toward the side of the home where Miss Adelaide's room was.

"He's looking for something," I explained, and knew I sounded foolish for offering any sort of explanation.

The man nodded and stepped back inside without comment, swinging the ornately carved doors shut.

I barreled after Colin and found him kneeling near the back of the building in a narrow row of box hedges. The cobbled parkway where Miss Adelaide's life had come to a sudden end was just behind him, and yet he seemed entirely disinterested as he rustled about in the shrubs. "Whatever are you doing?" I asked.

"Proving a theory."

"And just what theory would that be?"

"That either Miss Adelaide was up to something peculiar with somebody or else there was someone who was trying to undo her in the worst sort of way."

"What do you mean?"

"And given that she was eighty-three years old, it hardly seems likely that she was carrying on with anyone."

"What are you talking about?"

"Might I ask wot yer doin'?" A gravelly voice spun me around and I found myself looking down upon a dark-haired plug of a man who looked about as wide across the shoulders as he was tall.

"We've been hired by Miss Endicott to look into the death of her sister," I hastily sputtered as though we had been up to some mischief.

The man tilted his broad face and nodded. "That's just terrible, that is," he said. "I'm Mr. McPherson." He stabbed out a meaty hand. "I take care a the grounds fer Miss Eugenia."

"Ethan Pruitt," I replied, not in the least surprised by the power in his grip. "And this is Colin Pendragon."

"A course." He grinned. "Miss Eugenia always gets 'erself the best."

Before I could acknowledge his compliment, Colin stood up and thrust a handful of pebbles and small stones toward him. "I notice you've got this hedge turned in a layer of moss and wood shavings. Can you tell me where these stones might have come from?"

The man squinted into Colin's palm and gave a dismissive sort of shrug. "There's a border a them pebbles along the garden out back. Supposed ta keep the snails out, but I don't see that it does a fig a good."

"How do you suppose they've come to be all the way over here, then?" Colin pressed, and I wondered what he was driving at.

"Prob'ly them ruddy snails brought 'em round." Mr. McPherson snickered and, to my amazement, so did Colin.

"They can be pesky," Colin agreed, which struck me as amusing given that the only thing Colin knew about snails was how they tasted in butter and garlic. "I understand a bird flew into one of Miss Adelaide's windows recently," he hurtled right on to the next topic.

"Aye." Mr. McPherson gave an easy nod. "'Ad ta get the glazier out ta replace it."

"Did you find the bird?"

"Wot?"

"The bird that struck the window," Colin clarified. "Did you find its carcass?"

Mr. McPherson shook his head. "Nah. But ya can bet it knocked some sense inta the balmy thing." He laughed, as did Colin, who casually slipped his little trove of stones into a pocket as he stepped out of the hedge.

"We'll want to speak with you again tomorrow, Mr. Mc . . ."

"Pherson," I quickly supplied.

"Yes," Colin said as he brushed himself off.

"'At's fine." The man nodded. He walked back with us as far as the front edge of the house before bidding us good day and heading for the stable situated on the far side of the driveway.

"What was that all about?" I asked. "Dead birds and snails?"

"It is murder, Ethan," he proclaimed with steadfast conviction. "Miss Adelaide was, without a shred of doubt, murdered." He looked at me with a grim and determined expression. "And I am most certain that it was not by the hand of Mr. Nettle, either."

CHAPTER 2

Acting Inspector Maurice Evans was working out of a series of boxes from what had, until recently, been the tiny office of Inspector Emmett Varcoe. The Yard had still not decided whether to anoint Mr. Evans with the full title of inspector in spite of his clearly deserving it. The work he had done during the Connicle case, especially after the murder of his superior, Inspector Varcoe, made his promotion feel a forgone conclusion, yet such was not the case at the Yard. So though Colin and I had been summoned to discuss that very case, it was Superintendent Elflin Tottenshire who addressed us, leaving poor Mr. Evans to look quite ill at ease from behind his unfamiliar desk.

"... And while Scotland Yard does not expressly condone the type of investigative dabbling your sort practices, it does appreciate when men like you and Mr. Pruitt are able to pass along some occasional information that can prove useful to an investigation. After all, it is impossible for our good men to be everywhere." Superintendent Tottenshire gave a broad smile as he finished his diatribe, forcing his steely-gray pork-chop sideburns to flare out from the sides of his cheeks like great furry rodents. He was wearing a gray suit that had once been quite nice but now looked rumpled and over-worn, and stood leaning against a

bank of filing cabinets that lined the wall of the office behind where Colin and I were sitting. This was clearly a man who had risen to the highest level he would achieve and was, therefore, content to ride the last miles to retirement with what he had already earned.

"I have just been made to feel ever so quaint," Colin said as he fished a crown out of his pocket and set it into motion tumbling between his fingers.

Superintendent Tottenshire laughed, as did Maurice Evans, who seemed not to know what else to do. There was nary a single framed photograph or personal item arrayed in front of him, further attesting to the potential transience of his current position. He had even tried to scramble out of his seat when the superintendent had first arrived, but Superintendent Tottenshire had only waved him back down before planting himself against the row of cabinets. I kept trying to decide whether he had done so in order to force Colin and me to have to crane around to look at him or if he simply wanted to tower over us from where we sat in front of Mr. Evans. I suspected it was a bit of both.

"I have heard you referred to in many ways over the years, Mr. Pendragon," the superintendent quipped, "but never has the word *quaint* been used."

"And for that I am grateful," Colin responded and meant it in spite of the fact that Superintendent Tottenshire looked pleased with his jibe. "But do tell me, what exactly is it that you are imagining two such dabblers as Mr. Pruitt and myself might be able to do for you? Might it have something to do with the fact that your revered force allowed Charlotte Hutton to disappear onto the Continent at the very moment I was solving the Connicle case?" He looked up at the superintendent with a foul expression, the silver crown still swishing between his fingers. "Such an embarrassment for you and your men that has also left an unholy blemish on *my* record."

Superintendent Tottenshire gave a perturbed frown as h crossed his arms over his chest. "While your concern for the re gard of Scotland Yard is ever appreciated, I suspected you mig! be interested in working with us on the Hutton case, since it

clearly unfinished business for you as well. After all, I believe Inspector Varcoe was deferring to you during much of that case,
and had you notified him, or any of us, about your suspicions regarding Mrs. Hutton's complicity, then I can state quite emphatically that she would never have been allowed to evaporate into
France or Switzerland or wherever the hell she's gone." He stood
fully upright and looked at us with the same prickly sort of mock
innocence that Colin had just displayed. "Mr. Evans's report asserts that you were caught as unawares as we were."

The coin that had been so effortlessly tumbling between Colin's
fingers came to a halt. Not a moment after that, a razor-sharp
smile slowly twitched at one corner of his lips. "I will admit that
I did not recognize the depths to which Mrs. Hutton's con-
nivance fueled the very core of the Connicle case, but given that
two of the victims were her husband and young son, neither did
I *ever* imagine that your Yard would neglect to keep a watchful
eye upon her, if only because she was a critical part of the case."
He quickly started the crown twirling again. "It was a careless
presumption on my part that I shall be sure never to repeat."

"Then we have all learned something," Superintendent Tottenshire noted harshly. "And because of your father's artful
diplomacy we now seem to have the opportunity to set it right.
You must be sure to give Sir Atherton my regards when you
speak with him next."

Colin's face puckered ever so slightly. "I'm sure that will be
top of mind," he mumbled as he flipped his crown straight up
and swept it out of the air, slipping it into his vest pocket in one
smooth movement. "Unfortunately . . ." he started to say, and I
found myself wondering just what unfortunate thing he could
possibly be about to pronounce, since I knew nothing mattered
more to him than bringing Charlotte Hutton to justice, ". . . Mr.
Pruitt and I have just accepted a most intriguing case that we will
need to commit our fullest attentions to."

"A case . . . ?" The superintendent shot a quick glance at
Maurice Evans, who looked equally surprised, before turning
back to Colin and me. "What case might that be?"

"Eugenia Endicott has hired us to investigate the recent death

of her elder sister, Adelaide," Colin responded casually with a marked facetiousness in his tone, confirming what I already suspected, that he was rather enjoying taunting the superintendent. "Very mysterious business. Perhaps you've heard about it?"

"Heard about it . . . ?!" Superintendent Tottenshire repeatedly shifted his gaze between the two of us as though trying to gauge whether Colin was having a jest at his expense. "There's no mystery to Adelaide Endicott's death. That old bird either tossed herself from the window or else tottered and fell from it. There's no more to it than that." He let out a wary laugh. "Miss Eugenia has been hounding our hallways insisting we arrest her sister's male attendant." He swung his gaze to Mr. Evans. "What was that man's name?"

"Freddie Nettle," I supplied.

"That's right." The superintendent stared at me, a mixture of confusion, wariness, and disbelief on his face. "We spoke to the man. There's no motive. He's out of a bloody job now. Hardly the stuff to arouse suspicions. Really, Mr. Pendragon, do you mean to spend your time exploiting an old spinster? Have your funds become so tight . . . ?" He chuckled as he looked at our stoic faces before turning to Mr. Evans in search of a comrade who would share his incredulity.

I cannot say exactly why, but Maurice Evans did not allow a smile any more than Colin or I did. Instead, I thought Mr. Evans looked noticeably startled, aware that he was expected to support the conjecture of his superior officer and yet clearly caught by his better understanding of the reasons why Colin would accept a case.

"Really, Mr. Pendragon . . ." the superintendent said again, and this time I could see something uncertain rustling behind his eyes.

"I'm afraid I do not believe Adelaide Endicott's death so easily accounted for," Colin replied quite simply.

For the second time in as many minutes, Superintendent Tottenshire flicked his eyes between the two of us as though certain Colin was having a jest at his expense. "Really . . ." he repeated yet again, releasing a most ill-conceived sort of snicker. "I must admit I find that entirely perplexing. We looked into the matter when Miss Eugenia first brought her accusations to our attention, but after a conversation with Mr. Nettle and a brief examination of the room from which Miss Adelaide fell . . ." He shook his head with an expression of persistent disbelief. "There was an autopsy performed, you know. No marks were found on her body consistent with having been pushed, and there was no matter whatsoever found beneath any of her fingernails nor were there any scratch marks of any kind on Mr. Nettle's face or arms." He caught a breath and noticeably appeared to relax. "Now don't you suppose we would have found tiny chips of paint or slivers of wood from where she would have tried to grip the sill to keep from being thrown to her death three floors below? Or at the very least a bit of skin from where she had scratched Mr. Nettle while fighting for her life?!"

"I never said she did not throw herself from that window," Colin answered plainly. "I mean only to suggest that she may well have been coerced to do so."

"Coerced?! Whatever would make you think such a thing? Honestly . . . I'm truly starting to think that you are trying to make me the butt of some preposterous joke. Is that it? Is this your retribution for the errors Scotland Yard made in allowing Mrs. Hutton to slip away during the Connicle investigation?"

Colin's eyebrows bolted skyward. "While I will admit to some vindication with your acknowledgment of the Yard's fouling up that case, be assured I am not playing with you in the least." He gave an easy smile that only seemed to belie his words, just as I knew he meant it to. "So why are we quibbling about the Endicott sisters, a trifle in your opinion, when we have the matter of Mrs. Hutton to discuss. If we were to make ourselves available at some point, what is it you would wish from us?"

The merest suggestion of a scowl wafted across the superintendent's face before he gave his answer. "We already have a man en route to Zurich for a meeting with a senior official at Credit Suisse where, as I am sure you remember, the bulk of Mrs. Hutton's extorted funds wound up under the assumed name of Mary Ellen Witten, the name we learned she had been using when we lost her." He gruffly cleared his throat and paced around behind Mr. Evans's desk, trying to feign superiority by having that bulky piece of furniture between us. "Sir Atherton has achieved the impossible with the Swiss authorities, and we mean to make the most of it since those men at the bank will not freeze her accounts forever. Which is why we are moving with all due haste." He leaned forward, planting his hands on the desk, and stared at Colin. "We would like you to head right over there, Mr. Pendragon, and join that meeting."

"When is the meeting?"

"Thursday. We sent our man this morning so he can have a couple of days to work with the Zurich police. Sort things out with them . . . let them know what we're up to . . . a bit of international diplomacy, I suppose you could say."

Colin shook his head with a mock scowl. "I should fear for the whole of Victoria's empire if the Yard is tasked with our diplomacy."

Curiously, Superintendent Tottenshire seemed to take no offense as he continued to glare at Colin. "Will you go then? Can I get you to go to Zurich tomorrow?"

Colin stared straight ahead, his eyes locked on the thin manila folder Maurice Evans had shoved at us when we'd first entered: Charlotte Hutton's file. I knew Colin would never let this opportunity go. It did not matter that Eugenia Endicott was paying us an obscene sum to concentrate our efforts on the death . . . murder? . . . of her sister. Charlotte Hutton was a scourge to Colin's reputation and he would abide no such thing.

"I'll go," he answered just as I knew he would. "But I will only stay for the meeting on Thursday. I'll not dally to deal with your counterparts at the Zurich police. And as Mr. Pruitt will be left here to begin our investigation for Miss Eugenia, I would ask that you allow him access to Miss Adelaide's autopsy report." He fidgeted slightly and I wondered if he was concerned about my ability to adequately pursue the Endicott case in his absence.

"I shall do you one better." The superintendent stood up with a satisfied grin. "Not only will I allow Mr. Pruitt access to the autopsy report, but I will also give him a chance to review the notes we took at our meeting with that Nettle fellow." He gestured to Maurice Evans, who obediently got up and exited the office. "This is capital, Mr. Pendragon, simply capital!"

"Yes . . ." Colin answered with far less conviction as he slid his eyes toward me. "It will have to do."

I returned a smile and the faintest of nods. "You mustn't concern yourself with me," I blustered. "I shall try not to resolve the case before your return."

Colin arched an eyebrow. "I'll only be gone a single night."

"Actually"—Superintendent Tottenshire cleared his throat— "we should like to send you tomorrow afternoon and have you spend the whole of Thursday there. The meeting at the bank is midday, and I was hoping you might have a look about thereafter. We can get you on the first train back Friday morning."

"Don't hurry on my account," I said rather more glibly than I felt.

"I see. . . ." Colin muttered, his lips pulled thin even as amusement tumbled behind his eyes. "Apparently, I have been holding you back all this time."

"Well, there it is then." I shrugged.

Superintendent Tottenshire glanced at me. "Scotland Yard will be at your service while Mr. Pendragon is away, Mr. Pruitt. Should you require any assistance whatsoever with that Endicott business, you can see me personally."

"Your offer is very generous," I said as I glanced over to Colin and found him once again focused on Charlotte Hutton's file sitting at the center of Maurice Evans's desk. If he had heard the superintendent's offer he gave no sign of it.

"You are welcome to have a look," Superintendent Tottenshire said to Colin, having obviously noticed the same fixated look on his face that I had.

Colin rubbed a hand across the top of the folder a moment as though petting a lover before finally snatching it up and clasping it between his hands as if he could ascertain some sense of it by touch alone. "It's so thin," he said after a moment.

"It is. Which should give you some notion as to the level of interest Scotland Yard has in procuring your assistance on the case."

The tiniest furrow rippled across Colin's brow as he swept the folder open and quickly pawed through the few pages. "Is this truly it?" he muttered with a mixture of astonishment and gratification.

"The Swiss *are* rather prickly." Superintendent Tottenshire gave a shrug. "Were they not, there would be little need for us to seek your aid."

"And in that we shall forever have a parting of the ways." Colin sniffed, tossing the meager file at me just as Maurice Evans returned with another slim folder.

"These are the preliminary results on Adelaide Endicott's autopsy," he said, handing the file to Colin. "Mr. Ross is running additional tests on tissue samples he took . . . blood . . . stomach contents . . . I don't know what else. And I'm having one of the constables dig out the notes that were taken during Mr. Nettle's interview, but there wasn't much."

"I believe I made that clear," Superintendent Tottenshire reiterated with self-assurance, as though that would make any difference to Colin.

While Colin leafed through the autopsy details, I glanced down at the two and a half pages that comprised the totality of Charlotte Hutton's file. They consisted of a series of bank account numbers along with a litany of bank names and addresses that traced the movement of her embezzled funds from the Bank of England to Banque de Candolle Mallet & Cie, then Deutsche Bank, and finally Credit Suisse. She had been masterful in her planning, which allowed for nothing further in the file but a few scribbled notes interspersed here and there. It seemed doubtful that any of it was going to be of the slightest use.

"I must say . . ." Colin muttered as he handed Adelaide Endicott's autopsy to me, ". . . that if this is the assistance your Yard is offering, I do not hold out much hope for our partnership." He stood up and paced in a quick circle behind our chairs.

I opened the second folder and several photographs dropped

into my lap. Each of the grainy pictures showed the twisted remains of an elderly woman facedown on a cobbled walkway. Her death had clearly been sudden and brutal, and I could not imagine how the coroner, Denton Ross, could have been able to surmise anything beyond the obvious signs of trauma she had suffered when she struck that path.

I shuffled the pictures to the bottom of the file and quickly read through the descriptions of the contusions, lacerations, fractures, and defacement she bore, and noted at once the type of damage the report did not contain. Just as Superintendent Tottenshire had said, there were no abrasions around her wrists or ankles, no marks around her neck to suggest that she might have been dead before being cast from the window, and not a speck of detritus beneath her fingernails. If she *had* been shoved to her death, it appeared she had made no effort whatsoever to keep herself from falling. From the looks of this report it seemed that Mr. Nettle's story of Miss Adelaide having abruptly leapt to her death was almost irrefutable.

"I shall go to Zurich tomorrow," Colin was saying with a decided lack of enthusiasm, "but I'll not leave until late. I will travel overnight from Calais, so be sure to get me a berth. I am not wrong about Adelaide Endicott's death, and I intend to spend the morning at Layton Manor with Mr. Pruitt interrogating their staff."

"Yes, of course." The superintendent nodded with an unimpressed sniff. "We can get you to Zurich by dawn Thursday morning and you can meet the gentlemen for breakfast."

"*Early* breakfast," Colin corrected him. "I need to be on my way back by late morning."

Superintendent Tottenshire looked sideways at Mr. Evans before nodding his head. "Of course. Just as you desire it. Maurice will make the arrangements and get the tickets to your flat tonight. You won't mind attending to that, will you, Maurice?" He tossed a smile at his subordinate, but did not bother to wait for a response. "We shall have Mrs. Hutton paying for her atrocities in no time," he announced proudly, his great triangular sideburns bookending his grin like a furry ellipse.

"Indeed . . ." Colin agreed with far less vigor as he moved for the door. "So *we* shall." I heard the inference he was making, though I suspected that neither the superintendent nor Mr. Evans did.

I bid the two men good day and followed Colin out the door, but just before I was swallowed up by the hallway I overheard Superintendent Tottenshire order Maurice Evans back out to the Endicott house tomorrow afternoon to have another look around. He was not, it seemed, a foolish man.

CHAPTER 3

The tea was perfection and the red currant scones exemplary, but our questioning of the Endicott staff was getting us nowhere.

After speaking with three individuals over the last hour and a half, we had learned that Miss Adelaide was a dear, if enfeebled, old woman, who had never once been heard to make any remark about wishing she were departed. That Miss Eugenia was a tough but fair employer, who inarguably ran the household. And that there was an unusually high turnover rate for the staff. This last point, however, was only grudgingly admitted by the housekeeper, a compact woman in her early thirties named Clarice Somerall, who carried herself with the discipline of a headmistress even though she had the fresh beauty of a lovely young woman. She was one of the longer termed staff members and could only claim eighteen months herself.

Colin's patience had begun to fray somewhere near the hour mark, and he hadn't even attempted to be discreet when glancing at his watch over the last thirty minutes. If Miss Somerall had been of a mind to share anything in particular, I am certain her desire ebbed once he set his watch, its gold cover gaping open, onto his knee. At that point there was still three-quarters of an hour before he needed to leave to catch the train to Dover, which had left me wondering whether he was bored with Miss Somerall or if in fact he had grown weary of the entire process. Whichever the case, it had clearly not sat well with Miss Somerall, who clipped her already truncated answers before finally taking her leave, her every movement as tight and austere as the light brown bun she had tweaked her hair into.

"This is proving to be a bloody waste of time," Colin growled as we walked around the front of the house and headed for the stable off to the side just at the point where the driveway began to curve back down to the road. As with all estates of such distinction, the stable matched the house in style and construction, built from the same deep umber rectangular stone blocks that comprised the main building. There were three large doors across its front made from the same dark wood and bronzed hardware that adorned the home's front door. It looked large enough to hold a half-dozen carriages and better than twice as many horses, though it seemed unlikely that any such need had ever existed for the Endicott sisters. But then it was never about need. "If this groundsman . . . What the hell is his name . . . ?"

"McPherson."

"If this Mr. McPherson doesn't have anything of value to say, I shall be well pleased to be off to Zurich and leave all this to you."

"How very fortunate for me," I said, attempting to goad him out of his mood, but he only ignored me.

We entered the long single-story structure, dwarfed by the size of the main house and yet quite large in its own right, and I was struck at once by the earthy scent of wood, hay, and horses. While the building itself was stone, its interior was carved into sections by posts and beams that provided places for three coaches and one open buckboard as well as stalls for horses, whose number I gave up trying to figure after reaching ten. There was hay strewn about, both as bedding for the horses and general upkeep for any detritus that hit the creaking wooden floor, except in the farthest section of the stable on my right, which was comparatively clean and held the implements of Mr. McPherson's grounds work. It was there that we spotted the solid man stripped to his undershirt, sawing a hank of wood in half with sparse, precise movements that were nonetheless powerful enough to make short work of a girth of wood greater than the width of a large man's thigh.

"Mr. McPherson . . ." Colin called out.

"Aye," he answered without glancing over at us or taking even the slightest pause in his work. "A minute more . . ."

We paused and watched as the powerful muscles of his shoulders, arms, and back drove the saw blade through the section of tree trunk as if it were a slab of bread. I figured him to be somewhere in his early fifties and yet he moved with the grace and ferocity of a man still in his prime. He was clean-shaven and his short brown hair held little gray, but it was his eyes that gave away his advancing years, framed by deeply embedded crow's feet and containing an incisiveness that can only come with age.

At last the section of trunk he'd been cutting sprang free and dropped to the ground from the makeshift table he had contrived from boards laid across two wooden horses. He stood up and swiped an arm across his slick brow, settling his eyes on us. "Mr. Pruitt an' Mr. Pendragon," he said, striking me with the oddity of having my name mentioned first until I recalled that I had introduced us as such the day before.

"And you are Mr. McPherson," Colin said with the brief flicker of a smile as he seized the man's hand and shook it, testing, I was certain, how his strength compared to that of Mr. McPherson.

The two of them were equally broad of shoulder and sturdy of build, but Colin stood almost half a head taller than Mr. McPherson, leaving the older man looking very much like a cast-iron fireplug. "We apologize for interrupting your work," Colin went on, "but wondered if we might have a moment of your time to ask a few questions about Miss Adelaide?"

Mr. McPherson snatched a rag from his back pocket and mopped his brow, dragging the cloth around to the back of his neck as he squinted at Colin with something of a bemused expression. "Ya can ask me wot ya want, but I don't work in the 'ouse, so I can't tell ya much about either a the Misses."

One of Colin's eyebrows ticked up with what I presumed to be annoyance. "Are they good to work for . . . ? Fair . . . ?"

"Me pay's on time." A smirk stretched his lips. "That's fair 'nough ta me."

"Did you have many dealings with Miss Adelaide?"

"Nah. Miss Eugenia's the one runs things. She tells me wot she wants and 'ow she wants it ta be. I 'ardly talked ta Miss Adelaide. Didn't 'ave no reason."

"Was it always that way?" Colin pressed. "I know she's been unwell for the last year. . . ."

"I ain't said but 'ello ta Miss Adelaide long as I been 'ere."

"And how many years is that?"

Mr. McPherson shrugged a shoulder. "Don't remember. Twenty some, I s'pose."

"Twenty?!" And this time both of Colin's eyebrows lifted. "You've worked here for over twenty years."

"Aye," he answered with marked indifference.

"Then you are quite the anomaly, Mr. McPherson," Colin said, considering the man with renewed interest.

"Wot?"

"We haven't spoken with anyone yet who has served the sisters for greater than two or three years. You would seem to be the exception."

"That ain't nothin'," he grumbled with the wave of a hand as he slid the soiled kerchief back into his pocket. "Ya mustn't pay no mind ta that. People say all kinds a things they don't know shite about."

And now it was Colin who looked baffled as he asked, "What?"

"Mr. Fischer's been workin' 'ere somethin' like ten years," he continued as though he'd not just lost the two of us. "*Devlin!*" He took a step past Colin and called out to the far side of the stables where the horses were kept. "'E's the coachman and tends the 'orses. 'E'll 'ave somethin' ta say."

I glanced around to find a man of average height with a thick middle and round face that was well covered by a beard and mustache. His dark brown hair was slicked back and tucked behind his ears, and I pegged him to be somewhere in his middle thirties, though his cherubic cheeks made him appear possibly younger. Yet as with Mr. McPherson, this Mr. Fischer's dark eyes held a maturity and awareness that seemed to signify a youth left far behind. "What are ya bellowin' about?" he asked as he took his time striding over to us, all the while raking his eyes over Colin and me, obviously taking our measure.

"Mr. Pruitt and Mr. Pendragon." Mr. McPherson pointed to us in turn. "They're the ones I was tellin' ya Miss Eugenia 'ired. They come ta tell us wot 'appened ta Miss Adelaide. Why she done what she did." He peered over at the two of us. "'At about right?"

"Well . . ." Colin slid his eyes from Mr. Fischer back to Mr. McPherson, his face revealing nothing. "I suppose you could say that. Assuming she did anything at all."

"Bloody hell . . ." Mr. Fischer scoffed as he finally reached us. "Ya aren't gonna start blatherin' about devilish spirits throwin' Miss Adelaide to her death, are ya?" He waved an irritated hand toward us. "'Cause I got nothin' ta say if ya mean ta start in on that rot." He swung his gaze over to Mr. McPherson, who was clearly trying to suppress some sort of snicker. "Is that wot ya bellowed me over 'ere for, Denny? 'Cause yer a right fig if ya did—"

"Excuse me," Colin interrupted, rapt keenness igniting his gaze. "I meant only to suggest that perhaps some *one* had done her harm, not some *thing*." He slid his eyes to me and one of his eyebrows drifted for the ceiling. "You would appear to be referring to an entirely different sort of possibility . . . ?"

"Oh fie . . ." Mr. Fischer scowled at us. "Don't get me started on them jabberin' about things they think they see and hear. The lot a them runnin' around that blasted house like they was bein' chased by a devil. A ruddy lot a rubbish it is, ya ask me."

"Indeed," Colin responded at once, ". . . I am asking you. Spectral sightings, you say?"

"Huh?"

"Ghosts . . . ?" Colin hastily corrected.

And that was all it took for Mr. Fischer to burst out laughing, followed at once by Mr. McPherson. "Now don't tell me yer one a them blokes gets hisself all caught up in the gossipin' of a bunch a washerwomen?!"

Colin's lips pulled tight. "I make it a habit never to get caught up in anything while working on a case, other than the collection of as much information as possible. Which is precisely what I am trying to do right now, collect information."

Mr. Fischer shook his head with poorly concealed amusement. "You can do what ya want, but if you get yerself caught up in that load a shite yer as daft as them loons wot works in the house."

"Is that why there's been such a frequent turnover in staff?" Colin turned to Mr. McPherson. "Are you telling me people are afraid to work here?!"

Mr. McPherson shrugged one of his meaty shoulders and let out a small laugh, which was echoed much more forcefully by Mr. Fischer. "I don't talk ta most a the people wot works in the 'ouse," he said with his typical reserve. "I got me 'ands full with the grounds."

"You wanna know about wot goes on in that house, all ya gotta do is talk ta Mrs. Barber in the kitchen," Mr. Fischer interrupted. "She's a feisty one. Ain't no wonder she's a widow."

"A pox on ya," Mr. McPherson growled.

"Now, gentlemen," Colin spoke up, his tone edging toward that of a headmaster. "I am trying to conduct an investigation into the death of one of your employers, and I must tell you that I am finding it most peculiar that neither of you seems particularly interested in providing any assistance beyond making absurd statements and ribbing each other like a couple of schoolboys. I must ask you to either pay heed to the topic at hand or I shall be forced to inform Miss Eugenia that she has a pair of fools in her employ. Do I make myself clear?"

Mr. McPherson had the decency to look horrified, but Mr. Fischer only pursed his hairy, round face, looking rather like a wild animal that had just been poked with a stick.

"Good." Colin bit the word off. "I was asking you about the staff then, Mr. McPherson. Are these shadowy tales the reason there has been such an upheaval in staff over the past several years?"

I could tell that Mr. McPherson was loath to answer the question, just as it was obvious that Mr. Fischer found the whole matter preposterous. Yet with Colin's steely gaze fixed upon him, Mr. McPherson realized he had no choice but to respond as he finally spoke up. "Some people are jest daft," he allowed grudgingly. "They got no sense. Ya 'ave one person goes loose in the cogs and the next thing ya know ya got 'alf the bloomin' staff believin' a bunch a piffle."

"Piffle . . ." Colin repeated flatly. "And just what kind of *piffle* are you referring to?"

Mr. McPherson shuffled his feet and glanced down at his heavily callused hands, and I suddenly began to wonder whether perhaps, just perhaps, the topic made him uneasy because he harbored his own unspoken doubts rather than simply because he found it an embarrassment as I had initially presumed. "Some a them ain't 'ere no more claimed to 'ave seen a young girl in a white christenin' gown wanderin' the 'allways cryin' like she were lost, but if they tried ta talk ta 'er she jest disappeared like she were never even there. Others of 'em said they never saw 'er, but they 'eard 'er cryin' somethin' pitiful." He shook his head. "I ain't never 'eard or seen nothin'."

"A little girl?" Colin repeated. "Who is she supposed to be?"

"You ain't really askin' a question like that now, are ya?" Mr. Fischer groaned. "Don't tell me yer as daft as the rest a them. . . ."

Colin turned on the man with a scowl. "If you're not going to answer any questions, then I would encourage you to shove off."

"'E knows more 'bout it than me," Mr. McPherson demurred, shuffling back a half step. "I don't 'ear much. They got no cause ta talk ta me."

Colin sucked in a deep breath and shifted his gaze back to Mr. Fischer, leveling a pointed glare at the man. "Well, Mr. Fischer . . . will you tell me the stories you have heard or shall I extricate them myself through the many holes in your head?"

Mr. McPherson chuckled under his breath, which earned him a deep frown from Mr. Fischer. "Wot is it ya want ta know?"

"Who is this girl supposed to be?"

"Hell if I know. I ain't never seen her."

Colin's lips thinned. "Does anyone who works here now claim to have seen her?"

Mr. Fischer exhaled loudly, setting the hairs of his wiry mustache wriggling. "Nah, or they'd likely be gone too." He waved a hand as though the whole topic annoyed him, which it very clearly did. "Pitiful thing is it were Miss Adelaide wot started it all, as far as I can remember. I ain't sayin' nothin' bad about Miss Adelaide, I'm jest tellin' ya wot I know like ya so nicely asked me to."

"And I appreciate that," Colin replied in a matching tone. "So what was it Miss Adelaide started exactly?"

Mr. Fischer pursed his faced as though the conversation itself was a cause of irritation to him. "She was always talkin' 'bout spirits and ghosts and all that sort a rot. Claimin' all kinds a fanciful things like she were daft or somethin'. But she weren't," he was quick to add. "She were a good and kind woman. She jest didn't have no sense when it came to that kinda nonsense. That used ta drive Miss Eugenia balmy." He gave a chuckle, and I noticed that, in spite of himself, Mr. McPherson did too.

"Then Miss Eugenia does not share her late sister's predilection for spiritualism?" Colin asked.

Mr. Fischer shook his head resolutely. "Not in the least. I heard 'em have a row a time or two over it, but it didn't make no matter ta Miss Adelaide. She jest went right on believin' what she wanted. I think what riled Miss Eugenia was how they kept losin' staff over the years." He shook his head again and gave another chuckle, but this one was drier and carried little mirth. "Those stories scared half of 'em away."

Colin frowned. "Stories of seeing some little girl wandering about in tears? That hardly seems the stuff of nightmares."

"There were more things," Mr. Fischer added with a sudden note of defensiveness in his voice. "Crazy things. I don't know what all, but it didn't take long for some a them kitchen girls and upstairs maids ta start seein' their own potty things. Some a them went racin' out without even waitin' ta get their last pay. Daft . . . every one of 'em."

"You seem to know quite a lot about it all."

Mr. Fischer gave a smirk that was mostly concealed by his beard and yet still evident by the crinkling of his eyes. "Miss Adelaide used ta talk ta me about things when I'd be drivin' her here and there. Especially when I took her out ta see her spiritualist twice a month. Some woman over in Lancaster Gate."

"Lancaster Gate?" Colin repeated curiously.

"'At's right. But don't ask me her name 'cause I don't know it. I never went in. Jest dropped her off and waited outside for an hour till she was ready ta go home again."

"Forgive me, gentlemen," a sonorous voice interrupted from the open doorway behind us, "but your carriage has arrived, Mr. Pendragon."

Colin flicked his eyes to me with a look of exasperation. "Really . . ." he muttered under his breath, ". . . this is most inconvenient."

"Charlotte Hutton would be delighted to hear you say so," I reminded him, earning me a scowl for my efforts.

"Thank you," Colin called back before returning his attentions to the two men in front of us. "I do appreciate your assistance, gentlemen, however hesitant it was at times." He flashed the slimmest of smiles. "We hope to exonerate the good name and memory of your Miss Adelaide." Both men stared back at him with rather blank expressions. "To prove that she did not harm herself," he tried to clarify. "And most certainly to determine whether Mr. Nettle may indeed bear any responsibility."

The two men glanced at each other, but neither said a word nor did their faces betray any semblance of what had passed between them.

"Very well," was all Mr. Fischer said after a moment.

"I trust you will continue to provide Mr. Pruitt with your aid while I am away." Colin said it more like a command than a request. "We shall get this sorted at once." He flashed another stiff smile before glancing at me, which was my signal to follow him back outside. "This makes for a rather peculiar turn on things, wouldn't you say?" he summed up quite aptly as we stepped out into the sunny side yard.

"I would imagine it will only serve to muddle things. Apparitions and spiritualists? Whatever are we to make of that?"

"Whatever indeed?" Colin glanced at me with one cocked eyebrow. "Perhaps you will have the opportunity to discover whether it denotes anything at all."

We rounded the corner to the front of the house and spied the cab patiently waiting, its lanky driver hunched over with disinterest even as tall, elegant Mr. Galloway stood by the open door as though he owned the vehicle himself.

"I'm not so sure I'll have the time to be able to denote anything during your brief absence," I pointed out. "Besides, all of this is likely nothing more than the latest fashion of the idle sort."

"Perhaps." He gave a little shrug. "But there is no better way to manipulate another than to prey on their beliefs and fears. Too many governments and religions are masterful at it." He swung himself up into the carriage with a nod and a grin. "Good day, Mr. Galloway . . . Mr. Pruitt . . . Till Friday." He pounded a fist on the carriage's ceiling and the coach immediately lurched forward, and as I stood there next to Mr. Galloway I wondered exactly what the hell I was supposed to do next.

CHAPTER 4

The girl was frightened. I could see it in the way she held herself, her arms wrapped across the front of her body as though hoping to ward off something inevitable: a raised voice, a cutting rebuke, a pelting blow; her eyes huge and round, pupils overwhelming the whites as though there was almost no color to them at all. Yet it was not these corporeal sorts of mundanities that held the young woman in such a state, but rather very much the opposite.

"Me mum says I got ta stop listenin' ta stories and keep me 'ead down 'cause we need the money and she's afraid I'm gonna quit." She hugged herself tighter, hunching her shoulders forward as though a chill breeze had just wafted into the room. "I ain't gonna quit," she added in a way that sounded more for her own benefit than mine. "I got seven younger brothers and sisters, and me dad drinks wot 'e makes sure as the sunrise."

"That must be a difficult burden for you." I gave her a warm smile, hoping to get her to relax at least a little before I dared undertake the real reason for my interrogating her. "You must be such a blessing to your mother. But why does she fear you would quit?" I furrowed my brow and leaned in slightly in an effort to seem conspiratorial. "Was it Miss Adelaide? Was she a difficult mistress?"

"No, sir. . . ." she answered at once, casting her eyes down to the scuffed table in front of us, immaculately clean, but clearly it had seen its share of innumerable meals over the years.

The two of us were seated in the staff's small dining quarters, tucked in the ground-floor corner of the home just off the main kitchen. I had asked Mr. Galloway if I might have a word with an upstairs maid, and he had chosen to summon Miss Britten. She was, he had informed me, the woman who took care of Miss Adelaide's quarters. I thought she looked like a woman in her late twenties, but given that she had no husband and still provided income for her family, I decided that she was likely ten years younger than that. Her umber hair was pulled into a neat bun with a small white cap set upon it, not a lock out of place, and though she was of medium height and terribly thin, her broad, angular face looked stout and eminently readable.

"Miss Adelaide were a lovely woman. . . ." Miss Britten informed me with the staunchness that showed she meant what she was saying. "She never 'ad a 'arsh word fer anyone. She were always kind. Weren't nobody didn't think the best a 'er." She hesitated a moment and her eyes shifted around the room as though she hoped I might abruptly end our conversation and keep her from having to say whatever was clearly pricking at the back of her mind. "But sometimes it were like she could sense things none a the rest of us could 'ear or see. One minute she'd be talkin' like we are now, and then she'd jest go all quiet and look off. . . ." Miss Britten's eyes crinkled and it felt like she was trying to catch a glimpse of whatever had drawn Adelaide Endicott's notice.

"Did you ever question her about it?" I asked, though I knew what her answer would be.

"Oh no, sir. 'At weren't me place. I'd jest leave 'er be and she'd come round again when it suited 'er."

"And when she did . . . come around again, as you say . . . were there ever times she would confide in you about what had happened to her? What she had seen or heard?" I pressed.

Miss Britten shook her head mutely, tucking her elbows in with that same sense of self-preservation. "She'd tell me there were un'appy souls about. There'd been wrongs done ta people and somebody 'ad ta make it right. Sometimes I'd find 'er cryin' . . . she'd be so sad about somethin' . . . and the next minute she'd be shiverin' and lookin' all undone with 'er eyes flittin' 'ere and there. And then she'd ask me if I could feel 'em. That's what she'd ask—'Can ya feel 'em . . . ?'"

"Them . . . ?" I repeated quietly, anxious to keep her talking. "Who do you think she meant?"

The young woman finally turned her gaze to me, peering at me as though I had lost my senses. "The spirits," she answered with the simplicity of an exchange about the price of fruit at market. "The ghosts."

"Yes," I said with a soft smile that I hoped she would not mistake for disbelief on my part. "Of course. And did she ever tell you what the wrongs were that had been committed? Who these . . . ghosts . . . might be?"

"No, sir," she answered with a firm shake of her head.

"Did *you* ever see them . . . ? Feel their presence . . . ?"

"I ain't never seen nothin'. But sometimes . . ." She looked off again, her eyes not appearing to focus on anything. ". . . Sometimes I think I 'ear someone comin' inta the room I'm cleanin' and when I look up there ain't no one there. And there's been a time or two . . ." Her voice drifted off for a moment, and I watched her face flush ever so slightly. "I'll be workin' somewhere, not payin' any mind ta nothin', and I'll feel a coldness slide past me like I jest brushed up against death 'imself." She physically shuddered and I realized that her knuckles had gone white where she was still holding herself.

"Have you heard anyone else on the staff speak of feeling such things?"

She shook her head. "Mr. Galloway would 'ave our jobs if 'e 'eard us sayin' anythin' like wot I'm tellin' you."

"So Mr. Galloway does not give any heed to the things you have felt? What did he think, knowing that Miss Adelaide believed in them?"

"Wot did 'e think . . . ?!" She chuckled. "Don't matter a fig wot 'e thought. 'E worked for 'er. She could've stood on a street corner in 'er bloomers fer all it'd mean ta 'im, but 'e can mind the rest a us."

"Of course. . . ." I could not cover my discomfited smile at having made such an obvious blunder. "Forgive such a foolish question. Does Miss Eugenia hold to the same beliefs her sister did?"

Miss Britten shook her head and rolled her eyes. "Nah. She always got angry when Miss Adelaide brought it up. Wouldn't 'ardly even talk ta Miss Adelaide on the days she went ta see 'er spiritualist." She shook her head again and looked markedly uncomfortable before she continued. "I 'eard 'em 'ave a row about it a time or two, but Miss Adelaide wouldn't give in." She lowered her gaze to the table again, and just as I thought she was done talking she spoke up once more in a voice almost bereft of volume. "I think she were right . . . Miss Adelaide. Somethin' ain't right 'ere. Somethin's troubled. Can ya feel it?" Her eyes suddenly shot up to mine, and I was so startled by the abruptness that I found I had to look away.

While I have never truly given much consideration to such things, neither have I presumed to dismiss that which has been so far from my mind. And yet for reasons I cannot even begin to fathom, I would swear that I felt a curious sort of tickle rustle along the back of my neck and discovered myself quite at a loss for words. A flush rose up in my own cheeks, whether from embarrassment or discomfort I cannot say, but it was enough to get me to finally force my tongue back to action. "These old homes," I heard myself mutter, "are known to creak and groan rather precipitously."

"Yes," Miss Britten agreed, unfolding herself for the first time since we had begun our conversation.

"Do you know anything of the spiritualist Miss Adelaide had been seeing? Her name? Where she lives?"

"No, sir. You'd 'ave ta ask Mr. Fischer 'bout that. 'E's the one that drove 'er everywhere."

"Of course. And what of Miss Adelaide's footman, Mr. Nettle? Did you know him well?"

"I knew 'im. But 'e kept to 'isself mostly. 'Ad ta, I s'pose. It were 'is job ta be around whenever Miss Adelaide needed 'im. So 'e never ate with the rest a us and 'e slept upstairs in the antechamber outside 'er room."

"Was he close to anyone on the staff?"

" 'E only ever seemed ta talk ta them nurses wot was also carin' fer Miss Adelaide. But that's wot 'e were 'ere for anyway."

"Did you ever notice any sort of difficulty between Mr. Nettle and Miss Adelaide?"

"Miss Adelaide were the nicest woman I ever met," she answered at once. "Never 'ad a cross word fer anybody other than 'er sister, and I already tol' ya 'bout that. That's jest the way of it. I got five sisters meself."

I allowed a slight chuckle as I girded for the last question I needed to ask this young woman. "Do you ever recollect Miss Adelaide suggesting that she might do harm to herself? Perhaps when she was feeling most unwell?"

Miss Britten's eyes went round as she stared back at me. "No, sir. She were a God-fearin' woman and would never a done such a thing ta 'erself."

"Of course . . . of course. . . ." I hastily agreed as if the question was as ill-mannered to me as it clearly had been to her. "Then I will thank you for your time and leave you to your duties."

"As you wish," she said as she rose to her feet and gave a quick curtsy. "It's a terrible thing wot 'appened. And now I fear there'll be another restless soul wanderin' these 'alls." She impulsively rubbed at her bare arms as though the room had suddenly gone cold, and then she withdrew, appearing to take care not to meet my gaze as she did.

CHAPTER 5

That Mr. Galloway was displeased by my question was apparent, and that was before I could tell whether he meant to answer it or not. His face had puckered and his demeanor became even stiffer than what I had become used to seeing. I knew it was a risk to speak with him so pointedly but could not imagine trying to ask Eugenia Endicott these same questions. Doing so would simply have to wait until Colin returned. That I knew he would prefer it that way did give me some solace.

"Must we rummage through this topic, Mr. Pruitt?" Mr. Galloway queried in return, his brows having already caved in upon each other.

We were sitting across a small table in his spare but comfortable set of rooms downstairs, accorded him as the steward. From here he dispensed orders, critiqued daily routines, and reproached staff as necessary, just as I felt he was doing to me.

"I would not ask these questions if I did not believe them to be important," I responded, hoping it would be enough to elicit an answer from him, however begrudging.

"Very well. . . ." he said with notable distaste. "Miss Adelaide was indeed a proponent of spiritualism, but it was most definitely *not* a topic discussed amongst the staff. Such an undertaking would have been unseemly and most assuredly not tolerated."

"I understand. Yet having grown up in a home of some privilege myself, I also know that the staff did talk amongst themselves, and it is *that* chatter that I am most interested in right now." I gave him a congenial smile, safe in the knowledge that this man would never know that there was only the smallest measure of truth in my statement. With little more than twenty-four hours before Colin's return, I did not mean to have my time here be for naught. "Did you have trouble retaining staff, Mr. Galloway? Were people put off by the stories of Miss Adelaide's spectral convictions?"

"Anyone who harbored such convictions would not have been welcomed here. It is an honor to work at Layton Manor, and you can be assured that the entirety of the staff believes it to be so."

"Of course. But did anyone ever quit because of the things Miss Adelaide claimed to have seen or heard? Or perhaps they themselves confided an occurrence of their own that gave you even the merest pause?"

"Members of any staff come and go on a whim. I could not, nor would I care to, hazard the sorts of reasons any of them might have had." He sniffed, clearly intent on ensuring that I understood how banal he thought this conversation to be.

I nodded agreeably but kept my eyes on him. "And you? Have you ever, even once . . ."

The man's face hardened precipitously, seizing the remainder of the question in my throat. "I should say *not*." The words curled from his mouth as though laced with acid.

I offered a smile I meant to be conciliatory but could see that it did not have the intended effect on him. This was a man fiercely loyal to the household he ran, and for that I could not fault him, never mind that it did nothing to aid in my investigation. "How well acquainted were you with Mr. Nettle while he worked here?"

I could see at once that we were on smoother terrain, as Mr. Galloway's features eased ever so slightly. "I was the one who found Mr. Nettle for Miss Adelaide. I know the woman who runs a service that helps place finer household staff. She is the only person we use at Layton Manor. Though the requirements for Mr. Nettle were unique, I knew Mrs. Denholm would be able to procure such a man. And he did a proper job while he was here." He allowed his eyes to slide sideways. "Until the end, of course. . . ." He let his voice drift off, and I found myself feeling oddly sorry for him, for the accountability he now so clearly seemed to feel was his to carry.

"Do you also believe Mr. Nettle to be guilty of causing Miss Adelaide's death?"

"I . . ." He appeared to consider the question quite carefully before turning his gaze to me with an expression so perplexed it seemed almost childlike. "I don't really know what to think," he finally conceded. "Something happened to Miss Adelaide, and he has said himself that he was the only one in the room with her at the time."

"Indeed. But that does not mean that Mr. Nettle is responsible. Did you know him to have had any difficulties in his dealings with Miss Adelaide?"

"Never. Miss Adelaide was a gentle woman, quiet and soft-spoken. There was no one she did not get on with."

"Of course," I said, and at least it seemed that everyone was in agreement on that point. "Yet I have heard that Miss Adelaide and Miss Eugenia had some disagreements here and there with respect to Miss Adelaide's beliefs in spiritualism. Were you aware of that?"

As his gaze hardened I realized that I had once again pushed him too far. "I really could not speak to such things nor is anyone else on this staff at liberty to do so. Such queries are boorish at best."

"I understand, Mr. Galloway, but everything is admissible when confronted by the possibility of murder. Or are you perhaps suggesting that Miss Adelaide was predisposed to harm herself?" I knew my question for the ploy it was, but hoped Mr. Galloway would not.

"Never!" he answered at once, uncertainty marring the set of his tone. "It may have been an accident. I suppose that is your duty to decide, but I do not believe it necessary to discuss all manner of private matters to determine such a thing. You are a detective, are you not? That is what you do?"

There was accusation in his voice as he glared at me, and I decided I had learned all I was going to from this man. "Were you able to reach Miss Adelaide's two nurses for me? As I mentioned earlier I should very much like to speak with them."

"Of course." He pulled a folded slip of paper from his suit pocket, his demeanor concise and in control, and just that simply I could see that he was well in his element again. "I have arranged for you to meet the day nurse, Miss Bromley, late this very afternoon. She requested that you come to the Queen's Arms on Queen's Gate near the Victoria and Albert Museum. I took it upon myself to accept on your behalf."

"You did well," I said with a smile, pleased to have this so quickly accomplished. "And the nurse who tended to Miss Adelaide at night . . . ?"

"I have a message out to Miss Whit, but have not yet received her response." He yanked his watch from his vest pocket and glanced at it. "It is still early since I believe she continues to work at night. Given that to be the case, she may not have risen yet for the evening."

"Of course. I do appreciate your efforts on my behalf."

"I am pleased to be of assistance," he answered curtly, allowing me little sense that he was telling the truth. "I will get word to you as soon as I hear back from Miss Whit."

"Thank you," I said as I started to stand.

"Do you have a telephone, Mr. Pruitt?" He looked at me coolly. "Or will I need to send a messenger?"

I smiled at him, certain he knew the answer to his question. "It will have to be a messenger, I'm afraid. Technology is moving far too quickly to keep up with all of the changes. One can only wonder which things will truly improve our lives and which will only serve to annoy." I gave a chuckle that he did not reciprocate. "Please let Miss Eugenia know that I will be back tomorrow morning. Perhaps you will have had an answer from Miss Whit by then."

"Perhaps," he said as he too stood up. "I am sure you can appreciate that Miss Eugenia will not sit idly by for long. She will expect strides to be made without delay."

"And she cannot be blamed for that," I answered glibly, though I was reminded in that instant of Colin's inopportune absence. I would persevere as best as I knew how, following the tenets he had taught me over the past dozen years, but I knew it likely that I would only be treading water until he returned.

"Good day then, Mr. Pruitt," he said as if he were the lord of the manor himself. "I shall give your tidings to Miss Eugenia, and I can assure you she will look forward to whatever news you bring with you tomorrow."

"Yes . . ." I said rather more haltingly than I meant to as I backed out of his small suite of rooms. "Yes . . ." I said again. And I was suddenly struck by the ease with which he spoke for his mistress. He was her servant, the man who oversaw every facet of the running of her home, and yet he referred to her with the insouciance of someone who had dominion over her person. I was startled by it and jotted it down the moment I climbed aboard the cab he had ordered for me.

CHAPTER 6

"I beg your pardon?"

The Queen's Arms was overflowing with people and the volume was so intense that I could barely hear anything that Miss Bromley was saying. She had arrived not ten minutes before and been pointed in my direction by the barkeep as I had requested. I had specifically selected a table near the back of the pub for what I had thought would be its relative seclusion, but that was proving to be unobtainable as there was no seclusion to be found here and even less privacy. Still, I was determined to persevere and had gone ahead and ordered her a glass of cider while I continued to sip the ale I had ordered for myself. I knew it was crucial to conduct this interview the best I could, so I would not allow this pub's incessant clatter to keep me from my purpose.

"I was just asking how I can help you," she apparently repeated, offering a shy smile. Her pale brown hair was brushed tightly back, and though she'd removed the nurse's cap she had been wearing, it left a crease around the top of her forehead. Her face was slender and pretty, her brown eyes as rich as chocolate, and her lips were quite full, which made her smile, even with its hesitancy, both generous and warm. She was still dressed in the long skirt and blouse of her profession, which accentuated an immaculate figure, leaving me to wonder why this lovely young woman was not already married.

"Perhaps we'd do well to find a better place to speak," I fairly hollered across the table at her. "I don't think we'll be able to hear each other."

She held up a hand as her smile widened. "Leave it to me," she said in full voice before popping out of her chair and disappearing toward the bar.

I sat there a moment trying to figure what exactly I was leaving her to, when she suddenly reemerged through a crush of people with a tall, handsome man in tow. He was clearly someone of consequence in the Queen's Arms as the crowds moved aside for him and Miss Bromley as they made their way back to the table.

"Philippa tells me ya need a place ta talk," he bellowed at me, and for a moment I thought I detected a note of disapproval in his statement.

"Yes." I smiled at the young man, determining him to be at least ten years my junior in spite of the scruff growing along his jawline, and that's when I noticed that Miss Bromley was still beaming behind him. Given his casual use of her given name and the euphoric look upon her face, I deduced that the two of them were courting. Which left little wonder as to why he had sounded displeased at my wanting to be somewhere quieter with her. "I am investigating the recent death of Adelaide Endicott," I offered by way of explanation. "I am hoping Miss Bromley might be helpful."

"She might what . . . ?" He leaned forward, looking no less reassured.

"Be helpful," I shouted directly into his ear. "That she might be helpful."

He nodded and waved a hand, sweeping up our glasses before leading us through the door that let out into the kitchen. "You can sit at me desk," he said, and I noticed at once that the din was reduced almost twofold the moment the kitchen door swung back into place. "I'll ask ya not ta touch anything 'cause all the food comes outta here, but it'll be a quieter place."

The kitchen was humming with activity, men and women bustling about attending pots of stews simmering on two stove-tops, fresh bread going into and coming out of four small ovens, and a long counter upon which any number of items were being sliced, chopped, carved, or hammered. And yet even amongst all of this carefully orchestrated commotion, the level of noise was a fraction of what it had been in the pub itself.

"I hope ya don't think Philippa had anything ta do with that old woman's death," he said as we reached a cluttered desk shoved up in a rear corner of the room.

"Quintin . . . !" she gasped.

"Not at all." I gave another grin, but the young man still seemed unimpressed. "I am merely collecting information. Trying to find out everything I can about the late Miss Endicott."

The young man gave a mirthless nod and gestured toward two chairs set by the desk. "Make yourselves ta home then," he allowed in a way that almost sounded grudging. "And let me know if ya need anything more ta drink."

"Of course. Thank you kindly."

"Thank you, Quintin," Miss Bromley said.

The young man gave her a quick wink before his black eyes fell hard on me, and then he was headed back out to the pub, but not before whispering something to one of the thickly built men heaving cast-iron pots about as though they carried no weight. I caught the other man's gaze as it raked over to me, and then the young barkeep was gone.

"This is certainly an improvement," I said to Miss Bromley, determined to make the best use of our time together. "How fortunate that you are such good friends with that young man."

"Quintin and I are to be married," she answered with a shy smile, and I could see there was real excitement behind her eyes. "We were to have done so already, but his father suddenly got ill and died over the winter, and it's left Quintin to sort the business here at the pub by himself. He is the eldest boy, you see, and his family depends on him."

"I'm terribly sorry. . . ."

She cast her gaze down and then up again, and I was struck by her timidity given her occupation. "I believe that things happen for reasons beyond our understanding sometimes," she said after a moment. "Because of the postponement I was able to help several women I might not ordinarily have been able to assist had we already wed." She seemed to blush slightly as she shifted her eyes sideways. "We hope to have a very large family, you see."

"How wonderful. And with the business the Queen's Arms is doing, I should think you will be able to raise them quite well."

"I do hope so." She looked straight at me and her expression changed with the rapidity of a snuffed flame. "What was it you wanted to ask me about Miss Adelaide?" In the matter of a moment she had gone from a bashful soon-to-be bride to a confident woman of both wherewithal and intelligence.

"Ah . . ." I took a mouthful of my ale and turned back to the crux of my visit. "How long did you work as Miss Adelaide's nurse?"

"About a year and a half. Perhaps slightly longer. I loved working for her. She was a wonderful woman, always kind and patient, and yet she suffered so. I do suppose we all have our burdens to carry."

"I suppose we do," I said, struck by the thoughtfulness of this young woman. "How had she been faring lately?"

She pursed her lips and shook her head. "She had not been well. Her nerves were weak and her health was declining. When I started with her she could just barely get around with a couple of canes, but it didn't take long before she seemed disinclined to move on her own at all. I'm not even certain that she could. That's why they brought Mr. Nettle in—to carry her up and down the stairs and to push her in her wheeled chair whenever she required it."

"And her mood? How did it seem? Did she ever give you any notion that she might harm herself in any way?"

"Absolutely not, Mr. Pruitt." Her eyes locked onto mine. "Miss Adelaide would never have done such a thing. She was a God-fearing woman."

"Of course, of course," I said, unaccountably embarrassed for having suggested such a thing. "You mentioned that her nerves were weak," I pressed on, trying to be as delicate as I could. "Was there anything in particular you feel that may have contributed to that condition?"

Her lips went thin and her eyes narrowed almost imperceptibly, and I knew she had seen through my stratagem. "If you have gotten anyone at Layton Manor to confide in you, then you already know that Miss Adelaide believed in the occult. I am not saying whether I do or not, but I will tell you that it did her no good."

"How do you mean?"

"She hated to be alone in that house unless she was in her room sleeping, and even then Mr. Nettle was posted right next door in case she ever needed him during the night. And she needed him quite regularly. Many mornings I would arrive to find that poor man bleary-eyed from lack of sleep, having spent a good deal of the night running in and out of her room."

"Why? What was happening that caused her such distress?"

"I don't know. She would claim to have heard something unnatural or to have seen some inexplicable phenomena. . . ." She shook her head before settling her gaze on me once more. "You would really need to ask Miss Whit, Vivian Whit. She was the nurse on duty during the nights. And Mr. Nettle, of course. I'm certain he can tell you some stories."

"What did you think of Mr. Nettle?"

"He was a very patient man. He treated that woman like she was his mum. I found it rather sweet. And he was always there. He never had a day off."

"What do you make of Miss Eugenia's contention that he might have had something to do with her sister's death?"

"It makes no sense. Why ever would he do such a thing?" Her eyes continued to bore into mine. "I cannot explain what happened that night, but neither can I imagine that Mr. Nettle was in the least ways involved."

"Might there be someone in the household who harbored animosity against Mr. Nettle perhaps? Someone who might want it to appear that he had murdered her?"

Miss Bromley shook her head without an instant's hesitation. "Mr. Nettle kept to himself. . . ." she started to explain, and then took a breath and appeared to reconsider what she had been about to say. "Well . . . actually . . . he was always around Miss Adelaide— other than when Miss Whit or I were attending to her private needs, of course. Otherwise he was always with her and there really was no chance to get to know him very well. I suppose I saw him as much as anyone. Even so, his attentions were always on Miss Adelaide as they were required to be. I'm not at all sure anyone had enough interaction with him to have developed much of an opinion. Other than Miss Adelaide, and it was easy to see that she adored him."

"Miss Eugenia would be the exception then . . . ?" I pointed out.

"Oh!" Miss Bromley looked almost startled as she reconsidered her statement in light of Miss Eugenia's charges against Mr. Nettle. "I suppose she is only looking at the facts at hand. She knows her sister would *never* have harmed herself, so what else can she be left to believe?" The young woman stared at me, her eyes alive with the sensibility of her assertion, and I could tell she was just waiting to see if I would agree with her.

"What about Miss Adelaide herself?" I pressed ahead, unwilling to concur on something I knew Colin had already rejected. "Do you know of anyone who was angry with her . . . ? Upset in any way . . . ?"

"No, no," she answered again with great speed. "Miss Adelaide was a frail and delicate creature. She gave no one any reason to feel anything against her. Only a person without a heart could have managed such a thing."

I wanted to tell her that was precisely the sort of person who would wish to end Miss Adelaide's life but thought better of it. If someone had harbored any hostility toward Miss Adelaide it was obvious that Miss Bromley knew nothing of it. "Would you stake your reputation as a nurse on the fact that Miss Adelaide would never have brought harm to herself . . . ?" I asked again,

even though I knew Colin was convinced she had been murdered.

"Impossible," she replied with such determination that I could
not help but be convinced.

"You mentioned that Miss Adelaide could not walk on her
own. Can you imagine how she might have gotten to that window without someone's aid?"

Her eyebrows creased and her gaze drifted off as she gave the
question a moment's consideration. "She was not paralyzed, Mr.
Pruitt. It wasn't that she was unable to move her lower body.
Rather she had become feeble in her later years; her legs were
weak and her hips brittle. . . ." Her eyes came back to me in sharp
focus. "If she held on to the wall . . . I suppose it would have
been possible. . . ." But Miss Bromley did not sound particularly
convincing.

I drained the last of my ale before posing one more question.
"What did you make of Miss Adelaide's fears, Miss Bromley?
You declined to say a moment ago, but do you share her fascina-
tion with the occult?"

Her answer came with the speed of a hummingbird's wings.
"I am a nurse, Mr. Pruitt, and as such consider myself a woman
of science, which leaves little room for such follies as wandering
spirits and rattling chains." She gave a wry chuckle that lit up her
pleasing face. "I do not mean to disparage the beliefs of others,
everyone is entitled to hold their own, but I can put no stock in
something that cannot be proven, measured, or tested. Perhaps
that is my failing, but it is a failing I am well contented with." She
chuckled again and this time I could not resist joining her.

"You have been very forthright, Miss Bromley, and for that I
must thank you."

"It is my pleasure and my duty," she said. "I was very fond of
Miss Adelaide, and if there is the slightest hint of impropriety in
her death I hope you will be successful in bringing it to light. She
deserved that, no matter her eccentricities. They certainly did not
make her any less the gentle person that she was."

"Mr. Pendragon and I will do everything we can to ensure

that is the outcome. May I count on you to make yourself available again should we have any further questions?"

"Most assuredly."

And as the two of us stood up from the little desk in the far corner of the Queen's Arms' kitchen, I found myself considering the possibility that Colin could be mistaken, that Miss Adelaide had, in fact, taken her own life out of some terrible perceived fear. Yet what that fear was, to drive a woman described as nobly as she sounded to such a tragic end, I could not even begin to imagine.

CHAPTER 7

I pulled the collar of my coat up around my neck as I stared out for a moment at the settled night from the warmth of Shauney's Pub. While I would have rather gone directly home from my meeting with Miss Bromley, Mrs. Behmoth had announced quite resolutely in the morning that without Colin in town she would not be preparing dinner and I should attend to myself. And so I had come to Shauney's, as Colin and I often did when left to fend for ourselves, and had my fill.

I headed out into the night just as the wind started to rise in earnest, the portent of rain dense in the air. Tucking my chin into my upturned collar I hurried toward the alley that dissected the street leading to our flat, the clicking of my boots the only sound to keep me company. It was simply far too early for most people to be heading home, which is why I was surprised when I caught the furtive sounds of someone moving in my direction from not far behind me.

It is a curious thing—hearing footfalls when none are expected. What is the appropriate response? Should one crane around and gawk as though the street belonged to them alone? There seemed little sense in doing so. London is a city of almost five million people. That any block, no matter how insignificant, should ever be traversed by one person alone seemed most unlikely, and it was for that reason that I merely hunched farther down and picked up my pace as I darted into the alley. My companion, whoever he was, doubtless would not follow me through here as its only outlet was the end of our street.

As I had expected my escort did not follow, and curiously I could not deny that I felt myself relax again. It was a foolish reaction; I scolded myself, but nevertheless it did renew my determination to get home as quickly as possible. I told myself my nerves were thin because of my doubts around the Endicott investigation, and for a moment I believed that to be so, but then I heard a soft tread from somewhere closer behind me, faint and cautious, and I knew for certain that I was being followed.

My heart instantly amplified its beating before I could expel a single breath, leaving me to struggle to keep my movements unhurried and consistent. It seemed important not to allow my pursuer to know that I was aware of him, though I could not have explained precisely why. I suppose it gave me the only bit of an edge that I had. So I kept walking, huddled deep within my coat, striving to maintain my steady gait, all the while waiting for a sudden burst of sound to explode from behind me in a signal that the hunt had just become an attack.

The end of the alley loomed directly in front of me, the outlet to our street not twenty feet to my left, and I girded myself for what I knew must be coming. If I could just reach the corner, I hoped that I would be able to secrete myself in a nook or doorway and change from being the pursued to the pursuer. That, I well knew, was what Colin would do.

I reached the exit and took it, glancing back as I moved out and continued to my left. My furtive look had earned me nothing; the alley was as dark as midnight. There could have been a mouse or a mob behind me and I would not have been able to decipher either.

I yanked the low gate open that led onto the long, narrow park that sliced through the center of our street and moved quickly to try and fade into the shrubbery and trees. Almost at once my ears prickled with the sound of the gate swinging open behind me. The blatancy of this rogue quite suddenly stoked my ire, and I found myself coming to an abrupt halt and turning around before even realizing that I intended to do so. It took an instant for my eyes to adjust until I caught sight of a smallish figure moving toward me, swathed in a full black cloak with a cowl pulled far enough forward to conceal the face. While it was difficult to get an accurate sense of the man's build beneath the bulky cloak, I knew at once that I was broader and very much taller, and if he was not wielding a weapon I realized I had nothing to fear.

"Mr. Pruitt . . ."

As we were shrouded in darkness, I felt reassured that the woman could not see the surprise that overtook my face at the mere sound of her voice. The advantage, nevertheless, was clearly hers, for I could see nothing of her as I tried to decipher who she was and why she had been trailing me. She came to a stop when there were fewer than a handful of feet between us, a distance that immediately felt both improper and perilous, and then reached up and tugged the cowl from her head.

I watched the hood fall back from her face and hair, and for a moment felt even more confounded, as at first glance I did not recognize her. Yet before it could come fully free, settling around the back of her head, I heard myself audibly gasp.

"You recognize me," she said, sounding neither disappointed nor concerned that I should do so. "How could you not?" she added. "What do I know of subterfuge or concealment?"

I wanted to say that she knew a great deal, standing before me with hair as black as the very night itself hanging like a frame around her strikingly beautiful face. It made her look younger thusly arranged, whereas the last time I had seen her it had been curled atop her head and as yellow as straw. "I could never forget your face, Mrs. Hutton," I replied.

"I wish I could take that for a compliment." She spoke wistfully, her eyes parroting the somber tone of her voice. "Is Mr. Pendragon not with you?"

"He will be along shortly," I lied, not even certain why I had done so.

"Yes, of course," she muttered, though I wondered if she believed me. "I . . ." She seemed to be studying me, and as she did so I caught a quick flash of blue from her eyes in the shadowy cast of a nearby gas lamp. "I have been watching your flat from here for the better part of the past day and a half, trying to summon the nerve to speak with the two of you. This morning I finally had the presence of mind to pay a man to follow you." She dropped her gaze, but it was too dark for me to see whether she had flushed with the audacity of her statement. "He alerted me that you were having supper at that pub a short time ago." Her eyes shifted back to mine. "I hope you will forgive my temerity. . . ."

"I see. Well, you might have tried knocking on our door as most people would do," I bit back, trying not to let my vitriol against this murderous woman sink our conversation before it had even begun. She had sought me out for some reason, and I was determined to know it before I turned her over to the Yard for her complicity in six murders, including those of her own husband and infirm six-year-old son. And that did not even count the shooting death of Inspector Varcoe, who had lost his life during the arrest of her accomplice, Wynn Tessler.

"It is your understandable wrath that has left me cast out like a ghost upon your trail." I don't know whether it was the blackness of the hair around her face or the starkness of the night itself, but she looked sallow and drawn, and not at all the formidable woman Colin and I had run up against during the Connicle case. "Will you sit down for a moment, Mr. Pruitt?" she asked, the hint of pleading in her voice. She gestured at one of the iron benches nearby, all of them appearing cold and uninviting in the darkness.

"I should think we would be more comfortable if we went to my flat."

"Doubtlessly so," she responded at once, "but I cannot be so careless when I must presume that you would sooner see me in prison than hear me speak another word." She managed something of a smile that was so filled with weariness I could not help but be struck by it.

"Very well," I said after a moment, as enticed by curiosity as anything else. I followed her to the nearest bench and sat down beside her, leaving the largest gap between the two of us that I could so that any onlooker spying upon us would have thought we were not together at all.

"You know why I'm here," she stated so softly that the wind nearly carried her voice away.

"Tell me," I said, though I did have little doubt.

"You believe me a calculating woman who carries the responsibility of many deaths upon her heart. Am I right?"

I did not know what she was driving at nor did I have any desire to engage in her dubious games. Nothing would have pleased me more than to drag her to the nearest bobby so she could complete her self-assessment from within a cell, but that was out of the question. So I remained silent and decided to see if she would hang herself with her own words.

It took a full minute, the two of us sitting there like ornamental sculptures, awaiting the impending shower that even now was imbuing the night with the scent of ozone. "Is it too impossible to consider that Mr. Tessler drew the deepest wounds from me?" she spoke at last, her gaze having moved somewhere along the edge of the slender park. "I will not deny that I allowed myself to become entangled with him a few years ago, but it is not as you believe. My husband and I had become estranged in every way after the birth of our poor son, Will. It was evident almost at once that something was not right with him. He was always so docile. I would hold him and stare into his sweet face, but it was as if he could not see me. Like he was caught somewhere that the rest of us could not perceive." Her voice hitched the slightest bit, but she maintained her composure, neither dropping her chin nor turning to look at me.

"Arthur blamed me, of course," she continued. "Perhaps I *am* the one to blame. . . ." she added heavily. "I suppose that doesn't matter anymore. But it drove us apart, Mr. Pruitt, and it crushed my spirit. So when Wynn Tessler began to pay me gentle heed, enquiring after my health and setting himself to my well-being . . ." She made a *tsking* sound as she continued to gaze off into the darkness another moment before suddenly turning and glaring at me, her eyes clear and hard and full of anguish. "And like a fool I allowed myself to fall into him. It was weakness, Mr. Pruitt, and desperation, and I have paid for that ever since."

I chewed on the inside of my cheeks to keep from saying something unseemly. That she could imagine such a sordid confession might justify the murders of her husband and unfortunate son sickened me. Yet here she was sitting beside me, speaking as though she was nothing more than the victim of an impulsive decision she had come to regret, and hadn't she just been the thoughtless little gadabout? "Your son . . ." I started to say, taking pains to speak slowly and with as level a tone as I could achieve, ". . . was still missing when you took your daughter and disappeared onto the Continent. You had left an address and contact information with the Yard, and it was, all of it, lies. That would seem to be what you truly thought of your sweet-faced son." In spite of my best efforts I bit the words out more harshly than I had meant, expecting her to cower or look away shame-facedly. But she did neither. She held herself steady and continued to look at me, unabashed, or perhaps willing to accept what she knew she deserved.

"I do not deny a word of what you say," she answered boldly. "By the time I took Anna to Claridge's the night we discovered Willy missing, I knew what I was going to do. What I *had* to do," she quickly corrected.

"Was that when you also decided to embezzle all of Edmond Connicle's funds and those that Mr. Tessler controlled at Columbia Financial?"

"No, Mr. Pruitt," she said without blinking. "Embezzling Wynn Tessler's money had been my intention for several months. I was going to leave Arthur and take Anna and Willy somewhere safe where we could start over again. I had made a mess of everything, Mr. Pruitt. Arthur despised me and took every opportunity to flaunt his affections for other women where he knew I was sure to see. When Edmond Connicle set his eye on me I encouraged him. . . ." She hesitated a moment before seeming to force herself forward. "But it was a shameful decision, as I could not deny to myself that I was doing the same thing to Edmond's poor, delicate wife that my own husband had been doing to me, which only served to force me closer to Wynn Tessler." She stared off and shook her head. "Which was my final undoing."

My head began to tumble about as she spoke, the starkness of black and white getting whirled with an unexpected range of grays as, for the first time since Wynn Tessler had railed his outrage at the duplicity of Charlotte Hutton, a seedling began to niggle at the back of my mind suggesting that maybe, just maybe, there was more to this case then any of us had suspected. "Whatever are you talking about, Mrs. Hutton?" I asked, gratified to hear that I still sounded gruff and unmoved.

"My reckless liaison with Mr. Tessler turned untenable almost at once." She turned back to me, wrapping her arms around herself to ward off the rising cold, yet managing to look ever the more pitiable for it. "While I craved comfort and solace, Wynn Tessler was seeking control and financial gain. It started subtly: a passing word about how Arthur had squandered our money, how it was simply a matter of time before we found ourselves destitute. I was terrified, Mr. Pruitt. Not for myself but for my children. What would it do to Anna and most especially poor Will? He was going to need constant care for the whole of his life. I wept for fear of what would happen to them. Was he to spend his life in one of those horrid sanitariums?" She rubbed her forehead with a gloved hand and glanced away, still clinging to herself with her other arm. "I could not allow it. It terrified me to the core of my soul."

"Is that why your son was killed?" I asked, the callousness of my question striking me uncomfortably.

Her eyes bolted back to mine and I could see a glint of fury behind them. "Never." She spat the word as if it tasted of acid. "I was his mother, Mr. Pruitt. A mother does not kill her child, her own flesh and blood. It goes against the laws of nature and humanity. I would not expect you to understand."

But in that she was mistaken, for not only did I understand but I knew her assertion to be flawed. My own mother had been testament to that. "I am sorry for your son," I said after a moment, and in that I was telling the truth, "but I fail to see the point of what you are telling me or why I should not summon the next constable who happens by to put you in prison where you belong."

She finally released her grip on herself and raised a hand toward me. "Hear me out, Mr. Pruitt, and if you feel the same when I am finished then you may do as you please."

It was an undeniably seductive statement and yet it held a hollowness that I told myself to be wary of. "Go on."

"You see, Mr. Pruitt, Wynn Tessler preyed on my fears and then he preyed on me. At first it was with his words, vile and threatening, and then it was with his fists. Never to my face. He never left a mark on my face, he was not foolish, but he did what he wanted with my body." She suddenly reached up and pulled open the cloak she was wearing, dexterously unbuttoning the collar of her dress before I even realized what was happening. "Do you see, Mr. Pruitt?" she asked as she wrenched the top of her neckline apart, revealing a long, jagged scar that ran from her left bosom nearly fully across her décolleté where it disappeared beneath her camisole. "There are many others. Cuts, burns, scars . . ." she mumbled as she refastened her collar with tremoring hands. "He was savage. . . ." And for the first time her voice broke and she sagged slightly as she finished sealing the cloak around her throat. "I was helpless. There was nothing I could do. I was ruined. If Arthur had found out he would have cast me aside and forbade me to ever see our children again. And that was the hold Mr. Tessler used on me. I would do his bidding or he would destroy my life." She released a disdainful chuckle, full of anger and regret as she looked back at me. "Which is exactly what he did anyway."

"You ran, Mrs. Hutton," I reminded her, though even as I

said it I could not deny the shimmer of doubt that was still waft-ing along the farthest reaches of my brain. "People who are inno-cent, especially those who are victims, tend not to flee in the face of impending resolution."

"Wynn Tessler had already seen to the murders of Edmond Connicle and my husband, and at that time my son was missing. To say that I was terrified for my daughter's life—for my own life—would be a gross understatement. He was out of control, Mr. Pruitt, and you and Scotland Yard were no closer to a resolu-tion than you had ever been. So yes, I ran. I ran to protect my daughter, and I ran to free myself from his hateful grip. It was the only thing left I could think to do. And as I told you before, I had been planning it from the time Mr. Tessler first started black-mailing me."

"You should have sought out the authorities," I scolded, but could not help feeling unfair for doing so. It was ever the simple answer that took no measure of what she had been through. So it did not surprise me when she gave a sardonic laugh.

"And how might that have played out, Mr. Pruitt? Confess-ing to Scotland Yard my infidelities? Do you really suppose that group of men would have looked upon me with any sympathy?"

She paused, her eyes boring into mine, but I had nothing to add. I knew she was right. They would have summoned her hus-band and remanded her to his custody for admonishment. His responsibility, his burden, his shame. And there it would have ended. "No one would have died," I finally muttered, but even I recognized the futility of my own words.

She nodded and looked away again, her shame as evident as the crisp chill of the wind. "In the beginning Wynn talked only about stealing money. Taking enough to run off and set ourselves up somewhere for the rest of our lives." Her gaze flicked back to me. "I was always part of his plan. He'd convinced himself that he loved me." That biting laugh came again. "So I began to plot how I could get away from him. Him *and* Arthur. And then Wynn had Arthur murdered. He thought I would be pleased." She shook her head. "I never wished Arthur ill. Our marriage had withered years before, but I did not wish him ill. He was the father of my children. . . ." Her voice faded as she pinched the collar of her cloak closed and held it with a fist.

"And then Wynn Tessler handed me the keys to the kingdom," she said, her eyes drifting back and for the first time I could see that they were filled with a hard-edged triumph.

"He opened trade accounts with both of your names on them and began to siphon money over," I spoke up, knowing where her story was leading.

"You have done your research."

"Because of . . ." I wanted to say *you* but settled on, "this . . . a revered inspector from Scotland Yard lost his life, shot by your Mr. Tessler."

She sucked in a breath and her shoulders tensed. "I didn't know. . . ."

"You fled, Mrs. Hutton, and you stole nearly every farthing that Mr. Tessler had already extorted. What did you presume would be left in your wake?"

"I . . ." She shook her head and stared off.

A single raindrop struck my forehead and reminded me that this conversation had to come to an end. In spite of her story, there was no question what had to be done. "You need to come with me to the Yard, and you need to tell them what you have told me. All of it. You cannot keep running, and I suspect you have figured that out already." I knew it was the freezing of her financial accounts in Switzerland that had brought her here in the first place. What I could not figure was why she had come to see me.

"I cannot do that, Mr. Pruitt," she stated with the assurance of someone who believes they are speaking with the utmost sense. "Wynn Tessler remains a threat to me for as long as he is alive. Need I remind you that, other than your Scotland Yard inspector, he did not murder any of the people you hold me culpable for. He hired a man to do his bidding, and now that he knows how I have double-crossed him, he will most certainly not rest until he has had my life taken and, almost assuredly, that of my dear Anna as well. I cannot allow that, Mr. Pruitt. My daughter has already paid enough for my mistakes. I will not have her pay with her life."

"The Yard can protect you and your daughter. . . ."

She barked out a laugh that silenced me at once. "Why should they be able to do so now when they could never before? How you can say such a thing and not cringe, Mr. Pruitt. . . ."

A drop struck the side of my face and I angrily brushed it away. She was not wrong. I hated what she was saying, but even Colin and I had been of little use until far too long into the horrid affair. "What do you want from me, Mrs. Hutton?" I asked, but I was sure I already knew.

She swept a hand against her cheek. We were about out of time for sitting in this little bit of park, so I anxiously waited for her to say what I knew she had come here for. "You can have the money back. You, Mr. Pendragon, and Scotland Yard. I was frightened and I allowed myself to be enticed into doing something I should never have done. All I ask"—she turned to look at me once more, her gaze settling upon me like a great, burdened thing—"is that you leave me just enough to live on and take care of my daughter."

"It is not your money to keep," I said without a second's thought. "It was stolen from the Connicles, Mr. Tessler, and any number of investors from Columbia Financial. If you expect to keep any of it, you will need to prove that it is yours to do so."

To my surprise she gave a soft, low laugh. "I took you for a man of compassion and understanding, Mr. Pruitt." Her voice was flat and colorless as she gazed out across the narrow park, the raindrops beginning to pelt us with ever more conviction. "I am an aggrieved woman who has suffered the betrayal of her husband and the murder of her son and, while I do not presume to hold myself blameless, neither am I the fulcrum around which those other poor souls lost their lives. I too am a victim, scarred of mind and body, who seeks only to live a quiet life away from here where I can protect my only child." She pulled the hood of the cloak up over her head and her face instantly disappeared back into its shadows. "I thought you would understand. I certainly hoped you would. I see now that I was mistaken."

She stood up just as the rain began to spatter in earnest, and I too sprang to my feet, confused by everything she had told me and the marks she had revealed across her chest. Whether she was speaking the truth or playing me for a fool I was not sure, but I knew I could not simply let her disappear into the night. "You approach me unbidden in the dark of night after such a startling disappearance to tell me things I could not know, and expect that I might have some immediate resolution for you? I'm afraid you ask too much of me." My thoughts were racing as I stood before her, unable to see her face to gauge whether my words were having any effect. "I can give you my word that I will not confide our meeting to the Yard, but I will speak with Mr. Pendragon. If there is anything to be done, anything we *might* do to assist you, he will need to be involved. If all that you have told me is the truth, Mrs. Hutton, then you appreciate the generosity of my offer."

It took a moment for her to answer, a moment in which the rain assaulted me like an impertinent child, but eventually she said, "Of course."

I cursed the cowl of her cloak as I stared back into the blackness where her face should have been, wondering if there was relief to be found there or something else. "I will see Mr. Pendragon later tonight," I lied. "Where can we get in touch with you?"

Again there was more than a moment's hesitation in which I could not fathom what she was considering before she finally answered, "I will seek out the two of you."

"That will not—"

"Forgive me my misgivings," she spoke over me, "but I have already been amply deceived by too many men." She swept around me before I could respond and bolted for the nearest gate out of the park. "I trust you understand. . . ." she called back hastily.

The rain increased as I moved to follow her, and by the time I made the short distance to the small side gate she had used it had begun to pour. I squinted down the street and caught her scurrying into a cab waiting along the side of the road just down from where I was standing. "*Mrs. Hutton . . . !*" I called out, but the driver hammered the reins in an instant and his carriage took off.

As I watched it disappear around the corner, I was heedless of the fact that I was getting soaked through to the skin. It did not matter to me in the least anyway, as all I could think about was how shocked Colin was going to be when I finally had the chance to tell him what had just happened.

CHAPTER 8

As I stared out of Eugenia Endicott's carriage I could hardly believe my eyes. The sight before me seemed impossible, and I knew my jaw had unhinged, leaving me to doubtlessly look quite the comic vision, should anyone be staring back at me.

I had not started out this new day intending to make this particular journey. My first thought had been to visit Maurice Evans at the Yard to update him on my conversations with Mr. Galloway and the day nurse, Philippa Bromley. It wasn't that I felt I had achieved anything notable yesterday, after all I was, as Colin liked to say, merely assembling the facts around the case, but rather I was curious to see whether Mr. Evans had received any word from Colin. In truth, I could scarcely contain myself until the afternoon for wanting to report my encounter with Charlotte Hutton to Colin. And it was for that precise reason that I decided not to see Mr. Evans. I feared I could not hold my tongue and knew Colin would be furious if I confessed my contact with Mrs. Hutton to the Yard before telling him. Besides which I was all but certain he was unlikely to elect to confide in them anyway.

And so I was left to my own devices while I awaited Colin's return, offering me few alternatives but to set myself to the Endicott case once more. It was to that end that I had returned to Layton Manor that morning, to beseech Mr. Fischer to drive me out to meet the woman Adelaide Endicott had consulted on a twice-monthly basis for all matters spiritual. Which is how I found myself quite unexpectedly bolt upright in the back of the Endicotts' carriage on Lancaster Gate, staring at a house I remembered very well.

It did not appear to have changed in the least since I had last been here. Still looking ever so slightly woebegone with its densely thatched roof and the partial covering of ivy clinging to its oat-colored walls of twirling plaster. I could even spy a slip of the giant, curved wrought-iron letter, peeking out from beneath a waterfall of the same ivy running up the front of the chimney, that I knew formed the bottom part of the letter *S*. But it was the little flowers planted along the walkway of the tidy front lawn that confirmed the owner of this home, just as it had done for Colin the first time we had come here six months earlier. Brightly colored flowers with heads like English tea roses, but not roses at all; dahlias. For I found myself delivered to the home of Lady Dahlia Stuart.

"Thank you, Mr. Fischer," I called out as I climbed from the carriage. "You have done me a great service."

"Do you need me to wait for you?"

"No thank you," I answered as I headed up the short walkway to the front porch, remembering the first time Colin and I had come here during the Bellingham case. Lady Stuart had been a difficult woman to find at first, before ultimately proving to be pivotal to that case. For she, above all the men in the Queen's Guard, had proven herself to be as committed to finding the truth of the Bellingham murders as Colin and I.

I rapped on the door and watched Mr. Fischer steer the Endicott carriage back down the block and out of sight. Of all the potential characters I had girded myself to meet here today, I had never remotely conceived of the possibility that it would turn out to be this fine woman.

"Oh . . ." her elderly father and houseman—Evers, she called him—grumbled the instant his eyes fell upon me, before he'd even fully opened the door. "You . . ." His eyes flicked to my left and right and then he cast his gaze behind me as he peered down the walkway. "Where's the other one?" he asked, his tone as sharp as a knife's edge. "Did ya finally come ta yer senses?"

I took note of the fact that his well-practiced vernacular had slipped and could not help but be amused by it. "I am afraid not," I answered with great good cheer. "Is Her Ladyship at home? Might I have a word with her?"

He rummaged up a scowl, as he always seemed prone to do, before finally answering. "Ya know she doesn't like people just droppin' in."

"I am not people, I am a friend. You will announce me or I will announce myself," I said with a steady smile.

He curled his lips and stepped back, ushering me in with his usual dearth of enthusiasm. I took no heed of it as I made my way to the parlor, Evers starting off in the opposite direction to fetch tea, I presumed. As he shuffled away I felt content in the knowledge that he had no greater dissatisfaction with Colin and me than the fact that we knew the truth about him and his daughter. He refused to believe that we had no need or desire to reveal their complex pasts to anyone. The word of a gentleman meant nothing to Evers, which said more about him than it did about us.

I stepped into the parlor and found it just as it had been the last time I was here: brimming bookshelves lining the sidewalls astride a plaster-and-brick fireplace, a high-backed couch and four wingback chairs arranged just so, all of them covered in the most colorful fabric of leaves and thatch that spoke to the whimsy of Her Ladyship. I took a minute to look at the photographs while I waited for her, but I did not have to wait long.

"Mr. Pruitt . . ." I heard her voice before I saw her step out of the hallway from the opposite side of the room. "What a distinct pleasure."

"Lady Stuart . . ." She looked ever the beauty, her flawless skin and shining black hair accentuating a face that looked carved from marble, perfect in its angles and curves. "The pleasure belongs to me," I said. "And I am delighted to see you looking as well as ever."

She came into the room moving with the grace of a dancer, which I knew she had once been, adding to her distinction and refinement. "Please make yourself comfortable," she said as she gestured toward the chairs. "I trust my father showed you the proper courtesy. . . ."

"I don't believe he cares much for Colin and me."

She sat down with a pained smile. "I'm afraid he will forever find you and Mr. Pendragon something of a threat, given all that you know."

"That is absurd," I answered as I seated myself across from her.

"I know"—she gazed at me with her luminous smile—"but my father is quite a different matter. I hope you will forgive him his impropriety."

"Think nothing of it. You are fortunate to have your father still in your life under any circumstances."

As if on cue, her father returned with a tray of tea and biscuits and set them before us. "Thank you, Evers," she said, maintaining the charade that had been in place the first several times we had visited her. He loosed another grumble and ambled back out of the room, and I hoped he felt assuaged by the continuance of their normalcy. "I would say he means well, but it's really only insofar as it suits him," she said with a wink. "But I suspect you have not come here simply to check up on my father and me. You are by yourself; please tell me there is nothing wrong with Mr. Pendragon."

"Mr. Pendragon is quite well," I assured her, "and would send his regards if he knew I was here. But he is out of the country for a few days and I have been following up on a case. It is a case that has led me, amazingly, to you." I could not help the smile that overtook my face.

"Oh . . ." She finished preparing our tea and handed me a cup. "How extraordinary. Should I be concerned?"

I laughed and could tell by the twinkle in her eyes that she had not meant to be serious, either. "It would seem that we live in a time when your services are particularly desired. I suppose it should come as no surprise that more than one case might bring us to your doorstep."

She lifted her eyebrows and nodded. "I make a good living." She leaned forward, offering the plate of biscuits, and gave me a conspiratorial smile. "If they ever tire of my form of the truth I shall be quite done in."

"Or perhaps you will forgo the spirit world and make some use of this new thinking around the workings of the mind. You are already clever enough to ferret out what people wish to hear. And that skill is most definitely not something you divine from formless ectoplasm."

Her smile widened, once more illuminating her face. "You flatter me, Mr. Pruitt. So tell me, which of my clients is it that has crossed your path?"

"Adelaide Endicott," I said, and watched as her face slowly crumbled. "Ah . . . of course you have heard what has happened."

"The papers are implying that she took her own life, but I cannot imagine her capable of doing such a thing. Do you and Mr. Pendragon really believe it to be so?"

"We have only just begun our investigation, but Colin is decidedly of the mind that Miss Adelaide did not harm herself nor is it the matter of an accident. Though I will confess that I do not know exactly how it is he has come to that opinion so quickly."

"Really?! I would have thought you the one person privy to the machinations of his deducements."

"I suppose I am, but only as he sees fit to share them with me. So while I can assure you that Miss Adelaide did not bring an end to her own life, I cannot tell you how such a thing is known, and as I am sure you can imagine, there is much else yet to be solved."

"So how can I help you?" she asked as she refilled our tea.

"Did you know the young man who assisted Miss Adelaide, Mr. Freddie Nettle?"

"Of course. He seemed a bright and earnest young man who very much doted on her."

"Then I presume he came here with her?"

"Absolutely. My understanding was that she went nowhere without him. He pushed her wheeled chair, and if there were stairs or some other obstacle impeding her, he either removed it or swept her up in his arms and delivered her to wherever she needed to go. He was quite strong, though she was only just a slip of a woman."

"Yes . . ." I could not help the sigh that escaped from my lips. "Which does rather play against him. If Miss Eugenia can get the Yard to heed her suspicions against Mr. Nettle, it is not difficult to believe that he could easily have cast her from that window."

Lady Stuart frowned. "How awful. I simply cannot imagine him doing such a thing. You would have thought she was his own grandmother the way he fretted over her."

"Miss Adelaide must have been grateful to him."

"She adored him."

"I wonder if she made any allowances for him in her will."

Lady Stuart's brow creased as she clearly picked up on my inference. "Not that she mentioned to me, and we did talk about so very many things."

I waved a hand dismissively, finding my own imaginings ill-conceived and lacking merit. "If Mr. Nettle had harbored any desire to murder his mistress I am certain he could have found a more suitable way to accomplish it than in the middle of the night when the two of them were alone. Even the dimmest of criminals can usually conjure a better alibi than what little he has contended of that night." I looked back at Lady Stuart. "So what was it that brought Miss Adelaide to see you on such a regular basis?"

"She sought the same thing most of the women who come to me seek, freedom from the ghosts of her past."

I felt my eyebrows spring upward. It was not the answer I had expected, though at the moment, I wasn't at all sure what I had thought she might say. "Ghosts?!" I said after a moment. "Are you now a convert to your own chicanery?"

She laughed, as I had meant her to, and leveled her striking gaze upon me again. "Come now, Mr. Pruitt, we all of us have ghosts in our pasts. Things we regret but cannot change. Fears . . . misfortunes . . . burdens . . . all of which wriggle about our minds like burrowing worms. There are those of us who can abide it, shunting them back in place as it becomes necessary, and there are those who cannot. They are the victims of the decisions they cannot unmake and the deeds they cannot undo. Miss Adelaide was one such person."

The smile on my face disintegrated as quickly as a shiver from her words. These distant ghosts, these formless entities who insisted on having their due, were not foreign to me. "I see. . . ." I murmured, taking a languorous sip of my tea to further collect myself before speaking again. "And what was it that most affected Miss Adelaide?"

"It was a child."

"A child . . . ?!" I repeated. It was unthinkable that Miss Adelaide, a spinster, could have borne a child.

"Yes," Lady Stuart said, smoothly ignoring my obvious shock. "Not her own, of course, but that of a woman who worked for her family when she was young. Someone she felt she was in a position to aid but did not. This would have been some sixty years ago. Can you imagine the scandal?"

"I'm afraid I can imagine the scandal were it to have happened yesterday. And what became of this child or the woman?"

"As I am sure you assume, the infant was whisked off after its unfortunate birth. And the woman . . ." She shook her head and looked off toward the windows. "Adelaide said it destroyed the poor thing. I do not know how it could have been any other way."

"How awful." And yet I found my mind already twisting through a host of other possibilities. "*Her*, you said. The child was a girl?"

"Yes."

"Which might explain why she professed to having seen a vision of a young girl wandering around Layton Manor weeping. Did she tell you of that?"

"Many times. She said the visions started almost two years

ago. Perhaps a lifetime of guilt had finally done its damage as she began to face the waning of her own health. . . ." Lady Stuart let her voice drift off, and while I knew there was something to her assertion, something else had begun to rattle about my brain that refused to be stilled.

"Do you not suppose . . ." I began, taking great pains to sound casual, ". . . that there might not be the slimmest chance that she was, in fact, referring to her own indiscretion? Could that not speak to the level of intense emotion she still carried after all these years?"

A wistful smile brushed across Lady Stuart's lips as she looked at me, her eyes filled with aching and sorrow. "Perhaps, though I would find it hard to believe it to be so," she answered. "There is an irrevocable bond between a mother and her child that can neither be denied nor extinguished. It is sacred and true, and I can only tell you that Adelaide Endicott did not appear to have that fire in her soul when she talked about her regret."

"I see. . . ." I muttered like a man who knows nothing of a woman's heart. But in this Lady Stuart was mistaken, for my own mother had possessed no such bond. So while I felt compelled to remain unresolved about the possibility of Miss Adelaide's having borne a child, I also suddenly had the inkling that Lady Stuart had been speaking with the authority of one who has suffered the very thing she was talking about. "What did she tell you of her visions?"

"The woman in question was the lady's maid who cared for both her and her sister, Eugenia," she stated with a sigh, making it clear that the weight of the story impacted her still. "Miss Adelaide never told me the young woman's name nor did I seek it out. It made little difference since the woman was released from the Endicotts' employ at the time it happened."

"So I would suppose," I blurted, receiving a pained sort of grimace from Lady Stuart that made me curse my carelessness and vow to be more delicate.

"Yes . . ." she said evenly as she poured a bit more tea for both of us. "Apparently, the poor girl had been courting a young man who worked at one of the neighboring estates, and when her indiscretion became known she was whipped nearly to death by Adelaide and Eugenia's father. Miss Adelaide told me that it was through her intervention, and hers alone, that the young woman's life managed to be saved."

"And what of Miss Eugenia? Did she not also interfere?"

Lady Stuart looked at me with an expression that was at once as assured as it was discreet. "I do not know whether you ever had the pleasure of meeting Miss Adelaide; she was such a kind and pleasant person, but she and her sister . . ." Her eyes drifted off for a moment before she snapped them back to me with a gracious smile. "They were two very different women, and while I would not presume to state that one was any better than the other, they had their own perspectives on intolerance and propriety."

Even with the small amount of time I had spent with Miss Eugenia, I imagined that I understood precisely what she was telling me. "What do you think it was about this lady's maid that brought Miss Adelaide to your doorstep after all these years?"

"The woman's daughter," she answered with the same steady confidence she had shown for the whole of our discussion. "She was convinced that the beating her father had wrought upon the young woman had caused her child to be born with grievous injuries and that the girl could not have lived much past a handful of years at most. It tormented Miss Adelaide. I believe it's why she began to have the visions that first brought her to me." Lady Stuart set her teacup down and leaned back, a flash of something bolting past her eyes so quickly that I could not determine what it was. "She wanted me to contact the child," she finally went on, her voice softening and lowering in a way that made me suspect she was plagued by her own bit of guilt for having allowed herself to be contracted for such a grim and impractical duty. "She wanted me to beseech the child for forgiveness. Miss Adelaide had become terrified of dying because she feared the wrath that would surely be levied against her for what she had failed to do: to spare the life of an innocent child for the iniquities of its mother."

My heart felt leaden and I found myself shifting my eyes toward the windows as the thought of the remorse that had seized Miss Adelaide late in her life fully settled on my chest like a weighted coat. That she had carried such a burden for so many decades made her final schism with reality seem almost inevitable. "I hardly know what to say," was all I could manage to articulate before an insistent pounding at the front door interrupted us. "It would seem I have infringed upon the time that belongs to your clientele," I muttered as I stood up, relieved to be able to leave just the same.

Lady Stuart glanced at the clock on the mantel before looking back at me. "I have no clients at this time of the day. . . ." But she got no further before a great bustling in the hallway stopped her, and we both turned to find her father stepping into view with Eugenia Endicott directly on his heels.

"Mr. Pruitt . . ." she fairly hissed as she came around from behind Evers and planted herself just inside the parlor. "I am aghast to find you here with this . . . *woman*. . . ." She said the word as though its definition was that of a harridan or prostitute. "I am quite certain that I already made it well clear to you that she did nothing more for my sister than twist her gentle nature and torment her mind. When Mr. Fischer reported that you had insisted he bring you here, I simply had to see it for myself." She scowled at me with such a look in her eyes that I found myself forced to glance away. "This is intolerable, Mr. Pruitt. . . ."

"Miss Eugenia . . ." I started to say, though I had no idea what I was going to follow it up with.

"I do not wish to hear whatever it is you feel compelled to say to me, Mr. Pruitt. You and Mr. Pendragon will not spend my money on such frippery. You vowed to find the cause of my sister's death or oblige Scotland Yard to arrest Mr. Nettle, which is what I have insisted on from the start. But now I see that you are determined to scrabble through every dung heap you encounter until you have achieved some self-satisfaction that I will not abide. This is my sister, Mr. Pruitt. My good and godly sister.

You may submit a final accounting of your time to my solicitor and then the services of you and Mr. Pendragon shall no longer be required."

And just as quickly as she had arrived, Eugenia Endicott swept back out of the room, leaving my heart in my throat as I scrambled to think how I was ever going to tell Colin.

CHAPTER 9

After I left Lady Stuart's I made my way to Shauney's pub and spent the rest of my afternoon there, scribbling notes about the Endicott case and trying to figure out what I had accomplished in Colin's absence. As late afternoon turned to evening, I ordered supper for myself, aware that Mrs. Behmoth would not be going to such trouble just for me. I nursed a couple of ciders for most of the length of my stay and when Shauney asked if I expected to stay at his table through the whole of the night, I finally determined it was time to go home to wait for Colin's return. I was anxious to tell him about my contact with Charlotte Hutton. He was going to be amazed, or infuriated, I didn't really know which.

By the time I got home from Shauney's, I found Mrs. Behmoth in a mood amidst the unmistakable signs of Colin's return. Given that the time had barely ticked past seven-thirty, I was stunned to discover his valise already on the settee, flung wide with its contents scattered about as though they had been held under pressure. I hurried back to the stairs to yell down to Mrs. Behmoth about his whereabouts, as there wasn't a sound of him upstairs, and Mrs. Behmoth trudged all the way up to see me, and in that one action I knew all was not well.

" 'E's afoul," she had growled at me as though it was my responsibility now. "Came in 'ere like a ruddy tempest lookin' fer you and railin' on 'bout the Yard. You'd better get 'im settled down before 'e comes back or I'll see that 'e 'as somethin' ta grouse about."

I did not doubt Mrs. Behmoth, so I wasted no time in learning that he had immediately headed off for the Yard, his agitation and displeasure intact. And so it was that I now found myself hurrying up the front steps to the great brick turreted building with its white stripes of masonry, New Scotland Yard. I dutifully signed in on the ground floor and was up at the Detective Division two floors above with great haste. My stride only faltered and began to slow when I heard Colin's voice, clipped and thick with displeasure, as I neared Maurice Evans's office. While I could not yet make out what he was saying, there was no denying the mood with which he was delivering it. Each of the junior constables I passed averted their eyes from mine, though whether from embarrassment or amusement I could not be sure. All I knew was that for once Mrs. Behmoth had not been embellishing the truth.

". . . And where have you been . . . ?" Colin turned on me the moment I eased the office door open, before I could even fully get inside.

"Nice to see you as well," I answered with a lopsided grin, hoping to at least be able to partially cajole him out of whatever mood had thusly descended upon him. "Mrs. Behmoth said I would find you here."

"Ach . . . Mrs. Behmoth," he scoffed before turning back to Maurice Evans, who was seated behind his desk with his arms folded across his chest and a pinch to his lips that appeared to speak as much about defense as it did defiance. "He was a self-righteous little prig when we were working on the Connicle case," Colin carried on, clearly not about to be deterred from whatever was needling him. "You told him yourself to stand down a time or two. I remember it. Mr. Pruitt remembers it. And now you expect that we're to work with him as though he has the slightest wisp of usefulness to anyone other than himself?!"

"Mr. Pendragon . . ."

"Tell me"—Colin kept right on—"is he having it off with the superintendent's daughter or something?"

Mr. Evans sputtered as he bolted upright and began to choke, though he had been drinking nothing. "Keep your voice down," he commanded harshly as he continued to cough.

"He is." Colin sneered. "That little twit is courting Tottenshire's daughter. . . ."

"Who are you talking about?" I finally cut in.

"That little toady hanging around the Connicle estate during the initial investigation who decided it was his duty to tell us what we *could* and *could not* do."

"His name is James Lanchester," Mr. Evans supplied, as though that would make any difference. "*Sergeant* James Lanchester."

"Sergeant . . . ?" I repeated, immediately remembering the brash young man for both his pomposity and the fact that he had not known who Colin was. "I thought he was a constable . . . ?"

"He has been promoted," Mr. Evans said with notable distaste. "When they handed me this temporary assignment after Inspector Varcoe's murder, they moved Lanchester into my old place. *Permanently*." And there, quite evidently, was the rub. Young Mr. Lanchester was handed a new job while Mr. Evans was expected to earn his way into a position he had merited years ago. "I told you he was the one they'd sent ahead to Zurich," he reminded Colin curtly, his own mood having apparently soured. "It wasn't my call to make, but I will see what I can do about getting him reassigned."

"I didn't remember his name," Colin shot back, which was hardly a surprise, "but I certainly remembered his squirrely little haughty face the moment I saw him."

"How nice for you," Mr. Evans grumbled as he pulled a half-smoked cheroot out of the ashtray on the corner of his desk.

"You're not going to light that. . . ." Colin curled up his face.

"Well, I wasn't planning on eating it."

Colin snatched it out of Mr. Evans's hands and tossed it into the waste bin. "Not while I'm here. You and your Yard have already been offensive enough; I'll not stand here and let you blow that putrid filth in my face."

Mr. Evans gazed into the trash and for a moment I thought he might be about to fish his cigar back out. "You mustn't feel compelled to stay," he sniped back after a moment.

"What is going on?" I asked as I sat myself across from Mr. Evans in spite of the fact that Colin remained standing. "What happened at your breakfast in Zurich this morning?"

"*Nothing* happened." Colin answered first, swinging down into the chair next to me. "That little pox doesn't know when to keep his mouth shut, and if we had any opportunity to work with the Zurich authorities I can assure you it is now gone."

"Mr. Pendragon . . ."

"Do *not* patronize me. . . ." Colin snapped.

I cringed as I tried to catch his eye, but Colin was not paying the least attention to me. He was clearly well beyond my being able to offer any subtle reminder that we *needed* Maurice Evans. We had suffered years of animosity with the Yard, so working with Mr. Evans, who actually esteemed Colin's skill, was a change that could only serve him . . . us . . . well. "Would you mind, Mr. Evans, if I had a private word with Mr. Pendragon for just a moment? I have something of some urgency to discuss, and it could have a bearing . . ." I wanted to say *on his mood,* but decided to leave the rest of the sentence unsaid.

Mr. Evans ticked an eyebrow at me and I thought I spotted something like pity dashing across his eyes. "Very well," he said, and pushed himself up, striding to the door. "I will see if I can't enjoy a smoke where it will be appreciated." He glared at Colin, who did not bother to look back at him, and then tossed me that sympathetic look again before pulling the door shut behind himself.

"I know what you're up to," Colin barked before I could say anything.

"And what would that be?"

"You mean to scold me like some petulant child." He finally turned and looked at me, and for the first time I could see a great wave of fury continuing to bubble there just as I had known there would be. "You weren't there," he snapped. "To watch that sniveling, pompous little twat trying to monopolize the conversation and order me around as though *I* worked for *him!*" He gave a *harrumph*. "And then he has the audacity to suppose he can simply order the assistant commissioner of Credit Suisse to do his bidding . . . ?!" He screwed his face up until he looked about ready to spit. "It was appalling. All he did was offend everyone we met and ensure their unwillingness to help us any further."

"It does sound awful . . . and inappropriate . . . and a little like you at that age." I could not resist; it seemed important to remind him, though it only earned me a deeper scowl. "I'm sure it was terrible and I understand that you are incensed," I started again, giving him his due, which I knew was what he needed. "But I have some news that is going to astound you and could quite possibly change everything."

His eyes narrowed as he studied me a moment, making it feel as though he were attempting to see what game I might be playing at. "What . . . ?" he finally asked, sounding almost distrustful as he did so.

"I was walking home from Shauney's last night, and you will simply not believe who accosted me in the park outside of our flat."

"Charlotte Hutton?" he answered without a breath's hesitation.

My face froze, or perhaps it dropped just a touch, leaving me both stunned and the tiniest bit disappointed that he had guessed my fantastical news so simply. "Yes . . ." I sputtered.

"*Charlotte Hutton?!*" he said again, bolting up from his chair with such a look of exhilaration that it would have been impossible to believe he had been so angry just an instant before. "*I knew it! . . .*" he carried on, starting to pace the few steps across Mr. Evans's tiny office. Though what it was he knew I could hardly begin to imagine. "What did she say . . . ? Why didn't you wrestle her to the ground and drag her to the nearest bobby . . . ? What were you thinking?!"

I could do little more than blink foolishly as he rattled off his questions in rapid-fire succession.

He sat back down and leaned toward me, speaking in a soft, intimate way, his words still jumbling out quickly. "Where is she now? You haven't told anyone else, have you? Do *not* tell Maurice Evans or any of these other Yard nobs. Especially that spiv Lanchester. They can all scratch their buggered heads until we figure this out." He suddenly pulled up short and stared at me. "So tell me what happened. Speak up, Ethan!"

"She told me a very different story, Colin."

"What?" It wasn't so much a question as an expression of doubt.

"She admits to the affair with Mr. Tessler, but she claims that the money, the murders, it was all his plan and she was as much a victim of him as the very people he ordered killed."

"Of course she did," he sneered.

"I have to admit there was something compelling about her tale, especially after she—"

"Oh, come now . . ." he said dismissively, his expression going hard as he stared right into my eyes. "Tell me . . . did she tear up when she spoke about the horrible loss of her poor young son?"

I could only sigh in response.

He stood up again with a laugh. "It's brilliant! She is the devil." He took a few steps away from me as he dug a hand into his vest pocket and extracted a crown that he quickly began spinning through his fingers. "Let me guess. . . ." he muttered with a hint of gamesmanship in his voice as he started pacing around the tiny space, his gaze cast toward the ceiling in amused thought. "She's looking for us to release some money to her, just enough so she and her daughter can disappear somewhere safe and live out their lives in peace: America, Bolivia, the Far East. Somewhere Wynn Tessler and his supposed network of thugs will never be able to find her. Because she claims to still be terrified of him. . . ." He dropped his gaze to me, one eyebrow arced heavenward. "She said that, didn't she?" I nodded and he gave a pleased snicker. "That's why she didn't go to the Yard to straighten this matter out like a true innocent would. That's why she appealed to *you,* my dear Ethan. Because she knew damn well that if she stood any chance of selling her bag of twaddle it would have to be to a tender heart like yours. Did she ask about me? I'll bet she said she was hoping to speak with the both of us, didn't she . . . ?"

I swallowed hard at his apt relay of our conversation and managed nothing more than a light shrug.

"There is no doubt in my mind that she knew I was gone before she approached you. Cunning . . ." The coin spinning around his fingers was moving so quickly it seemed conceivable that it might soften from the friction. "Did you follow her . . . ?" he asked after a second, keeping his back to me.

"There was a cab . . ." I started to say.

"No doubt she had arranged to have it waiting for her." He turned back to me and seized the coin in his hand as he fairly blurted out, "Did you see a livery number on the carriage? A name of any type?"

"It was pouring rain. . . ." I started to say, realizing how feeble an excuse that sounded, so I left it at that.

"No matter. Likely there was neither. She would have made certain of it." He came and settled back down next to me, his expression full of fire.

"There is something else," I finally had a chance to say, though I could tell his mind was already racing well ahead. "She opened the neckline of her dress and revealed her décolletage." I gestured with my hand to the delicate area below the neck.

Colin scowled. "Well, that was a foolish miscalculation on her part," he drolled, but I ignored his inference.

"The skin is covered with scars," I said. "Horrible marks and such disfigurement that it appeared to bolster her contention of the sort of relationship she suffered under Mr. Tessler."

His scowl deepened as he continued to stare at me. "How do we know she did not receive those from her late husband? Or that they were the product of makeup and putty? You said it was night and raining out. That is a perfect combination for such trickery of the eyes."

"Well . . ." But I had nothing else to add. His point was keenly made and certainly in keeping with the sorts of lies I would have believed her capable of before the previous night.

"Tell me. . . ." Colin interrupted my thoughts in the most off-hand way. "When did she state she would contact us again?" And all I could think was that of course he knew this was how she had left it.

"In a few days," I answered. "Once you got back and I had a chance to speak with you."

"Of course. . . ." he muttered, pursing his lips and casting his gaze far out the window.

"There is one more thing that has nothing to do with Mrs. Hutton. . . ." I spoke up again, eager to deliver all the news I had while he was in his current contemplative state. "I'm afraid Miss Eugenia has fired us from her sister's case."

"What?!" And this time it was a question filled with surprise. "Well, no matter." He quickly dismissed this news with a wave of his hand as he got to his feet again. "We shall just go back to the service of Mr. Nettle then. He brought us into that case any-way." He took the few steps to the office door and swung it open. "Let's go. We've much to discuss, not the least of which is how you got us fired by Miss Eugenia in such a brief period of time. I do fear I may be rubbing off on you. . . ." He chuckled.

I started to protest before quickly deciding to hold my tongue and quietly follow him out, all the while thinking how grateful I was to have him back.

CHAPTER 10

———◆◇◆———

Colin and I talked without pause from the moment we took our leave of Scotland Yard. He poured out his frustrations with the Zurich trip while I filled him in on the details of Charlotte Hutton, our firing by Eugenia Endicott, and the happenstance of discovering that Lady Dahlia Stuart was the medium Miss Adelaide had been consulting.

We had gone back to Shauney's and I had an Earl Grey tea and currant scone while Colin ate dinner, and we did not run out of conversation until nearly nine. It was fortunate timing since Colin had sent word from Scotland Yard to Freddie Nettle that he should meet us back at our flat at nine sharp. We needed to tell him that he was to be our employer on the Endicott case again; never mind that it also meant we were once more working gratis.

As Colin and I walked home I was not in the least surprised that he was leading us along the exact same route I had used when Charlotte Hutton had stopped me. And when he pushed the short gate open that led into the narrow park stretching the length of our street, I knew he meant for me to narrate precisely what had occurred yet again.

"Where did you sit?" he asked as he followed me onto the flat stones that led through the slender bit of woodland.

"Just there," I said, pointing to the iron bench as though it were the site of something profound. "She sat on the nearer end and I sat opposite." To my surprise he quickly ran a hand along the seat of the bench before stooping down and peering beneath it. "Whatever are you doing?" I asked with some distaste as he slid both hands underneath it before dropping one palm down the front leg on that side while the other skirted across the ground.

"I'm checking to see if she dropped anything. . . ." he answered, and I knew I should have known that.

"And did she?" I asked, even though I could see his hands were empty as he stood up.

"Where did she catch the cab?" he pressed on, ignoring the obviousness of my question.

"Around the corner. Tell me you're not about to go rooting through the dung. . . ."

He glared at me with a wholly unamused expression. "Are you quite finished?"

It was my turn to ignore the question as I took him through the opposite side of the park and pointed to the area where I had seen Mrs. Hutton climb aboard the carriage. "It was raining," I reminded him. "And it did so for most of the night. I doubt there is anything left behind."

He scanned the area and knelt down only once to poke at something near the gutter before giving a quick shrug and standing up again. "Clearly, you are right. Still . . ." he added, and I was sure he meant to remind me that I had not done everything I could have.

I followed him up the few steps to our tiny porch and made it inside just in time to find Mrs. Behmoth thudding down from upstairs with an empty tea tray in one hand. "Well, thank bloody 'ell," she grumbled. "Ya got a visitor and I ain't paid enough ta amuse 'em."

"Is it Mr. Nettle?" Colin asked as he started up.

"It is. . . ." She glared at him as she watched him bound up the stairs before finally turning her gaze to me. "Did ya get the burr outta 'is bum?"

"It was the Yard," I answered by way of explanation. "You know how he gets about them."

"Them and everybody else 'e ain't got the patience ta tolerate." She started off toward the kitchen. "I don't know 'ow 'e got like that," she muttered. "'Is father ain't that way and 'is mum sure weren't neither."

I stared after her for a moment, thinking she might turn back and give me a chuckle or wink to show that she understood her own jest, but she only pushed her way into the kitchen, and I realized she'd meant what she had said. Had we been alone I might have chased after her, but under the circumstances I had no choice but to shake my head and hurry upstairs.

Mr. Nettle was seated on the settee across from Colin, who was pouring the tea with a magnanimity that assured me he was quite pleased with how his day had improved. "Mr. Nettle, thank you for coming out so late."

"Mr. Pruitt," he said, bouncing to his feet to shake my hand. "I am always at your service. I cannot tell you how pleased I was to receive your message. How is the case progressing? Have you made any strides in clearing my name?"

"We make strides every day," Colin replied archly as he handed a cup of tea to Mr. Nettle. "In fact, we have already managed to ruffle enough feathers that Miss Eugenia has had a change of heart and decided to relieve us of her support in investigating the case."

"Oh . . ." Mr. Nettle's color drained with astonishing speed. "When you sent me that message informing me that she had decided to hire you herself, I hoped it meant she had second thoughts about my guilt. I see now that my optimism was misplaced." His body sagged noticeably. "Does she persist in calling for my arrest?" He slid his teacup onto the table and folded his arms across his chest as though attempting to defend himself from an attack that he alone could sense. It seemed odd for a man of his robust sturdiness, and it made me feel ever more sorry for him. If he actually did prove to be guilty of any malfeasance I was going to be astonished by it.

"You mustn't worry yourself about Miss Eugenia and what she rails on about," Colin reassured. "You need only be concerned with what I think." He flashed a quick smile, and I could tell that Mr. Nettle didn't know whether Colin was kidding or not. "Right now all you have to do is answer some questions for me, and then I shall need you to do me a service."

"Of course, Mr. Pendragon," the young man answered without hesitation. "I shall do anything you ask." He hesitated and I could see a kernel of something uneasy pass behind his eyes as he flicked them down and then back up again. "But I must remind you that, as before, I won't be able to pay you very much. I shall assume whatever expenses you require, but I will have to beg your understanding . . ."

"Please . . ." Colin waved him off before handing over the plate of biscuits Mrs. Behmoth had included on the tray. "I do not solve crimes simply to be paid," he explained offhandedly as he slid a biscuit into his own mouth. "Isn't that right?" he added with a sideways glance at me.

"Without question," I answered at once, eager to reassure Mr. Nettle. "Unless of course we are talking about the guilty or the very rich," I added with a chuckle and was glad to see Mr. Nettle do the same.

"Absolving an innocent man is payment enough," Colin said as he took a sip of his tea, though I noticed he kept his gaze on Mr. Nettle and I wondered whether he had been reconsidering the potential of this man's involvement in Miss Adelaide's death. "May I assume you were well acquainted with the nurses who worked for Miss Adelaide?"

"Yes, of course. Miss Bromley assisted during the day and Miss Whit arrived about seven o'clock each evening. Neither of them worked on Sundays, so we had to make do with the women of the household staff that day. It seemed to be working out." He grimaced and shook his head slightly. "I cannot help feeling that I failed Miss Adelaide and shall never forgive myself for it." His despondence was thick in his voice.

"How old are you, Mr. Nettle?" I asked.

"Thirty-one."

"Which makes you too young a man to hold such reproach against yourself. We are none of us clairvoyant. We cannot know what the future will hold, which leaves us at a decided disadvantage. You must remember that."

"You are very kind, Mr. Pruitt. . . ."

"Yes, yes . . ." Colin interrupted. "But Mr. Pruitt does bring up an interesting point. Lady Dahlia Stuart is said to be clairvoyant, is she not? And I understand your mistress made twice-monthly visits to her?"

"That's right, sir. I went with her every time. Her Ladyship does have a lady's maid, but she is quite a bit older and could not have managed to assist Miss Adelaide in getting into and out of the house."

"And though it would have been far easier to have Lady Stuart come to Layton Manor to counsel Miss Adelaide, I understand her sister would not permit it?"

Mr. Nettle flinched slightly, making it evident that this was a topic he did not like discussing. "Miss Eugenia forbade it. She could not stop her sister from visiting Lady Stuart, but she could keep Her Ladyship from coming to their home. It was forever a point of contention between them."

"Of course"—Colin shot a glance in my direction—"so I have been told. And what did you do while Miss Adelaide was consulting with Lady Stuart?"

"I sat with her valet, Evers is his name, in the kitchen. It left us far enough away that their conversations were private but close enough that I could quickly be summoned if the need arose."

"And did Miss Adelaide ever confide in you the reason for her visits to Lady Stuart?"

Mr. Nettle shifted the slightest bit before snatching up his teacup and fussing over it with undo attention. "Not particularly . . ." he said after a moment, but I knew he wasn't being entirely honest and shot Colin a look to be sure he saw it too, though I needn't have concerned myself.

"Not a very compelling answer," he pointed out. "Perhaps you might be more specific and allow us to judge the particulars."

Poor Mr. Nettle blanched, and once again I found myself feeling pity for him. That he could be conceived of as a murderer was lost on me, but then I had been fooled before. "It was a little girl," he finally said with marked trepidation, his eyes falling to the cup he still held in his hands. "I believe the child died and she felt responsible for her death. I don't know who she was, but Miss Adelaide confessed to a lifetime's regret for what had befallen the child."

"She gave you no name?"

"Nothing. I swear it, Mr. Pendragon." And as he looked back up at Colin I would have sworn to the depths of the man's sincerity myself.

"Any hint as to her connection to the child? Why she was driven to feel such responsibility?"

"She did not confide any such details to me and I dared not ask," he explained and, of course, he was right. Such impudence would never have been tolerated.

Colin sucked in an agitated breath and appeared to be measuring his patience, though what he had expected to hear I could not imagine. "So you believe she was troubled by the death of a child who had no obvious connection to Miss Adelaide. Doesn't that strike you as odd?" he pushed ahead, and given the circuity of this conversation, I could not help admiring his persistence.

Mr. Nettle blinked as though perceiving a question thick with trickery before quite suddenly blurting, "Well, it's always particularly sad when a child dies."

"We all have to die at one time or another," Colin said with a sniff, and I could not help cringing.

"I really don't know anything about the girl or her death," Mr. Nettle blurted in a great flurry of words, "but I know that Miss Adelaide blamed herself. She told me she had not done enough for the child when she'd had the chance to do something at all."

"There now, you see . . ." Colin said as the ghost of a grin fleeted across his lips, ". . . that all sounds *quite* particular to me. This was obviously a child who not only was in her life but upon whom she appeared to have been able to make something of an impact at one time. You mentioned a lifetime's regret; may I assume these events around this child happened some years ago?"

"Indeed." Mr. Nettle nodded, setting his teacup on the table and tugging nervously at his sleeves as though they had ridden up improperly. "She told me once it was a child she knew when she was just a young woman herself. I remember because I tried to convince her there is so little any of us can do when we are but young ourselves. But she was not to be consoled. By then she was already suffering the visions. She had become convinced the child's spirit had come to Layton Manor to avenge the wrongs that had been done to her when Miss Adelaide was young."

"And what of Miss Eugenia? Did you know her to suffer these regrets or ethereal sightings?"

Mr. Nettle shook his head and pursed his lips. "I should say not. Such talk made her angry. She would not tolerate it. Not even from her sister."

"Yes . . ." Colin agreed, one eyebrow arching up. "So Mr. Pruitt and I have come to realize. What did you make of your mistress's relationship with Lady Stuart?"

"It is not my place . . ." he began to demur.

"It is with us. I will remind you that we are trying to warrant that no murder charges are brought against you, Mr. Nettle. I would assume you are well aware of the reach the Endicott family wields. It is only a matter of time before we hear from Lord Endicott himself. You would be a fool if you believed him willing to endure the perception that his eldest sister might have put an end to her own life."

"Yes . . . of course. . . ." Mr. Nettle sagged back into the settee and I caught sight of a thin film of perspiration on his upper lip. "You understand that I had no personal quarrel with Her Ladyship. She was always kind and patient with Miss Adelaide. But neither did I believe her ministrations to be of much use. Sometimes when we would leave I did find Miss Adelaide's mood considerably brightened, but most often it seemed to have little bearing at all. I could not help but think that the visits did little more than reopen the wounds Miss Adelaide was unable to stanch. And it brought no end to her deliriums."

"You are referring to her visions of the young girl?"

"Yes, sir."

Colin leaned forward and set his teacup down, leveling a steady gaze on Mr. Nettle. "You must think about this next question very carefully," he began, "as your answer needs to be the truth as you know it rather than the product of anything you think others wish us to believe."

Mr. Nettle nodded with the gravest of looks, the discomfort in his eyes matched by the grayness of his pallor and I knew what Colin was going to ask: a question we had already posed countless times before. But this time I wondered if the answer would be different.

"During your tenure with Miss Adelaide, were you ever aware of, or hear any rumblings about, or even come to suspect, that she had ever tried to cause harm to herself?"

The breath seemed to rush out of Mr. Nettle as he stared back at Colin, this broad, powerful man appearing almost stricken at the thought. "I . . ." He paused a second and cleared his throat. "I know I would do myself a great service were I to answer yes, but it would be a lie." He shook his head. "There were times I would find her weeping, or she would be terrified by a thing she was certain she had seen, but never, not ever, did I hear her say she wished she no longer lived. It simply is not so, even if I am hung for the lack of it." He stared back at us, his eyes filled with aching, and I wished for his sake that it had been otherwise, but even so, I knew Colin would not care. "Will you still work this case, Mr. Pendragon?" he asked in a voice so frail it was nothing more than a whisper.

Colin sat back with a somber smile. "Of course. A thing too easily done can be borne by the Yard, so I relish the opportunity to ferret out the truth of your innocence. And so I shall." He stood up and paced over to the fireplace where he poked at it despite the fact that it was already roaring. "Might you know where Mr. Pruitt and I can get into contact with Miss Adelaide's former night nurse, Miss What . . . ?" He glanced over at me.

"Whit," I said.

Both of his eyebrows rose. "Really . . . ? So close." He glanced back at Freddie Nettle. "Mr. Galloway has been having little luck in reaching the young woman thus far."

"I have an address for her," Mr. Nettle answered. "I kept the information for both Miss Whit and Miss Bromley lest we ever had to summon either of them early."

"We shall only need that of Miss Whit," Colin said as he walked over to the landing. "Mr. Pruitt has already met with Miss Bromley. Thank you for your time, Mr. Nettle. We shan't hold you up any longer."

Mr. Nettle looked from Colin to me, clearly surprised by the abruptness of the conversation's end. Nevertheless he readily pushed himself off the settee, looking ever more out of place for being so summarily dismissed. "You may count on me to be available whenever you require. I shall bring Miss Whit's information by first thing tomorrow morning."

"The sooner the better," Colin concurred, cuffing the man's shoulder as he started down the stairs. "And do not lose hope, Mr. Nettle, for it is sunshine that follows every storm."

"Thank you, sir," he called back, his tone having returned to something akin to normal once again.

"Sunshine follows every storm . . . ?" I repeated after we heard the door slam shut downstairs. "Where did you come up with treacle like that?"

"I overheard it on the ferry from Calais. You don't like it?"

I frowned. "What I don't like is that we are getting nowhere on this case."

"Nowhere?! We're making enormous advances. Your getting us fired is proof enough of that."

My scowl deepened as I pursed my lips. "I wish you would stop going on about how I got us fired."

"But it amuses me so," he said with a snicker as he yanked off his vest and tie and started across the room. "I am going to take a bath. You're welcome to join me, but you had best stop brooding if you do." He paused at the door and peered at me with renewed fire behind his eyes. "This has been a remarkable day," he said with great pleasure, tossing me an incorrigible smile before disappearing down the hallway. And all I could wonder was what the bloody hell he had to be so pleased about.

CHAPTER 11

Vivian Whit was a small, curvaceous woman with a wild raft of curly blond hair beneath the crisp white cap still atop her head. She was also not the least bit hesitant to speak her mind, which, I presumed, was a result of the fact that she depended on no one but herself for her livelihood or security. "It was a rogue's night last night," she was telling us. "I'm working for a grand dame now as batty as the belfry at Saint Paul's. This one can't keep straight if I'm her sister, her mum, some daft playmate she calls Trudy, or the headmistress of a school she probably hasn't set foot in for over sixty years. She's called me everything but what I am." Miss Whit leaned forward and gave Colin and me a ready wink. "Of course sometimes that does make my job easier."

"How so?" Colin asked as he coaxed his spoon around the inside of the second soft-boiled egg he'd been served.

Miss Whit's smile took on a mischievous edge. "The lady is much more cooperative when she thinks I'm her mum or headmistress. I can usually cajole her when I'm her friend as well, but when she takes me for her sister . . ." She shrugged and gave a lopsided smirk. ". . . Sometimes I just have to leave the room and come in again. She doesn't seem very fond of her sister."

"And how long have you been working for this woman?"

"I picked up the assignment right after Miss Adelaide's death." She poured herself more tea, which was apparently the only thing she consumed for breakfast, though I had to remind myself that this was actually the end of her day, not the start, as it was for us.

"Did you not take any time off after Miss Adelaide's death?"

"I don't get paid to take time off," she answered. "Thirty-six hours after Miss Adelaide's fall I was already working for this one in Notting Hill. It's not that I wasn't sad for Miss Adelaide; it's just the way of it. One person dies and there's another right behind her who needs your help." She gave a tiny shrug as her eyes drifted out the window of the small café off Bond Street where Freddie Nettle had arranged for us to meet with her.

"Where do you get your assignments from?" Colin asked as he snatched another slice of toast from the caddy at the table's center.

"From a woman who does all sorts of placements. Her name is Mrs. Denholm."

"Yes . . ." Colin said with a sideways glance at me, "I believe Mr. Galloway mentioned her to us."

"That he did," I reassured. "He said all of the placements at Layton Manor come through her."

"I wouldn't know about that." Miss Whit's smile blossomed again. "But I'm registered with her. A lot of the other nursing girls are. So when one job is completed, all one has to do is stop by Mrs. Denholm's flat and she has another one as good as waiting to be taken on. That's why I like nursing. It's good steady work and it allows me to look after myself." Her grin grew impishly. "I don't intend to do the bidding of any bloke unless I *want* to." She gave a ready laugh that we both could not help but join, given the infectiousness of her high spirits.

"Good for you then," Colin said. "Perhaps this suffrage movement of Mrs. Pankhurst's is having an impact on some of our younger women after all."

"It certainly is on the ladies who have any sense." Miss Whit beamed. "Let us not forget that our sovereign is a woman. What more proof of the capabilities of women should anyone need than that?"

I could see by the clarity and defiance in her eyes that she truly believed a change of such magnitude should be as simple as that.

"And it is women like you who shall see to that revolution." Colin tipped his head as he pushed his empty plate to the side of the table.

"Revolution . . ." she repeated with an exhalation of breath. "That makes it all seem so much more romantic."

"Romance, is it?" Colin said, managing not to laugh. "I'm afraid you must remember that the fabric of a society is never easily rewoven." He flashed a meager smile. "But we have gotten rather far afield, so permit me to return us to the topic at hand. All the sooner that we can leave you to end your day, which I can only assume you must be eager to do."

She waved a quick hand at him as she continued to sip at her tea. "I find it nearly impossible to sleep after the end of a shift. With everyone else just starting their day, it feels somehow more difficult to give up my own." She let out a sigh.

"How did Miss Adelaide manage during the night? Do you believe she regularly suffered a greater degree of difficulty during that time?"

"She did. But then I most often believe that to be the case. As soon as the sun sets and the shadows lengthen, anyone with a propensity toward fancy tends to find themselves all at odds."

"Is that what Miss Adelaide suffered then . . . ?" Colin cut in, "flights of fancy?"

"Oh . . ." Miss Whit put a hand to her mouth and looked momentarily chagrined. "I didn't mean to suggest that of Miss Adelaide. Miss Adelaide was the victim of her advancing age and the sort of hysteria that has crippled so many women for as long as it has existed."

One of Colin's eyebrows snaked up as he flicked his gaze toward me before settling it almost immediately back on Miss Whit. "Whatever would Mrs. Pankhurst think to hear you spout such a diagnosis?"

Miss Whit's shoulders set squarely as she stared back at Colin. "It is fine for Mrs. Pankhurst to say whatever she wants, but she is neither trained in the science of medicine nor the mind. Miss Adelaide saw things and heard things that simply were not there. So unless you are about to tell me that you are an advocate of spiritualism, Mr. Pendragon, I believe the only other outcome you will be able to derive is that of hysteria." Her self-satisfaction was evident as a slight smile cracked her lips.

Colin did not even try to contain the laugh that burst forth. "You, Miss Whit, are most refreshing. Now tell me the truth, did you and Miss Adelaide get on well?"

"Of course we did," she answered at once, as though any other suggestion could hardly be conceived. "I wouldn't have stayed with her if we hadn't. I have already told you there is no shortage of people to work for."

"And how did Miss Bromstad—"

"Bromley," I corrected.

"Yes . . ." He sniffed with disinterest. "How did Miss Bromley manage with Miss Adelaide?"

"Miss Adelaide loved Philippa. She is the most patient person and ever so lovely. You simply must speak with her as well."

"And Mr. Nettle? How did he and Miss Adelaide get along?"

"Well . . ." She hesitated an instant and glanced away as though trying to think of the right thing to say. "He was entirely indispensable, wasn't he? She could hardly make a move without him. I'm sure they were very close under those circumstances."

"Circumstances?"

Miss Whit swung her eyes back to us and looked almost startled. "He is a man after all, Mr. Pendragon. Propriety . . ."

"Never mind propriety," Colin pressed. "Did they get along? Did you perceive that Miss Adelaide was relatively close to him as one might expect, given the nature of his service to her . . . ? Or was there some level of tension between them?"

"He tended to her," she said again as though Colin must surely not realize what he was asking. "They were not companions or colleagues. She told him what to do and when to do it, and he followed her orders."

"Yes . . ." Colin bobbed his head, and I could feel his patience losing its moorings. "I am fully aware of the nature of the relationship between an employer and an employee. But I find it hard to believe that a woman of medical science, such as yourself, did not take note of any underlying tensions that may have existed between two people she spent a great deal of time around if she had, in fact, seen it."

I held my tongue and fought to keep my expression steady, certain she would find his ploy as overwrought as I had, but I was fooled. Her back stiffened and her eyes looked startled, almost to the point of offense, and it made me realize that I must commend Colin on our way out for recognizing this flaw in the young woman's character.

"I see that I have not made myself entirely clear," she backtracked with the smoothness of glass. "Mr. Nettle was not so foolish as to permit any sort of disgruntlement to impact his tenure with either Miss Adelaide or Miss Eugenia. He is not an imprudent man. But neither can you suppose that he could have been wholly satisfied being at the perpetual will of an elderly woman who was not herself of sound mind. I am sorry, gentlemen, but it simply has to be said. It does not matter what Miss Eugenia wishes to be so; her older sister was a sorrowful case." Miss Whit tugged at the pristine white sleeves of her uniform and ran a quick hand along the sides of her barely contained rabble of hair. "So given those circumstances, I do believe Mr. Nettle handled himself as well as anyone could dare hope for. Even so, I cannot admit to having spotted any particular affection there. It would be unlikely in any event: We are professionals, after all. Even Mr. Nettle, in his own way."

"He did not harbor any animosity toward Miss Adelaide then . . . ?"

"That would be as useless as raining fury upon a kitten or pup. What would be the sense in it?"

Colin scratched at his chin and nodded thoughtfully, and I knew what his next question would be. "Then do you believe, given the seriousness of Miss Adelaide's deteriorating condition, that she might have been capable of doing harm to herself?"

Miss Whit cringed, the stiffness of her spine as rigid as it had been just a moment before. "That question . . ." She cast her gaze off across the café for the second time and looked to be lost in her thoughts once again. "I have asked myself that same question too many times since her death." She shook her head and she shifted her eyes back to us. "Miss Adelaide was in a great deal of torment," she continued. "We can say whatever we please about mysticism, but I can attest to the fact that she was haunted by what she believed she had seen and heard."

"Then you think it is possible . . ." Colin repeated, unwilling to finish the question for a second time.

"How could it *not* be a consideration? She was quite terrified, Mr. Pendragon. There were members of the household staff who quit because of her ranting. And it was only growing worse—the visions coming more often. It had gotten so bad that on most nights I had to stay in her room with her, sitting right next to her bed, until she could fall asleep. Only then would I sneak out and leave her to the care of Mr. Nettle in her antechamber."

"I see. Was there anyone at all with whom you noticed Miss Adelaide having a strained relationship?"

Miss Whit seemed to ponder that question a minute as I hastily settled the bill with the waitress. "The only cross words I ever heard from Miss Adelaide were directed at her sister," she answered once the waitress had hustled off with a stack of our plates cradled in her arms. "Miss Eugenia had no patience for talk of tortured spirits prowling the hallways of her home."

"Was that the crux of their arguments? Do you recall what was said?"

"Oh . . ." She shook her head. "I would never listen to such things. It was no concern of mine."

I suspected she was lying and felt certain Colin thought the same. A raised voice is an invitation to eavesdrop, and few are more capable at it than the upstairs staff at a great house. "But of course," Colin said, tossing her a polite smile. "You have been most accommodating, Miss Whit. I hope you will permit us to contact you again should the need arise."

"You may depend on me, gentlemen." She gave a generous smile of her own as she stood up and brushed at her uniform. "I was very fond of Miss Adelaide."

"It must be difficult to work so closely with a client for whom you know there can only be one eventual outcome."

"And so it is. Good day, gentlemen." And with a simple nod of her head she turned and exited the café on nimble feet, her deportment as light and composed as her manner had been.

"She certainly seems to be the right woman in the right job," I said as she disappeared down the street.

"Do you think?" Colin shifted his gaze to me. "I thought her something of a conundrum. But what really interests me are the rows between Miss Adelaide and Miss Eugenia. I think it time we pressure Mr. Fitzroy for some answers."

"Fitzroy? You mean Mr. Galloway?"

He gave a dismissive wave of the hand as he pushed himself to his feet. "If you say so."

"I should hardly think we'll get much from him," I warned as I followed him out. "We have been fired from the case, so I doubt he will even let us into the house. He does seem quite fond of Miss Eugenia."

Colin waved me off yet again, tossing me a playful grin. "Oh, come now, Ethan. Do you really think I would allow such a triviality to get in the way of our solving this case? Do you not know me better than that?"

"She was livid with me," I hastened to remind him. "I don't think there is anything I will be able to say or do to convince her to change her mind."

"Considering that you are the one who got us fired, I can

hardly expect you to reacquaint us to the case," he agreed as he raised an arm to hail a cab.

"So *you* intend to persuade her then . . . ?" I said with untempered disbelief. "Perhaps I really *don't* know you."

He chuckled. "You underestimate me. Neither one of us will have to act the conciliator."

CHAPTER 12

—⟫—◦—⟪—

Colin had not played fair.

"The Yard appreciates your willingness to meet with us this afternoon, Miss Endicott," Maurice Evans said as the three of us rose to our feet as she swept into her parlor. Displeasure marred her face the moment her eyes fell on me, tamping the obvious interest she had shown only an instant before.

"And why ever would I not be willing? Heaven knows I have been trying to get the attention of Scotland Yard since my sister's murder at the hands of that scoundrel Mr. Nettle."

"Which is precisely why we are here," Mr. Evans replied with gentle patience, a feat I found rather extraordinary, given how little Colin had confided in him when we'd scooped him up from his office. "Mr. Pendragon has been quite persuasive around the potential for a shortsightedness on our part, and I intend to ensure no such error is made," he added, though far less convincingly so, in my opinion.

Nevertheless, Miss Eugenia's icy glare appeared to thaw the thinnest sliver as she raked her gaze across me once more before settling it on Colin. "Has he?" She sniffed, maintaining a measure of disregard.

"You see me here," Mr. Evans volleyed back, turning his hands palm up and giving a smile that was nothing if not spirited.

"Now you see . . ." Colin spoke up resolutely, ". . . you have presumed that your money has earned you nothing from us, and yet have I not now delivered an Acting Inspector of Scotland Yard to your parlor when you yourself were unable to accomplish such a thing?" Miss Eugenia blanched and stiffened as she continued to stare at Colin, but she did not speak a word. "I am quite certain I told you at the outset that I would need to ferret through every improbability around your sister's death in order to be sure to arrive at the precise circumstances under which she was murdered. Perhaps that will ultimately lead us to your Mr. Nettle; at this point I cannot say. But in the meantime, you simply must permit me"—he threw a passing glance in my direction—"us . . . to speak with whomever we choose about your sister . . . this household"—he waved a hand glibly, as though to include the whole of the United Kingdom, which is exactly what I knew he meant to do—"or I shall have no other recourse than to suspect that you must have something to hide." He abruptly leaned forward and studied her. "Do you have something to hide, Miss Endicott?"

I thought she was about to seize up as her jaw unhinged and her shoulders sprang up around her ears. "*What?!*"

"Why would Mr. Pruitt's speaking with Lady Stuart provoke you to so abruptly end our services?" he pressed.

"Because"—her eyes flew between the three of us, her body as rigid as if she had been physically struck—"that woman is a charlatan and a thief."

"A thief . . . ?" Colin's eyebrows bolted for the ceiling as he slowly settled back again. "Her soothsaying may be something of a lark, but I have never known her to swindle anyone."

"I fail to see the difference. . . ." Miss Eugenia shot back.

"She tells people what they want to hear for a nominal fee. They're happy, she's happy, where is the harm? A swindler, Miss Endicott, will rob you of your heart and hearth. Quite frankly, I fail to see the similarity."

Maurice Evans sucked in a quick breath and I wondered whether he was trying to suppress a wince or a guffaw. This was not going at all as I had anticipated. "Miss Endicott . . ." I began with all the gravitas I could muster, ". . . you cannot be faulted for doing what you believe to be correct, but neither can you fault us for doing what we must in pursuit of the truth. Mr. Pendragon has already assured you that he does not believe your sister took any action to harm herself. Now you must allow him to determine precisely what it was that *did* happen that night."

"I am certainly not seeking to have you hire us back," Colin pointed out with just a hint too much satisfaction. "We are on retainer with the Yard now," he lied, "so I should very much appreciate the cooperation of both you and your staff. That is all I ask."

Eugenia Endicott gave another sniff as she ran an idle finger up to poke at the gold-and-diamond necklace draped at her throat. It looked as carefree a gesture as I was convinced it was calculated, for Miss Endicott was far too polished to not realize exactly what she was doing. "Very well," she finally agreed, acting every bit the condescending dowager we all knew her to be. "But you will get no accommodation from me with regards to that pretender."

"Nor shall any be required," Colin answered indifferently. "However, I should quite like to know the true origin of your disregard for Lady Stuart. . . ."

"Disregard . . . ?!" she repeated as though he had said something absurd. "You may be assured my antipathy toward that woman runs much deeper."

"And the reason . . . ?" Colin prodded with an inelegant fracture to his patience.

"Really, Mr. Pendragon," she huffed. "I should think that would be immediately evident. That woman did nothing but torment my sister. There is no secret that Adelaide was a delicate sort her entire life. It is simply the way of it. And that parasitic woman did nothing but fill Addie's head with the type of nonsense and recklessness that stained the last years of her life. . . ."

She snapped her mouth shut, pausing as if words alone were failing her. "Her behavior was unconscionable."

"I understand the nonsense of it," Colin said, allowing the briefest flick of a tight-lipped grin, "but recklessness? Whatever do you mean by that?"

Miss Eugenia looked momentarily startled as she dropped her glare and folded her hands tightly across her lap. Even so, her spine and shoulders seemed to steel themselves as she glanced back up again and spoke in a tone laced with frost. "I fail to see what any of this has to do with my sister's murder."

"You have never told why you are so certain that Mr. Nettle murdered your sister. Whatever would his reason have been?"

"Reason . . . ?" she echoed with her usual indignation. "Because he was the only person in the room with her when he *claims* that she jumped to her death. Is that not reason enough?! Now really, Mr. Pendragon . . ."

"I am talking about motive, not circumstances," Colin fired back with the assurance of having known precisely how she was going to answer him. "You have never given me any sort of indication as to *why* Mr. Nettle might have wanted to murder your sister. Was he set to inherit something of value . . . ?"

"Inherit . . . ?" She repeated his words yet again, screwing her face up as though something quite foul had happened. "How unseemly. Tell me, Mr. Pendragon, am I to supply every nuance of your investigation? Because I fail to see what they pay you for if that is to be the case."

I watched Colin's jaw clench, ticking at the spot just below where it attached by the ear. I considered that I should speak up lest he say something regrettable, but it was Mr. Evans who beat us both. "Without a motive it is nearly impossible for a solicitor to successfully prosecute a case," he explained with unaccountable patience. "So it is common to seek the opinion of a person who is intimately involved in the case. It has been known to be exceedingly helpful."

She remained quiet for a minute, making it evident that she was weighing what sort of response she should give, and all the while her eyes remained on the three of us, defiant, willful, and filled with exasperation. "I cannot say what may have been in that man's mind," she pronounced at last. "Do you have a motive for your Ripper killings, Detective, or is that why your men never solved them?"

"You do the Yard a disservice with such a statement," Colin said. "After all, did those killings not cease over six years ago?" He waved a dismissive hand at Eugenia Endicott while I marked the event of his having defended the Yard. "But we are wasting our time here. What I am interested in hearing about is this lady's maid whose offspring apparently haunted the whole of your sister's life."

Just as I could have predicted, Miss Eugenia's face soured as she drew herself up within her chair. "So you prove yourself no better than the basest of household gossips, seeking to scrounge through the detritus of a good and noble family for any hint of misdeed, no matter its origin." Her lips, in spite of the color she had put upon them, looked nearly colorless, her eyes having gone quite black. "Very well then—Addie and I shared a young lady's maid when I was nearing my late teens and she was either nineteen or twenty. I do not recall her name as it was a very long time ago," she added unnecessarily, though I suspected she had said it to make a point. "This foolish woman compromised herself, which earned her a deserved lashing at the hand of my father for the dishonor it brought upon our household. The proof of which"—she flicked her eyes between the three of us, making certain we each saw the vitriol coiled therein—"can be seen in the fact that we are discussing it still today. My sister interceded and believed she saved the woman's life if not that of her unborn child," she scoffed. "My father was not a killer of women. He was a good and decent man. But Addie . . ." She finally slid her defiant gaze away from us.

"And you believe Lady Stuart inflamed your sister's guilt around that event," Colin added.

"All that woman did was contribute to my sister's hysteria to the point that Addie began to have visions and became ever more unsettled with each passing month. It was intolerable. That woman is as much a murderer herself."

"I'm afraid the events leading up to your sister's death are far more complex than that," Colin stated with simple finality. "I have found a pattern of scratches and pitting outside your sister's bedroom window, and your groundsman, Mr. . . . ." Colin's voice slowed and stalled.

"McPherson," I quickly supplied.

"Yes, Mr. McPherson. He tells us that a pane had been replaced recently. "Something about a wayward bird, despite no carcass being found. . . ."

Miss Eugenia scowled with a look as much of confusion as distaste. "What is your point, Mr. Pendragon?"

"I believe there was a great deal more to your sister's haunting than the workings of her own imagination."

"*What?!*" And for the first time Miss Eugenia looked profoundly startled. "What are you saying?"

"I am saying that I need to investigate further and will continue to require your cooperation," he answered succinctly. "And that is how we shall find the truth, the whole of it, around your sister's murder."

"Murder . . ." she repeated soberly before releasing a burdened sigh. "Yes. At least we can agree on that fact." Her eyes instantly regained their resolute focus and she once again bore her gaze into Colin. "Perhaps Mr. Nettle and that disgraceful Stuart woman had some sort of alliance? They may well have been allies against my sister. Do you suppose it so, Mr. Pendragon? He drove with dear Addie to those appointments without fail. He and that woman would have had every opportunity to cobble their vicious plot."

Colin nodded with a feigned sort of grimness. "At this moment everything you can conceive and everything you have yet to conceive is a possibility. Which is why we must now pursue our investigation again, with your goodwill, of course," he added, and while I could not believe she would find a whiff of credence in such a banal statement so poorly delivered, she actually looked quite gratified.

"Most certainly." She shook her head stiffly. "I may have spoken a bit hastily with my initial conclusion."

"There it is," Colin said as he bounced to his feet. "Then we should very much like to speak with your Mr. Fitzhenry."

"Galloway," I corrected with a stiff smile to Miss Eugenia.

"As you see fit," she responded, a familiar note of displeasure sneaking back into her tone. She stood up and cast her gaze upon the three of us, one after the other, before she spoke again. "I do hope you will bring an end to this quickly. I simply cannot abide the thought of Mr. Nettle"—she paused and released a stilted breath—"or whomever . . . roaming about freely while my poor Addie is gone. It does not sit well with me at all." She did not wait for any of us to answer before moving to the door and disappearing from the room completely, her final words as much a threat as a statement.

"I must say"—Colin turned to Mr. Evans with brimming magnanimity—"that your presence here this afternoon has made every bit of difference. But we mustn't delay you from your official duties another minute. May I see you out?" He gestured in the general direction of the front door as though this was his house and therefore his obligation to attend to. The very sight of it made me want to laugh, though I managed to hold my peace until Mr. Evans released a great guffaw of his own.

"Not for an ounce of gold," he said.

To my surprise Colin sloughed it off with a disinterested shrug before muttering, "I thought it worth a try. . . ."

Mr. Galloway joined the three of us just a few minutes later, his tall ramrod frame looming in the doorway with his face set in its usual somber way. I could not tell whether he was displeased to have been thusly summoned or if perhaps this was simply the best of his nature. Either way I noted that it took a moment before he finally deigned to step into the room. "Madam instructed that you wished to speak with me?" he droned with all the decorum of a proper steward.

"Indeed," Colin answered at once. "And may I presume that the discerning Miss Endicott also informed you that we require nothing less than the utmost in forthrightness on your part? For if she did not, rest assured that is both our need and her intention." Colin flashed a tight-lipped smile that left little room for misinterpretation. "Now, why don't you come in and attempt to make yourself comfortable? We shall promise not to take a moment more of your time than is absolutely necessary."

Mr. Galloway came fully into the room, stopping near our chairs as he clasped his hands behind his back. "I prefer to stand," he said, his eyes focused somewhere above the tops of our heads.

"And I"—Colin waved toward the chair across from us next to where Maurice Evans was seated—"prefer that you sit. As a guest in this house I hope you will indulge me."

The poor man looked quite taken aback, his brow knitting noticeably before he gave a perfunctory nod and took the chair with the ease of a cat in a puddle of water.

"Now then . . ." Colin pushed himself to his feet and wandered over to the enormous carved marble mantel on the center of the far wall before quickly realizing that he would never be able to rest his arm atop it without having to reach uncomfortably high. "Yes . . ." he muttered as he casually dove a hand into his vest pocket and extracted a coin that he smoothly began twining between his fingers. "What we find ourselves in need of is *your* understanding of the disagreement that Miss Endicott herself has admitted existed between her and her sister."

"Disagreement?" He looked wholly astonished. "I can assure you I have no notion of what you are referring to."

"No notion?!" Colin repeated with a twinge of mockery. "Surely the distinguished steward of such a place as Layton Manor would be aware of any amount of dissension within his purview, and most especially that between the mistresses of his household." The coin in Colin's hand whirled effortlessly as he took several steps toward Mr. Galloway, his face relaxing and the hint of a smile tugging at one corner of his mouth. "And given that Miss Eugenia herself has confessed to the truth of it . . ." He shook his head and snatched the coin into the palm of his hand just as he moved past Mr. Galloway, startling the man as he had meant to. "Perhaps we would do better to speak with one of the chambermaids . . . ?"

I could see that Colin had hit his mark, though Mr. Galloway was clearly not a man to give up his restraint so readily. "If

Madam has already confided in you, then whatever do you need from me?"

"Perspective, my dear man," he said with relish as he swung back around and dropped back into his chair, leaning forward so that he was still very much in Mr. Galloway's sphere. "As the man in charge of this household I fully expect that you have an opinion on everything that transpires here. Miss Eugenia has acknowledged that she did not approve of her sister's consulting with Lady Stuart. What did you make of it?"

"Me?!" He looked startled again. "It was none of my affair who Miss Adelaide chose to visit. I simply run the household—"

"And you were instructed never to permit Lady Stuart entry into Layton Manor," Colin interrupted, waving him off. "Even though such an order may have been out of your realm of questioning, I am certain that you have an opinion, Mr. Galloway, and I shall have it."

"I was rather glad of it, if you must insist," he finally answered, shifting his weight uncomfortably. "Miss Adelaide's visits to that woman seemed troublesome to me. At the very least they left Miss Adelaide's temperament very much the worse for it."

"Her temperament? Whatever do you mean?"

"She became more frightful . . . tremulous . . . and she would speak about hearing things that were not there and having visions that did not exist. It got so I could hardly keep any staff."

"We have become such a gullible society," Colin acknowledged as he finally sat back. "But not you? Miss Adelaide's musings did not stir your imagination?"

Mr. Galloway scoffed before hastily rearranging his stern features, yet even so, in that instant I knew I had caught a glimpse of the man behind his well-honed façade. "I am not a man who gives credence to such things."

"Did you ever speak to Miss Eugenia of your concerns around Miss Adelaide's visits to Lady Stuart and your difficulty with the staff?"

"Never," he said with distaste at Colin's having even suggested such a thing. "I am not here to air my grievances. Were that the case, then I should think any sort of half-wit could run a household."

"Of course. And what of the other staff? Has anyone ever confided their feelings around Miss Adelaide's convictions?"

Mr. Galloway's gaze curdled. "Their feelings are not sought," he said indignantly. "Anyone confiding such impropriety would have been dismissed."

Colin nodded once, his lips pressed tight and his blue eyes narrowing ever so slightly. "And what do you know about the root of Miss Adelaide's fears? The lady's maid who brought shame upon the Endicott family when your mistresses were but young women themselves."

"That is no business of mine," he answered perfunctorily, though his brow notched the thinnest tick, assuring me that he knew.

"Yes . . ." Colin nodded again and leaned forward. "We have already well established that you are a man who tends to his own and for that I commend you. So let me ask you, *how* did you know about the lady's maid who brought such a lifetime of regret and terror to Miss Adelaide?"

Mr. Galloway's mouth pursed so tightly that I thought it might disappear from his face completely. "A staff hears things. . . ." he reluctantly allowed.

"Indeed . . ." Colin sat back.

"There were arguments between Miss Adelaide and Miss Eugenia. Things were said. . . ." He cleared his throat. "Sometimes I was privy . . ."

"Yes. And did the rest of the staff also know or were you the only one with such knowledge?"

"There have been many such conversations over the last couple of years—"

"Then everyone knew," Colin cut him off, having reached what I suspected he'd been after from the start. "You have been helpful in spite of yourself, Mr. Galloway," he announced as he got up and threw a glance back at Mr. Evans and me. "I should like to poke around outside for a bit but would appreciate it if you would show Mr. Pruitt and Mr. Evans to Miss Adelaide's room again."

Mr. Galloway pushed himself up and straightened the tails of his coat. "I shall need to inquire with Madam."

"That will be a courtesy," Mr. Evans spoke up, "as I shall remind you that this is official Scotland Yard business now. Just as your mistress wanted."

It was a generous statement by Mr. Evans, as this was neither official nor exactly what Miss Eugenia had been after.

"Yes . . ." Mr. Galloway said, his voice rife with his unease, "yes, of course."

We all started toward the parlor door, though I made certain to fall back so I could sidle up to Colin. "And just what am I looking for upstairs?" I asked out of the corner of my mouth.

"Signs of ghosts," he muttered.

I wanted to protest but knew nothing would come of it, so I followed Mr. Evans and Mr. Galloway through the towering foyer while Colin shifted his trajectory toward the front door. The three of us climbed up the sweeping staircase to the third floor and moved down the wide hallway resplendent with original portraiture on either side that appeared to mark many lifetimes of Endicotts, given the variations in dress and manner. Just as we rounded a bend to the right, Mr. Galloway came up short and swung open the door that I remembered from our first visit led to the rooms belonging to Miss Adelaide.

"Should you require anything further . . ." he said as we entered.

"You have done more than enough," I quickly answered. "Thank you."

He nodded his head once and stepped back out, leaving the door conspicuously open, and I was sure he would alert one of the chambermaids to keep an eye on us.

"So what exactly have we been sent here for?" Mr. Evans idly asked as he began to stroll around the large bedroom.

"We are looking for signs of ghosts." I repeated Colin's directive with amusement as I went over to the door that led to the antechamber where Freddie Nettle had spent his nights. "Surely you can manage that," I quipped. He mumbled something from across the room, but I paid him little mind as I edged into Mr. Nettle's compact sleeping quarters. There was a single bed shoved against the shared wall with his mistress to my right, a tiny round bedside table with an electric lamp next to it, and a small armoire that looked well used on my left. It was only when I focused on the meager single window set high upon the outside wall that I realized the space had been intended as a dressing room. That Mr. Nettle had slept here spoke as much to the needs of Miss Adelaide as it did to the station that he fulfilled.

The armoire was empty, which I had expected, with nothing personal left in either it or the space. That a young man had spent the better part of a year and a half dwelling here was undetectable. I could not help but find that inexplicably sad.

"Find anything?" Mr. Evans startled me as he poked his head through the doorway.

"Not so much as a dust mote." I moved forward and stood on my tiptoes so I could just manage to peer out the bottom of the sole window and spotted Colin far below in the side yard with Mr. McPherson, the two of them muscling a long ladder out from the stable. "Did you see anything of interest?" I asked as I joined Mr. Evans back in Miss Adelaide's room.

"Nothing that caught my eye, but I would dare not presume to speculate on what might catch yours," he answered with a chuckle.

I glanced over at him to gauge what sort of jest he was trying to insinuate and decided I had every right to be suspect, given the rogue's grin he returned.

"Allow me to take you through Miss Adelaide's last moments as they were relayed to Colin and me by Mr. Nettle," I said as I went back to the doorway that led to Mr. Nettle's tiny quarters. "Some time well into the night, we have not yet been able to pinpoint exactly when, Mr. Nettle claims to have heard a series of great anguished cries coming from Miss Adelaide. He says he rushed into the room"—I swept my hands out in front of me—"which would put him somewhere about here . . . and says he spotted Miss Adelaide quivering by that window all the way over there." I instantly launched myself across the room, passing a nearer window, Miss Adelaide's four-poster bed, a second window, and a large straight-backed chair with a small side table beside it before finally arriving at the spot where the poor woman was said to have been found cowering. "He says he called out to her, but before he could take a single step forward she turned and flung herself out the open window." I turned toward the window with a dramatist's flair, intending to heighten the story by pretending to cast myself out, but nearly let out my own shout when I abruptly found myself inches from Colin's face.

"Get me off this bloody damn ladder," he demanded as he reached out and seized one of my wrists in one hand and the waist of my pants with his other, effectively pinning me against the inside windowsill.

To my relief, Mr. Evans appeared beside me before I had even heard him start to move, and between the two of us we were able to lever Colin in through the window until he finally landed in a rather unsightly heap on the floor. He bounded up before Mr. Evans or I could offer him any further aid and leaned back out the window and called down, "There you are then, Mr. McPherson. I won't be needing your ladder anymore. You have done a fine service for me and I thank you most kindly."

A muffled reply drifted up from below, but I could not make out any of what he said.

"Are the front stairs too monotonous for you, Mr. Pendragon?" Mr. Evans ribbed.

"You aren't a bit funny." Colin sniffed, forgoing any sort of laugh, assuring me he was mortified. "How have the two of you fared up here? Find anything of interest?" He pressed forward as he hastily brushed at his jacket and slacks. "Or am I the only one here who is actually doing some work?"

Colin stared at the two of us from his position at the window as though expecting an answer, the sun blazing in from behind him, when I suddenly caught sight of something cobalt blue and emerald green flickering ever so subtly from one shoulder of his coat. At first I thought it must be a trick of the sunlight, an optical illusion caused by its angle as it began to tease its way into the tops of the nearby trees, but when it happened again, those same peacock hues glittering in an instant like a speck of pixie dust, I could not hold my tongue.

"What have you got on yourself?" My question earned me blank stares from both of them. "Give me your coat," I prodded as I grabbed Colin from behind and yanked it off his shoulders. "If you don't see what I'm seeing you can send me back to Needham Hills," I quipped, though the joke still managed to catch in my throat. "Now look." I gestured to the left shoulder with my chin as I held the jacket up to the sunlight. "Do you see those colors . . . ? The blues and greens . . . ? It's a gray suit. Where are these ludicrous colors coming from?"

Colin nearly shoved me out the window as he rushed forward and raised his left leg as high as he could in an obvious effort to catch the sun's rays. "Bolt the door," he commanded over his shoulder to Mr. Evans, but before the man could even cross the room Colin was kicking his shoes off.

"What are you doing?" I asked, afraid that I knew what his answer would be. He did not respond but instead unfastened his pants, just as I had suspected he was about to do, and carefully slid them to the floor.

I heard the door click and in the next instant Mr. Evans spoke up. "Should I be here . . . ?" he asked, his tone, curiously, having dropped an octave.

"Don't be a prig," Colin scolded as he stood there in his underdrawers, his pants held well up into the sunlight, an anxious scowl upon his face. "There . . . !" he barked quite suddenly, minutely turning the left knee of his pants, the knee that had initially struck the floor of Miss Adelaide's room, all the while gazing at it as though it were an ancient wonder. "You are my clever one, Ethan," he said, but if I was clever I had no idea why.

"What is it?" Mr. Evans asked as he moved toward us, decency be damned.

"The remnants of a powder," Colin said.

"Powder?" Mr. Evans repeated, stealing the very word from my own lips.

"Undoubtedly phosphorous powder," Colin shot back as he

thrust his pants at me before pulling a white handkerchief from the pocket and dropping to his hands and knees, slowly dragging the small cloth along the floor and baseboard beneath the window. "Just look at the way it glows when the sunlight catches it. Any bright light can serve as an accelerant. Or it can be lit with a match where it will flare up and burn with the most distinctive tones. Very much like what you noticed on my jacket." He sat back on his haunches and twisted the handkerchief first one way and then another and, sure enough, scattered traces of those blazing colors flared to life. "It's a parlor trick. Done mostly by seers to mystify their audiences and the poor dupes who seek them out. Though I would suspect they much prefer oil of phosphorous, as it gives a more ghostly appearance when ignited and sprayed through the air." He stood up and delicately entrusted me with the handkerchief for the minute it took him to slide his pants back on. "I would bet that Lady Stuart always has a supply on hand," he added, and I did not miss the pointed look he tossed my way.

"You cannot mean to suggest . . ." I started to say before stopping myself. Of course he meant to suggest it.

"Who the devil is Lady Stuart?" Mr. Evans asked, his curiosity now clearly piqued.

"An old friend of sorts," Colin supplied with the usual rudimentary flash of teeth. "She was a confidant of Trevor Bellingham."

"Oh . . ." He grimaced. "What an appalling set of circumstances that was. She wasn't privy to what happened, was she?"

Colin reached into my coat pocket and pulled my handkerchief free. "She is not a foolish woman," he answered as he shook out my handkerchief with one hand before carefully wiping the inside and outside of the windowsill with it. "She knew enough to be vital, but not enough to solve the case." He turned back and flashed another condescending bit of a smile. "I did that," he reminded Mr. Evans with the arch of an eyebrow. "Now if you will excuse us, Ethan and I have other matters to attend to."

"Other matters?" Mr. Evans protested even as Colin started for the door. "What other matters? And just what are you planning to do with those handkerchiefs? You cannot merely usher me in and boot me out whenever it suits you."

"Perish the thought," Colin replied with the first honest grin he had given since his graceless entrance. "I promise you are always top of mind, Mr. Evans," he reassured thinly as he disappeared into the hallway with the two handkerchiefs held out before him, one in each hand, as though they contained the Holy Grail itself.

"He is maddening sometimes," Maurice Evans sputtered at me.

"I am . . ." I said as casually as I could, ". . . aware of that fact."

CHAPTER 13

We were met at the door with a glare and a frown, but never-theless, the man allowed us entry just the same. I suppose he knew Colin would not have it any other way. He had proven that nearly a half year before. Never mind that we had arrived well past teatime, since Colin had insisted we stop by our flat to drop off the handkerchiefs.

Evers deposited us in the same parlor as always, informing us with some degree of pleasure that his mistress would be with us when she was ready. It was an arch statement that we both ig-nored, and in nothing greater than a single minute or two her voice rang out as welcoming and warm as ever.

"Gentlemen!" she said, her eyes lighting up at the sight of Colin.

"Lady Stuart." He stood up and gave her a gentleman's bow, which made her absolutely beam. "It is a delight to see you again."

"Likewise, Mr. Pendragon." She swept into the room, her smile as radiant as her father's greeting had been frosty. "I did not expect to see either of you so soon after the regrettable end to your visit here the other day, Mr. Pruitt."

"Things do change quickly on some cases," I answered.

"Then I hope you bring good news. Do sit down and let me ring for some tea."

"You mustn't put your father to any trouble," Colin said. "We have come far too close to dinner to be amenable and don't wish to unsettle your schedule any more than we already have."

"Nonsense," she answered at once as we all sat down, the tiniest smirk tugging at the corner of her lips as she leaned forward and picked up a small bell, giving it a sound ring. "My father could use some unsettling. I'm afraid he forgets himself at times."

He appeared almost at once, and I supposed he had been lurking in the hallway. "Yes, ma'am."

"Tea, if you please," she said with grace. "And a few of those ginger biscuits, I think."

"It is quite late . . ." he started to say.

"I do not require a lesson in timekeeping. That will be all." Her voice was firm and yet undeniably kind. She did not condescend, but neither did she permit him any leeway, leaving their charade recognizably strained since we knew the truth of it. Still, appearances mattered, and I was sure none of her clientele had the least awareness.

"As you wish," he grumbled before moving off.

Colin and Lady Stuart caught up for a few minutes, sharing pleasantries before it was Lady Stuart herself who finally drove the conversation directly to the heart of our visit. "Have you learned anything further about Adelaide Endicott's death then?" she asked.

"We are learning new things every day." Colin leaned back and plucked a crown from his pocket and set it to spinning through his fingers. "Just this very afternoon we have found traces of what I believe to be phosphorous powder along the sill and floor by the window she is said to have leapt from. I believe the coincidence too much to ignore."

Lady Stuart looked surprised even as a spark of amusement lit her eyes. "And you thought of me. . . ."

Colin's eyebrows ticked up as the coin halted in his hand and he stared back at her. "I did," he answered simply before starting the coin on another rotation. "I do not mean to imply the powder was delivered by you, but I would be willing to wager that you have a supply of it here in your home."

Lady Stuart nodded. "You would win that bet, Mr. Pendragon. I have phosphorous powder *and* oil, and a few other tricks I am certain would not surprise you. Some of my clients do need to feel the touch of a loved one from time to time, so I do what I must." Her eyes flicked quickly between the two of us. "I do hope you don't think me the worse for it. As I have always said, I mean to do no harm."

"You needn't explain yourself to us," I hastened to answer lest Colin not bother. "In the case of Trevor Bellingham I believe you did him a kindness indeed."

"That may be." Colin nodded as Evers came back into the room carrying the requisite tea and biscuits Lady Stuart had ordered. "But Eugenia Endicott seems quite convinced that you had no such positive impact on her sister."

Evers dropped the tray onto the table with a disapproving clatter, earning him a scowl from Lady Stuart. "That will do," she warned, sounding as if she were speaking to a petulant child. He returned the shadow of a grimace but left us without a word. "I make no excuses for him," she said lightly as she poured our tea. "No matter the role, he will always be my father."

Colin nodded and gave a soft chuckle. "I have the same with my Mrs. Behmoth. She brought me up and is as maternal as if I had sprung from her, yet remains just so to this day. It is a curse and a blessing, I suppose." He shifted his eyes to mine and I returned the smile, though I had never enjoyed any such relationship in my life.

"If you are wondering whether it is possible that I might be involved in any way with Miss Adelaide's death"—Lady Stuart tipped Colin a knowing look as she handed out our tea—"You may rest assured that I have never, not once, set foot in Layton Manor. For that matter, I have never even been on the grounds of the estate. As you might imagine, Miss Eugenia would not permit it. It was one thing for her sister to come here, but she was certainly not about to accede to having me there."

"I'm afraid you have misunderstood," Colin said, flashing a tight smile even as he sipped his tea. "I think I know you well enough not to suspect your hand in murder. Besides, given where we found the phosphorous powder, I believe it to have been thrown into Miss Adelaide's room from atop a ladder outside. So while I do not doubt your vigor, I also do not imagine that you would ascend to such a height for any reason."

Lady Stuart laughed. "A lady would not ascend a ladder to any height with these great skirts bunched around our ankles. Such an endeavor would be ill-advised for many reasons."

"I most certainly found it to be so when I did it," Colin agreed. "What I was actually wondering was whether you may have noticed any of your *supplies* missing or being pilfered through?"

"Supplies . . . ?" She gave a hearty laugh. "Tricks of my trade, I believe you mean," she answered smartly as she snapped up the little bell again and rang it. "Such things are kept in the pantry where they have little chance of drawing attention. My father should know better than I do."

Just as before, the elderly man was in the doorway with remarkable speed. It made me wonder if he spent the whole of his day eavesdropping on his daughter. "Yes . . . ?" he mumbled as his eyes quickly raked over the tea and biscuits remaining on the plate, a telltale sign that even given his present disgruntlement he did still understand his place.

"Have you noticed any of our potions or powders having been rifled through of late? Anything missing or unaccountably pinched?"

"Potions or powders . . . ?" he repeated with noticeable irritation.

"Don't be cheeky," she scolded.

I am quite certain I saw the man grit his teeth before he answered. "No, ma'am. No one touches anything but me."

"And has anyone been in your kitchen besides yourself?" Colin piped up. "Would they have cause to know you keep such things in your pantry?"

"No one . . ." he replied with finality before noticing that his daughter had raised her hand toward him. "Eh . . ." He seemed to begrudgingly remember something at the signal. "That young man sat in there with me when his mistress was here."

"Young man?" Colin pressed. "Do you mean Freddie Nettle? He waited in the kitchen with you in case he was needed?"

"S'right."

"And did you ever leave him alone in there? Perhaps while you answered the door or fetched something for your mistress, or even if the duty to nature tapped your shoulder?"

"What . . . ?"

"The WC," Colin clarified.

"No," the man snapped before heaving a perturbed sigh. "Maybe . . ." he allowed with all the enthusiasm of one about to face a tooth extraction.

"And is it at all possible that some of the material could be missing and you not notice it?"

"I don't use those things much," Lady Stuart responded before her father could. "I don't find much need with my clientele. So I really cannot say with any assurance that either one of us could truly tell if some small amount had been taken." She was studying Colin and I could see that she was troubled. "But neither do I mean to suggest that Mr. Nettle would have done such a thing. He seemed to be a very kind young man, and he quite doted on Miss Adelaide. Even so, the answer to your question is yes—it is possible."

"Of course . . . of course . . ." Colin quickly fired back. "These are only questions. The assemblage of facts. No one is being accused of anything at this time." He stood up, but not before snatching one of the ginger biscuits. "As always you have been most generous with your time," he said, "and I have little doubt that we will be back to see you before this case has reached its inevitable conclusion."

"Whatever I can do to assist," she said with a delicate smile, the surety of her offer evident in the concern that colored her eyes.

"Good day, then." Colin gave a swift bob of his head as he slid the crown he had been fiddling with back into his pocket and took an eager bite of the biscuit. "We shall see ourselves out. There is no need to trouble your father."

The sound of Lady Stuart's laugh followed us to the door, and in a matter of minutes we were aboard a hansom cab being ferried back to our Kensington flat. I tried pestering Colin with a few questions about Freddie Nettle, but he seemed disinclined to engage my curiosity, so I finally settled back and left the matter alone. There was no use in hounding a subject he did not wish to pursue as I knew it would only earn me the usual assertion that everyone was a suspect and it was too early to speculate on theory. Yet, if opportunity was the tinder that sparked the embers of motive, then I could not help thinking that Freddie Nettle was distinctly in its sights.

"I wonder when Charlotte Hutton is going to show herself again?" Colin asked out of nowhere as we turned onto our street.

"Whatever made you think of her? Don't you have enough on your mind without thinking about *that* woman?"

Colin turned and stared at me as if I had lost all sense. "*That* woman . . ." he repeated with a glower, ". . . is the worst sort of devil. It isn't simply that she consented to the murders of her husband and young son, a horror bad enough in its own right, but that she has now come back with these lies, these inventions, all for the single purpose of extorting the money she severed these lives for in the first place." He swept his gaze back out the carriage window and I saw his jaw clench. "And you can be sure my father will not be able to hold the Swiss off for long. We are only fortunate that she does not know that. But they will release the funds to her whenever they tire of our diplomacy and she will be lost to us again and *I'll not have it!*" he barked, striking the side of the cab with his fist.

"'Ere, 'ere," the cabbie scolded as he pulled the horse to an immediate stop. "Ya can git out if yer gonna be poundin' on me livli'ood."

Colin leapt down and barreled off the rest of the way to our flat as I paid the man, adding a generous tip for his troubles. By the time I reached our flat it was to find our front door gaping with no sign of Colin. It was, I supposed, enough that he had left the door open for me. I eased it shut and went upstairs, and was startled to find Colin and Mrs. Behmoth seated in the parlor staring at the two soiled handkerchiefs wadded up on the coffee table as if they were about to shoot up once-a-millennia blooms.

"I been watchin' 'em like ya said," she was explaining with remarkable seriousness. "Not even a puff a air 'as touched 'em."

"Very good," Colin said, his voice equally grim. "Then let us see . . ." he murmured as he carefully touched the uppermost corners of one of the handkerchiefs, cradling its bottom with the small silver tray it had been deposited on almost two hours before, ". . . if my supposition is right." He moved with the stealth of a thief as he crept toward the fireplace and then, without the slightest pause, threw the handkerchief directly into the rage of flames.

"*ACH . . . !*" Mrs. Behmoth hollered as she burst to her feet. "Wot in the bloody 'ell are ya doin'? Ya jest 'ad me sittin' 'ere watchin' this shite fer the last—" But that was as far as she got before her mouth snapped shut and her eyes nearly bulged from their sockets.

I turned at once and saw that the fire around the handkerchief was spitting out licks of luminescent green, turquoise, violet, and blue flame. It looked ethereal and disconcerting and, as it began to sizzle and spark like a hunk of meat on a cast-iron skillet, also unnerving.

"Phosphorous powder . . ." Colin bothered to say. And I could see why such a ruse would be so compelling. "Our Mr. Nettle would seem to be compromised," he added. "Or perhaps Lady Stuart is, as she was before, failing to be entirely truthful." He turned his gaze on me and I could see a cold heat flickering deep within his eyes.

CHAPTER 14

Morning broke with a hammering of rain and a deep-set chill. As a result I felt no compelling desire to extract myself from the warmth of our bed until Colin ultimately sat up and gave a huge leonine stretch, heaving an attendant yawn from the base of his soul to go along with it.

"There is much to be done today," he said in the next breath, "and none of it will be accomplished if we stay in here." He turned and gave me a quick peck. "Though it would certainly be more amusing." He chuckled as he pushed himself off the bed and headed for the WC.

The necessity of running around the city on such a dreary day did not entice me in the least, so it was with little enthusiasm that I washed and dressed and padded out to the parlor to get the fire stoked. I was only just coaxing it to an acceptable roar when a sudden pounding rattled the door downstairs. "Who . . ." I heard myself grumbling to no one, ". . . could be arriving so blasted early in the morning?"

"Don't trouble yerself," Mrs. Behmoth called up the stairs.

As if I had been about to, I wanted to holler back, but kept my peace instead. I caught a glimpse of myself in the mirror over the mantel and thought myself a distressing sight with my unruly hair and my eyes puffy and bagged. A squeal from downstairs thankfully stole my attention just as Colin strode into the parlor finishing the knot of his tie.

"Sounds like my father is here," he noted as he came up next to me and began rubbing his hands in front of the fire. "What do you suppose he's here for?" His expression suddenly fell as he turned his eyes to me. "I do hope it's not to inform us that the Swiss have released Mrs. Hutton's accursed funds." Before I could even think to respond, Colin spun away from me and stalked toward the stairs. "Tell me you're not here with some pitiful news about those ruddy Swiss...." he hollered down from the landing.

"And good morning to you." I heard his father's voice, as calm and affable as ever. "Would you be so kind as to bring some tea up, Mrs. Behmoth?" he muttered. "I can tell my son is in a rich mood, and I've not even spotted poor Ethan yet."

"I'm here...." I called out with a woeful lack of enthusiasm as I forced myself to move away from the warming fire's embrace.

"Yes." Sir Atherton sounded as if he was chuckling. "Perhaps we shall need a couple of pots."

"Don't ya worry," Mrs. Behmoth was quick to answer. "I got plenty a tea and a fresh batch a currant scones. Ya picked the right mornin' ta stop by."

"Outstanding," he said with genuine delight, and not a second later I heard him beginning to make his way up.

"If this is about those Swiss . . ." Colin said again as he turned back for the fireplace.

"Calm yourself," I hissed as I tried to coax my hair into place before settling into my chair and praying that wasn't why Sir Atherton was here.

"Late night?" Sir Atherton teased as he rounded the landing and headed for the wing-backed chair beside me as he always did, Colin's chair. "On second thought"—he gave a mock sort of sputter—"I'm not at all sure I want to know."

"Is this about Mrs. Hutton's Swiss accounts?" Colin asked

yet again with nary a hint of amusement as he leaned against the mantel, effectively blocking the fire from doing much good for me. "Because if it is . . ."

"Do settle yourself, boy." Sir Atherton waved him off. "I've had warmer greetings from people who despise my politics. Now I am not here about our goodly Swiss allies, but I'll be damned if I'm going to start any sort of discussion without a spot of tea first."

As if on cue I heard the thundering footsteps of Mrs. Behmoth as she began to make her way up the stairs. While I was immediately relieved that he was not here to bear ill tidings of Mrs. Hutton's funds, I could not help but begin to wonder exactly why he had come so early. Sir Atherton Pendragon was not known for his social calls.

"I've got yer favorite clotted cream," Mrs. Behmoth announced as she rounded the top of the stairs and came into the room with the tea tray and a plate of steaming scones.

"I told you not to keep that in this house," Colin reminded her with a lack of patience as he crossed to her, thankfully allowing the warmth from the fireplace to freely radiate into the room again. "It isn't good for any of us. I've told you that repeatedly."

"Don't you bark at me," she scowled as she batted him away from the tray. "I ain't done nothin' ta git yer arse up. I'm jest servin' a fine man who's always done right by me. Where's the 'arm in that?"

"Could we please have the tea?" I cut in over both of them.

"An outstanding idea." Sir Atherton chuckled, sitting back and watching Mrs. Behmoth prepare our repast with the assurance of one who has done so a thousand times before. She handed him his cup and a scone, but I noticed that neither of them touched the little dish of clotted cream. "You are most kind," he said with a smile.

I was served next, with Colin relegated to the settee normally reserved for our guests, receiving his last. "Let me know if ya need anythin' else," Mrs. Behmoth offered directly to Sir Atherton before finally leaving the room and trundling back downstairs.

"You really should go easier on her, you know," Colin's father said as he sipped at his tea. "She is advancing in years and won't be around to take your guff forever."

"She will outlive us all," Colin shot back over the rim of his cup. "Now what has brought you here? If someone has requested my father to come and set me in my place, then I will know it at once."

Sir Atherton shook his head, a faint smile tugging at his lips. "You are your mother's son. Very well . . ." He set his teacup down but continued to nibble on his scone. "Thomas Endicott practically tore my door off its hinges late yesterday. I must say you have His Lordship quite riled. Whatever are you up to at his sister's estate? I have been as much as ordered to set you straight, just as you supposed." He shook his head again and gave a low chuckle.

"We are investigating the death of his sister Adelaide."

"Ah. A dear girl. Gentle soul. But whatever is there to investigate? I thought her attendant pushed her out the window in a fit of pique. . . ."

"Is that what Lord Endicott told you? Because it is certainly what his sister believes, though I have yet to find even the thinnest of motives. Pique, did he say? A curious notion when it seems Adelaide Endicott was every bit the delicate blossom you and everyone else have painted her to be. It is certainly how I remember her. So whatever could she have done to push her man to such a horrible act against her? A woman he had been devoted to for the better part of a year and upon whom his very livelihood depended."

Sir Atherton blinked twice before shifting his gaze to me, his eyes filled with astonishment. "Why are you asking *me*? I am most certainly not the detective here."

"I am simply trying to tell you that the circumstances around his sister's death are not so concise. While I most certainly cannot rule out Mr. Nettle's involvement, there are clues we have unearthed that would point to at least one other accomplice."

"Clues?"

"We have discovered a residue of phosphorous powder around

the window she is said to have been pushed from, and on the outside there are marks along the sill and rails that almost assuredly point to the fact that someone had been pitching small stones from the ground below, no doubt in an effort to attract her attention. And when I climbed a ladder myself there yesterday, I can tell you it came as no surprise that the ladder's stiles fit snugly into the two small notches I had spotted there. So while Mr. Nettle may be as guilty as night, he most assuredly did not act alone."

"Do believe this Nettle fellow is a part of it?"

"I do not know yet, and that's my point. Eugenia Endicott is convinced of the man's complicity, and while she may be right, she may also be wrong. And when last I reviewed the law, you cannot indict a man on supposition."

Sir Atherton gave a slight nod and picked up his tea again, taking his time to sip it even as he also snatched up another scone. When I thought perhaps he might be done with the topic, he spoke up in a thoughtful tone filled with introspection. "Your point is well made. You will have to go back with me to His Lordship's estate to state your position."

"I am not going out to explain anything to that old gas bag."

"I will remind you that he is an esteemed member of Parliament. . . ."

Colin popped off the settee and pounded back over to the mantel, snatching up the small, intricately carved derringer he had left there days ago and buffing it with the soft cloth he'd set it upon. "I don't care if Victoria herself is going to be there," he groused irritably, burnishing the pistol as though its very existence depended on it. "I have much to do today. I am not going."

"I'm afraid Her Majesty is at Holyrood Palace and will therefore be unable to attend your accounting," his father said, shifting his gaze to me and casting his eyes heavenward.

"I didn't mean literally."

"I know what you meant."

"Why don't you tell me what needs to be tended to first," I quickly spoke up, "and I will take care of it. I handled this case on my own while you were in Zurich," I reminded him.

"Whatever became of that Hutton woman?" Sir Atherton asked as he glanced back at Colin, who was still feverishly polishing the pistol. "Shall I send word to the Swiss Federal Council that they can have those funds released?"

"*No!*" Colin blurted, his hands recoiling in the same instant. "You mustn't do that. I need more time. *We* need more time. . . ." he corrected, as though my involvement would have any greater impact on his father.

"Oh . . ." Sir Atherton sounded genuinely taken aback. "Then I shall be certain to delay them for you when they contact me, which I am sure will be any time now. . . ." He sniffed and cast his eyes back to me, and I could see a spark of mischief lying therein.

It only took a minute longer before Colin released a snarl and shoved the gun and cloth back onto the mantel. "I'll not stay to tea with that pompous oaf nor will I promise to be anything more than civil," he warned.

"I could hardly ask for more than that," Sir Atherton responded ever so agreeably. "Fetch your things then. I told him we'd be by midmorning at the latest. I see little reason to delay."

"I've not even eaten yet," Colin protested, the depth of his displeasure wholly evident in his tone.

"Then grab a couple of Mrs. Behmoth's scones," Sir Atherton directed. "You could hardly do better than those. And once we're finished, since you won't take tea at His Lordship's, we can stop somewhere and get a meat pie and some chips." His eyes lit up. "I haven't had a good steak-and-kidney pie since I can remember."

"I deplore steak-and-kidney pie," Colin griped. "It smells like absolute rot."

"Then I shan't share mine with you," his father answered smoothly as he reached forward and wrapped two of the currant scones in a napkin. "Now hurry up," he chided, "we've all got things to do, and you cannot expect Ethan to continue covering for you for the whole of this case." He glanced over at me from beneath his silvery-white eyebrows. "Not that I don't think you wouldn't be perfectly capable, of course. In fact I'm quite certain I wouldn't be on this fool's errand if *you* were leading the charge."

Thankfully, Colin did not hear his father, as he had already struck off for our bedroom. "You like to goad him," I pointed out.

Sir Atherton gave a little snicker and a shrug. "It is a father's prerogative." His face slowly sobered. "Do you agree with Colin? Do you believe Adelaide Endicott was murdered?"

"Without a doubt."

"Always so loyal," he said with a wistful sort of smile. "I admire you for that."

Not an instant later Colin burst back into the room, shrugging into his jacket and fumbling with the last buttons on his vest. "If we're going to do this, then let's get it over and done with," he grumbled before turning to me. "I'll need you to go and see Mr. Nettle again," he continued as he paused on the landing while his father ambled over. "I don't much care what he has to say for himself, but I want you to check his flat. See if you can find anything that would lead us to believe he might have had something to do with that phosphorous powder."

"Check his flat?!" I repeated with disbelief. "And how am I supposed to accomplish that while he's sitting right there?"

"Well, now . . ." Colin turned toward me though I could tell he was actually glaring at his father. "You are perfectly capable of leading the charge. You needn't ask a fool like me." And with that he bolted down the stairs, his black coattails snapping their admonishment in his wake.

"Oh . . ." Sir Atherton said as he released a prolonged exhalation. "This is not likely to go at all well."

CHAPTER 15

As though to further antagonize this day, the rain picked up in both ferocity and resolve, adding a wind that whirled about the city like a rabid dog. Even my umbrella was barely serving its purpose as I had it yanked all the way down against the top of my head, clutched in both hands, as I tried to keep it from eviscerating itself.

I had come all the way out to Shandy Street and as I descended from the cab was at once reminded of how close I was to Maw Heikens's old building; the place where I had lost so much of my youth. For a moment I thought perhaps I should go by and check on her, but my clearer head prevailed and I kept to the task at hand. I knew Colin was counting on my not failing at this charge and did not wish to conjecture at his mood were I to have nothing to say for my undertaking. It was enough to imagine where his disposition was going to wind up once he had finished his accounting for Lord Endicott.

My boot sank into a fetid puddle that almost assuredly contained equal parts horse urine and rain, and I cursed as the liquid splattered across the cuff of my pants. There was little consolation in the fact that they were already well saturated halfway to my knees.

I crossed White Horse Lane and slowed as I clawed the scrap of paper from the inside coat pocket where I had written Freddie Nettle's address. It turned out to be a rather sorrowful-looking boardinghouse, and I supposed I should have expected nothing more. What else could the man possibly have procured for himself on such quick notice considering that he had been residing at Layton Manor for better than the last year? No doubt the bulk of his compensation from the Endicotts had been paid in room and board. And now he was consigned to a three-story brick building wedged in between more of the same, all of whose faces were blackened by the thick, oily residue of coal smoke belching from the countless chimneys stabbing up into the dull gray sky.

There was a small, sagging wooden porch tacked on the front that did not appear to have ever seen a coat of paint. The windows that faced the street were either cracked or boarded up, making the conceit of a view absurd at best. Not that there was anything else to look out upon other than more of the same dilapidation. If this had ever been a desirable neighborhood it took a vivid imagination to envision it. There was nothing left now but poverty and rot and indifference.

I huddled under my umbrella as I pounded on the front door, snatching a quick glance above to find the porch's decomposing roof as protective as a colander held over one's head. So it was a relief when the door was finally forced open, sticking mercilessly at its upper corners, by a boy of about nine or ten who looked nearly as disheveled as the building he lived in. "'Oo are you?" he asked with a surly little scowl.

"My name is Ethan Pruitt," I answered, my eyes scanning the dimly lit room behind him to see if there wasn't someone better suited that I might have this conversation with. "I am here to see Mr. Freddie Nettle."

"'E ain't 'ere," he said as he shoved against the door, clearly intending for our discussion to be over.

"Now just a minute . . ." I quickly got out even as I stabbed my foot in between the door's trajectory and the jamb. "Might I speak with the landlord for a minute?"

"Ya might pull back a bloody stump if ya don't git yer buggered foot outta me door," the boy warned, and then wagged a fireplace poker through the gap in the stalled door to back up his threat.

I cannot say exactly why, but the sight of this scrawny rascal with his smudged face, unkempt heap of wiry black hair, and dockworker's glower suddenly infuriated me. Or perhaps the problem was that he reminded me of myself at something near that age, so that I could not stop myself from reaching out and yanking the wielded poker as I heaved against the door, effectively springing it open and sending the young scamp sprawling backward onto the floor. "I am a gentleman and will not be threatened," I announced as I stepped inside.

"Ain't no gentleman I know wot sends a mere boy to the floor like a worn boot," a harsh, gravelly female voice informed me.

I glanced to my left and found an emaciated elderly woman in a shabby nightgown with a raggedy knitted shawl of indeterminate color clutched across her shoulders and a foul cheroot clenched between her lips.

"Madam . . ." I started to say, which made her laugh and reveal that she had no teeth. Even so, the cheroot hung to her lower lip as though it had been sewn there. "I meant no disrespect to the lad. . . ." I forced myself to continue as the fetid smell of unwashed bodies and ill-kept food began to swirl into my nostrils. "But I am here on official business, and this youngster would not permit me so much as an explanation. . . ."

"'E weren't taught ta wait fer no explanations," she sneered, plucking the slim cigar from her mouth and staring at the opposite end of it. "Get me a light, ya little bugger," she snapped at the boy, who immediately scrambled back to his feet and fled the room. "So wot's this official business . . . ?" she said with a sniff as the boy rushed back and dutifully put a match to the end of her cigar.

"Mr. Nettle has been implicated in the recent death of Adelaide Endicott," I began to explain, even though I had no idea what exactly it was that I hoped to get from her. "I have some further questions for him. I'm afraid they are critical if we have any chance of proving his innocence in the matter."

"Wot makes ya think 'e's innocent?"

Her question surprised me because I had not expected it, and for that reason I acted the fool. "Do you believe him capable of murder?"

She puffed on her cigar and swatted the boy away. "You ain't no gentleman. . . ." she pronounced as she studied me over the glowing end of her cigar, ". . . you're an arse." The boy giggled and the old woman turned on him. "Git outta 'ere, ya little pox. You ain't worth a shite yerself. Lettin' this big, wet oaf inta me 'ouse."

The boy bolted from the room and I cursed myself for having been so brusque with him. He was, after all, only trying to take care of himself, and in that I could not fault him. "How long have you been renting to Mr. Nettle?"

She gave a dismissive shrug of her bony shoulders and coughed a minute before answering. "Week or so, I s'pose. Ya'd 'ave ta ask the little nob. 'E remembers things better'n I do."

"Which room is his?"

"Top a the stairs and to the left. Keeps it nice and neat. I like that in a man. Most of 'em is pigs." She glared at me and did not bother to smile.

"I'd like to see the room."

"I'd like ta 'ave tea with the feckin' Queen," she shot back, starting to laugh again before it quickly turned into another hacking cough. "Bring me a drink a somethin'. . . ." she hollered toward the tiny kitchen as she caught her breath again.

I was still standing at the front door, dripping rain onto her filthy, greasy floor, and I didn't imagine she would notice the difference. Or care if she did. The boy's swift return stilled my thoughts as he handed her a glass of dark ale that she slugged back as though it were water.

"I'd offer ya a drink," she said as she sloughed the emptied glass back at the boy, "but you ain't stayin'." She gave a raspy chuckle that exposed her blackened gums again and my stomach curdled. "Now git outta me 'ouse or I'll shoot ya dead where yer standin' and 'ave this little shite 'ere toss yer arse onta the street for the curs ta fight over."

And sure enough, somewhere during her wheezed diatribe she pulled a well-used pistol from beneath the cushion of the lopsided chair she was reclining on, and I could only curse myself for not having considered it. Of course she was armed. And even though the weapon looked hazardous to fire, there was no doubt that it would leave a wound as likely to become septic as it was to kill.

"Forgive me," I said, nodding curtly but keeping my eyes riveted on the old woman. "Perhaps you can tell me when Mr. Nettle is expected back, and I will return at that time."

"I ain't 'is keeper," the woman answered sharply.

I cast a glance at the boy but could tell he wasn't about to contribute an unbidden word to what was left of this conversation. "Of course," I managed to pry out of my throat as I took a careful step backward, reaching for the door behind me. "I am sorry to have disturbed you." Neither of them responded as I swung the door wide and stepped back through it, popping my umbrella up and feeling relieved by the cold, fresh air that immediately snapped against my face. The house was a horror, and I hoped the boy would have a chance to break free as I had.

The rain had subsided to a drizzle during my brief visit inside the boardinghouse though my mood had not similarly lifted. I had come all this way and learned nothing without even managing to gain access to Mr. Nettle's room. Colin would be disappointed, but what really needled me was that I had made such a point of how capable I was back at our flat. The thought of returning home with nothing but the stink of tobacco on my clothing was enough to spur me to action. I would not allow that to be the case.

So with nary a glance back at the decrepit building I had just been evicted from, I headed to the end of the street and took two quick turns into the alley that ran parallel to it. This would not be the first time I had done what I had in mind, though it had certainly been many years. Not since Maw Heikens had used me for just this sort of clandestine activity had I dared attempt such a thing. And as I stared up at the harsh metal fire escapes clinging to the backs of the buildings, I could not deny that I was twenty years past the wispy boy of middle teens who eagerly bowed to Maw's every whim for the solace of the opiate she doled out.

Everything about the alley was dull and gray, and even the incessant rain could not diminish the inherent level of its dreariness or filth. Garbage was piled against the backs of the buildings as though it had sprouted from the very earth and begun to grow there. So much grime and filth clung to the compressed structures that it was difficult to tell where one ended and the next began. I was finally forced to count the fire escapes until I came to the seventh set, knowing this was the building where Mr. Nettle resided.

It almost came as no surprise when I realized there was no ladder from the bottom landing to the ground on Mr. Nettle's building. These places were as ill-kept as the people who lived within.

The next building over had a ladder hitched up into its ribbing, but it looked better than eight feet off the ground and I doubted I could get purchase on it even with a running start. The metalwork on the building next to that one had its ladder extended almost all the way down, so I decided I would make my way up to the roof from there and then come back to the building where Mr. Nettle lived. I would use the ladder on his building to descend back to the second floor where I knew his room to be.

My ascent proved to be more arduous than I had anticipated given the wetness of the rungs. As I rose up the ironwork, my boots persisted in slipping, leaving me no choice but to drop my umbrella back to the cobbles so I could grip the ladder with both hands. By the time I reached the third-floor landing I was wet enough that I no longer needed to care about the drizzle.

A variety of black pipes, both straight and curiously angled, rose up from the roofs around me like stiff dark weeds, each one belching a mixture of smoke and soot that was instantly seized by the spitting rain and flung back down in an oily sludge. My coat and hat would be ruined, but I didn't care.

I made my way back to Mr. Nettle's building, stepping easily over low-slung brick dividers that served no other purpose than as a demarcation between the buildings so that work done on one rooftop would not also mistakenly be done on another. Though I doubted there had been any work up here in my lifetime.

The ladder that led down the back of Mr. Nettle's building looked dubiously attached to the roof's lip, but I had no other choice, so I decided to ignore the possibilities. I carefully made my way down to the landing of the second floor, lowering myself hand over hand as my boots fought to make purchase. Although the whole structure groaned and rattled under my footfalls, I paid it little mind since the few windows that faced the alley were all closed against the wind and rain. I imagined myself the first person on this contraption since its assembly and only hoped it would not abruptly give way, pulling free of the building and pitching me to the hard cobbles of the alley below.

It was a relief to finally reach the second floor. I stood a moment with my back to the wet brick and felt the cold rolling off it in spite of my layers of clothing. Its dampness was the least of my concerns, as only a bathtub could have made me wetter than I already was.

I sucked in a quick breath and peeked through the single window that let onto the fire escape landing, spying a dingy hallway on the other side with no one about. There was one door on the left and one to the right, which I knew from the woman downstairs was where Mr. Nettle was staying. A staircase led up to the floor from the far end of the hallway and another beside it rose up to the next level. Thin, well-trodden carpet covered the landing and short hallway, threadbare to the floorboards beneath in many spots, but it would likely be enough to dampen the sounds of my footfalls.

I waited another moment to be sure I heard no movement from within, no one coming up the staircase or descending from the floor above, but there was nothing. If anyone was about, they weren't up here. I hesitantly reached forward, my heartbeat drumming in my ears, and grabbed the window, giving it a gentle tug. It m___ ___irly easily though not smoothly. I had expected it might, as ___ ___ly spent the whole of the summer months wide open.

I prodded it about halfway before cautiously sliding in through the gap and delicately nudging it back down. There would be no hasty exit from this place unless I burst through the glass and swung down the ten or so feet to the ground, no simple feat if the landlady was also firing her corroded old pistol at me. It was enough to give me pause, though it was far too late for that, and so, after pulling in a deep breath in an effort to cease my thundering heartbeat, I crept to Mr. Nettle's door and pressed an ear to it.

No sound issued forth, but then I had not expected it to. Though my ingress had been circuitous it had not been time consuming, and beyond that I could not fathom a reason why Mr. Nettle would ever hurry to return to this place.

I eased the door open just enough to glimpse inside and still felt relief when I found the tiny space unoccupied. I slipped in and coaxed the door shut with the utmost care so that the click of its latch reseating itself could not have been heard by a passing mouse.

The room, such as it was, lay before me. A single space with a small bed pushed against the wall opposite me, so close one full step would bring me right up to it. There was a small window on the outside wall, barely larger than one foot square, with a requisite crack running across the lower left corner. A plain wooden stand, well worn with nicks and scratches, stood beneath the window with an old pitcher and bowl atop it, both looking as misused as the piece of furniture they sat upon. These things, I was certain, came with the room. Hardly a recommendation to live here.

I glanced around, but there was little else to see beyond a trunk on the floor flung open and brimming with neatly folded clothing, a straight-backed chair beside it piled with items clearly waiting to be laundered. It appeared, given what little Mr. Nettle had, that I was on a fool's errand. As I took in this meager assemblage of possessions, I could imagine no reason why he would have murdered Adelaide Endicott, for surely her death had brought him to the lowest form of subsistence other than living on the street.

Determined to complete my undertaking, I hurriedly riffled through his trunk, taking care to leave it precisely as I had found it. There was mostly clothing inside, along with a few books and a ledger that bore the truth of how little he had been paid by the Endicotts, and a small framed picture of a pretty young girl.

I attacked the items piled on the chair next, but made short work of it as I did not relish pawing through someone else's soiled garments. I hastily held his jackets and shirtsleeves up to the little window to see whether there might be any reside of phosphorous powder on them, but the grayness of the day did not cooperate in allowing me to catch any glimpses of those startling colors. In desperation I even forced myself to fumble through his pant and vest pockets in hopes of finding some damning note, but there was no such thing, and I was left to feel I had accomplished nothing more than a respite from the rain.

A cursory glance beneath the bed revealed, as would be expected in such a diminutive space, a single pair of shoes; polished and tended that had obviously been worn while serving Adelaide Endicott. I pulled the pair out and stared at them a moment. The care and attention that had been bestowed upon them spoke of a man who both understood his place and took pride in it. These were boots I would slip on my feet without hesitation and yet here they sat, buffed and shined and shoved under a dilapidated little bed to await their time once more.

So thorough was the devotion paid them that a slight mar, something I doubt I would ordinarily have noticed, caught my eye near the right front of the outer sole on the right shoe. It looked like a smudge that reached up no more than a half inch toward the toe cap, and though I could see a dab of polish had been applied to it, it was still evident due to its slightly duller sheen.

I stood up and took the shoe to the window in an effort to get a better look, turning the shoe over and finding a similar but larger mark on the bottom of the sole, approximately the size of a half crown but with edges that looked as jagged as an eggshell. I brought the shoe toward my face to take a quick sniff, and that was when I heard the door open behind me.

"Ain't that a fine sight," a boy's voice clucked.

It took a long moment before I could finally get myself to lower the shoe and glance around. I felt as if I had been caught at a most inglorious task and, in some ways, I suppose I had. "Aren't you a clever young man," I said as I turned fully around to face him. "And I thought I was being ever so quiet."

"Yer makin' enough noise ta wake up me wretched ol' auntie downstairs. An' if ya do that I'll as likely let 'er shoot ya as not."

A tight smile came easily to my lips as I realized that the woman downstairs had not sent him up and that his first inclination was not to tell her he had discovered me here. "My apologies," I answered with a small nod of my head. This lad was no fool and I was certain I knew what would earn me his silence. "You must allow me to pay you for your trouble," I continued as I slowly reached my free hand into my pocket, pulling out several shillings and a farthing.

The boy snickered. "Ya think ta give me a 'andful a change? Auntie's gotta gun an' you can believe she'll fire it. I'll take a pound or I'll start 'ollerin' so loud you'll 'ave the 'ole buildin' and the one next door down on yer 'ead." As though to assure me of his threat he took a half step backward, halting just outside the threshold where his youthful scream was bound to have its greatest impact.

"A bloody pound . . ." I heard myself repeat even as I dug into my vest pocket again and pulled one free.

To my surprise, rather than take it from me, the boy stepped back again, now fully out in the hallway. "Ya done in there?" he asked.

"Yes," I grumbled, taking the shoe still clutched in my right hand and shoving it and its mate back under the bed where I had found them.

"Then get outta there and be quiet, ya ruddy tosser."

This boy, I could not help thinking, was masterful. He would probably end up owning half the row houses in Whitechapel if left to his own devices. So I did precisely as he instructed, moving the few steps out of Freddie Nettle's cramped quarters and delicately easing the door shut behind myself. "Now what?" I asked, the pound note still held in my other hand.

"Drop the pound on the floor and git yer arse back out the winda ya came in through," he hissed.

"Back . . . ?" I gaped toward the window and the rickety fire escape beyond and realized there was no other way. I could not simply toddle down the stairs without risking a lead pellet from the woman he called Auntie. "Yes," I had to agree, staring into a young face as filled with amusement as it was with gratification.

The pound note fluttered to the floor without a care, landing between us, and the boy's eyes filled with such yearning that I felt a tug of regret at my throat. He looked up at me and his face went hard again. "Go on. . . ." he commanded, obviously not willing to collect the pound until I was gone. And again, I thought him ever the smarter for it.

With nothing left to do, I turned back to the window and pried it halfway up just as I had done before, only this time I was struck by the groan it released as the stiles scraped against the jamb. No wonder the lad had heard me. Wearing a sheepish look, I glanced back over my shoulder and found both the boy and the pound note gone.

I hurried out the window and was down in the alley in nothing more than a minute, having decided to jump the ten feet to the ground rather than climbing up and over as I had done before. Though I landed harder than I had intended, nothing was incurred beyond the injury to my pride and disappointment at having accomplished little more than having spent a pound.

My umbrella was still right where I had tossed it, for which I was grateful, as the rain had begun to pick up again while I was inside. I strode out of the alley's mouth with my eyes down, holding the umbrella low over my head even though there was scant risk that I could get any wetter than I already was. I kept debating whether to omit the charge to our pocketbook in the retelling of my dubious journey to Colin.

I charged across White Horse Lane, trying to pick my way carefully through the detritus adrift along the edges of the street, intending to head back to the Underground. It was difficult enough to get a cab to come down here on the best of days but perfectly impossible on a day such as this. So it came as a great surprise when a short young man with a cap on his head publicizing his profession as a cab driver began to wave wildly at me from just up the street. At first I thought he must surely be calling to someone else, somebody behind me, but he kept his gaze rigidly set on me even as he started to jog toward me.

"Sir . . ." he called as I came into earshot. "It's the lady. She needs you right away, sir."

He beckoned me and started back the way he had come, and for some reason my heart immediately began to ratchet with unease. There was only one reason Mrs. Behmoth would ever be forced out on such a day as this to fetch me—something had happened to Colin and his father. I took off after the diminutive man, letting the umbrella slip down to my shoulder as I rushed to the black coach he was now standing beside. Rain was dripping off the poor man's cap, nose, and chin, and I knew the same was true of me, but none of it mattered in the least as he yanked the coach's door open with welcomed precision, allowing me to scramble inside at the same instant that I pulled my useless umbrella closed.

But it was not Mrs. Behmoth's round face that stared back at me through the muted gray light of this oppressive day, but the startlingly delicate features of Charlotte Hutton.

I fell into the seat across from her at the same moment the driver heaved the door shut, trying to collect my breath and thoughts. "What . . . ?" I started to say before deciding to let her speak first.

"You must forgive me," she spoke softly. She was wrapped in a black cloak from neck to toe and had a plain black hat pulled low over her face so that not so much as a strand of her hair could be seen. Her alabaster skin looked like a single point of light in the midst of an otherwise starless night.

"Forgive you . . . ?" I asked. For of all the things I could have imagined her saying, those words would not have been amongst them.

"I had you followed when you left your flat this morning,"

she explained without artifice. "I am convinced that your Mr. Pendragon has already made up his mind about me, so I am hoping that you are a man of reason who will listen to what I have told you and hear the truth in my words. There is nothing more that I seek than a chance to start anew, away from here, with my daughter. A simple life, Mr. Pruitt. I do not ask for more than a small house and the funds to keep us safe and cared for. We are only two women; we shall not require much."

I stared back at her, enfolded in her firmament of blackness, her blue eyes the only color showing against the paleness of her face. But those eyes were wary and watchful, and I knew she was measuring me, searching to see if I was, in fact, the man she hoped me to be. "For a woman who asserts the simplicity of her needs, you managed to end up with an extraordinary amount of money at your disposal. I wonder what would have become of that wealth had the Swiss not cut your access to those funds."

The thinnest of glimmers flashed behind her eyes as one corner of her mouth nudged the tiniest bit. "We both know I would be lying if I tried to answer that question, Mr. Pruitt. When I arrived in Geneva and realized what Wynn Tessler had done . . ." She let her voice trail off and glanced out the window a moment. "I thought for the first time in my life I was free of any man." She slid her eyes back to mine and gave a wearied exhalation. "You cannot understand. It is impossible for you to know. So I would indeed be lying if I told you I did not look at that money as recompense for everything I had endured—by Arthur, by Wynn Tessler. The loses I suffered, the cruelty . . ." A hand moved up and touched the throat of her cloak, and I was reminded of the scars she had shown me, and I wondered if that was her intent. "I would like to say that I would only have taken what I needed and left the rest behind, but I dare not admit any such thing." Her eyes bore into mine. "Could you assure anything further than what I have said, Mr. Pruitt, were you to have trod on the same path that I have done?"

I found that I could not answer. Had she continued to stare out the window I might well have been able to cobble some nonsense together to insist otherwise, but her gaze did not waver, and I was certain she would see that I was a man who would have fled with the money in an instant were I still the person who lived on these very streets. "It is not for me to give any of that money away. . . ." I started to say, but got no further when I noticed her stiffen in her seat, her eyes instantly clouding over.

"Would you have me take you to my rooms to disrobe so that you can see the full extent of what was wrought against me?" she demanded. "Or perhaps you would prefer that I do it here and now?!" And in that same instant she began to fumble with the tie at the collar of her cloak.

"*No, madam!*" I yelped. "I have already seen your wounds. I do not doubt my eyes any more than I require further proof of what befell you. Nevertheless, seven people were murdered, including an inspector of Scotland Yard. . . ."

"And I murdered *none* of them!" she hurled back, her voice low and hard. "Do you forget that my own *son* was one of those victims?"

"Of course not." A heavy exhalation escaped me as I rubbed at my eyes, trying to think how I could rescue this conversation. "If there is some arrangement to be devised for you and your daughter with regards to this money, it can only be earned if you come with me to the Yard."

"I have already told you that Wynn Tessler would have me murdered before I could even finish my statement. You are foolish if you think he is to be dismissed simply because you have him behind bars."

"And I gave you my word that Colin and I would protect you. . . ."

"Your word . . ." She gave a harsh, dry chuckle. "I cannot see what difference you word will make when my throat has been sliced from ear to ear."

"Then come with me to my flat to speak with Mr. Pendragon," I offered, my eyes as beseeching as my voice. "He will know what other options we might pursue. After all, it was his father who procured the sequestration of your Swiss funds in the first place." And the instant the words left my mouth I cursed their very formation on my tongue.

Charlotte Hutton leaned back, surprise and satisfaction appearing to fight for control of her gaze. "Of course," she said, and I knew how seriously I had blundered. "Then I have been right all along about Mr. Pendragon. But I have been mistaken about you." Her eyes held such accusation that I had to look away. "So I am just another hysterical woman who likely earned what she received . . . ?"

"You have misunderstood my intention," I answered, and yet I sounded weak and unconvincing even to my own ears.

"Have I?" She continued to grip the neck of her cloak with one hand as though it was the only thing between myself and her honor. "I think not, though I can see now that I have wasted your time. You must forgive me."

She stared at me with a look as much filled with regret as it seemed to be rife with betrayal. I knew that I needed to say something, something that might bind her here while I tried to discern a way to bridge the chasm that I had stupidly flung us into. There had to be something I could say that might give her pause, if not to meet with Colin then at least to talk with me again, but as I sat there, slack-jawed and empty, nothing would present itself. And before the span of another moment could pass she leaned forward and burst out of the cab, slamming the door behind herself with such force that it momentarily froze me to my seat.

That was all the time it took before some baser instinct screeched across my brain so that in the next moment I too leapt for the door, fumbling to twist the handle and yet finding it inexplicably unyielding. I threw my shoulder against it and still it did not give. Had she slammed it so hard that the mechanism had broken?

I slid across the seat and shoved the opposite door wide, jumping out into a fresh downpour even as I skittered around the coach and up onto the sidewalk. The cab driver was standing there, looking every bit the drowned rat, staring at me with astonishment, but I had no interest in him. I scanned the street one direction and then the other, trying to spot Mrs. Hutton, but there were too many people moving about, all hunched beneath umbrellas as they scurried to get out of the downpour.

"Where is she?" I hollered at the driver. "Which way did she go?"

He stared at me with shock and fear in his eyes, and it was only then that I noticed his arm closest to the coach was gradually sliding back down to his side. The bastard had been blocking the door.

Rage exploded in my brain, for my failure at Freddie Nettle's, for my failure with Charlotte Hutton, and for the way in which this wretched man had stymied me. And without a single thought, as the rain and wind pounded against me as if to finally seep directly into my bones, I reared back and punched him in the jaw.

CHAPTER 16

"I wouldn't believe it if I 'adn't seen it for meself," Mrs. Behmoth said with a frown as she set a bowl of warm, salted water onto the table in front of me. "Fightin' like a street cur. You've been livin' with that one too long," she added with a nod of her chin toward Colin.

I was sitting at the kitchen table in fresh undergarments with my robe flung loosely over my shoulders, trying my best to ignore her as I delicately coaxed my right hand into the water. It felt soothing on my fingers up to the point when it began lapping at my knuckles, and then it was as though the water had abruptly burst into flame, licking at the raw wounds and severed flesh there. Without even meaning to I yanked my hand out, intending to have another go at it once I better girded myself, but before I could release even a single yelp I heard Mrs. Behmoth release a *tsk* and then her meaty hand came down over mine, shoving my fist fully into the water.

"Some kind a ruffian you are," she scolded.

"Leave him be," Colin said as he came over to me, tossing a set of barbells around as though they carried no weight at all. "I'm proud of Ethan."

"You would be," she grumbled, folding her arms across her chest in an unmitigated display of her obvious disapproval.

"No one is going to get the best of us," he went right on as though she hadn't said a word. "That sod has learned his lesson, and when we pay him a visit later today, I'm sure he'll sing like Jenny Lind used to."

"You sound like a bloody rooster." Mrs. Behmoth scowled.

Colin ignored her again, turning to me with an eagerness I had never expected, given how truly unsuccessful my morning had been. "Next time you need to punch someone do it from below so you won't do as much damage to your hand."

"Next time . . . ?" I started to say before opting to hold my tongue. If some newer, more compelling perspective of who I was had suddenly blossomed in Colin's mind, then who was I to fiddle with that?

"If you have the misfortune of speaking to that Hutton woman again you should be sure to make *her* your next target. That woman is an infuriating passel of lies." He hoisted the barbells with renewed vigor as he stalked repeatedly around the table. "She means to seduce you with her lies. She has an answer for everything and yet *refuses* to meet with me. Hers is a dark bloody heart."

"She claims you have already condemned her and would sooner see her in prison than investigate the possibility of some truth on her part. I tried to convince her otherwise, but you must remember that she has had a sorrowful time of it with the men in her life. Don't forget that I have seen some of the wounds and scars left behind on her body attesting to that very thing."

"And I will remind you that there are many ways to become scarred," Colin fired back.

"Wot married person ain't got a scar or two from their 'usband or wife?" Mrs. Behmoth added. "It's jest the way of it. Means ya love 'em."

I looked at her with a mixture of disbelief and horror. "I really don't think that's true."

"Wadda you know. Ya ain't even married." She shoved herself up from the table and began puttering at the sink.

"Your husband was just cowed," Colin said to her back, his mouth ticking up at the corners. "You didn't scar him, you drove him to an early death."

She gave a peevish shrug and glanced back, tossing Colin a wearied look. "That man could be tryin'. But we 'ad our fun when 'e did as 'e was told."

"There it is." Colin snickered as he finally plopped down in the seat she had vacated, though he continued to pump the barbells as though to stop might cause his body to cease functioning. "And now I believe it is high time for us to pay a visit to that Mrs. Denmark we keep hearing about." Colin's cerulean eyes were hugely round and full of verve. "If there really was dissension in the Hutton household, then there is staff who will know about it. I can only presume that the Denmark woman will have placed at least some of them there. Or she will be likely to know where any former staff may have ended up."

"Denmark?" I repeated. "Do you mean Mrs. Den*holm?* The woman who places household staff that Mr. Galloway and Miss Whit mentioned?"

"Yes." He waved me off as though I were addled. "We shall check in with her and then we will find your cab driver. I am most eager to see if he won't be much more cooperative now. Go get yourself dressed and Mrs. Behmoth will bandage your knuckles." She gave another *tsk*, but Colin only chuckled.

His amusement did nothing for my state of mind. Why I had decided it acceptable to strike a man who most certainly had no idea of the magnitude of his actions I could not say, but it left me feeling neither proud nor satisfied. The shredding of my knuckles and the ache it left behind was something I knew I deserved. Nevertheless, I dutifully went upstairs and dressed as quickly as I could before allowing Mrs. Behmoth to fuss over my hand with some gooey salve and a bandage I was certain she took great pleasure in binding too tight.

Colin hailed a cab while I shrugged into a dry coat, my first still hanging like a drowned carcass in front of the fireplace on the far side of the kitchen. I would be lucky if I could wear it again in a week's time. A moment later we were on our way to Mayfair to meet with Mrs. Denholm.

"How did it go with Lord Endicott?" I asked as we clattered around Hyde Park.

"Well, I didn't punch him in the jaw, if that's what you mean," he answered with a snort.

"You aren't funny."

"Do I need to watch myself to make sure I don't make you cross in the future?"

"You'd best," I shot back. "Now tell me about Lord Endicott."

"I know this will come as something of a surprise to you," Colin said with a thick dose of mockery in his voice, "but Lord Endicott is a pompous blowhard who loves nothing more than to hear the sound of his own voice."

"Shocking," I replied flatly.

He chuckled. "My father did his share of the talking, of course. He really is a master at spinning gold out of straw. I said as little as possible and treated His Lordship with the deference he feels he deserves, and after we had finished tea and my father had exhausted his inquiries into all of their common chums, we were allowed to make our escape."

"And what did you tell him about the investigation into his sister's death?"

"That while I did not believe she had killed herself, I was not yet willing to state that Mr. Nettle was necessarily involved, either."

"And . . ."

He shrugged his shoulders lightly as we pulled up to a four-story brick building in a row of similar structures. "It seemed to suit him for now."

"How long is now . . . ?" I pressed, even as Colin reached for the carriage door.

"Until the next time his sister calls him up to complain about us," he answered as he popped out and strode purposefully away.

I gave the driver half of his fare, which proved something of a challenge as I could barely slide the fingers of my injured hand into my pocket, and bid him wait for us. Far better to have him at our call than to try to find another cab on such a dismal day as this. The rain had let up but the wind still howled, forcing me to hold my hat in place with my good hand as I made my way up the front porch to where Colin was already disappearing inside the flat.

"Mr. Pruitt . . ." An elegant woman in her late middle years ushered me inside a few steps behind Colin, her figure immaculate beneath a form-fitting ivory dress with bold navy stripes and a high collar of lace that wrapped around the back of her neck. Her brown hair was a pile of finger-sized curls situated just so, but it was the warmth in her eyes that most caught my attention. "I cannot tell you what an honor it is to invite two such notable men into my house," she said as she led us into her front parlor just off the small entranceway.

The room clearly served a dual purpose, as along with a large sofa and two delicate, matching French chairs there were two desks situated along the wall astride the fireplace. One was tall and open with an array of cubbies along its inside face, and the other was a large flat table with swooping swan's-neck legs. It held a collection of small baskets stuffed with papers while at its side stood a large wooden cabinet whose contents, I was sure, were yet more papers and files.

"Please make yourselves comfortable, gentlemen." She gestured us toward the sofa as she went over to a side table beneath the front window and picked up a tea tray. "You are just in time to share a small repast," she said with a smile as she set it down on the table across from us and seated herself in one of the fragile-looking French chairs. She looked to be the only one of us slight enough to use it. "I have egg sandwiches and some spinach-and-cucumber sandwiches, and I bought this shortbread from the bakery down the street if you are willing to splurge a bit."

"You offer us far too much," Colin said with a smile as he reached forward and lifted a couple of the sandwich triangles onto a plate and handed it to me. "We certainly do not mean to put you to any trouble," he went on as he made a similar plate for himself.

"It is no trouble at all," she said as she poured our tea and handed the cups across. "I would be remiss if I did not treat everyone who enters my home as a potential client."

"Ah . . ." Colin gave her a sheepish smile as he poured a bit of cream into my tea and then his. "Then I am sorry to have to inform you that we are not here to avail ourselves of your fine services, though perhaps one day we shall," he added with a crooked grin, "but rather to ask you some questions about a few of your former clients. It is for an investigation we find ourselves entangled in, and I would hope you will be able to furnish us with some much-needed information."

"Oh . . ." She looked startled as she sipped at her tea. "Well, yes, of course. You may count on me to assist in any way that I can, but as I am sure you can imagine, discretion is an integral part of my business. . . ." She let her voice trail off, and I knew we would have to tread carefully if she was going to be the font of knowledge we hoped her to be.

"We would expect nothing less," Colin replied with great expansiveness as he grabbed two more sandwich quarters for himself. "How else could you be relied upon by this city's finest families if discretion were not an integral requirement of your services?"

She beamed at his compliment, reminding me that he could be wholly charming whenever he was so inclined.

"Then do tell me what your questions are," Mrs. Denholm said as she picked up one of the egg sandwich triangles and nibbled on it like a church mouse.

"Mr. Galloway of Layton Manor tells us you are the person who has populated the Endicott sisters' household with most of its staff over the last good many years. I was hoping you might share with us any difficulties you have had in accomplishing that."

"Oh!" Her eyes went wide and she set the mostly uneaten bit of sandwich back onto her plate, dabbing at her mouth with the delicacy her inconsequential speck of eating deserved. "Miss Eugenia and Miss Adelaide are two of the most genteel women I have ever had the pleasure of doing business with: kind and fair, and Mr. Galloway maintains the household impeccably. It is such a shame about Miss Adelaide's passing." She leaned forward and glanced quickly to her left and right as if making certain no one would overhear her, though, to the best of my knowledge, the three of us were the only ones in the flat. "It cannot be true what they're saying, can it? That Miss Adelaide brought about her own demise?"

A taut grimace tugged at Colin's lips, and I was certain he was thinking the same thing I was: This woman's definition of discretion ended with her enunciation of its three syllables. "If she did," Colin said slowly and without the hint of distaste that I could see shuffling about behind his eyes, "then our goal is to find out what drove her to it." He allowed a hint of a smile to play at one corner of his mouth. "Or who."

"Oh," Mrs. Denholm said again, a hand coming up to cover her mouth as she leaned back in what looked almost to be a swoon. "I can hardly breathe for the thought of it."

"You mustn't upset yourself," I spoke up, though I couldn't help feeling there was a degree of exhilaration to her reaction. "Your assistance, as you can give it, will be a critical part of this investigation and something I am certain Miss Eugenia and her brother, Lord Endicott, will be most pleased to hear of."

"And how might I be of any service?" She flicked her eyes between the two of us, her enthusiasm sharp and evident. "Most of my dealings were with Mr. Galloway. I cannot claim any but the most cursory acquaintanceship with Miss Eugenia and have never even met His Lordship."

"Nevertheless"—Colin sniffed as he picked up a piece of the shortbread—"I would presume you have missed little. But at the moment I would simply like to know if you had any difficulty filling the positions at Layton Manor? People not staying or refusing to accept work there perhaps?"

"There were some issues, but you mustn't blame them on Miss Adelaide or Miss Eugenia. People get such preposterous notions in their heads sometimes it becomes virtually impossible to lead them to reason."

"Notions . . . ?" Colin pressed. "What sort of notions might you be referring to?"

"Well, I am not one to gossip, but it was said the household was quite dogged with all manner of spectral malfeasance. Objects moved about when no one was there, inexplicable sounds, passing coldness in a hallway or room as though an unsuspecting person had stepped right through some poor tortured soul. And there was a most persistent rumor that Miss Adelaide herself had suffered terrible visions."

"Do you know what sort of visions?"

"Oh no. I never pried into such things." She leaned forward and scooped up her teacup and saucer again. "But I do remember someone telling me they had something to do with a young girl. A poor sorrowful thing in search of her mother. Calling out or crying . . ." She waved a hand as quickly as a hummingbird. "I really didn't pay the story any mind. But it has been said their father was indiscriminate," she carried on, flashing a pointed gaze that made both the insinuation and her feelings behind it well obvious. "The sad little creature was likely the unwanted product of such a union left searching for her place in this life and the next." She released a protracted sigh that resulted in both of Colin's eyebrows heading skyward.

"Are you a believer in such things then?" I asked before Colin could comment.

"Oh no." She gave a lilting sort of laugh that ridiculed the very suggestion. "If such a thing were true, there would be phantom children in nearly every manor house in this country. I should think those caught wandering in the spaces between our world and the next would have greater concerns than their earthly pedigree."

"But you did find some people unwilling to accept employment with the sisters?" Colin asked.

"Most would take the positions. Such employment is not easy to come by, especially when it involves serving only two elderly women. Far easier than a large family. But I had a devil of a time keeping people there. Some lasted a few months, others less than that." She shook her head and set her teacup down and I noticed it still looked practically untouched. "There is just no sense in some people. I felt quite sorry for Mr. Galloway."

"And I understand you also placed the two nurses who worked for Miss Adelaide." Colin moved along, tossing a quick look at me. "What are their names?"

"Philippa Bromley and Vivian Whit."

"I did. I found them at the Royal London Hospital. They were set to enter Tredegar House to begin formalized nurses' training but were sadly passed over for the inaugural class. I could see they were skilled and level-headed girls, so I snatched them up for Miss Adelaide at once. And you can see I was right. They stayed with her right up to her untimely death."

"And Freddie Nettle?" Colin continued without a moment's delay. "You found him a place there as well, didn't you?"

"Yes. He had done some work out at Bristol House for the groundskeeper there and had proven himself strong, amiable, and trustworthy. When Miss Eugenia contacted me about Adelaide's failing health, I knew right away that Mr. Nettle would be an ideal fit. His tenure at Bristol House had been completed and he was quite at loose ends—"

"You said Miss Eugenia contacted you," Colin cut her off again. "So it was not Miss Adelaide herself who sought the assistance?"

Mrs. Denholm gave a wry smirk as she looked back at Colin. "You mustn't underestimate a woman's pride, Mr. Pendragon. It can be every bit as ferocious as a man's."

"I see. . . ." he said tepidly, and I knew he had little notion of a woman's pride. "And what exactly did Miss Eugenia tell you her sister required?"

"A nurse to care for her at night and a strong, able-bodied man to tend to her activities, such as they were. Someone capable of pushing her around in a wheeled chair when necessary, or to carry her upstairs when she wished to retire. He didn't need any medical knowledge because they would have the nurse for that. So I placed Vivian Whit first." She sat back and thought for a moment before continuing. "I sent Mr. Nettle there not a week after Miss Whit started, and it couldn't have been more than another month before Mr. Galloway came around to say they would require another nurse to assist during the day. I must admit"— her brown eyes sparkled with self-satisfaction—"I wasn't the least bit surprised. The deterioration of the elderly is never but one direction. I had already spoken with Philippa Bromley and another young woman to see if either of them might be interested in the duty at Layton Manor should the necessity arise, and Miss Bromley was quite receptive. So when Mr. Galloway came back to see me, I was able to fulfill the second requirement at once." She grinned, quite pleased with herself, which I found rather distressing under the circumstances.

"You had some knowledge of Mr. Nettle then before you placed him at the Endicotts'?"

"Oh yes. I wasn't about to send just anyone there. It was quite a coup for my business to be able to serve the Endicott sisters. I was determined that they would be entirely satisfied because if I were ever called upon to supply staff to Lord Endicott . . ." Her eyes flashed like a child's on Christmas Day. "I'm sure you can imagine how that would affect me."

"And Mr. Nettle . . . ?" Colin prodded, barely concealing his lack of interest in the trajectory of her business.

"I've known of him since he was hawking newspapers on the street. He caught my eye because he was bigger than the other lads. A handsome boy who looked already a man and I wondered why he hadn't procured some better employment for himself." She gave a fluttering sort of laugh as she snapped off a small corner from a piece of shortbread. "My late husband would buy a paper from him most days, and finally I could not contain myself and began to speak with him, and you can imagine my surprise when I learned he was not quite sixteen. I'd thought him nearly ten years older." She shook her head with a laugh as she set the untouched bit of biscuit back onto her saucer. "He was living in one of the workhouses not far from Limehouse. No family. Not even a sibling that I know of. But he was trying to make something of himself, and I recognized a certain quality in him." Her expression went soft, and she stared past us, and for a moment I thought I sensed something of a maternal bent from this woman for Mr. Nettle.

"So you started finding him work . . . ?" Colin asked, his impatience with her remembrance beginning to leak through.

"Not right away." Her eyes snapped back and she picked up her tea again and took the most delicate sip. "My husband became ill around that time, and I didn't work for almost two years while I took care of him." She flashed a brief, mournful smile that made the outcome of that story obvious.

"And after that?" Colin pushed, though his voice had notched back.

"I ran into Mr. Nettle again. He was doing some courier work, odds and ends, whatever he could land for himself, I suppose. So I decided to test him out and gave him to a man who was handling the green space at several rows of houses in Marylebone before procuring a place for him working on the grounds at Bristol House." Her smile came easily again. "He did beautifully in both positions, just as I had known he would. Never late, never missing, and so very bright." She set her teacup down and leaned forward again, speaking in a charged whisper as though about to share the most extraordinary thing. "So I did something I have never done before or since. I started tutoring him in the etiquette of working for a proper family: the customs, protocols, and routines. Everything from the way he spoke to the way he handled himself. It was thrilling. He was the most eager pupil."

"I would say you did your job well, as he was quite polished on the occasions when Mr. Pruitt and I met with him."

"Oh"—she grinned—"he deserves all of the credit, not me." But I could see that she was well pleased by Colin's compliment.

"Do you review the backgrounds of the people you place?"

"Yes, of course. What sort of businesswoman would I be if I did not?"

"And what does that process constitute?"

"I interview past employers whenever practicable and procure letters of recommendation when not. I also collect and maintain brief biographies about the people I place: where they were born, what sort of education they've received, who they've worked for, that sort of thing. I think it's important to know something about the people I place."

"Commendable," Colin said, and as his eyes drifted back to the piles of file folders on the table there and the wooden cabinet against the wall I knew why he thought it so. "And might we avail ourselves of your meticulous records at some point? I should think we might find them most useful."

"Well . . ." she demurred. "That would be highly irregular. . . ."

"These are highly irregular times," Colin reminded her perfunctorily.

"Yes . . ." She nodded. "Yes . . . I suppose they are." She seemed to give it some thought as she sipped at her tea for a moment. "I would certainly not want them taken from here. . . ."

"There would be no need." Colin flicked a brief, tight smile at her, well pleased. "Mr. Pruitt can work right here."

There was no surprise in his statement, though I was annoyed just the same. That I would be consigned to this woman's parlor for what would amount to several hours was as good as forgone, and yet still I wished that I was not always thusly condemned.

"I suppose that will be fine then," she agreed with a note of hesitancy.

"Wonderful." And now Colin's smile came more easily. "We shall arrange a suitable time for him to come back, as we have other business to attend to and his right hand is not as dexterous as it should be just now." This last he said with a chuckle that only further riled my mood. "But let me ask you something on a wholly different topic, Mrs. Denholm. Did you ever have occasion to place staff at the home of Arthur and Charlotte Hutton? They had a rather large house north of the city. . . ."

"By the widow Connicle," she interrupted, her eyes going wide. "A terrible thing, that. I placed staff at the Connicle household over the years until the poor widow lost everything, but I never had cause to send anyone to the Huttons. I believe"—her voice dropped and her hands fluttered up around her face as she tilted her head slightly forward—"that they were living beyond their means. I don't even know what's happened to Mrs. Hutton after the death of her husband. But such things are not my concern." Yet her tone suggested that it was very much of interest just the same.

"They had a nurse who cared for their son," Colin continued, ignoring Mrs. Denholm's obvious fascination. "Might you have helped to settle her elsewhere?"

"Janelle Godwin," she said at once. "She did come to me, but I didn't have anything for a woman with her experience. She dealt only with children who weren't quite . . ." Her voice trailed off, and it was clear she was at a loss to explain any further.

"Did you happen to collect her contact information, by any chance?"

Mrs. Denholm looked pleased, or perhaps relieved, to have her statement dispensed with. "Why, yes. Yes, I did." She pushed herself off the chair and walked to the brimming table of files and sorted through one corner quickly before pulling out a single sheet. "Would you like me to copy her address for you?"

"We would be most grateful," Colin said as we both stood up. "And though you did not place anyone in the Hutton household, did you ever hear any chatter from anyone who did work there? Nurse Godwin perhaps . . . ?"

"Really, Mr. Pendragon." She glanced over at him with an expression as filled with determination as it was with facetiousness. "You must believe me when I tell you I do not partake in such idylls. If I have heard things it is in spite of my wish not to do so."

"And if I have given the slightest indication that I think you guilty of such trifling, then I do indeed owe you an apology," Colin said with a slight bob of his head and such smoothness that

I knew his father would be proud. "It is simply that, given your position in the community, I would suppose you *must* hear things, and while I would not expect a woman such as yourself to perpetuate such chatter, it could be useful to know what has been said. Ofttimes there are sparks where there is smoke. . . ." He let the suggestion hang in the air as he accepted the piece of paper she handed over, her eyes never once leaving his face, and I could see she was well in his thrall.

"Yes . . . of course . . ." she muttered, finally tearing her eyes away and twittering a self-conscious sort of laugh as one of her hands flew up to flutter about her lacy collar. "I believe I did hear that there were some frightful rows between Mr. and Mrs. Hutton. I could not even speculate as to the cause, but it was enough to elicit comment on more than one occasion. But such things . . . A staff can be privy to such things in even the finest homes."

"Was there ever the suggestion of physical altercations?"

"Physical . . . ?!" She stopped herself from repeating the phrase and looked quite drained of color as she flicked her eyes between Colin and me. "I am sure I would not know. The very idea of such a thing happening in one of our city's finer homes. It is too repugnant to even consider."

"My apologies," Colin said airily as he headed for the door. "If you would be so generous as to arrange a time with Mr. Pruitt to review your files . . . ?" He gave a thin smile and nodded before sweeping his hat back onto his head and disappearing outside.

I turned to find Mrs. Denholm staring at the blank entry where Colin had just been, her eyes as filled with bewilderment as intrigue. "He's rather an extraordinary man, isn't he?" she mumbled under her breath, her gaze unmoving.

"Oh yes." I gave a smile she did not notice. "He has been called many things."

"Forgive my ill manner, but is he married?"

And at last she turned to look at me so that I had to struggle to keep my expression impassive. "He is not. Might you be available for me to return tomorrow morning then?"

"I attend church at nine, but you are welcome to come back between eleven and noon. A widower?"

"A confirmed bachelor. Then I shall see you just past eleven. Thank you."

I hurried for the door but did not manage to make my way out fast enough before she could fling one more statement at me. "I have the most darling niece. . . ." she began to say.

"As do I, madam," I lied as I quickly let myself out.

CHAPTER 17

⟶◦⟵

The carriage depot was a hive of activity. Hansoms, landaus, hackneys, cabriolets, and even a few broughams rolled in and out of the huge warehouse in a clatter of horses' hooves, jangling bridles, and bellowing voices. If someone was conducting this mêlée I could not tell, and yet it all appeared to be moving with a fluidity that was undeniable. For there were neither collisions nor quarrels around who was going where, with even the detritus left by the horses dealt with by a small group of boys who darted around the floor with such efficiency that there was barely time for the stream of great spinning wheels to become soiled before they headed out onto the streets.

The foreman, a gruff, hairy man named Rawley who was of diminutive height but spoke in a sonorous roar, did not bother concealing his contempt for me in the least. His dark eyes practically bored out of a beard that seemed to start somewhere beneath his collar and rose up almost to the tops of his cheeks, which was made worse by eyebrows so wild and overgrown that I had to wonder how he could see through them.

"I remember," he was saying to Colin, his disdain wholly evident even though he had turned his gaze out onto the floor. *"Watch yer bleedin' arse, Mullen,"* he suddenly shouted, *"or I'll have ya pickin' up shite with them guttersnipes. They're horses, not puppies, ya bloody arse.*" He flicked his eyes back to Colin and his scowl actually deepened. "I tend ta remember when one a me men takes a fist from a customer."

If I could have melted into the floor I would have eagerly done so.

"Your driver was willfully impeding a Scotland Yard investigation, Mr. Rawley, and even now it is fortunate that he has not been incarcerated for his collusion."

"What?" Mr. Rawley glared.

"For helping the woman get away," Colin snapped.

Mr. Rawley stared back at Colin, continuing to ignore my presence, and if he cared in the least about Mrs. Hutton's escape he did not give the slightest hint of it. "He coulda lost a tooth," he said after another moment. "He may still."

"I hardly think you can blame the state of any man's mouth on Mr. Pruitt. Now you will tell me where we can find this man or I will have the whole of Scotland Yard down here within the hour to audit every record you and your laudable company have ever set to paper." It was a persuasive argument that instantly caught Mr. Rawley's attention even though there wasn't a whiff of truth to it.

"He's in the little office up them stairs on the back wall," he growled like some sort of feral beast. "He wanted nothin' more ta do with yer street lout here," he added, wagging his chin in my direction, though his eyes continued to avoid me.

"Very wise," Colin sneered as he began to head for the back wall, moving with enough speed that I started to suspect he didn't want to be caught laughing.

"You might counsel your men on the alliances they choose to make," I scolded Mr. Rawley for no better reason than I was still mortified by what I had done as well as by his reaction to me. And then I hurried after Colin lest this man suddenly decide to exact his own revenge for his driver.

The open stairway led up some twenty-five feet or more, allowing an avian view onto the bustling scene below. There was a glass-walled office at the top with sliding windows where I could imagine Mr. Rawley shoving his head through to holler down whenever the need suited him. Certainly, he would miss nothing from this perch. But for some reason he did not accompany us up so that the only other person here was the driver I had struck. The poor man's eyes were wide, and the left side of his jaw was mottled in red, orange, and a most unnatural shade of blue. Shame immediately washed over me as we continued to approach him, compelling me to furtively remove the pristine bandage Mrs. Behmoth had wrapped around my knuckles, which had suddenly begun to feel indecent. Quickly stuffing the soiled dressing into a pocket of my trousers, I followed Colin into the cramped glass office.

"You ain't gonna hit me again . . . ?" the man pleaded in spite of his thick tongue and badly swollen jaw.

"I should never—"

"Don't give him any reason to," Colin hastily cut me off. "You've already seen how ill-controlled his temper can be."

"I heard you was a bully," he murmured, his eyes filled with accusation, "but I never thought ya'd lay inta a man wot was jest standin' there."

"A bully—?" I started to protest.

"Let us not forget that you are hardly an innocent man," Colin interrupted me again. "You held the carriage door closed and allowed a fugitive from justice to escape. Remarkably bad form."

"Who said I was a bully?!" I could not help myself.

"I didn't know any such thing. She tol' me you was threatenin' her and she was afraid a you, and then she paid me ta hold the door shut if things went badly and she had to get away. Paid me a right tidy sum too," he added, as though that would clarify everything. "I didn't even know you was that poxy detective till you came in just now and Mr. Rawley spotted ya. Tol' me right off who ya was and that I should stay here while he took care a things." He scowled as he flicked his eyes between me and Colin. "I'd say he's done a shite job a that."

"And just who is it exactly that you think I am?" I continued to object with possibly more vitriol than was necessary.

The poor man's eyebrows collided as he stared at me as if I had lost my mind. "Colin Pendergan."

"Pen*dragon*," I corrected with satisfaction. "And that would be him." I hooked a thumb at Colin.

"Well, then . . . who the hell are you?"

"Ethan Pruitt. I am Mr. Pendragon's associate."

The unmolested side of the man's mouth curled down as he glared at me. "I mighta guessed he'd have some nob throw his weight around for him. But I ain't done nothin' wrong but help a lady out wot paid me ta do it. That's all I know and that's jest business."

"And for that you can hardly be faulted." Colin took a breath and I could feel his demeanor soften. "I hope you will forgive my man here. The issue is that our business with this woman goes all the way up to the very highest reaches of Scotland Yard. We believe she may be embroiled in as many as seven murders, including that of her own young son, so as I am sure you can understand, it is of the utmost importance that we find this woman. That is why my partner could not restrain himself earlier and it is the reason we are here now. You, my good man, may very well hold the key to this most gruesome case."

The parts of the man's face that were not already marred by bruising noticeably paled, leaving me struck by Colin's sudden eloquence. "I didn't know any a that," he explained. "She were jest a woman I picked up wot said she were scared a some man and would I help her? She weren't but a slip of a thing. Lovely. The kinda face ya ain't likely ta forget. I felt sorry for her."

"As you were meant to," Colin assured him, sliding his eyes to me with a look that was intended to remind me how she had done the very same thing to me. "Where did she flag you down?"

"Off Park and Seymour. Right at Portman Square. She were out at the curb standin' in the rain and she caught me eye. I said she were lovely. So I picked her up."

"And where did she wish to go?"

"Some flat in Kensington."

"Kensington . . . ?!" I parroted, knowing that it was going to turn out to be our flat.

"Yeah. A building on Gloucester Road. Across from the skinniest damn park I ever seen. A good dog could piss from one side ta the other." He chuckled. "The place weren't nothin' special."

"And what did you do while you were there?" Colin asked, not deeming to notify this man that it was indeed our home he was talking about.

"We sat there for hours and waited, watchin' the comin's and goin's like we had all day." He shrugged. "Didn't matter ta me 'cause she was payin' fer me time same as if I were drivin' her around."

"And what did you see?"

"First, a great black carriage drove up and some old squire got out and went inside. Had ta be somebody high-flyin' 'cause he had a crest on the side a his carriage like I ain't never seen before with a lion and a griffin on it. Like he were royalty or somethin'."

"He only thinks he is," Colin muttered under his breath. "Then what did you see?"

"After a while the old guy came back out with some other bloke on his heels. I didn't catch but a glimpse a him 'cause it were startin' ta rain, and he looked like he weren't happy 'bout somethin', stompin' his feet and slammin' the carriage door. Made me wanna laugh, but the lady, she didn't make a sound. The whole time she was jest sittin' there, I couldn't feel her movin' at all, like she was testin' herself or somethin'."

"And then . . ." Colin continued to prod.

The driver's eyes shifted to me and began to darken with his evident displeasure. "Then yer man here came out," he said, gesturing to me with his chin. "Course I didn't know it were him at first 'cause he were all hunched up under an umbrella. But that's when the lady came ta life. Ordered me ta follow him, which weren't easy in all that blasted rain, but I'm good at wot I do. Even after he got inta a cab I never lost him. Not even close." The man stopped and gave a self-satisfied smile, clearly believing he had finished with his story.

"And . . ." Colin said for the third time, and now I could tell his patience had become brittle.

"We followed him ta Whitechapel. All the way down ta Shandy Street." His eyes began to flick between me and Colin and I could see he knew he was being tested. "This one went in fer a bit and then came out all riled up. It were pourin' and he were a helluva sight. And then he went round back, and the lady had me pull the cab inta the mouth of the alleyway and we watched him climb up the fire escape and let himself in the back winda. I knew you weren't up ta no good. Sure as hell you weren't up ta no good."

Colin turned to me with a frown creasing his brow. "You *broke* into Mr. Nettle's flat? You didn't tell me that."

"I was going to get to that part, but I hardly think now is the proper time."

The driver gave a halfhearted laugh and I could see he was well pleased at this change in attitude. Nevertheless, I refused to let it bother me, given the damage I had already caused him.

"He weren't all that long. Came back out the rear too, which was a good thing 'cause the lady was startin' ta fret that we might lose him, and I weren't interested in runnin' from front ta back in that bloody storm no matter wot she was payin' me. But he came out soon enough, and as soon as he turned onta Shandy again she had me pull over and pick him up. Right before we did was when she told me how she feared for her safety. That's when she asked me ta hold him in the carriage at the end a their meetin' so she could get away if she had to. And after wot I'd just seen him do, breakin' into that old buggered building, I could see why she was worried."

Colin heaved a wearied breath as he watched the man carefully. "Do you know where the lady was staying or where she was headed?"

He shook his head and winced, stopping the motion in an instant as he unwittingly retriggered my guilt. "Nah. She paid me before we picked him up." He cocked a thumb toward me. "And when she run off . . ." He shrugged, and I knew there was nothing else to be said.

"You didn't see where she went?"

"Down the street. Ducked inta the first alley on the right and then . . ." His eyes landed on me again. "This one came out swingin' and I couldn't tell ya nothin' more."

"There aren't a lot of cabs that work down there," Colin said. "If you brought her all the way from Marylebone and Oxford, somebody had to have taken her back. It would have been too far to walk in that rain."

"I s'pose."

"Will you speak with the other drivers?" Colin asked in such a way that it sounded less a request than an order. "It's a very specific area and it only happened late this morning. And if the lady you described is as memorable as you say she is . . ."

"Well . . ."

"There would be a reward for proper information that assists us in finding her."

"A reward?"

"We shall ask your Mr. Rawley downstairs to do the same thing," Colin announced as he turned and headed for the door.

"All right then, but I'll ask ya ta keep that one away from me." He leered back at me.

Colin glanced around and gave the man a curious sort of stare, managing to look both deadly serious and yet somehow quietly amused. "Then you had best set yourself to accomplishing the task at hand with all due haste. I will certainly do my best to contain Mr. Pruitt, but I believe you are already well familiar with his temper." He turned back and flung the door wide with noticeable bravado. "Why don't you stop by the *nothin' special* flat tonight that you spent so much time in front of this morning and bring us word of what you've managed to learn over the course of this afternoon. There is absolutely no time to be wasted."

"Tonight?!" He looked startled at the very idea, as Colin had meant him to be. "Wait, why do I have ta go ta that place again?"

"Because that . . ." Colin called back as he started down the stairs, ". . . would happen to be our home."

CHAPTER 18

———◦———

Janelle Godwin lived in a small but scrupulously clean flat out in the Haggerston area on the east side of the city. As before, our driver had waited for us while we'd been at the carriage depot and had uttered nary a complaint when we had bade him take us by Freddie Nettle's boardinghouse on the way to Miss Godwin's. We had stopped just long enough for me to give the shrewd lad there a half crown to find Mr. Nettle and tell him that we wished to call upon him within a couple hours' time. The boy had been only too happy to help, and was ever more heartened to learn there would be another half crown for him if Mr. Nettle was indeed available upon our return. I had every faith that he would succeed.

Mr. Nettle's Whitechapel neighborhood proved a brief detour on our way to see Janelle Godwin. She immediately invited us in even though we had arrived unannounced and in the hours too late for tea but too early for supper. Nevertheless, she insisted on setting a kettle to boil despite our protestations, and by the time she brought the tea atop a well-used pewter tray, had even managed to hunt up a small plate of butter biscuits.

"I must admit I didn't imagine I would ever see the two of

you again," she said, a quick flush coloring her pale, round cheeks as she added, "I don't mean any offense. I simply meant . . ."

"No explanation needed," Colin responded, waving her off with a warm smile. "Most people who meet us during the course of an investigation assume, if not desire, never to cross paths with us again. You can hardly be faulted for feeling the same. Which is why I must thank you for your kindness and hospitality in meeting with us now."

"Think nothing of it." She smiled as she poured tea for both of us and held it across. "If there is anything I can do for you gentlemen, you have only to ask. After all, the two of you are to thank for what justice was brought to young Willy Hutton. Such a poor little lad. All drawn into himself like he was locked inside his own head. He was a special soul." She eased back in her chair, and it was easy to see that she still grieved for the unfortunate boy she had attended when his own mother had been unwilling to do so.

"You are being too generous," Colin replied grimly, "given that we failed in the completion of our duty. I am sure you are aware that Charlotte Hutton has yet to be brought to justice for her part in that ghastly case."

"Oh . . . !" Miss Godwin shook her head and set her tea aside. "I read in the paper that Mrs. Hutton had gone missing on the Continent, and I feared that perhaps she and Anna had come to some harm as well. Now I see that you mean to infer something quite different."

"Indeed." Colin flashed a slight grin. "You must forgive the boldness of my statement, but it does not seem to me that you are particularly stunned by my insinuation. Might I be correct in presuming that perhaps you may have harbored some concerns with respect to Mrs. Hutton's involvement in the deaths of her husband and son?"

"Oh . . ." she said again, though this time it was less with surprise than discomfort. "A mother could never be blamed for the death of her own child," she stated resolutely. "However, the bonds that hold a marriage together can be tenuous at times."

"I see." He nodded as though she had honestly enlightened him in some fashion. "And what of the Huttons? What did you observe of them?"

"That would hardly be for me to say. I was brought into their home strictly to look after their son. My association with Mr. and Mrs. Hutton went no further than the aid I tried to bring to little William."

"Yet you were in their home nevertheless," he pressed, and as with every other conversation we had endured this day, I could tell his patience was already beginning to ebb.

"I only ever spoke with Mr. Hutton in the context of his son," she explained.

"Then he was much involved in his son's care?"

She shook her head, but there was neither censure nor condemnation in her expression. "The rearing of children is hardly the domain of gentlemen. I'm sure I needn't tell you that. Are either of you fathers?" A warm smile softened her face.

"We are not, but your point is well made," Colin allowed. "But if I may speak frankly, I must admit that I found Mr. Hutton to be rather churlish in his manner. Perhaps you knew him differently?"

"He did come to fatherhood somewhat later in life. He was a dozen or more years older than his wife, you see. Having young children can be tiresome at any age, but it is ever more so when one gets older." She chuckled. "But I cannot say anything untoward against Mr. Hutton. He treated Anna like any doting father would, and it cannot have been easy to have sired a son who would never be able to care for himself."

"Yes, of course." Colin nodded, and I understood that we had finally led her to the crux of what had brought us here. "That must have made things difficult between him and his wife at times . . . his disappointment with her for having borne him such a son."

Miss Godwin's face flickered with something taut and unsettled, and for a moment I thought she might choose not to comment, though it was evident that something simmered just beneath the surface of her inscrutability. After another minute, however, her eyes clamped onto Colin's as she answered, "Mr. Hutton was no different from any man with the responsibility of a family and an estate to run. But I'm afraid it was Mrs. Hutton who could make me cringe at times. There were occasions when she treated him with such cruelty. . . ." Miss Godwin shut her eyes and drew a slow breath. "He would leave without a word, and I thought it all so terrible."

"She provoked him?" Colin prompted.

"She bore her own burdens."

"And did you ever know him to lay a hand upon her?"

"Oh no. Never," she said at once, her repugnance at the mere suggestion clear on her face. "I would not believe it. He was a gentleman."

"Then you never saw marks upon Mrs. Hutton's person that her husband may have caused, even by accident?"

"Marks?" she repeated as though trying to fathom the very idea of it. "You make the Huttons sound as though they were street brawlers. Really, sir, I cannot profess to imagine where you have come to such a thought."

"Gossip," I put in before Colin could supply his own answer. "We hear many things from many quarters and are required to verify all of it lest we should ever proceed to an inaccurate conclusion."

"Ah . . . well . . ." She gave an acknowledged sigh that contained a fair amount of perception in it. "Was there ever a marriage that did not contain some modicum of hardship and conciliation? I have been witness to a great many of them and have yet to see one such example that did not comprise nearly as much discord as it did adoration. But I have never . . . *never* . . . been witness to the sorts of behaviors you suggest. I would not work for such people. I could not."

"It was not my intention to suggest that you would," Colin answered with such an excess of sincerity I thought surely she would recognize it for the pretense it was, ". . . which is why I will ask you to consider very carefully the next several questions I am compelled to impose upon you."

Miss Godwin's face went slack and her pale blue eyes darkened under the intensity of whatever she supposed Colin might be about to put to her. "Of course, Mr. Pendragon. I will answer whatever questions I can. It is the least I can do for Willy."

"Did you ever know Mr. Hutton to raise a hand against his children or household staff? Were you ever witness to any display of temperament that could have caused you to wonder what he might be capable of?"

She shook her head. "He was like any other man. Mostly, he had little to do with his children, though he sometimes would read aloud with Anna, but William . . ." She glanced down and rustled her hands uncomfortably. ". . . I think William made him endlessly sad. He never said so, but I could see it when he looked at the boy. I suppose it was inevitable."

"And the household staff?"

"I'm sure you must remember that they had very little staff. When I first started with them there was a girl who came to clean three times a week and two women who worked in the kitchen, but by the time of Mr. Hutton's death there was only me and one woman left in the kitchen. I tried to help out whenever I could if William was napping or indisposed." She released a sigh. "It was such a difficult time."

"And Mr. Hutton . . . ?" Colin prodded.

"I really don't believe I ever saw Mr. Hutton utter two words to the other women in the household. He had no reason to. They were Mrs. Hutton's concern, of course."

"Of course," Colin allowed with frustration. "And what about you? Certainly, you claim to have reported to Mr. Hutton about his son from time to time?"

She nodded. "I did. He was very much interested in how I thought his son was doing." Once again she looked down at her lap and fiddled with her fingers, and all I could see was the helplessness of a woman who had been unable to make much of a difference. "He was always very kind to me. I cannot say a harsh word about him. And my reports, I'm afraid, were never what he could take any solace in. Little William was never going to be right, and I know that burden weighed heavily on Mr. Hutton. One could hardly blame him if he had shown a bit of temperament at times. . . ." She let her voice trail off, and I felt both chilled and unaccountably sympathetic to her point.

"And Mrs. Hutton?"

"I've already told you—"

"You misunderstand," Colin cut her off. "You mentioned that Mrs. Hutton caused you some consternation?"

Miss Godwin shifted uncomfortably as she leaned forward and took one of the biscuits. "It is such an impossible thing to surmise what strains a woman must bear when she has brought a broken child into the world. It is almost as though he was a living testament to her failure, there for all to see . . . to judge."

"Then you seek to make concessions for Mrs. Hutton? Do you feel she needs them made?"

For the first time Miss Godwin looked truly ill at ease, bunching her napkin in her lap, though it did not seem she noticed she was doing so. "She was stern with all of us, but then it was her duty to be. She had a household to run and the circumstances were far more difficult than those which most of us will ever have to confront."

"You are speaking of something beyond her son's poor health, aren't you? Are you referring to her husband's financial missteps? You were aware of their dwindling prosperity?"

"It was a large home and yet there was so few staff to maintain it," she answered simply. "I have already told you that during the two years I worked with William I watched what staff they had contract to almost nothing." She reached forward and topped off our tea before pouring some more for herself. "But I would be dishonest if I did not admit to overhearing them argue about money on several occasions."

The ghost of a smile fleeted across Colin's lips. "Such conversations could be expected in almost any home," he said, and I knew he was baiting her. "What would make theirs any different?"

"Once in a while . . ." She took a sip of tea and glanced off toward the far side of the room, looking like she was either remembering something or measuring her words of that memory. "As I said before, Mrs. Hutton could be very harsh with her husband. I would hear things I did not mean to, did not *want* to, but

I heard them. He had apparently made investments of some kind, I really don't know, which had lost them a great deal of their money. I began to fear they would ask me to work for less pay, which I really could not afford to do, but they never did." She winced slightly. "Perhaps I should have suggested it myself."

"Did you ever know Mrs. Hutton to raise a hand against her husband?"

Miss Godwin paled. "She never did any such thing to anyone. She is a lady."

"And what if I told you that she now claims to have been the victim of abuse by her husband? Would that change your mind about him? Make you search your memory again?"

"Oh . . ." she said with a sort of sigh that made me wonder whether Colin's question had forced her to ruminate over something she did not want to consider. But after another moment she surprised me with her answer. "I am afraid I would have to question Mrs. Hutton's memory of such an event. Her husband was quiet and somber, I will not deny that, but I witnessed him with his children. He was kind and ever so patient with Willy. It seems unlikely to me that he would treat his wife any the less, though, as you yourself suggested, Mr. Pendragon, she could provoke him at times. But on those occasions, at least when I was there, he would simply leave."

"Yes, yes . . ." Colin muttered, and I knew his mind had to be whirling in a thousand discordant directions. What I could not imagine was whether any of it was going to help us find Charlotte Hutton. "And you say it was money that most embroiled them?"

"That was all I ever heard. She blamed him for their difficulties. Said some awful things. I never heard him yell back, but it was obvious that he was angry. It would upset Willy so. He didn't understand, of course. And what could I say? It was none of my business."

"Of course," Colin said as he stood up, his face grim. "I must thank you again for inviting us into your home unannounced and allowing us to prod you with such questions. Rest assured that you have been most helpful."

"Then I am pleased that you came by," she said rather wistfully as she walked us to the door. "If there is anything else I can do for you gentlemen, you have only to let me know." She paused at the open door and looked at Colin keenly. "I was always very fond of Anna. She is such a dear girl and had the most tremendous heart. She was extraordinary with her brother, flawlessly patient and kind. Have you heard anything of her?"

"We have not." Colin bit the words in a display of his own personal frustrations.

"You must find her," Miss Godwin murmured in a voice edged with despair. "You must make sure she is well and happy. It is the least that young girl deserves."

Colin gave a single nod of his head and I could see the weight of her request stirring within his eyes. "We will not consider this case settled until Anna Hutton is exactly as you wish to see her." Which was an assurance I could only pray we would be able to keep.

CHAPTER 19

⟫•⟪

When the crafty lad at Freddie Nettle's boardinghouse led us past the chaotic front room to the stairway beyond, I must confess that I was relieved to find the elderly landlady asleep. She was slumped over and snoring lightly in the very same chair she had been occupying earlier in the day, and I was fairly certain this was precisely where she would be found throughout the night. It would not have surprised me to spy a chamber pot tucked away somewhere beside or beneath her seat. The very thought sent me scurrying after Colin and the scruffy lad, keeping my eyes focused on the way the boy was flicking the half crown I had just handed to him. Such exuberance, I knew from my own youth, was likely to cost him his treasure if he was not careful.

"Yer bloke weren't 'ard ta find," he was telling us. "Ya got any more a these silver ladies ya wanna get rid of, ya jest let me know." He gave a wink and a snicker as we crested the landing of Mr. Nettle's floor, and I was reminded, just as I had been earlier in the day, that this lad was regrettably beyond his years.

"If you're asking for a job," Colin answered before I could do so, "we would be happy to assist you in finding one. There are many legitimate things a resourceful young rascal like you could do for a bob or two."

The boy gave a snort as though Colin had meant to be funny. "Yer a right pip," he tossed over his shoulder before taking his fist and slamming it against Mr. Nettle's door. And if I wasn't already certain how meager this lad was, the pitiful sound his meatless fist made on the door would have confirmed it. "Ya got yer blokes 'ere ta see you," he called out.

The door opened at once, but then how could it not, given that the entirety of his room was no more than a handful of strides in any direction? "Mr. Pendragon . . . Mr. Pruitt . . ." Mr. Nettle stepped back and bade us enter, and for the first time I thought he looked gray and tense. He mumbled something I did not catch to the boy before swinging the door partway shut. "I'm sorry you have had to come all this way," he continued. "I'd be lying if I said I wasn't worried about what has brought you here."

"Worried . . . ?" Colin repeated as though it were the most curious thing for Mr. Nettle to be feeling. "Why ever would you be worried?"

Mr. Nettle appeared to be at a momentary loss for words, but was saved when the room's door suddenly sprang open. "'Ere's yer chair," the boy announced as he dragged in a dilapidated straight-backed chair with sagging rattan on its seat.

"You've done me a great service," Freddie Nettle answered as he took the chair and quickly swept it inside.

"And . . ." The urchin held out his hand.

"Here," I said as I quickly flipped two farthings at him. "Your kindness was for us. I really must insist."

"Oh . . ." Mr. Nettle answered, and I could see he was both embarrassed and relieved.

"You'd best keep this little scamp in your good graces," Colin said, "as I suspect he will own this boardinghouse one day."

"Nah—I'll get me somethin' better 'n *this* place," the boy sniped before disappearing back out the door with a high-pitched guffaw.

Mr. Nettle tossed the pile of clothing from the chair near the window and pulled it next to the one the lad had brought in, offering the two of them to us. As we pretended to make ourselves comfortable, Freddie Nettle settled himself onto the edge of the bed, making it squeal like a trapped mouse as he did so. "You must forgive my meager surroundings," he said with a slight flush. "My earnings with the Endicotts were slim since they provided me with room and board. I was able to stash a little bit away, but . . ." He splayed out his empty hands with an embarrassed wince.

"There is no reason for you to feel the least bit shy about your home," Colin answered smoothly. "You are a hardworking man who is doing his best in turbulent times. In my mind, that is the very definition of success."

"You are very kind, Mr. Pendragon."

"Well, that is hardly my intention," he said right back, and I found myself having to suppress a chuckle. "As to our reason for being here, I should very much like to see your best shoes."

"My . . ." Freddie Nettle stared at Colin, certain that he had not heard him properly.

"Best shoes," he said again. "The ones you wore when you were working at the Endicotts. I would assume they are here somewhere. . . ." Colin added, looking about the tiny space with a preposterous innocence, since I'd already told him they were under the bed.

"Why . . . yes . . ." he said with every bit of the confusion one would expect. "I keep them under here." He leaned forward and stuck a hand beneath the coverlet that hung to the floor, and for an instant it occurred to me that maybe, just maybe, he could be as likely to fish out a revolver as a pair of shoes. "Here you are, then," he said tentatively, holding them out and leaving me to wonder why I had suddenly doubted him.

"Ah, very good," Colin said with the flicker of a smile as he reached forward and plucked them from Mr. Nettle's hands. They were the shiny pair I had inspected earlier, well kempt with the one exception Colin's eyes fell to immediately. He brought the right shoe to his nose and took a quick sniff of the smudge I had mentioned to him on the outer sole. "Sulfur . . ." he murmured before returning his gaze to Mr. Nettle. "It would seem you have not been honest with us."

A startled look dashed over his face as a battle between mortification and guilt appeared to be vying for the prominent position. "I . . ." he began to say before abruptly clamping his mouth shut. It was evident that he was weighing some level of truthfulness, and I knew the next words out of his mouth would be critical in determining just how deeply mired he really was in Adelaide Endicott's murder. In the next moment he released a burdened sigh and collapsed in upon himself like a deflating balloon.

"Come now, Mr. Nettle," Colin said casually, though there was not a trace of ease in his voice. "Is it all that bad, then?"

"I am afraid you will think me unsound," he answered in the gravest of tones. "And perhaps I am." He swiped a hand across his forehead as he diverted his gaze to the floor in front of his feet. "I have told no one the full extent of what I saw the night of Miss Adelaide's death, and yet the other facts of what I have detailed are all true."

"Then perhaps you had best start from when you awoke that night."

"It was as I said." He spoke breathlessly, the words beginning to tumble from him with impending speed. "I awoke to the sound of Miss Adelaide crying out. There was a bang, like something heavy falling over, and then she cried out again. I did not even have time to think what might be happening before I leapt up and swung open the door between our rooms." His eyes rose, clamped on something in the distance that we could not see, as he continued. "She was standing near the window, just as I have stated to anyone who will listen, but hanging in the air in front of her was a spectral glow of deep, translucent colors, like I would imagine the northern lights must appear. And even as I struggled to understand what I was seeing, I heard a child's voice."

"A child's voice?" Colin repeated.

"You must think me mad."

"You will know if I think you mad. What did the child say?"

"I couldn't tell. She was crying and sounded so pitiful, and I thought I must be losing my mind because she sounded like she was right next to me, but there was no one there. It was only me and Miss Adelaide. And as that luminescent light began to fade, I saw that Miss Adelaide was crying. She was tormented. And even though she was looking right at me, I don't believe she even really saw me because in the next instant she grabbed for the window with such an agonized cry and was . . . gone. . . ." His face had gone pallid, his lips as white as the collar of his shirt, and there was no hiding the shame and misery brimming from within his eyes. "You may say whatever you will, as I fear for my own sanity now."

"Which is why you hide in this squalid place," Colin scolded, "rather than confide in the two people who have been trying to help you from the start. Really, Mr. Nettle, your choices since that night have been most wretched."

"But how could I tell such a fantastical tale to anyone without being vilified? I would have been thought of as daft. Scotland Yard would have seized me for guilty at once."

"The Yard . . ." Colin dismissed it with a wave of his hand. "I'm talking about Mr. Pruitt and myself. We could have assuaged your mind at once and gotten a good deal farther along with this investigation by now if you had only told us the truth."

"Assuaged my mind?"

"Now instead we have wasted valuable time pissing about to learn the very things you could have told us at the start. I must say I am very disappointed."

"And for that I do apologize," he said quickly. "But how could you have assuaged my mind?"

"Phosphorous powder, Mr. Nettle," Colin snapped back with nary a hint of patience. "It is used in theatrics and by those for whom such trickery can prove persuasive. I think it fair to call them charlatans. And here is a small mark of it on your shoe. What that tells me, Mr. Nettle, is that either you were close enough to Miss Adelaide at the point of her death to have gotten your shoe scorched by the burning powder, or you have some other use for it, which I have as yet to figure out. Now which is it?"

Freddie Nettle's despair was so dense I would have sworn I could feel it bristling against my skin. "I was next to Miss Adelaide when she fell," he admitted in a voice almost without sound, "but I did not push her. It was an accident. I was only trying to help her."

"From the beginning, Mr. Nettle," Colin prodded peevishly. "And I will caution you not to leave anything out lest you drive Mr. Pruitt and me from your room without a backward glance. I can assure you I am quite finished having you deceive me."

"Mr. Pendragon . . ." He shook his head pitifully, taking pains not to meet Colin's gaze. "I meant no such disrespect. I was terrified. Can you not understand that?" His eyes drifted up, and I could see fear and shame there, although Colin chose not to answer him. "I heard a scream and raced into Miss Adelaide's room, as I have said. She was already over by the window, staring out into the darkness. If she could see something, I do not know what it was. I started toward her, but before I could reach her there was a sudden flash of intense light, blues and greens that simply exploded into the room and hung there like an unworldly spirit had somehow found its way inside. And then I heard the little girl.

"She was crying for help and calling Miss Adelaide's name. It was as though she was standing right next to me, only . . . there was no one there." He rubbed his forehead again, finally clenching his fists to his eyes. "I thought I must be losing my mind. I don't believe in such things. I have *never* believed in such things. And yet . . ." His voice trailed off and still he did not look at us.

"And then what happened, Mr. Nettle?" Colin pressed after what felt like a full minute had passed.

He dropped his hands and stared at the floor, a hollow of a man. "I was terrified. I will not lie. I was terrified and I feared for my life. And I feared for Miss Adelaide. I did. There was a smell in the air, a pungent, burnt smell, and that child's doleful voice calling to Miss Adelaide through a flood of sobs, and the eerie light that seemed to be hanging everywhere around me, swamping me. . . ." He tugged in a ragged breath. "It felt like the gates of Hell had burst open and we were standing at the very heart of it."

"And then . . . ?" Colin said for the last time.

"I tried to reach out and grab Miss Adelaide. All I could think to do was get her out of that room—get us both out of there. But she pulled away from me. I don't know if she meant to, or if she even realized that it was me reaching for her, but she pulled away so savagely . . . so suddenly . . . that she stumbled backward and . . ." He held his hands out in front of himself, palms up as though wondering how they had failed to catch his mistress, and I could see that his eyes were wearied and ringed with red. "And then she fell. It was like she disappeared right into that cursed luminescent fog. Only she hadn't. She had fallen from that window even as I stood there like a bloody helpless fool."

CHAPTER 20

Neither one of us spoke on the ride back to our flat. There seemed nothing to say in the wake of everything Freddie Nettle had confided. I did not know what Colin had expected Mr. Nettle to confess, but I suspected nothing of what we had heard. That his story had always felt incomplete was undeniable, that he would have such a tale of spectral lights, disembodied cries, and watching poor Adelaide Endicott stumble out the window, without lifting a hand, was both damning and disturbing. For if he was spinning an account with the intent of proving his innocence, he was failing unquestionably.

I had thought Colin and I might discuss what we had heard, but he fell silent the moment we climbed into our waiting cab, turning his gaze to some far horizon, his lips pulling taut, and I knew it was best to leave him be. And so we remained until we arrived back at our flat to find another cab pulled to the curb by our porch. "Are we expecting someone?" I asked as our driver brought us to a smooth stop.

"We most certainly are," Colin answered quickly, his eyes instantly taking in the waiting carriage and flashing with a sudden, keen interest. Without another word he hopped out before we had drawn to a complete stop and bounded for the steps with profound determination. What, I could not help but wonder, was I forgetting?

I made quick work of paying our driver and hurried in to the sound of several men's voices drifting down from above. Mrs. Behmoth was nowhere to be seen, though I could smell roasting chicken and potatoes. My stomach growled as I slung my coat onto the hall tree, reminding me that it had been too long since I had eaten last.

"Ethan!" I looked up to find Colin leaning over the landing staring down at me. "It's the gentleman from the taxi depot that you manhandled. He has found the man who picked up Charlotte Hutton after your altercation this morning. Do hurry up."

I bolted up the stairs at once, cursing myself for forgetting such a thing. As I reached the landing and went through to the parlor it was to find two men standing just inside, one I recognized—the left side of his jaw looking swollen and mottled in deep reds and purples, a frayed top hat clutched in his fingers—the other man I did not. The second man stood nearly as tall as me, though he had the skinny body of a boy and the face to match. He too held a well-used top hat in his hands, and I thought I noticed him flinch when my eyes fell upon him.

"Please," Colin said, clearly not for the first time. "Do come and sit down. There is no need for such formality, gentlemen."

"We'd just as soon stand, thank you," the man I had regrettably slugged answered, his voice coming out thick and slightly garbled, and I feared that his tongue must be swollen as well.

"Please," it was my turn to say, taking pains to keep the sounds of guilt from my voice. "Let me get you both a brandy to warm yourselves."

The two men glanced at each other before the poor battered man gave a stiff nod of his head, probably all he could manage without causing a shock of pain. "We just come like ya asked," he said rather morosely. "This is the bloke what picked up yer lady near Limehouse this mornin' after she ran off."

"That is outstanding news." Colin grinned as he moved over to the fireplace and threw on a few pieces of wood, quickly poking it back to roaring life. "You remembered her, did you?" he asked, and I knew he was testing the man even though he appeared to be fully engaged with the fire.

"Yes, sir."

Colin stood up and turned toward the three of us as I handed them their brandy, and carefully slid the poker back into its stand. "And what did you remember about her?"

The taller man blinked once . . . twice . . . staring back at Colin as though he must be either daft or ribbing him. "She were a right beauty. There are plenty a lovelies, but she were one a them ya don't forget."

"Describe her to me."

"She had long black hair. . . ."

"Black?!"

"She has dyed her hair black," I interrupted, realizing I had never shared this crucial detail with Colin. "Clearly, she has done so to be less conspicuous."

"She had the bluest eyes I ever seen," the taller driver spoke up again. "'At's one a the things I couldn't forget. Hair as dark as night but eyes blue as the ocean. Ya don't see that. People with black hair got dark eyes, but not her. She were small and pale and delicate like one a them tiny birds, and she had them blue eyes. Ya don't forget a woman like that."

"Lucky for us." Colin flashed a razor-thin smile as he stalked over to where the three of us had remained standing just inside the room, his sudden enthusiasm bristling with every step. "And where did you take this most memorable woman? Where did you drop her off?"

"A boardinghouse just outside Regent's Park. I can take ya there if ya want. I remember it."

Colin's smile broadened. "Then we are indeed most fortunate for you and your memory. I presume now is a good time?"

"Now?" It was evident as the man flicked his eyes to his injured friend that he had not considered making the run tonight.

"We will pay you for the journey, of course," Colin added smoothly, which appeared to assuage the man's hesitation in an instant.

"Very well, then." He popped his frayed top hat onto his head. "If yer ready?"

"Ya don't need me. . . ." the first man said, less a question than a statement. "We're good, right? I'll be goin' home, then."

"I do hope you will forgive me," I felt compelled to say to him once more, the state of his jaw a reminder that my own right hand still ached. "I am mortified—"

"You have made it right," Colin interrupted, stepping in between me and the two drivers, herding them back to the staircase even as he reached out and snagged his suit coat off the hall rack. "But you really should watch yourself in the future," he could not resist adding. "Be careful who you make arrangements to assist, as I presume you do not wish to be perceived as an enemy of Scotland Yard."

The man paled, at least the part of his face not blotched by bruising did. "Oh no, sir. I would never want such a thing. I'm a God-fearing, law-abiding man," he explained even as the three of them trundled down the stairs with me in their wake. "I learned me lesson. Some things ain't worth an extra shilling."

"You are correct," I heard Colin reassure him. "You should never sell your soul for less than a crown."

The three of them laughed as they burst out into the night ahead of me, and I only hoped Colin's great good will was well founded. It seemed impossible to believe that we would arrive at some boardinghouse not two miles from where we lived to catch Charlotte Hutton unawares. I was desperate to believe it could be the case, yet did not allow myself to think it might truly prove so simple. Which gave me a start as I climbed into the cab. "Did you bring a gun?" I asked Colin as we got under way.

"A gun? Whatever for?"

"We don't know what we will find," I answered, trying to sound indifferent. "But a cornered animal is the most ferocious."

Colin chuckled. "And that is why I will have you and your merciless right hook at my side."

"You are not amusing." I scowled. "Don't you think we should at least fetch Maurice Evans?"

"If we get him then we will necessarily be involving the entire

Yard. It would be callous to expect him to help us without alerting his force. I'm certain it has to be against some regulation or another. They're like an ant colony: If you summon one you get the whole bloody swarm. Now settle yourself." He reached over and patted my knee and once again I hoped his mood was justified.

We turned another corner and I felt the cab begin to slow, reminding me just how absurdly close she was apparently staying to our flat. "Here it is, then," the driver called down from the seat above us as we glided to a halt.

"Splendid," Colin answered at once, swinging out of the cab. "And which building did she enter?"

I climbed out just in time to see the driver toss off a slight shrug. "I dunno. I don't stay around ta watch people enter buildings. I ain't paid ta do that."

"Then what address did she give you?" Colin asked, making no attempt to hide his annoyance.

"'At one." He gestured with his chin toward a Gothic-looking brick-and-white-stone building several doors down, complete with turrets poking up from the topmost floor at either end of the structure and a half dozen gargoyles looming over the street from above the roofline.

"Fitting," Colin mumbled as I paid the driver.

"Well, good luck to ya," the man said as I stepped back from his carriage. "She's a right pretty woman ta have business with." He snickered as he shook the reins, causing his horse to lurch forward. "Ya let me know if ya need any help." He outright laughed as he clattered off.

"Ass," Colin grumbled as he started for the building, his stride as filled with determination as it was with eagerness.

I followed him without saying anything, though I wondered how he intended to find out which flat was hers. From the look of the building I guessed there were greater than forty apartments within. That the name Charlotte Hutton would be plastered on one of the doors was ludicrous, likewise the name she had used to flee England, Mary Ellen Witten. She already knew we had traced that name to the accounts she'd opened in Zurich, that was yet another of my blunders on this case, which meant she would never be reckless enough to use it again.

We pushed our way into the lobby, and I was almost surprised to find a doorman in attendance. Yet, upon careful consideration, why would I have expected anything less of Mrs. Hutton? Did I truly imagine she might come to London and take up residence in a hovel? Wasn't it enough that she had taken a flat in a public building?

"Good evening," Colin was already calling out to the doorman, a tall, slender man of late middle years resplendent in a long dove-gray topcoat. There was a black top hat sitting on a counter behind which he was sorting through a stack of notices and papers.

He glanced over, his face well lined and tired, and a look of surprise abruptly stole across his visage. "Aren't you Colin Pendragon . . . ?" he asked almost reverentially, as though the very question were almost too astonishing to verbalize.

"Indeed," Colin answered with the flash of a smile, his pleasure at being thusly recognized forever a source of pride. "And this is my associate, Ethan Pruitt."

"Good evening," I said with a tip of my hat.

"Gentlemen," he replied with a nod, one hand flying up to his head before remembering that his hat was already on the counter between us. He gave a self-conscious chuckle. "Whatever might you be doing here?"

"We are looking for someone. A woman we believe may live here. Probably arrived within the past few weeks. She almost certainly lives by herself, although it is possible that she has a young daughter with her. She is quite lovely to look at, the kind a man will notice. Black hair, pale features, eyes an unusually brilliant blue. No more than her middle thirties, though you could not be faulted for thinking she could pass for younger."

"She has a black cloak with a hood that she's fond of wearing," I added. "It hangs almost to the ground and she often pulls the hood up to completely cover her face." I kept expecting the man to nod or grace us with a knowing smile, but instead found myself confronted by a burgeoning frown.

"We have no such lady here," he said after another moment's thought. "There's not been a vacant flat in quite some time and certainly no one of that description who has come to stay recently. From the sounds of her, I should think I would have noticed."

Colin heaved a sigh and I knew he was as disappointed as me if hardly surprised. "You're quite certain? Is it not possible she could have gotten past you?"

He shook his head slowly and I thought he looked almost regretful. "I know everyone who lives here. I've not missed a day of work since our youngest was born the winter before last. Can't afford to." He shrugged his shoulders and gave an uneasy smile.

"I see." Colin flicked a thin smile, his eyes narrowing ever so slightly. "I wonder, might I impose upon you to show me a roster of the building's occupants? I'm certain a conscientious man such as yourself would maintain such a thing . . . ?"

"Oh . . ." The man's smile widened. "I'm not supposed to share it with anyone, but then you're not just anyone, are you, Mr. Pendragon?" His eyes shifted from Colin to me. "I mean either of you," he added with a noticeable cringe. "Let me just get that for you." He sidled over to a short cabinet behind his counter with two locked drawers, pulling a key from a clipped ring hanging at his waist. With a quick turn he sprang the lock and reached in to extract a leather-bound ledger from the top drawer. "Here you go, then," he said, flipping it open and turning it to face us.

Colin stepped forward first and ran a swift finger down the list of names. "Miss Eldemeier and Mrs. Schriffen?" he read.

"Sisters living in flat 304," the man answered. "Lovely ladies but neither could be considered a beauty."

"Mrs. Newcastle?"

"A widow in 210. She's lived here for years."

"And Miss Holloway?"

"Aged and not well, I'm afraid."

"When was the last time you saw her?" Colin pressed, and I knew he was trying to consider every possibility.

"Just this morning. There are a few of us who take turns going to the market for her. Saturday is my day."

"Blast it. . . ." Colin blurted as he stalked back toward the front door. "Of course she would not be here. . . ." he grumbled as he continued right on outside.

"She's important to us," I said rather feebly, hoping that would be enough to keep from fully piquing this man's curiosity. "She could be the key to a situation she has no idea about."

"Well, I do spend a good deal of my day out in front of the building. Should I spy anyone who fits the description you've given me, I will be sure to send word round. It would be an honor to know that I've helped the great Mr. Pendragon. And you too, Mr. Per . . ." His voice drifted off as he failed to place my name, finally settling for a weak shrug and awkward smile.

"Then we can ask for no more," I answered with false gusto as I headed for the door. I went outside and found Colin standing at the curb with one arm out, the wind having kicked up again and a light patter of raindrops just beginning to fall.

"What kept you?" he asked as a cab drew up in front of him.

"I asked the man to keep an eye out for her."

Colin waved me off. "We don't need him. We'll get the young lad who was so helpful to us during the Connicle case."

"You mean the boy Paul? That little hooligan who kept an eye on the Guitnus' house when you were trying to figure out who was pilfering their jewels?"

"Hooligan?!" He turned on me with rounded eyes and a well-placed smirk. "Is that anything to call an enterprising youngster? He was quite resourceful, as I remember it. Helped lead us directly to the culprit." He shook his head but his eyes never left mine. "I rather think he reminds you of yourself when you were his age."

I felt my lips curl with displeasure. "I may have been many things back then, but I was hardly a hooligan. The only person I was hurting was myself."

Colin glanced out at the street. "Whatever the case, I think we need him and I trust him. So we will get Paul and some of his mates to start hunting for Mrs. Hutton. After all, it would have been too easy if she'd had a cab drop her right in front of the very building where she was staying. I'm afraid she's far too clever for that. But I would wager a bet that she is not staying far from here. In fact, I will even go so far as to say that wherever she is, she almost certainly has an unimpeded view to the front of this blasted, ruddy building, just so she can keep an eye out for us."

"Do you think so?!"

"Saint Paul's Cathedral . . ." Colin hollered up to the driver as soon as we'd settled in.

"You mean to find Paul tonight?"

"If I'm right about Charlotte Hutton then we have no time to waste. She will not loiter around while we stumble about trying to find her. Besides, that boy has nothing better to do with his time. We'll be paying him for good, legitimate work."

"It seems like it's going to be one helluva rainy night. . . ."

Colin looked back outside before releasing a sigh thick with his annoyance. "Fine. Then we can arrange to have him meet us in the morning, but we *must* get word to him tonight. We need him, Ethan. He'll be glad for the money and work just as he was when we had him watching the Guitnus' house. We simply haven't the time to do this ourselves, and I'll not get the Yard involved until I'm bloody well ready. They'll only bollocks everything up if we do."

I shook my head and pursed my lips, cursing myself for having let Charlotte Hutton get away the second time. "All right . . ."

"Then let us hope we can find him as readily as we did the last time we needed his assistance."

CHAPTER 21

Mrs. Denholm was being perfectly gracious about allowing me access to her files, and yet it was quickly becoming clear to me that her graciousness came with an ulterior motive.

"It is a wonder," she was saying, "that Mr. Pendragon has never married."

"Hmm," I bothered to say as I finished flipping through Freddie Nettle's file, the seventh such file I had already slogged through.

There was nothing of interest to be found there. It mimicked the story Mrs. Denholm had already told us—and why wouldn't it? From spotting him hawking newspapers to setting him up working with a gardener in Marylebone until the day she had decided to try him at the Endicott residence, it was all detailed with dates and crowing notes. The handwriting was clearly all done by the same feminine hand, swirling and light and leaning ever so elegantly to the right.

"Mr. Pruitt . . . ?" she said as though she had been repeating my name, and I very much suspected she had.

"Yes?" I looked up as I pulled Vivian Whit's file toward me, all the while wondering why Mrs. Denholm could not simply leave me be.

"I was telling you about my niece. . . ." she said, as though I should already know that.

"Of course," I muttered with what I hoped would be construed as an interested smile. "She sounds like a lovely young woman," I quickly added, hoping this to be the appropriate response.

"And so she is." Mrs. Denholm returned a generous grin, and I refrained from heaving a sigh of relief. "Which is why I thought she might make a most winning companion for Mr. Pendragon. You simply must help me arrange a meeting for them."

"Oh . . ." I was already jotting down fruitless notes regarding Vivian Whit's upbringing in Highbury ward, Islington, where she still lived with her family. I'd already captured her tenure at the Royal London Hospital and her failure to make it into the new nursing program at Tredegar House when Mrs. Denholm made her plea. "You must understand that Mr. Pendragon is quite slavish to his work," I said, just as I had done on previous occasions when this topic came up. "And he is known to be rather fond of his own opinions," I added, giving a chuckle as though the two of us were sharing a secret, but she did not join me. Even so, I acted as though the subject were closed, quickly making a note of how Miss Whit had met the Endicotts' coachman, Devlin Fischer, during her time at Royal London Hospital after he'd gotten pinned by a cantankerous mare, nearly crushing his chest beneath her pounding hooves. It turned out to be a fortuitous event in that it ultimately led to her meeting Mrs. Denholm and gaining employment with the Endicotts. I glanced back up at Mrs. Denholm as I pulled Philippa Bromley's file toward me, desperate to be done with this chore and out of here. "There really are terribly good reasons why some men never marry," I pointed out, hoping to close the conversation.

"You are talking nonsense, Mr. Pruitt," she shot back. "There isn't a man alive who wouldn't be better for it to have a wife take care of him and, quite frankly, see that he tows the proper line. Now your good Mr. Pendragon may well be a man of stout determinations, but that is only because he is yet to have the good fortune to meet the woman who can set him to rights. That, Mr. Pruitt, is precisely where my darling niece Hattie excels."

Mrs. Denholm's lips continued to move, and I nodded infrequently even as I continued to eye Philippa Bromley's file, learning little more than that she rented a room at a single women's boardinghouse in the Canonbury ward of Islington, and that she and Vivian Whit had become friends during their commute to Royal London Hospital where both had decided to try their hand at nursing. Apparently, they had shared visions of tending the city's downtrodden, which Mrs. Denholm had noted with some apparent amusement along the margin of her document. Nevertheless, it had undoubtedly been a great disappointment when both of the young women had been turned down for the Tredegar House program, though almost assuredly the position with Adelaide Endicott would have softened that blow.

"Mr. Pruitt!" Mrs. Denholm stated with such force that I knew I had been caught ignoring her again.

"Mrs. Denholm . . ." I said with equal force as I pushed the useless file away and popped to my feet, glaring down at my watch. "I fear I have overstayed my welcome and that I am late for another appointment. You have been most kind to me and I will certainly make mention of that to Mr. Pendragon," I hastened to add. "And if we should have further need of your files, I shall not allow Mr. Pendragon to miss the opportunity to return with me," I put in rather carelessly.

"Oh, would you?!" she answered at once, eagerness filling her gaze. "You must make it an absolute point to return then. I will have my Hattie here, and before you know it she'll have your Mr. Pendragon charmed and far more agreeable than you will ever have believed him to be."

"How could I refuse such an entreaty?" I tucked my notes and pen into the pocket of my coat as I pulled it from her hall tree and made a hasty retreat, avoiding setting any future date in spite of her obvious desire to do so. If we did have to return, it was going to be a most uncomfortable occasion.

I flagged down a cab and had him deliver me to the corner of

Regent's Park Road and Fitzroy, just down from Primrose Hill and a couple of blocks north of where the cab driver had taken us the evening before. Colin was to meet me here after he checked in with our young accomplice Paul, so I was not at all surprised to find the corner empty when I stepped out of the carriage. I had little recourse but to wait with feigned patience, and was ultimately startled when I finally caught sight of Colin heading in my direction with Maurice Evans at his side.

"Good day, Mr. Pruitt," he called out to me.

"And to you, Mr. Evans. What a pleasant surprise."

He laughed as the two of them drew up to me. "You are ever the diplomat, Mr. Pruitt."

"When I stopped by the Yard to beg for a photograph of Mrs. Hutton"—to my relief, Colin spoke up—"Mr. Evans refused to believe that it was simply for you to do a spot of research."

That, I thought, was the best story Colin could come up with? There was no wonder Mr. Evans had decided to tag along. "It isn't that I've forgotten her face," I tried to explain convincingly, "but it can be tricky when you're looking through old newspapers and such."

A slight furrow creased Mr. Evans's brow. "And why ever would you be going through old newspapers in search of that woman? She is missing *now*, not fifteen years ago."

"A woman with a young daughter does not just disappear onto the Continent without some forethought," I said, giving the only excuse I could spontaneously muster. "So I will be looking to see if there might not be some particular city, or town, or person that she might have some relation to. Anything that could give us a clue, however small, as to where she might have fled."

"There, you see . . . ?" Colin said rather more smugly than I thought the moment deserved, ". . . I told you we would let you know as soon as we have any information worth the Yard's time and efforts."

"And that is precisely what concerns me, Mr. Pendragon. Your disregard for Scotland Yard is exceedingly well known. How you used to infuriate poor Inspector Varcoe. Which means

I cannot even begin to imagine whatever might move you to decide to include us should you gain a footing on Mrs. Hutton's whereabouts."

Colin appeared to consider his words before giving a small shake of his head. "You do have a point."

"Colin . . ."

Colin waved me off. "You have always treated us with respect and fairness, Mr. Evans. That is something of a rarity coming from your quarters. So I shall never do you the disservice of putting you in a position that could compel you to act outside of the boundaries you swore to uphold and serve."

The poor man's brow furrowed. "I'm really not certain whether I should thank you or curse you."

Colin flashed a tight grin. "Most people choose the latter." He stabbed a grainy tintype of Charlotte and Arthur Hutton into my hands—the two of them looking equally ill at ease as their unsmiling portraits were captured for posterity. It was a good likeness of Mrs. Hutton even though her hair looked white as opposed to the black she was currently wearing. Still, with even the smallest amount of imagination, a person would be able to recognize her from the image. "I presume this will help you in your endeavors," Colin said.

"It should do nicely," I answered, belatedly realizing that he meant for me to go and meet with Paul.

"Very well then."

"And where are the two of you going?"

"I cannot speak for Mr. Evans," Colin said, "but as for myself, I will be heading over to Layton Manor. There are a few things I should like to review to satisfy my curiosity once and for all."

"Don't tell me you're still harping on that nonsense," Mr. Evans blurted with disbelief. "Why is it the gentry cannot believe one of its own might harm themselves? Do they really imagine such a thing to be solely driven by economics?"

"They shall believe it if I tell them," Colin stated flatly, though we both knew that would not be the outcome. "Perhaps you can meet me there if you have time later," he added, making it clear that he expected me at the Endicotts' as quickly as possible.

"I'll see how the afternoon goes," I replied, giving Maurice Evans a look I hoped he would construe as disinterested.

"You two are wasting your time," Mr. Evans reiterated. "You must be receiving quite the stipend for your troubles."

Colin's eyebrows vaulted toward the blue sky. "I find your inference offensive, Mr. Evans. Our efforts are not predicated on the ability of our clients to pay."

Mr. Evans chuckled as he waved Colin off. "I meant no offense, I am sure. Just do not let me discover that you've contrived a way to find Mrs. Hutton and have not shared it with me."

"Perish the thought."

"I am dead serious, Mr. Pendragon," he said, his face losing any hint of levity. "I'll not stand for it. I'll not be made a fool of as you did to Inspector Varcoe."

"You cannot blame another man's foolishness on me."

"Mr. Pendragon . . ."

Colin held up a hand and flashed a placating grin. "You have had your say. Now shall we head back to the Tube? I know the Yard won't authorize cab fare."

"You're a pip," Mr. Evans grumbled as they turned back in the direction they had come from. "Are you coming, Mr. Pruitt? I do believe I could benefit from spending a bit of time with someone less exasperating."

"I'm afraid you'll have to continue to fend for yourself, Mr. Evans. Now that I have this picture of Mrs. Hutton, I must get started at the archives." I held my ground while the two of them started off, Colin walking with his usual determination while Mr. Evans was at his side looking far less certain of anything.

Long before the two of them were out of sight I circled around onto the parallel block and headed in the same direction, south toward Prince Albert Road. From there I crossed onto Albany Street until I could cut between several of the buildings that led out onto the north end of Cumberland Terrace. Somewhere here, within this well-kempt if unremarkable area, Charlotte Hut-

204 / *Gregory Harris*

ton was in hiding. The very thought of it made my pulse quicken and caused me to pull myself back into the gloomy shadows cast between the buildings.

I glanced along the street as far as I could see, searching for any sign of Paul, knowing he would be along here somewhere. Between his admiration for Colin and relentless pursuit of sterling, I knew he would not fail to be here. The young scruff had proven himself both resourceful and dogged in watching the Guitnu home and following their middle daughter, Vijaya, when it looked as if she could be involved in the systematic pilfering of her parents' treasure trove of jewels. I only hoped that he would again prove as indomitable in helping us to find Charlotte Hutton.

A cool breeze whipped around the bottom of my coat, tugging at the flaps and sending a chill racing up my body. I yanked my collar up and stepped out of the gloom, trying to look as though I were a natural part of the day's activities, which proved difficult as it was Sunday and there was a frustrating dearth of commotion. I knew I could not simply stand about and was considering a quick jaunt down the length of the street, something I really did not wish to do lest Mrs. Hutton catch sight of me, when I spotted Paul. He was across the street and several doors down, leaning against the blackened stone and wrought-iron fencing of a dreary apartment building, his arms folded across his chest and a cap tugged low on his head. Dressed in his usual well-worn, dark, baggy clothing, he looked more a part of the fence than a living boy.

He crooked his head at me and I noticed a lopsided grin split his lips. No doubt he had spotted me long before I had seen him. How could I have forgotten how smug this lad could be?

A scowl tried to take root on my face, but I fought it off as I gave a quick nod before crossing the street and heading into the short alley across from where I'd been standing. I moved back into the shadows just far enough to avoid being seen from the street and waited. That Paul did not immediately follow me seemed considered on his part, but that I waited a full five minutes before his thin face poked around the corner was infuriating.

He dug his hands into his pockets and finally came trundling back toward me, moving with the nonchalance of one who rules the city. "Where's Mr. P.?" he asked as soon as he drew close to me. "'E tol' me I was ta meet 'im 'ere today."

"He is caught up in something else," I answered, trying to tamp down my annoyance. "He sent me instead."

"Oh." His face fell.

"You needn't look so disappointed. You'll still be doing his bidding. We all do his bidding," I quipped, only half in jest, but drew nothing from the lad.

"'E said 'e wants me ta look for some lady?"

"That's right." I reached into my coat pocket and pulled out the photograph from Maurice Evans. "She is a clever and dangerous woman, and you must not make the mistake of forgetting that."

He looked down at the picture and frowned. "'Oo's the bloke?" he asked, ignoring my warning as though it did not deserve comment.

"That was her husband. Was. He's deceased. Hence my remark that she is a dangerous woman."

"She's a right bird," he snickered with a lecher's grin, which looked comical on a boy for whom puberty had yet to take hold. "'Er 'usband were a toad. Ain't no wonder she got rid a 'im."

"If you are not going to listen to what I'm telling you, then your assistance will not be needed," I groused.

Paul glanced up at me, his expression wholly unperturbed. "Is that what Mr. P. says?"

I could not help but roll my eyes. I would not let this boy get to me. "Your safety is of paramount importance to both Mr. Pendragon and me, Paul. If something were to happen to you—"

"Ain't nothin' gonna 'appen ta me," he cut me off with a snort. "I can take care a meself. Been doin' so since the moment I were born. So you can stop bein' a twat."

"I am well aware that you are capable of fending for yourself," I said with a growl, "but you will learn that the people who care about you will worry just the same. It is a good thing, not a slight on your character."

Paul stared back at me, his hazel eyes round with surprise and, for an instant, void of the arrogance that always seemed to shield him. "What's it Mr. P. wants me ta do?"

"Find her. There is a boardinghouse just down the way that she was dropped in front of yesterday. Unfortunately, we have learned that she is *not* staying there. As I mentioned, the lady is clever and not about to be so easily netted. So we need you, and perhaps one or two of your more capable blokes, to do a bit of poking about in the buildings along this block and the next to see if you can get any information on her without arousing any suspicion. It is most critical, and I am afraid time is of the essence."

"Time is wot?"

"Short. We are short on time. It is possible that she is about to flee the city at any moment. In fact, she may have already done so."

"Me and the boys'll find 'er," he said with all the assurance of one who has earned a lifetime's living doing just that. "Ya ain't got nothin' ta worry about."

"I will worry about you and the other lads, Paul, if you do not heed my warnings about this woman. You must take care at all times and never presume that she does not know we are looking for her."

"Hmm . . ." He shrugged. "With this one soundin' so tricky and all, I jest may need ta charge ya somethin' extra."

I could not help but admire the lad's enterprising spirit, especially if it assured me of the safety of him and his brood. "If you and your boys find her without any of you getting caught or hurt, I will see to it that you each receive an extra stipend for your efforts."

"A wot?"

"Pay . . . pay . . ." I hastily corrected. "I will pay you extra. And there is one more thing: The woman has dyed her hair black now. She is no longer blond."

He beamed as he stabbed the photograph into his pocket. "Not ta worry. You jest be off," he said with a bob of his chin toward the alley's exit. "Me and the boys can't get nothin' done with you hangin' about. Bugger off, now." He chuckled as he backed up toward Cumberland Terrace again with a decided bounce in his step. "I'll be by yer flat the second we find this ol' witch." He chuckled again and disappeared around the corner with a sudden burst of speed.

I knew young Paul was clever, and worked hard to convince myself that he and his chaps would be fine, yet that was something I dared not presume where Charlotte Hutton was concerned. Which left a knot in my stomach at the thought of what we were asking Paul and his boys to do. If something were to happen to any of them . . . but I stopped myself from completing that notion and instead made my way out of the area as quickly as I could.

CHAPTER 22

Eugenia Endicott did not bother trying to hide her displeasure at seeing us. Granted it was Sunday, not that she gave any indication of being on her way to or from church, but I had thought she might at least feign satisfaction that we were actively working on settling the manner of her sister's death. Even though Colin had already made it clear that he did not believe Adelaide had jumped from the window, I could not shake the impression that Miss Eugenia still did not trust us, which put me in mind of the spectral child's disembodied voice. I wondered at Miss Eugenia's fervid dismissal of the topic. And in the next instant young Paul's resolute face popped into my head. That we had left him searching for Charlotte Hutton still did not sit well.

"Are you paying attention?" Colin interrupted my ruminations, highlighting the fact that I was obviously not in the least.

"Yes," I answered anyway.

He was leaning out the window of Adelaide Endicott's bedroom yet again, and I wondered at his tenacity in doing so, given that he had already been through it from both directions. Could there still be anything of note that he had not already discovered?

"What did I say?" he asked out of nowhere.

"Pardon?"

He glanced back at me from his ratcheted position halfway out the window. "If you were paying attention just now, then what did I ask you to do?"

"Really?!" I had no recourse but to affect offense. "Do you really mean to quiz me?"

He chuckled as he turned back around. "That's what I thought."

I heaved a sigh. "All right then, what is it you want me to do?"

"Look around the room. If Mr. Nettle says he heard the voice of a child, then it had to be coming from somewhere."

I glanced at the large, cold space and tried to imagine how such trickery might have been accomplished. There were two spindle-legged side tables beside the huge four-poster bed, which was draped with a heavy maroon fabric that had been pulled tightly back and tied to the posts, revealing the perfectly made bed as though it were waiting for the room's occupant to return at any moment. A large, intricately carved, three-door armoire stood across the room, the center door covered by a mirror, and it had laughing cherubs in fine relief along its top corners with sprays of carved roses and buds peeking from beneath delicately hewn leaves that ran fully across the top and partway down its sides.

The walls of the room were a dusky pink with dark wood wainscoting covering the bottom third. A vanity of the same stately design as the bed stood against the wall that separated Miss Adelaide's room from the anteroom where Freddie Nettle had slept, and while there was a space beneath it for a woman's legs, it was otherwise open and therefore seemed an unlikely spot for a child to hide. Not to mention that it was on the wrong side of the room and quite a distance from where Mr. Nettle had claimed to hear the pleading waif.

It was obvious that the only place for a child to hide, assuming one had done so at all, was either beneath the bed or inside the armoire. Though it too was some distance from the window, I yanked the doors to the armoire open and peered inside. To my surprise it was a clutter of clothing and accessories, speaking to a lifetime of accumulation. Dresses of all types were wedged in so tightly they barely gave when I pushed against them, with shoes, hatboxes, and handbags of every imaginable color and size stuffed along the shelf across the top and all over the floor so that they were piled two and three high, with extra bags on hooks that had been screwed into the inside of the doors themselves. A moth looked unlikely to be able to breech this space let alone a child of any size, so I swung the doors shut again and turned back to the bed.

With a tug at my trousers I got down on my knees, peering underneath at what appeared to be a veritable wall of darkness. With one hand I scrabbled a small box of matches from my shirt pocket, hastily lighting one, though only managing to cast more shadows than light across the claustrophobic space that looked quite filled with more hatboxes anyway.

"What are you doing?" I heard Colin from behind me, his voice soft and calm but with an undeniable hint of mirth to it.

I glanced back up at him. "I'm looking to see if someone might have hidden under here. . . ." It made sense to me, but nevertheless, a crooked grin tugged at one corner of Colin's mouth. "You told me . . ." but I didn't bother to finish the sentence. Clearly, I had failed at his greater meaning, so I blew out the match and stood up. "What?"

"Do you recollect Mr. Nettle saying the child's voice was coming from beneath the bed?"

"I don't recall him saying he knew *where* it was coming from," I answered curtly. "I'm certain he didn't have any idea, given the pyrotechnics making him question his own sanity and the fact that Miss Adelaide was hovering in front of the open window."

"He said it sounded as though it was emanating from out of the colored mist, which would be by the window," he reminded me. "But we know it can't have come from the window itself. That's where the phosphorous powder had been ignited and tossed from. I've already seen that the rails of Mr. McPherson's ladder fit the notches left in the casing on that window perfectly. And given that there *are* notches I would say that this game against Miss Adelaide has been going on for some time." He turned away from me and strode back to the window. "And I do not believe for an instant that this is the sport of a child. So the voice"—he knelt down by the window and rapped against the wainscoting—"it *had* to have come from inside this room. . . ."

I stood there while he crept along the floorboard, knocking against the wainscoting every few feet as if waiting for someone to knock back. It seemed a preposterous exercise and I could hardly imagine that he truly expected to find anything, so I was not in the least surprised when he straightened up after having gone as far as the nightstand by the bed to no avail. Rather than giving up, however, he stalked back to the window with a burgeoning frown and repeated the same exercise, heading in the opposite direction. The sound, when it came, was as distinctive as the difference between the timbre of a man's voice and a woman's.

"Oh . . ." I said before he had even stopped tapping on the dark rectangle of wood rising just off the floor.

"Indeed," he answered back, carefully running his fingers along the bead molding that outlined the panel itself. "So allow me to make my earlier point again. . . ." he said as he fanned out from the panel and began slowly poking at the adjacent woodwork before dropping his hands to the baseboard itself. ". . . You have been preoccupied today, and I wish you would come out with it already." The words had scarcely left his mouth when a soft click suddenly registered, barely above a whisper, springing the panel he was kneeling in front of no more than a finger's width. He looked up at me with a wry smile. "And there you have it."

As I stood there staring at the unlatched panel, I had to admit that he was right. I was distracted and needed to pursue this case as I would any other. Disembodied voices, spectral visions, pleading souls: Their sources had to be as tangible as the phosphorous powder Colin had already discovered. And now this, a small black cubby just large enough for a child to hide inside.

"This Endicott business has me vexed," I muttered as Colin swung the little entry door fully open. "I'm not thinking right."

"Yes," he said mundanely as he peered inside. "But why?"

"If you must know, I am worried about Paul. We have left him and his mates to search for a woman we have every reason to believe is dangerous. We still don't even know for certain the level of her complicity in her own son's death. It bothers me. That boy idolizes you, and I worry that he'll do something impetuous to try and earn your praise."

Colin lit a match and stuck his head inside the tiny space, leaving me to wonder if he'd even heard what I had been saying. "You're fretting over nothing," he replied after a moment, not bothering to turn his head, so that his words came out muffled and dismissive. "That little shite is more clever than you and I together. He'll probably be elected prime minister one day and we'll be working for him in our dotage." He leaned back out and extinguished the match with a single puff, holding his other hand up as though it were made of glass. Before I could ask what he was doing, he brought his fingers to his nose and took a hesitant sniff. "Ginger," he said.

"What?"

"It would seem our poor, pleading, phantom child has a predilection for ginger biscuits."

CHAPTER 23

The scents coming from the Endicott kitchen were heavenly. I could smell a roasting chicken with root vegetables, a fair amount of rosemary, and just the right amount of garlic. Above it all was the warm, doughy scent of baking bread and something sweet and thickly infused with cinnamon and cloves. We had not been invited to this part of the house, though that fact did not concern Colin, who had insisted we go down to see the cook the moment we had left Miss Adelaide's room.

"I am reminded that we have not had any lunch," he said with a note of regret as we rounded the last step down the back stairway that let directly into the kitchen. I knew Mr. Galloway would be positively undone if he found us using this route.

"I will never understand how you can forget to eat," I started to grouse just as a lovely young woman of diminutive proportions with strands of straw-blond hair peeking from beneath a cook's cap strode into the kitchen carrying a tray of the most perfect fruit tarts I had ever seen. She yelped as her eyes fell upon us and came to so sudden a halt that the dozen miniature tarts were nearly lost to the floor.

"My sincerest apology for causing you a fright," Colin said as he steadied the tray from the opposite side. "I am Colin Pendragon and this is Ethan Pruitt. . . ."

"I know who ya are," she answered with a scowl. "I just didn't expect ta find ya skulkin' about me kitchen."

Colin's smile froze and a single eyebrow arched. "We have come specifically to speak with you," he explained crisply, as though that should make everything all right.

She set the tray of tartlets onto the table and wiped her hands on the full-length apron tied around her slender waist. "Mr. Galloway know you're down here?"

"No," Colin answered, "though I suspect there's a good chance he will have heard your cry of a moment ago."

"Well, we don't normally entertain guests in the kitchen," she shot back as she yanked open the oven and peered inside, her interest in us appearing to wane by the instant.

"As it should be," Colin agreed smoothly. "However, I would hardly consider either of us guests, given that we are here to investigate the murder of your mistress." His words brought her up short as he'd intended them to, causing her to finally return her attentions fully to us. "I assume you are Mrs. Barber?"

I was astonished that he remembered her name.

"I am," she answered with a pride that caught me by surprise. "Go on, then, sit yourselves down." She gestured toward a couple of chairs shoved behind the large preparation table at the room's center and farthest from the stove and ovens. With a paucity of motion she took a kettle from the stove and poured two teas before scooping a couple of the tartlets onto plates and setting them on the table near us. "Come on, then," she said by way of invitation, "they ain't gonna eat themselves."

Neither of us needed a second summons before we dragged our chairs across the floor, landing in front of the two places she had prepared for us. "Mincemeat," Colin practically purred as he tucked into the pastry. "I don't believe we could have timed our visit any better."

Mrs. Barber chuckled as she poured herself a cup of tea and sat down across from us. "I'm glad ya like it, but I doubt you've come creepin' about me kitchen in search of it. So why don't ya tell me why you're here."

I remembered the coachman, Devlin Fischer, referring to Mrs. Barber as a feisty woman, and now I understood precisely why.

"I only mean to trouble you with a few simple questions," Colin said, a look of contentment flashing behind his eyes as he finished the pastry. "Are you the only cook at Layton Manor?"

"I'm the only one they need," she fired right back.

"Of that I can attest." A slight grin played at his lips. "Do you ever make ginger biscuits?"

She smiled. "They another of yer favorites?"

"Not like mincemeat. But I am more interested in whether they are a particular favorite of someone here?"

"Miss Eugenia likes 'em. She says they help settle her digestion. Mostly I make them when His Lordship comes because they're about the only biscuit I've ever known him to eat."

"Does Lord Endicott visit often?"

"I don't believe I've seen him in some months. . . . Other than the night Miss Adelaide died," she was quick to correct.

"Certainly. And anyone else? Anyone on the staff have a special penchant for ginger biscuits?"

"Mr. McPherson is awfully fond of them," she said with the faintest flush as she referred to the groundsman. "And Mr. Nettle used ta enjoy 'em, but then a man his size enjoyed everything I put before him." She chuckled again.

"What about Miss Adelaide's former nurses?"

"Miss Whit and Miss Bromley?" She appeared to give the question some consideration before answering. "I can't say I remember either of them makin' a fuss over anything I cooked. They're practically just girls, ya know?" She gave a curious sort of smile as though her reference should mean something to us. "But nobody has access to the kitchen anyway. This spot belongs ta me and I don't take well ta visitors." She took a quick slug of her tea. "Do ya really suppose Mr. Nettle had somethin' ta do with Miss Adelaide's death?"

Colin grimaced as he leaned back and finished his tea. "It is a complex and sordid affair," he said after a minute, "but I am still inclined to believe that Mr. Nettle is himself a victim in this case, as he lacks a motive. That most essential component in any crime." He abruptly pushed himself up from the table with a quick flash of a grin. "I must thank you for your time, Mrs. Barber, but most of all I am grateful for your culinary generosity."

"It's my pleasure," she said as she stood up. "If there is anything further you need you know where I'll be. But next time you might send for me rather than slinkin' into me kitchen." She snatched up our cups and plates and carried them to the large sink near the door. "You can go out this way if ya'd like."

"That would be ideal, as we are headed out to the stable," Colin said at once.

Mrs. Barber gave a shy smile. "Will ya say hello ta Mr. McPherson for me?"

"Consider it done."

I followed Colin outside and around the corner, walking the length of the house with thoughts of this case, Charlotte Hutton, and Paul fighting for attention in my head, and as a result walked right into Colin. "Oh!" I muttered foolishly.

"You must stop fretting so and have some faith in me," he said, and his voice no longer sounded patient or understanding. "I am trying very hard to make sure Mr. Nettle does not end up hanging for a crime I do not think he committed, and you are ever mentally elsewhere." He shot his arm up. "Did you even notice that we are standing at the very spot where Miss Adelaide died?" I looked up and realized that we were indeed standing just beneath the window where she had fallen. "I need you present, Ethan, because every time I speak to someone in this infernal household, no one looks guiltier than that blasted Freddie Nettle."

Having thusly vented his own frustration, he quickly rounded on his heels and stalked off, cutting across the cobbled side yard toward the stables near the porte cochere. I gritted my teeth and cursed myself for not paying enough mind to what was happening, vowing to contribute to the solution of this case and to that of Charlotte Hutton as well. For it was that villainous woman, more than anything else, that I knew most enflamed his mind.

Before we could reach the stable, Mr. McPherson came out with a short ladder on one beefy shoulder and a bow saw in his other hand. For a man in his later forties or early fifties he was in remarkable shape. I suspected it would amuse him to know that Colin was hoisting weights around to accomplish a form that Mr. McPherson achieved in the normal course of his day.

"Mr. McPherson . . ." Colin called out, quickening his pace. "Might I have a word with you?"

The man pushed his cap up off his forehead and gazed at us. "I ain't sure what else I can tell ya," he answered as we caught up to him.

"You needn't worry," Colin said, and I was relieved to hear that his voice was once again calm and steady. "Why don't you let me tell you something instead. The other day you helped me set your tallest ladder against the side of the house all the way up to Miss Adelaide's room. . . ."

"So we did." He gave a soft chuckle and I was certain he must be remembering the sight of Colin awkwardly disappearing in through the window.

"The rails of your ladder were an exact fit for a set of grooves in the paint just below the window. I am quite certain your ladder has been rested against that same spot repeatedly over the past several months. Have you been working up there?"

He scratched his forehead with a meaty paw as he peered at Colin. "A couple a times. You saw the winda was replaced. I had ta caulk the outside and paint it after puttin' it in." He shook his head and rearranged his cap. "I ain't much fer heights, but it had ta be done."

"Yes, you said that a bird had hit the window some time ago and cracked the glass?"

"S'right."

"But you found no carcass on the cobbles below. Were there any smears of blood on the window?"

"Blood?"

"On the window."

He shook his head after a moment. "No."

"Could you see a point of impact? A central place where the bird had actually struck the glass out of which the cracks appeared."

Mr. McPherson nodded at once. "'At I did." And I could tell he was pleased to be able to say so. "I could see right where the little bugger had hit. Left a nick in the glass and there were several small cracks rose up from there, but one of 'em went clear across to the far side a the pane. So the winda had ta be replaced."

"A nick in the glass?" Colin pressed. "How big? The size of my thumb . . . ?"

"Nah." He shook his head and scrunched up his face as though trying to remember. "Not that big. It were jest a small thing. Maybe like a pebble or somethin' small. . . ." and even as he said the words his eyes drifted past us to the cobbled drive running along the side of the house where a velvety coating of emerald moss and a thousand tiny stones filled the slender crevices between the brickwork. "Oh," he said with sudden understanding. "You don't think it were a bird at all. . . ." he added as he continued to stare toward the side drive before letting his eyes drift up to Miss Adelaide's window.

"I see that you and I have come to the same conclusion." Colin spoke quietly, allowing a small, taut smile to ghost across his lips.

"But why?" Mr. McPherson asked in the next moment. "I don't understand why someone'd wanna be tossing rocks up at Miss Adelaide's room. Why would someone do that?"

Colin started walking toward the stable again, forcing Mr. McPherson and me to follow along behind him. "That is the question, isn't it."

As we reached the stable Mr. McPherson finally slid the small ladder off his shoulder and leaned it up against the side of the building before setting the bow saw beside it. "I noticed some little divots along the outside a the winda when I was paintin' it. Thought they were just wear. . . ." He shook his head and scowled, and I knew he meant it for himself. "That weren't wear," he scoffed. "That were somebody throwin' a bunch a shite up there ta rattle the winda, weren't it?"

"To rattle the window . . ." Colin repeated thoughtfully as he began walking around the stable's entry space where most of the equipment for the grounds and horses were kept, including several ladders of varying sizes, saws, and rakes all mounted to the far wall. "You are close, sir, but I believe the intent was to get Miss Adelaide's attention, not merely to rattle her window."

"Her attention?"

Colin spun around from his study of the paraphernalia hanging along the wall and looked directly at Mr. McPherson. "Where do you sleep at night?"

The man looked startled. "Sleep? I go home. By the time it gets dark I go home. Got a bunch a kids I gotta look after."

"Yes, of course. I forgot that you're a widower."

"Huh?" The man looked startled again, but I realized what Colin was referring to. "Who told you that my wife died?"

"No one, Mr. McPherson. They didn't need to. It was evident when Mr. Fischer ribbed you about your awareness of the comely Mrs. Barber. I have no doubt that a man such as yourself would never allow such an interest to be observed if he had a wife at home."

"That's right," he said. "I loved my Mary, but she and me youngest died of a fever 'bout two years ago and left me with the other four. Still miss her, but I ain't gonna deny that I notice Mrs. Barber."

Colin chuckled. "Then let me assure you that I believe she has noticed you as well." In spite of his sun-darkened skin, I was certain a slight blush colored Mr. McPherson's cheeks. "Tell me, does anyone in the household ever come out to the stable or ask to use any of the"—he gestured around at the abundance of tools—"equipment?"

He shook his head and I was certain he was glad for the change of subject. "Nah. They've no reason to. It's all mostly women workin' here 'cept for Mr. Galloway, and I doubt that man's had any sort a yard tool in his hand in the whole a his life."

Colin nodded. "And what about Mr. Nettle?"

Mr. McPherson gave a smile. "Freddie were always good. Fit and smart. He used ta come out from time ta time and do some work, a bit a whittlin' or fixin' a piece a Miss Adelaide's furniture when it needed somethin'. One time he sanded and waxed both a her bed tables when they was lookin' sorrowful, and another time he made himself a small wooden bookcase ta hold books and papers he kept in the little room where he slept. He were good with his hands, that one. I didn't mind him comin' out and usin' me stuff."

A sudden noise from the stalls where the horses were kept caught our attention, and not a moment later Mr. Fischer stepped out of the darkened hallway dragging a muslin tarp with a great pile of foul-smelling used hay atop it. "Well . . . !" His eyes lit up as he spotted the three of us. "Didn't know we had company."

"Hardly a visit," Colin corrected as he glanced back to the contents of the tarp Mr. Fischer was pulling. "If we were interested in a social call, you can be certain we would not choose the day you sluice the stable to do it."

Mr. Fischer gave a hearty laugh as he continued to heft the contents out into the sunlight, bringing instantaneous relief to the air we were trying to breathe. "Well said, Mr. Pendragon. It isn't everyone who gets the chance to appreciate the scents from a horse's nether end." He laughed again as he rubbed his hands against his breeches and walked back to us. "And what it is that brings you out here? Have you finally brought an end to this business about Miss Adelaide's death?"

Colin's face curdled. "I have not. It remains regrettably obstinate in its conclusion, but I will get there."

"Let me know if there's anything I can do to help," Mr. Fischer offered before giving a sideways nod to Mr. McPherson. "Course, Denny and I aren't privy to much since we work out here." He gave a mild shrug. "Although I am the one who brought you to that clairvoyant lady's house. I suppose that was helpful, wasn't it?"

"Lady Stuart," I filled in for him. "Yes, it was a useful service indeed."

"Tell me something," Colin spoke up as he continued to study

Mr. Fischer, his brows remaining continuously furrowed. "Did Mr. Nettle always go inside Lady Stuart's home when the three of you went there? Did he never stay out in the carriage?"

He immediately shook his head. "Never. Miss Adelaide couldn't have made it inside on her own, and the lady's houseman is elderly himself. Besides, Freddie had to be there in case she needed him. But he always stayed in the kitchen. It's not like he were allowed anywhere else in the house. He couldn't listen to what the women were talkin' about, if that's what you're gettin' at."

"So we have been told. . . ." Colin let his voice drift off with irritation.

"Does anyone else have access to the stable?" I asked, going back to Colin's earlier assertion. "Perhaps when either of you is ill?"

Mr. Fischer laughed as he slid an amused glace at Mr. McPherson. "I've curried these horses even when I was too sick to keep so much as a morsel in me own gut. And there have been days I've taken one or both ladies out in the pouring rain even though my head was burnin' with fever. So no . . ." He shook his head with another chuckle. ". . . Nobody else touches these horses or carriages without me."

"Not even Mr. Nettle?" Colin asked, and I imagined he was looking for some assurance, however small, that Freddie Nettle did not have free rein around the whole of Layton Manor and its grounds.

"Certainly not Freddie." Mr. Fischer smirked. "I never saw him show much of an affinity for the animals."

"Well, that is something," Colin groused under his breath, though it made not the slightest bit of difference to the case. "Where do you sleep nights, Mr. Fischer? Do you stay here or do you have a room elsewhere?"

"I rent a room out in Lower Holloway. I've had it for just over a year. It's not much, but it suits me fine. I spend most of my time here anyway."

"As do we all," Mr. McPherson agreed.

"Were either of you ever called to do any work in Miss Adelaide's room?" Colin asked.

"Nah," Mr. McPherson answered. "That were Mr. Nettle's job. I already told ya he were good with his hands."

"Then are either of you aware that there is a false panel in the wainscoting in her room?"

The two of them looked at each other and I could see they were startled. "It don't surprise me." Mr. McPherson was the first to answer again. "These old houses got all kinds a crazy shite build inta 'em."

"It doesn't surprise me, either," Mr. Fischer agreed. "Goes back to the days when the nobles were up ta no good. Not like now. . . ." He cocked a deliberate grin.

"Thank you, gentlemen," Colin said as he pulled out his watch and glanced at it. "You have both been very helpful, and we have taken up enough of your time." He took a step back and signaled to me. "We must be off. We have another appointment to make."

I followed him outside before I asked, "What appointment?"

"Maurice Evans is expecting us," he said, as though I should know it already.

"Whatever for?"

"He has arranged for us to speak with Wynn Tessler. I may be making little headway in this blasted case, but I will not lose Charlotte Hutton."

"Wynn Tessler . . . ?!"

"The man is waiting to be put to death," Colin said, though I was already fully aware of that fact. "I should very much like to hear what he has to say about Mrs. Hutton now."

"What of Freddie Nettle?"

Colin flicked a glare at me before picking up his pace toward the street. "At this point, in spite of my own declarations to the contrary, I am about to arrest Mr. Nettle myself." He pulled away from me and I let him go, a fist curdling my belly as the magnitude of his words reverberated through my brain.

CHAPTER 24

The stench of the place was the first thing one noticed upon arrival. It was impossible to have it any other way. Even on a day like this one with a chilled breeze whistling along the streets, the stink would not be contained by the massive, four-story, granite, brick-and-cement structure. Newgate Prison had been standing on this corner for more than a hundred years, and there was nothing about its soot-blackened exterior, nearly windowless façade, or permanent reek that suggested it was anything other than what it was.

Countless men and women had been housed and hung here over the course of that century for every crime from arson to high treason to horse stealing and murder. It was the latter that now brought us to this wretched place. Six men and one enfeebled boy ruthlessly slaughtered for the most heinous reason. But while Wynn Tessler waited in this unspeakable purgatory to be put to death for his part in that savagery, Charlotte Hutton remained unforgivably free.

I trailed behind Colin and Maurice Evans, who were themselves following a great bear of a man who had been introduced as a senior guard. He easily stood over six feet and had a barrel of a chest that was so solid and menacing that even Colin looked almost diminutive in his wake. If there were a hell on earth I felt like I was visiting it.

"How long did you say . . . ?" I heard Mr. Evans repeat to the warder as he led us down a narrow brick hallway, his head less than a foot below the curved stone ceiling.

The man tugged mechanically at his wooly black beard as though actually giving the question some thought. "Ten minutes," he finally said. "More than that tends ta get a bit fiddly. Doesn't do anybody any good ta get a condemned man riled up."

"I cannot see why anyone should care," Colin mumbled.

"You'd care if you was watchin' over 'em. Makes it that much harder for us when these nobs get riled up. Doesn't make much sense bangin' their heads together when they're all gonna wind up at the end of a rope soon enough anyway."

"Yes, I suppose," Colin answered, his distaste at the sentiment evident. "But of course this is Yard business," he reminded.

"Bugger the Yard," the man responded casually. "No offense, Mr. Evans. Your boys may throw 'em in here, but we're the ones keepin' 'em in line until their time's up. Which means the rules inside Newgate belong ta us. So ya got ten minutes with yer man unless ya get him into a lather and then ya got less." He turned as we reached a metal door covered with iron straps bolted along its width in a regular pattern, with a smaller sealed inner door, no bigger than a man's hand, at its center. "You boys hearin' me?"

"You are the only one talking," Colin answered with a smile so tight I doubted air could pass across his lips. "Now shall we?"

The man's eyes pinched ever so slightly before he reached out and unhooked the latch on the inner door, yanking it open. "It's me, Renny," he called out. "Got the company for our distinguished Mr. Tessler." He gave a soft snicker that none of us joined in on as he shut the little door.

A moment later the jangle of multiple keys rattling about followed by a series of locks sliding free could be heard from what sounded like a considerable distance, which was obviously a testament to the thickness of the door before us. Just when it seemed we might never actually gain entry, the door finally began to draw open, moving at such a ponderous pace that our chaperone leaned forward and put his considerable girth against it. A plain room of medium size was slowly revealed, with a matching door on its opposite wall and two heavily barred windows astride it, though what they looked out upon I could not yet see.

"We got ever'body locked down," the man opening the door alerted us. I presumed he was Renny, though we were not introduced to either him or the other warder pacing the room, whose eyes were fixed on the two barred windows. "Go ahead and let him through," he called over his shoulder to his compatriot.

"I trust you boys will have a nice visit with yer friend." Our escort chuckled, giving a wide grin that exposed far too many spaces where teeth should have been.

"If you please . . ." Colin rebuked dismissively.

The warder who had been pacing immediately stopped and set himself to releasing the copious locks upon the opposite door. As the last one slid back, he gripped a metal rod attached at the midway point of the door and leaned back with his far less considerable weight than our attendant until the door began to move.

"Here, ya little runt, let me give ya a ruddy hand." Our burly usher snickered as he stepped up and gripped the edge of the door with both hands so that between the two of them, it began to move more easily. A most wretched stink rolled out the moment the door was halfway open, reminding me of a mix of bad hygiene and inept plumbing. It was staggering in its strength, and I had to open my mouth slightly just as I did whenever I was forced to visit the morgue.

The cellblock behind was three stories high with rows of cells along opposite sides numbering sixty or greater on each floor. A circular metal stairway rose on either end with a metal walkway connecting them across the fronts of the cells on the second and third floors. The space on the ground floor separating the two facing rows of cells was no more than twenty feet across and had several benches bolted to the floor in a haphazard array, with two similarly secured small tables and a half dozen chairs around each. That none of it was meant for comfort was easy to see.

"Welcome ta beautiful Newgate Prison," the towering guard

sneered. "Yer man is fourth down on the left, second floor. Let's try not ta get picked off on yer way to him, huh?!"

I thought he meant for us to find Wynn Tessler on our own, but he led us into the vast space and up the closest staircase, trudging heavily as he went and leaving me to wonder at the soundness of the old structure. If nothing else, it provided me something to concentrate on beyond the pervasive smell that only thickened as we rose to the second level. I could not imagine how I would have tolerated it had we been forced up to the third.

"Leave some room between yerselves and the cells ya pass. If I gotta wrench ya free from one a these buggers you ain't gonna be happy." This time the man did not smirk or chuckle in the least as he set himself just to the right of the walkway's center and began making his way down the row of cells arrayed on his left.

Little was said as we passed the first three cells, though one man gave a sonorous whistle. For an instant I feared that it might signal something untoward before remembering that both our attendant and Mr. Evans were visibly armed. I also knew that Colin had secreted a two-shot derringer under his arm as well, and I was suddenly well pleased for it. I did not shift my eyes to the left but kept them riveted on the back of Colin's tawny head, determined not to make eye contact with any of these men.

"Wake up, Tessler," our guide said as he drew up to the fourth cell, drawing a ring of keys from his waist that was bigger than my fist. "Ya got some admirers wanna have a word."

I drew up to the cell and turned to face it, finding myself staring at a brick space no more than five feet across and eight feet deep with a curved ceiling that stood barely six feet at its highest point. The walls were whitewashed and there was a bucket and a metal pitcher chained to the floor against the back wall with a roll of bedding beside it. A single chair and a table no larger than it stood near the front of the cell, and I realized that if the bedding were left unrolled it would dominate the tiny space. It reminded me of the cells the monks at Whitmore Abbey lived in, although theirs were a choice while these were meant to demoralize at best.

It took a moment for my vision to adjust to the dimly lit space so that the first thing I spied of Wynn Tessler were his eyes reflecting the glow from the buzzing electric lights mounted on the ceiling outside his cell. He looked hollow and haunted and had obviously lost weight, as his cheekbones appeared to be cutting across his face like razors, his eye sockets sunken and dark. His hair was shorn almost to the point of baldness, and the gray uniform he was wearing hung from his frame as though there was almost nothing beneath it.

"Mr. Tessler," Colin said with the same easy deference as if we had run into him in Green Park.

"Ah..." Wynn Tessler's voice came out stilted and cracked, a sign that he did not use it much. "... Mr. Pendragon and Mr. Pruitt. Come to gloat, have you?" He took a step into the refracted light, and to my surprise I saw that he wore an expression that was neither disdainful nor caustic.

"We take no solace in another man's downfall," Colin said. "We are here with Mr. Evans of Scotland Yard because we have made precious little progress on the whereabouts of Charlotte Hutton. I was hoping you might be more eager to reveal any further details you might know about her before you suffer the blame of these crimes solely on your own...." Colin abruptly turned to the warder and gestured at the barred door. "Open this door so that we may speak with Mr. Tessler properly," he ordered, as though the right was his to do so. "We are civilized men here, not barbarians."

The bearish man looked taken aback as he slid his eyes to Mr. Evans. "I don't think so," he rumbled.

"You'll do it," Mr. Evans spoke up, "or I shall have your badge and uniform before nightfall."

I had no idea whether he could make good on his threat, but the hulking guard moved forward and instantly unlocked the great barred door, pulling it open with one hand. "If ya try ta make a move over this threshold," he growled at Wynn Tessler, "I will crack yer skull before ya know I'm there." And to ensure that his threat was taken seriously he removed the billy club from his waist and smacked it into the palm of his hand.

"There is no need for that." Colin scowled at the man as he stepped inside the cell himself.

Neither Mr. Evans nor I followed. I doubted there was room for either of us anyway. Nevertheless, I did manage to place myself between the door and the warder so that I would not miss anything being said.

"You are welcome to the chair, Mr. Pendragon," Mr. Tessler said derisively. "You might notice it is one of the few luxuries left to me."

Colin waved it off as he stood right in front of Mr. Tessler. "I will be satisfied simply to hear your claims of Mrs. Hutton—"

Mr. Tessler held up a hand and silenced Colin. "Allow me to tell you what you will hear if you ever do manage to find her," he started, his tone dry and harsh. "She will claim to have been a victim of my cruelties. I will have bribed her into complicity by raising my fists against her until she had no choice but to cuckold her piteous husband." He smirked, but there was no humor in his look. "Poor Arthur. Such a pitiful man. Everything he touched he fouled. Except for her. She was already venomous."

"So you and her husband were innocent victims of her whims, then?"

"Do not mock me, Mr. Pendragon."

"Do not play me for a fool."

Wynn Tessler sneered. "I am already paying for my part of this . . . this . . ." He seemed unable to name what he had done, though I did not have the sense that it was because his conscience bothered him. "If I knew where she had gone . . . if I had the slightest notion of where to send you, I would make you a map myself. Nothing would bring me more pleasure than to walk to those bloody gallows knowing that harpy as going to dangle beside me." His eyes drifted sideways and lost their focus for a moment. "I tell you quite honestly. . . ." he said wistfully before his gazed snapped back to Colin's face. "I would die with a smile."

"She never mentioned anything to you? Someone on the Continent she knew? Somewhere she was fond of? Was there nothing, however idle, that gives you any thoughts on reflection? She took her daughter, Mr. Tessler. What would she have done with Anna? Where would she have taken her?"

Mr. Tessler tilted his head back and closed his eyes, and I noticed his body sag. "I have nothing for you, Mr. Pendragon. How I wish that I did. She is the most devious creature I have ever had the misfortune to know." He fell silent a moment before looking back at Colin again. "Do you know that one evening when she was delayed in returning home to her boorish husband after we had enjoyed a full day's assignation, I watched her gouge a knife from the midpoint of her forearm to the elbow just so she would have a story to tell Arthur of the accident that had made her so unaccountably late." His face soured. "She is a horror, Mr. Pendragon. She is the very plague itself."

"All right . . ." The warder loomed into the doorway, shoving me out of the way as he stuck a finger into Colin's back. "That's enough now. It's time for you to be on your way."

To my surprise, Colin backed out at once rather than argue against the abrupt end to our time here, which was nowhere near the ten minutes we had been promised. I watched as Colin gave a small nod of his head to Wynn Tessler from the doorway. "You paint the woman with a very black brush indeed, and yet you yourself admit to having fallen well under her influence."

"And so I did," he said. "And for that I am on the cusp of paying with my miserable life."

The warder leaned back and seized the door, swinging it shut and bolting it back in place with the fluidity of someone who has done so too many times before. Even so, Mr. Tessler did not move. With the shadow of the bars painted across his face he remained right where he was, staring out at us, his hollowed eyes no longer able to reflect anything. I found it difficult to look away from him, but as the warder and Colin and Mr. Evans started off, I forced myself to follow them.

CHAPTER 25

Colin was pacing in front of the fireplace while riffling through the pages of notes I had taken at Mrs. Denholm's house. It was his third time through them for the simple reason that there was nothing to be found there. So I was hardly surprised when not a second later his arm holding the pages suddenly went limp, hanging uselessly at his side, the papers dangling perilously close to the fire. For a moment I thought he might be about to pitch them in, but he did not. Instead he just stood there like that, stock-still, glaring at the lapping flames for what seemed several minutes before just as suddenly bringing the pages back to his face and starting to reread them again.

I could not help the sigh that escaped me as I tried to turn my attention back to the observations I was scribbling about our visit to Wynn Tessler. It seemed important to record the recollections while still fresh before further conversation and time began to soften the edges of what we had actually seen and heard there.

The one memory that would not release itself from my mind, however, was the fact that Wynn Tessler had known exactly the story she would tell—*did* tell me, the first time she approached me. Such a tale of abuse and fear, just as he had said she would. Which put me in mind of the scars she had revealed to me, and of

Mr. Tessler's story of seeing her slash her own arm open for wont of an excuse. Was it truly possible that she could have done such things to herself? It seemed unfathomable even as a foreboding shiver ripped down my spine.

"Oh . . ." I heard Colin exclaim at the same instant a sudden pounding rattled our door downstairs.

I set my pen down and watched Colin hustle over from the fireplace to the windows, yanking the curtains aside and gazing out, my notes still dangling from his other hand. "Oh, bloody buggery hell," he grumbled.

"What? Who is it?"

"Lord Thomas Endicott in all his blustering glory," he answered, his tone sarcastic and annoyed. "I just spoke to the ruddy man yesterday morning and now he has come here, and you can bet it's not to thank me for the work I've been doing to find his sister's murderer." He let the curtain fall back into place before stalking over to me and thrusting my notes out. "And just as I've discovered that you may be onto something here." He tossed the notes on top of the page I had been writing and yanked our suit jackets from the rack, tossing mine to me even as he shrugged on his own. "Look proper. The old prig is a pisser for details."

"Why on earth would Lord Endicott come here . . . ?" I asked, sounding foolish even to myself and wholly ignoring the fact that Colin had just claimed some value in my slipshod notes.

"Keep yer bloomers on. . . ." I heard Mrs. Behmoth holler below us as her heavy footfalls trod toward the door. "Ain't nothin' worth all that racket."

"That oughta warm him up nicely," Colin sneered.

I shoved all of the loose papers into the desk drawer and quickly pulled my coat on, yanking my tie up to my collar. Before I could get across the room I heard the door open, followed by the sound of Mrs. Behmoth.

"Why, Lord E . . ." she said to Lord Endicott, as though he were the dairy delivery boy. "I ain't seen you since I don't even know when. Come in . . . come in. . . ."

I shot my gaze over to Colin, parked in front of the fireplace again, and could not help but roll my eyes. He gave me a shrug and shook his head. "She worked for my father for a very long time," he explained needlessly. "She knows everybody he knows."

I heard the sound of two people plodding up the stairs, their voices sibilant and affable, before Mrs. Behmoth appeared on the landing with an older gentleman on her heels. He was broad chested and of medium height, with bushy gray hair that was thinning at the front, and two of the longest, fattest muttonchop sideburns I had ever seen. For a moment I was struck by the fact that he wore no mustache where it seemed one ought to be, given the preponderance of facial hair he was wearing, but in the next instant I was distracted by the thin, grim turn of his lips.

"Lord E ta see ya," Mrs. Behmoth bothered to announce as she swung her arm toward the settee. "Ya know Colin, a course, and this 'ere 'is Ethan Pruitt. You'll find 'e ain't so moody as that one," she added with a thrust of her chin in Colin's direction. "Now sit yerself down and I'll bring ya up some tea and biscuits."

"You mustn't put yourself out," Lord Endicott answered with a scowl as he seated himself without so much as a glance toward either me or Colin. "This isn't a social visit."

"Ah," she scoffed as she headed back for the stairs. "I were jest makin' some for meself. Gettin' another cup or two ain't nothin'."

She had barely disappeared from view before Lord Endicott turned his exasperation toward Colin, and I watched as his expression, astonishingly, became even more irritated. "I must say that I am extremely disappointed to find myself here."

"No more so than we are," Colin volleyed back in a way that could conceivably be construed as an apology for having dragged him out on whatever duty had soured his face so, though I knew, and I suspected His Lordship did too, that it was no sort of an apology at all.

"Nevertheless . . ." Lord Endicott continued, ". . . you can imagine my displeasure at having my sister telephone me this morning, a *Sunday morning,* to tell me that you were there snooping about Addie's room yet again when all you really need to do is get Scotland Yard to arrest that blasted piss pot Mr. Nettle. Really now, I thought when you and your father came to see me yesterday that we had an understanding. Does he have any idea what you've been on about?"

To my surprise Colin actually took a moment before he leaned back against the fireplace and allowed the worst sort of pinched smile to settle onto his face. "While my father and I are tremendously close, I do not tell him how to do his business and he does not tell me how to do mine."

"No," Lord Endicott practically snarled. "I would say that is evident."

"As a man of the law I should think you would demand justice to be brought to bear on your sister's death first and foremost. That you seem just as eager to see this case closed as your sister—damn the truth—makes the force of your determination seem both inexplicable and suspect."

I cringed, but not before Lord Endicott had heaved himself to his feet and howled, "How *dare* you! I will not be spoken to in such a manner by anyone, I don't care whose son you happen to be."

"My parentage has no bearing on the resolve I bring to my cases. So why don't you tell me why you are so resolute that Freddie Nettle be arrested for a murder that I am not convinced he even committed?"

Lord Endicott looked momentarily taken aback as he glared at Colin, his brow furrowing as he appeared to finally be considering at least some of what Colin was saying. "You said murder." His tone was sharp as a razor, his wariness almost palpable. "Then you do believe Addie was murdered?"

"I don't believe it. I am *certain* of it."

"Well, then . . ." Lord Endicott huffed as he lowered himself back onto the settee, ". . . then at least we agree on something."

With unaccountably fortunate timing I heard Mrs. Behmoth begin her trek back up the staircase, her tread slower and more methodical than usual, assuring me that she was bearing refreshments. All I hoped was that the pause might allow the two men to settled themselves a bit.

"Are ya still partial ta shortbread?" Mrs. Behmoth asked as she came in and set the tray onto the low table in front of me.

He managed to stir up something of a tepid grin. "Indeed I am. And I seem to remember you were quite skilled at making them."

"Still am," she answered, stepping back so that Colin could take his seat and do the honors. "'Cept I ain't got any for ya today. This here's me rhubarb cake. And I got a couple a raspberry-and-lemon tarts wot that woman next door makes. They'll suit ya if ya like that sort a thing."

"It all looks wonderful," he said with the first earnest smile I had seen since his arrival.

Mrs. Behmoth grinned back as she started for the landing. "Next time ya stop by ta give these two a bawlin' ya gotta let me know yer comin' and I'll make up a nice warm pan a shortbread."

Lord Endicott looked momentarily startled before he appeared to quickly collect his wits and, still retaining that amused grin, said, "I wouldn't wish it any other way."

"Right, then." Mrs. Behmoth chuckled as she started back down the stairs.

"Perhaps I have been a touch abrupt in my demeanor," His Lordship began once he had his tea and a great slab of rhubarb cake in his hands. "You simply cannot understand what it means to have Genie phoning me up on a Sunday in an absolute dither. It is a helluva thing. A helluva thing."

"No doubt." Colin ghosted a thin smirk. "You might want to reconsider the telephone. They could prove more trouble than they are worth."

"I think it's a bloody ripe invention. If I'd been able to phone you, I might be eating shortbread right now," he added, though he hardly seemed to be suffering the loss as he devoured his cake.

"I hope you understand that Mr. Pruitt and I are not trying to vex your sister. Our only aim is to ensure that the right person pays for Miss Adelaide's death. And while I realize that Mr. Nettle is the most obvious perpetrator, I simply cannot convince myself that he is, in fact, responsible. I must ask you to permit me to follow this through until we can reach the truth."

Lord Endicott sipped his tea a minute, his face revealing nothing, as it was hidden behind his teacup and those monstrous muttonchops. After another moment he set his cup onto the tray and rose to his feet, popping the last bit of rhubarb cake into his mouth before wiping it brusquely with his napkin. "It is Sunday," he announced incongruously. "I should like to see this affair settled by Tuesday at the latest. We are laying Addie to rest that afternoon, and I see no reason why the entire matter shouldn't be completed by then. Nothing would be more fitting then to have her murderer charged and behind bars the very day of her services." He tossed his napkin onto the tray. "Do we have an understanding?"

"I understand that you wish to set a clock on the truth," Colin stated so simply and smoothly that Lord Endicott did not appear to take the least offense at it.

"I suppose you could say I do, but then I am well aware that you have a sizable reputation, young man," he said, his eyes fixed on Colin and his tone unaccountably light. "I cannot begin to number the times I have heard your father crow your praises, so I do not think it unwarranted to expect the unexpected from you. Have I mistaken your renown for something less than what it is purported to be?"

Even before His Lordship finished his declaration and posed his needling conceit, I suddenly understood precisely why he was indeed such a longstanding member of Parliament and the diplomatic corps. Not only had he discerned the extent of Colin's formidable ego, but he had also ferreted out how best to incite it. So I was not in the least surprised when Colin nearly stumbled over his words to respond.

"You may certainly take solace in the fact that your beliefs are not ill-placed. I am indeed nearing the end of my investigation, and I should think that Tuesday morning will be as good a time as any to put this case to rights." I longed to shake my head and rub my brow, but it was what Colin said next that most astonished me. "Will you meet Mr. Pruitt and myself at Layton Manor midmorning on Tuesday, then? We shall need to bring Freddie

Nettle along, and it will do no good if your sister refuses him entry to the house."

Lord Endicott's face pinched as he stared back at Colin. "Will that really be necessary?"

"Imperative, I'm afraid."

"Very well, then. But I will caution you not to turn this into an exercise in self-aggrandizement. My family will not serve as fodder for your diversion."

Colin's eyebrows shot up even as I girded myself for his response. "My diversion? And whatever have I done to earn such a scornful rebuke?"

Lord Endicott's lips thinned. "I said yours was a sizable reputation. I did not say all of it was good." And having thusly spoken he turned on his heels and plodded down the stairs, and not a moment later I heard him call his farewell to Mrs. Behmoth before the door opened and slammed shut.

"That pompous old prig," Colin barked as he tossed the undrunk portion of his tea into the fire, causing it to flare up angrily.

"Tuesday morning . . ." I lamented. "Whatever made you agree to such a thing?"

"You heard him. How dare he speak to me like that. And to drag my father into it as well! And what is with those ridiculous muttonchops? Have you ever seen anything so pretentious in your life?!"

" *'E's a good man,*" Mrs. Behmoth hollered up from the bottom of the stairs.

"*He's a self-important bore!*"

I thought I heard her snicker, but after a moment she called out, "*You want yer dinner up there?*"

"*We don't have time for dinner tonight,*" he fired back. "Get your overcoat, Ethan. We've got work to do."

"*Suit yerself. But I ain't warmin' it up later,*" she warned as I heard her amble back to the kitchen.

I stood up and grabbed my overcoat from the hall rack.

"You'll tell me where we're going . . . ?" I prodded as we started down the stairs.

"You should know," he shot back, his voice thick with annoyance. "I got it out of your notes."

He pulled ahead, tackling the steps two at a time, and though I could not imagine what he was referring to, I decided to let it pass until we were well on our way.

CHAPTER 26

The vestry of St. Mary Islington stood on the northern boundary of the city and was divided into eight wards in 1855: Upper Holloway, Lower Holloway, Highbury, Thornhill, Barnsbury, St. Mary's, Canonbury, and St. Peter's. I knew all of this. I was as aware of the city's wards and parishes as anyone could be, having moved frequently in my youth, both before and after my parents' premature deaths. And yet I had missed something so fundamental and obvious that I was left to feel ashamed at my lack of diligence and wished we would reach our destination already so I could do something other than sit in the back of a cab like a fool.

"Do stop your sulking," Colin said when we finally entered Highbury ward, heading for the address I had copied out of Mrs. Denholm's files.

"I'm not sulking." But I sounded petulant even to myself.

"Isn't it enough that you may have found a key even though you didn't recognize it as such?"

"No, it most definitely is not."

"If you figured everything out for yourself, then what need would there be for me?"

I rolled my eyes. "You are not making me feel better," I groused. "Just leave it be and let us see what comes of this."

He reached over and gave my hand a quick squeeze. "*This will do*," he called out to the driver, banging on the roof of the carriage with a fist. "Let us walk the rest of the way and have a look around," he said to me. "Perhaps you can coax this driver into waiting for us?"

"Of course." It hardly took any coaxing when I only gave them half their fare. Such was a perk of Colin's reputation; they always knew we would be good for it.

Colin did not wait while I made arrangements with the driver, so I hurried to catch up to him as he strolled down Liverpool Road toward Paradise Park with a white linen tea towel filled with the baked goods Colin had coerced Mrs. Behmoth into giving us dangling from his right hand.

"I have such hopes," he said as I drew up alongside him.

"I know you do." And it occurred to me that if his supposition did not pan out as he expected, we would be in dire straits indeed.

"It is sound reasoning," he went on, and I suspected he was trying to convince himself as much as me. "Speaking strictly in terms of opportunity, the only people who had access to spirit a child into and out of that cupboard are Mr. Nettle and Miss Whit. Even that upstairs maid was off her post by then."

"Miss Britten."

He glanced at me. "What?"

"The upstairs maid . . . her name is Winifred Britten."

"How lovely for her. . . ." he answered in a way that assured me he did not care in the least. "And who are the two people with the likeliest access to the ladders in the stable?"

"Mr. McPherson and Mr. Fischer," I answered dutifully.

"Indeed. And we know from Mrs. Denholm's files that Mr. Fischer and Miss Whit were acquainted prior to her and Miss Bromley going to work for Adelaide Endicott."

"Yes, because of his accident. They met at the hospital."

"Which would appear to suggest some sort of prior relationship between Miss Whit and Mr. Fischer, and yet neither of them ever mentioned any such thing." He turned to me with a scowl. "I find that curious." He glanced down the row of brick buildings smeared with the same soot and grime that colored the evening air. "It does not sit well with me, and this evening we shall find out if there is good reason for it."

It all sounded conceivable in its pieces, but the whole of it failed to reveal the crux of what Colin had been calculating Mr. Nettle's innocence against: Whatever would their motive have been for conspiring against Miss Adelaide? I did not voice my concern, however, but quietly shadowed him up the steps to the door of the building where Vivian Whit and her family lived. He swung the door open and I followed him into the vestibule, a sparse but well-tended space that nevertheless showed its years with its yellowed paint and the blackened grout between the tiny grayish-white hexagonal tiles beneath our feet.

He started up to the second floor without bothering to check the mailboxes, turning back once to hiss, "I had rather hoped to find a group of small children running about."

"Children? Whatever for?"

He cast a frown in my direction as he rounded the top of the stairs and headed down the hallway as though he knew precisely where he was going, and not a second later came to a stop directly in front of a darkly varnished wood door that still managed to show its age in spite of its nearly blackened patina. The number 23 was marked at the center of the door, the 2 bent out of some thin metal and the 3 painted next to it in white paint.

Colin knocked on the door before tugging at the bottom of his vest and straightening his tie. "Stay on your toes," he whispered, though what I was keeping myself thusly prepared for he did not have time to explain before the door drew inward to reveal a tiny elderly woman with a swirl of gray curls on her head and a face as heavily lined as a map.

"We ain't int'rested in whatever it is yer sellin'," she announced, revealing a mouth with nary a tooth in it.

"'Oo is it, Mater?" a woman called from somewhere behind her.

The elderly woman turned her face and glanced back over her shoulder and called back, "A couple a natty rogues wot thinks we got money ta spend."

"Excuse me . . ." Colin started to say.

"Natty? They ain't solicitors, are they?" the woman asked, both concern and curiosity coloring her words.

Our aged assessor turned back to us. "Ya ain't solicitors, is ya?"

"Perish the thought. . . ." Colin answered.

Before he could explain who we were, the door was abruptly yanked open to reveal an ample woman of middle years with short, curly brown hair that was quite unruly in spite of the ribbon she had tied into it in an obvious effort to keep it out of her face. She had round, rosy cheeks that bloomed the instant her eyes settled on Colin, her lips stretching into a full, if tightly sealed, smile.

"Yer Colin Pendragon," she squealed, her eyes remaining fixed solely on Colin, as though I were a part of her dilapidated door. "Viv told us she met you, but I never dreamt you'd come ta our 'ouse." She quickly elbowed the older woman out of the way. "Come on, Mater, let 'em in, for 'eaven's sake."

She ushered us inside a small flat that, while it showed the same wear present in the rest of the building, was immaculate in its upkeep. The furnishings, a sofa and two mismatched chairs, were worn and sagged precipitously, but there wasn't a speck of dust to be found and everything looked precisely in its place. A razor-thin man of middle age looked like he had been dozing on the sofa as he hurriedly ran a hand through his thinning hair even as he struggled to re-button his shirt with his other. Two rangy-looking boys and a pretty young girl of fifteen or sixteen were each studying books in front of the fireplace, and a younger boy of probably about ten was leaning up against the man on the couch, but there were no young children here. No little girl who would fit inside of a cupboard.

"I'm Viv's mum," the woman explained as she urged us inside, introducing us first to her husband and then the four children, none of whom seemed even the slightest bit interested in

who we were or why we might be there. "And ya met me mum."
She gestured dismissively toward the elderly woman, who was
still standing by the front door. "Ya must forgive 'er manners,
but we don't get a lot a visitors."

"There is nothing to forgive her for," I spoke up, certain
Colin would not bother to do so. "At least she had the kindness
to refer to us as natty," I added with a chuckle, which only Mrs.
Whit appeared to find even remotely amusing.

"I'm sorry ta tell ya that Viv ain't 'ere jest now. She's off at her
new job. But I've got some water boilin' if ya'd like ta stay for
some tea."

I was positive Colin would beg off, so I thought I had misheard
when he answered, "If it wouldn't be too much trouble...."

"Trouble...?!" she scoffed as if Colin had said something
patently comical. "It would be a pleasure." She hurried into the
adjoining kitchen, which, from what I could see, looked far too
small for a family of this size. "I'm sorry I've not got any biscuits
ta give ya, but me boys eat everything I make, sometimes before
it's even finished." She gave a soft chuckle that sounded as weary
as it did mirthful.

"Then you have nothing to worry about," Colin said as he
held up the small linen bundle he'd been carrying, "for we have
brought some biscuits with us."

"Oh, Mr. Pendragon," Mrs. Whit gasped as she returned to
the sitting room carrying a battered tray with a large worn and
chipped teapot in the shape of a laying hen and four mismatched
cups and saucers beside it. "You do us an honor comin' to our
home. You needn't offer us a thing," she continued as she shooed
the children out of the room before setting the tray down.

"We insist," I answered with a smile, finally understanding
why Colin had been disheartened not to see a bevy of children
playing about in front of the flat.

The two of us delicately lowered ourselves onto the wilted
chairs while Mrs. Whit and her mum sat down on the sofa next
to Mr. Whit.

"You are both so very kind," Mrs. Whit enthused as she began to prepare the tea for all of us.

"I can see why your Vivian is such a genuine person," Colin said. "You must be very proud of her."

"Indeed we are," Mrs. Whit beamed, though she still managed to keep her lips sealed together. "Our Viv is the first person in the family who's ever finished school."

"Pardon?" Colin said with the innocence of one who has misheard, although I was quite certain he had not.

"Didn't ya know? Our best girl got 'erself inta the first nursin' class at . . ." She suddenly paused and turned to her husband. "What were the name a that school?"

"Tredegar 'ouse," he supplied, his voice soft and innocuous.

"That's right. I don't know why I can't remember that name. That's 'ow come she 'as ta work at night. She goes ta nursin' school most days."

"Is that right?" Colin gave a generous smile and nod of his head, glancing over to me long enough to make sure I'd caught the lie Vivian Whit had told her family. Though whether it added up to anything greater than an invention meant to save her dignity was impossible to say.

"Why'd ya come ta see 'er?" Mrs. Whit's mum suddenly asked.

"Mater!" Mrs. Whit gasped.

"It's a fair question," Colin responded, holding his smile as he accepted his tea from Mrs. Whit. "We wanted to ask her a few questions about her time working for Adelaide Endicott."

"Oh . . ." Mrs. Whit sagged slightly. ". . . That poor woman. A reg'lar tragedy that is."

"She were old," Mrs. Whit's mother piped up again. "Weren't no more of a tragedy than if it were me."

"*Mater!*"

Colin allowed a chuckle, though I managed to swallow mine. "I am sure you are not alone in your thinking, dear lady," he said, "but Mr. Pruitt and I believe that any murder, no matter the age of the victim, demands a just and swift conclusion."

"Murder?!" Mrs. Whit cringed. "I thought she . . ." Her face reddened as she struggled to find a suitable way to describe what it was she thought.

"That she was the cause of her own demise?" Colin supplied. "And you are hardly alone in that supposition, which explains why Scotland Yard has yet to make any arrests. Mr. Pruitt and I have been retained to ferret out the truth. And I believe the truth to be a much darker thing."

"Oh dear . . ." Mrs. Whit shook her head.

"Wot's 'e sayin'?" her mother asked.

"Quiet, Mater," she scolded again before turning back to Colin. "I just don't see 'ow our Viv could be any 'elp."

"She tended to Miss Endicott and was familiar with her state of mind," Colin explained. "And she was also there the night of Miss Endicott's death."

"Terrible, that." Mrs. Whit nodded. "Our Viv came 'ome later than usual that mornin'. Said the Yard 'ad been called ta speak ta everyone, but as ya say, they didn't arrest nobody. Didn't seem like there were no one to arrest," she added with a shrug to her husband.

"I presume she told you what had happened . . . ?"

"She told me and Mum." She hooked a thumb toward her mother, who was gumming one of the biscuits we had brought. "Me 'usband were at work already."

"And what exactly did she tell you?"

"The old lady jumped," Mrs. Whit's mum answered first, a mischievous glint in her eyes.

"Mater!" Mrs. Whit admonished for the third time. "I'll not tell ya again. Ya gotta mind yerself." She looked back at us with a flush in her cheeks, but did not correct what her mum had said. "We were sorry ta hear it, is all."

"Do you know how it was Vivian came by that job?"

"That cheeky beau a 'ers . . ." Mrs. Whit's mum answered first yet again before she fished the biscuit out of her tea where she had dropped it a moment before, popping it into her mouth.

"That is the last time, Mater. Ya got manners worse 'n the kids." Mrs. Whit handed a spoon to her mum, but the older woman only set it, unused, on her lap. "Viv's been seein' a young man fer about a year now. 'E got 'er the job tendin' ta Miss Endicott. Got it fer 'er and one a 'er friends."

"Miss Brownley . . . ?" Colin started to ask.

"Bromley," I corrected. "Philippa Bromley."

"Yeah, that's 'er . . . !" Mrs. Whit giggled behind one of her hands. "Ya really are a detective, ain't ya?"

"And your daughter's beau . . . ?" Colin pushed ahead. "Would that happen to be Mr. Fischer?"

"*Mr. Pendragon . . . !*" Mrs. Whit's eyes looked ready to burst from their sockets and even her benign husband appeared momentarily shocked. "Now how could ya possibly know that?"

"It is my business to know such things," he answered cryptically. "Do you see much of Mr. Fischer?"

" 'E's an arse," Mrs. Whit's mum grumbled.

And before Mrs. Whit could rebuke her, Colin held up a hand and allowed a sympathetic smile to cross his face. "You mustn't trouble yourself about your mother, Mrs. Whit. She is entitled to her opinions, and I see no reason to take the least offense in them."

Mrs. Whit gave something of a smile in return, but it was easy to see that hers was tinged with shame. "Yer a right thoughtful man, Mr. Pendragon."

"You don't like Mr. Fischer, then?" Colin said right to Mrs. Whit's mum.

" 'E's a right nob," she fired back. "Full a 'imself, that one. Flashin' a bit a jewelry wot is filled with diamonds and sayin' it were 'is mum's, and yet 'e ain't got shite jest like the rest a us. Stole it, is wot I think. All 'e does is boss Viv 'round like they was married." She turned to her daughter. "They ain't married, is they?"

"Mater." Mrs. Whit flushed, and I couldn't help feeling embarrassed for her. "You know they ain't married." She turned back to Colin. "Mr. Fischer is good ta us," she explained, though once again I noticed she did not contradict her mum's statement. " 'E brings us food from time ta time and gave me the loveliest little necklace fer Christmas last year."

" 'E knocks Viv about." Her mother spoke up as she reached for another biscuit. "Not that she don't deserve it, mind ya. Gotta mouth on 'er. . . ."

"*Please . . . !*" Mrs. Whit's tone was tinged with begging. "What you must think a us. . . ." she said to Colin and me.

"Mama . . ." a hesitant voice called from behind us, and I turned to see a girl of five or six in a nightshirt, rubbing her eyes as if she had been asleep.

"Emmy." Mrs. Whit jumped up and took the girl by the hand. "Say 'ullo ta these gentlemen. They're famous and come all this way ta talk ta yer oldest sister." The little girl shied behind her mother, and I could see that Mrs. Whit meant to whisk her back to bed.

"Biscuit?" Colin popped up with the linen in his hands, moving the few steps toward the door with delicate strides so as not to further unnerve the little girl. "Take it back to bed with you. They're ginger biscuits. Do you like ginger biscuits?"

The little girl's shy smile widened as she nodded her head even as she carefully avoided looking directly at him.

"Well, go on then, Emmy," Mrs. Whit prodded. "And you'd best say thank you fer it too." She glanced back at Colin. "This one loves 'er biscuits. Especially me butter and ginger."

Little Emmy darted an arm out and snatched a biscuit from the cloth, quickly muttering something in a high singsong voice that I took to be a stand-in for her thanks.

"You are entirely welcome," Colin answered, giving her a dazzling smile as he stood upright and turned back to the other adults in the room. "You have all been most gracious with your time and hospitality." He spun back to little Emmy and held out the remaining biscuits. "Why don't you take the rest of these and share them with your brothers and sisters tomorrow."

The girl giggled and clung to her mother's leg, but even so, still managed to reach out and take the proffered bakes. "What do ya say to the nice gentleman?!" her mother hissed.

The child gave another sort of mumbled response, which earned her a quick tousling of her hair by Colin as he folded and slipped the empty cloth into his coat pocket. It was easy to see that he was well pleased; I only hoped he had real cause to be.

A few minutes later as we climbed back into our waiting cab, I could not hold my tongue another second. "You seem awfully gratified considering all we've learned is that Vivian Whit's little sister likes ginger biscuits."

Colin glanced at me with a single raised eyebrow as he called up to our driver. "Regent's Park, if you please. Albany Street just up from Redhill."

"Ay . . ." the reply drifted back.

"We have the means now," Colin answered as he settled back in the seat. "That was critical."

"The means? By that I assume you are referring to the connection between Devlin Fischer and Vivian Whit?"

"That's part of it. But we also know that with Miss Whit working nights at Layton Manor, she also had the opportunity to do whatever she pleased against Miss Adelaide. With or without Freddie Nettle's knowledge. No one would have given a second thought to Miss Whit moving in and out of Miss Adelaide's room at any hour. She, more than anyone else, had every right to be there. And now we know she has a little sister with a preference for ginger biscuits who, if I am not mistaken, would fit nicely into a small cupboard. And I'd bet she wouldn't put up a fuss if her elder sister asked her to do it. Especially if she was rewarded with biscuits for her efforts."

"And what of Mr. Fischer?"

Colin curled his mouth as if he had tasted something unpleasant. "He has access to the ladders in the stables. Who's to say he couldn't easily have implemented a campaign against Miss Adelaide from outside, tossing pebbles and small stones against her window." He turned to me and his eyes were steely. "You felt the pits along the jamb. Not an easy target. But he needed to draw Miss Adelaide's eye outside so she could see the crying child . . . lost . . . calling out to her." His eyebrows knit. "Until that was no longer having the effect he and Miss Whit were after." He sank down into the seat, his expression darkening. "That's when they decided to bring the girl inside. . . ."

"And then what?" I could not stop myself from pressing him. "Mr. Fischer started putting the ladder up against the window so he could rap against it . . . ? Or throw ignited powders inside . . . ? Don't you think Miss Adelaide would have seen him?!"

"It was the middle of the night, Ethan. She was a woman in her eighties woken from sleep. Why are you being so belligerent?"

"I'm not trying to be, Colin. But I cannot figure out why. Why ever would Devlin Fischer or Vivian Whit want to do such a thing?"

Colin gave a feral growl as he shifted his gaze outside and silently watched the passing scene for a few minutes as gas streetlights gradually gave way to electric, marking our passage into the more gentrified area of Regent's Park. "You ask the one question I cannot answer," he muttered long after I'd thought he was going to.

He kept his eyes leveled on the brick flats passing by, one huddled against the next, all of them soot stained if better tended than the area of Highbury where we'd just been. People were still trundling about: men with spats and canes and woolen coats, and women in long, deeply hued overcoats, some with fur around their collars, all of them unaware of the conundrum that had cost a wealthy elderly woman her life.

"Where do ya want me ta stop?" the driver called down.

"This will do," Colin said.

We were halfway up Albany Street, perpendicular to Cumberland Terrace, which was the last place Charlotte Hutton had been seen. I paid the driver his full fare and sent him on his way, and then waited for Colin to say or do something. He was standing at the curb, his hands held behind his back as though he had all the time in the world and was content to merely watch the city clatter past. The humming streetlights cast opaque shadows against the settling fog that had begun to drift in with the night's chill. If his intention was to spot our young spy, Paul, or one of his chums, I couldn't see how he expected to be successful at it.

"Mr. P.?" a boy's voice chirped from behind me, and I turned to find a small lad of not more than nine staring at us.

"Yes . . . ?" Colin answered, his expression still grim.

"Yer ta falla me," the boy instructed, and without further explanation turned and scurried across Albany and up a nearby alley toward Cumberland.

We followed without comment, though as we entered the alley and the boy began to slow, I could not resist asking Colin, "You knew Paul would have someone looking out for us, didn't you?"

"He is a resourceful boy. I assumed he would be watching out for us as well as Mrs. Hutton. We are, after all, his employer of the moment."

The young lad scuttling along in front of us suddenly pulled up short and held a finger to his lips. Even in the darkness of the alley it was still evident that his face was as smudged with grime as the clothing he wore, from the oversized cap atop his head to the waist-length coat and breeches I found it impossible to discern the original color of. His shoes were scuffed and while they appeared black I decided they could just as easily have started out their life some shade of brown.

"Back 'ere," the boy said, pointing toward a metal bin overflowing with trash.

I felt my face cave with my displeasure, unsure exactly what he was pointing at, but Colin did not hesitate in the slightest, immediately following the boy behind the huge bin and disappearing from view. "Ethan," he called after a second, and it was the first moment I realized I had not followed him.

In spite of how desperately I wanted to pinch my nose, I refused to allow myself such a finicky luxury as I moved around behind the bin, the last of the fresh air clamped tightly in my lungs. To my surprise there was a rectangular gap in the brickwork at the bottom of the building that was covered by the bin. I assumed it had been constructed as a window originally, but the glass was long gone and there was no sign of a jamb anymore, either. The boy dropped to the ground and slid through the opening with the ease of a resident mouse, Colin squirming in right behind him.

I knelt down before realizing I would have to get on my hands and knees, and even then I was too tall to wriggle through. With an exasperated groan I dropped to my belly and pushed myself through the gap feet first, my feet dangling out over unknown space before my waist finally slid through and I was able to lever my legs downward and find purchase on a ladder.

"'At's got it," I heard the boy's encouragement from inside.

I found myself perched atop a ladder of indeterminate height, and it took my eyes a moment to adjust to the dim candlelight below me. The room was obviously a cellar, as there were wooden crates and boxes stacked along every wall all the way to the ceiling and many more were randomly placed throughout the space, though I suspected Paul and his boys had done a fair bit of rearranging themselves.

"Welcome ta me 'eadquarters," Paul said from the center of the room, a broad grin on his face. There was one other boy in the room besides the cap-wearing lad we had followed here, and Colin was already standing beside Paul, though his eyes were riveted to the floor just beyond.

"I am . . ." Colin started to say, continuing to stare at the floor as he began to walk in an arc behind where Paul stood, ". . . amazed."

I reached the bottom of what I realized was a makeshift ladder, old boards tied together with rope that had been plucked from somewhere else, and hoped we could exit via a proper staircase rather than the way we had entered. Colin, Paul, and the other two boys were all gathered just a short distance away, all glaring at different places on the floor behind where Paul was. As I came up to them, I finally realized why. Sketched across that part of the floor in chalk was a map of Cumberland Terrace, with both Albany Street on the far side and Outer Circle on the near. The map showed precisely where Cumberland Place dissected Cumberland Terrace, and how Cumberland Terrace Mews paralleled a short portion of Cumberland Terrace. Every building and every alleyway was denoted, though many of the buildings had large *X*'s running through them.

"I finished this place 'ere and 'ere," the third boy said to Paul, pointing at two buildings just up from Cumberland Place on Outer Circle. "Ain't neither of 'em got a lady wot lives by 'erself and matches the photograph ya got."

"Shite," Paul cursed as he knelt down and *X*'ed out the two buildings. "Then ya go and take these two next," he instructed, gesturing to three buildings farther down the street. "And don't take yer eyes off the street. She could be anywhere and I'll not 'ave us miss 'er 'cause you lot 'ave yer 'eads up yer arses."

The young boy who had ushered us here snickered, which earned him a glare from Paul.

"I ain't missin' nothin'," the first boy assured, a tall, skinny chap who looked slightly older than Paul and had black hair and a sharp nose. "You ain't got nothin' ta worry 'bout with me."

"Then get on," Paul commanded firmly, and the boy took off, scrambling up the flimsy ladder and out the gap in an instant. "You too, Charlie." Paul glanced over at our young guide. "You done good." He looked over at Colin. "Ya s'pose you can give Charlie 'ere a little somethin' for spottin' ya?"

Colin flicked his eyes to me and I reached into my pocket and pulled out a shilling. "Here you go," I said as I handed it over, and to my surprise the boy swept off his cap and gave an exuberant bow. The chivalrous gesture caught my fancy, making me quickly add, "And there will be more once we find this woman."

"I'll take care a the pay," Paul quickly reminded him. "Now git. And keep yer eyes open."

Little Charlie seated the cap back onto his head, still clutching the shilling in one hand, and was up and out of the cellar with even greater speed than the boy before him.

"You have quite an operation here," Colin remarked with what I took to be a hint of admiration. "How many lads do you have working for you?"

"Six. Seven if ya count Charlie. But 'e ain't much good 'cept fer watchin' the street. I 'ave 'im lookin' fer your lady and, a course, I 'ad 'im lookin' fer the two a you. Were ya waitin' on Albany?"

"We were."

"'At's where I told 'im ta be. Knew you'd prob'ly come there so's ya won't be seen on Cumberlan'." He looked over at me. "And I 'membered wot ya said about the lady bein' dangerous, so I keep me lads rotatin' around. Sometimes askin' questions at the buildin's and sometimes jest beggin' fer a bit a change while keepin' an eye out fer that woman." He half turned back toward the ladder and gestured. "I keep the picture ya gave me of 'er hangin' right by the ladder so's the blokes can see 'er face every time they go out." He pointed to his head. "I aim ta keep 'er face right fresh in their buggered little minds." He laughed, but it was easy to see that he was pleased with himself, and well he should be.

"So you and your crew have ruled out all of these places?" Colin asked with a note of concern in his voice as he stared down at the boxes that had already been *X*'ed out, which was clearly the majority of them.

"That we 'ave," Paul said with pride.

"Well, then . . ." Colin stepped back and managed a smile. "I can ask no more." He started back toward the flimsy ladder and my heart sank.

"Colin," I called to him. "Do you think we might leave up the main stairs?" I nodded toward the dilapidated steps that led into the building itself.

"Ya can't do that," Paul answered before Colin could. "Door's locked and we can't 'ave nobody knowin' we're down 'ere. I've already 'ad ta redraw me map once."

"There you have it," Colin said as he heaved himself up the hanging ladder and, while he was not as dexterous as the lads, he still managed to make a quick exit of it.

I pulled four crowns out of my pocket and handed them over to Paul. "Can you split these between your boys?"

His eyes went huge and round. "A course."

"There will be more when this is done," I assured him. "Thank you, Paul."

He gave a casual shrug, but I could also see a small smile tugging at his lips. This suited him, and it occurred to me that we would need to find something better for him once this case was over. How could we simply walk away and leave him to the streets again?

I made my way up the feeble ladder with far less grace and skill than I had seen everyone else use, so I was glad when I felt Colin's hand clamp onto my shoulder to help pull me back through the gap. "That's a muck of a place, isn't it?" I said as I got up and tried to brush my clothes off, a hopeless gesture at best.

"That boy is resourceful," Colin muttered.

We headed back out of the alley and turned down Albany in the direction of our flat. I assumed Colin was going to hail a cab but he did not, and I realized he meant to walk the nearly four miles back to Kensington. "They'll find her," I said after a minute.

"Eventually. Or at the very least they will find where she has been."

I was glad the darkness covered my disappointment so he could not see it. "At least you have your little girl in the Endicott case," I was quick to point out. "And we have the alliance between Vivian Whit and Devlin Fischer. . . ."

"Do we?" He kept his gaze steadily forward, his stride as determined as the dourness that I could feel descending upon the both of us. "Without a motive I'm not so sure we have anything. In fact, with every hour that passes I'm not sure we actually have anything on either case at all."

I opened my mouth to answer before realizing I didn't have the slightest notion how to respond. Not even an inkling. Because I too had begun to fear the very same thing. And so we walked the rest of the way to our flat, all four miles of it, in abject silence.

CHAPTER 27

I was running as fast as I could, my lungs heaving, my feet rocketing across the cobbled stones as if they were hot enough to burst into flames, my heart pounding with such desperation it seemed sure to portend its very cessation. No matter how hard I tried, I could not catch my breath, and the only sound I could hear was the hammering of my own heartbeat edging ever closer to its very pinnacle, and then I heard the voice—

"*Are ya bloody dead in there, fer shite sake?!*" it called out with exasperation just before another savage pounding pelted the door. "*Don't make me come in and drag yer sorry arse outta there. Neither one of us would like the sight a that!*"

"Yes . . ." I groaned at Mrs. Behmoth as I rolled onto my back to find myself alone in bed. "Where's Colin?"

"'E left over an 'our ago. Said ta leave ya be. But ya got a ruddy urchin downstairs and I can't get 'im ta bugger off."

"An urchin . . . ?" I repeated through my fog before suddenly pushing myself up into a sitting position as the pieces of my addled brain finally began to shift into place. "Bring him up to the parlor," I instructed as I threw the covers off and leapt to my feet, immediately seized by the inexorable cold. "And get a fire going. That young man is a guest in our home, and you will please bring us up some tea and biscuits and treat him as such." I hurried over to my armoire and began yanking out clothing, my jaw clenched against the chill. "Thank you, Mrs. Behmoth," I belatedly called out.

I heard her *harrumph* as she moved off, her methodical footfalls echoing as she headed back up the hallway.

I dunked my head into the sink and almost yelped when the icy water cascaded over my hair and neck. This was not how I liked to start my day, and I only hoped it was not indicative of whatever was going to come next. I was unsettled at finding Colin already gone and wondered if the boy being shown in might be bringing instructions from him. Something for me to do so that the two of us would not look the fools tomorrow morning when Colin assembled Eugenia Endicott's household and Lord Endicott himself.

With my vest still unbuttoned and my jacket thrown over an arm, I dashed out to the parlor to see who had been sent, while hoping that Mrs. Behmoth had already gotten the fire stoked and the tea upstairs. To my surprise it was the same young boy who had escorted Colin and me the evening before. He was dressed in the same grubby clothing with the same oversized cap yanked down on his head.

"Charlie . . ." I said with what I could muster of a smile so soon after waking, my fingers fumbling with the buttons on my vest even as my eyes registered the lack of a tea tray anywhere in sight. "I didn't expect to see you this morning," I confessed as I sidled up to the fireplace to warm myself until the tea could be brought up.

"Paul sent me ta fetch ya," he answered in one great explosion of words. "Says ya gotta come right away 'cause we think we found yer lady."

"What?!" I heard myself gasp, nearly toppling into the fireplace I swung around so fast. "Mrs. Hutton?! You think you've found Charlotte Hutton?"

The boy's eyes went huge and round as he stared back at me, looking as though he feared for his safety in the face of my immediate elation. "I don't 'member 'er name," he answered. "Paul jest said ta bring ya back." He glanced toward the hallway I had come from before looking back at me. "Is that other man 'ere too?"

"No. He's out right now, but we shall leave him a message and you can be certain he will join us just as quickly as he is able." I pulled my jacket on and snatched up a piece of paper and pen from the desk, scratching out a quick note for Colin.

"Wot's goin' on?" I heard Mrs. Behmoth say as I turned to find her standing in the doorway holding a tray of tea things with a generous supply of shortbread.

"This lad and I must leave at once." I waved Charlie to the landing and dropped my note onto the tray. "I'm sorry we haven't the time to drink the tea, but please see that Colin gets that the minute he comes in. It is most urgent."

Her face dissembled into a scowl. "Ya tell me ta drag all this shite upstairs and now yer jest gonna run out?"

"Try not to curse in front of the boy, Mrs. Behmoth. He has enough bad habits already. Go on now, Charlie." I prodded him down the steps before I grabbed the tray from her hands and whisked it back down the stairs, setting it on the hall stand by the front door. I grabbed a handful of shortbreads and pressed them on Charlie. "There now," I called up, trying to keep the sarcasm from my voice, "I should think we can all be happy now." Charlie beamed as the two of us hurried out the front door before Mrs. Behmoth could respond, and I was sure we were all the better for it.

"Can ya run?" Charlie asked as soon as we got outside, the overcast sky doing little to warm me.

"I can. I am not *that* old," I admonished. "However, there will be no need of it, as we shall take a cab." Once again the boy's eyes went wide and I realized he had likely never been inside a carriage.

We were on our way at once, and as I had suspected the ride proved to be entirely new to Charlie. He perched himself on the edge of the seat across from me and seized the grab bar to his right as we got under way, clutching it as though it was the difference between a sound ride and the possibility of his being pitched out onto the street. I cannot say I blamed him, as the cobbled streets and well-worn springs of the old buggy did make for a treacherous combination. Nevertheless, we arrived back at Albany and Redhill without incident and a far sight faster than if we had run.

I paid the driver and we were on our way across Cumberland Terrace before I recollected how I was going to need to scramble back down into Paul's burrow. I cursed myself for not changing into something older and worn as I followed Charlie into the same alley, and was instantly relieved to find Paul and two other youths of similar height and stature standing at the far end of the passageway as though they lived there and had no better place to be.

Paul turned on Charlie with a scowl, glancing behind me as he pushed himself off the wall and headed back into the shadows where Charlie and I were. "Where's Mr. P.?"

"Mr. Pendragon was called away on urgent business early this morning," I answered in a tone more clipped than I had meant it to be. How was it that I continuously let this lad make me feel superfluous? "I left a message for him to join us as quickly as possible," I added after pulling a deep breath. "He will be upset to not be here if what Charlie has said is true."

"Oh, it's true," Paul fired right back. "I seen 'er meself this mornin'. She came outta a buildin' we ain't gotten to yet, all covered up in 'er black cloak with the 'ood up, jest like ya said, and off she went."

Now it was my turn to frown. "Do you know where she went? Did you have anyone follow her?"

I thought Paul looked stung until a crooked smile cantilevered across his lips. "Well, a course I did. I 'ad two a me mates follow 'er. We'll know everythin' ya wanna know as soon as they come back."

"You really are the most clever lad."

"Well, ya don't pay me ta be a nob." He laughed, well pleased with himself, and deservedly so. "Now ya'd best 'urry up if ya wanna have a look at 'er rooms. I don't know when she's comin' back."

"A look at her rooms . . . ?!" I repeated, instantly warming to the idea. "That would be . . ." But I couldn't even think of the word before Paul turned to the two boys on his other side and rapidly barked out instructions on exactly where they were to post themselves on the street.

"And don't forget the signal," he called after them as they sprinted off in their disparate directions.

"Call a the balmy birds," one of them trilled back with a snort.

Paul ignored the boy as he looked back at Charlie, who was still standing with us. "And you, Charlie, you got the most important job of all. You gotta post yerself at the door to the buildin' with yer cap in yer 'and and stall that lady fer as long as ya can."

"Ya know I'm good fer it," Charlie enthused eagerly.

And as I stared at his smudged and resolute face, his eyes sparkling with determination, I thought he would surely be an able distraction for anyone with his cap in hand. But then Charlotte Hutton was not simply anyone. She seemed just as likely to ignore him as to give him even a moment's pause. "You must watch yourself with this woman," I warned him. "If she is not inclined to stop, then you must let her pass. You mustn't do anything foolish."

"Ya ain't gotta worry about Charlie," Paul insisted as he led me across the street, Charlie in our wake. "'E can take care of 'imself."

We reached a four-story building, all dingy brickwork and peeling black paint around the windows that I suspected had likely been a color when originally applied. There was nothing unique or compelling about the place, leaving it as inconspicuous as every other building on the street. Charlotte had chosen wisely, but then I found no surprise in that.

Paul pulled up short at the two steps that led to the building's entrance: a single door that was a muted gray, with two sidelights running along either side that were grimy enough to make their original purpose irrelevant. "Now you stay down 'ere and see what kind a coin you can fetch. And if that lady don't pay you no mind, then you jest be sure ta let out a good clear call after she passes you and we'll be fine."

Charlie's face scrunched up. "And ya don't want me ta call yer name, do ya?"

"Me *name*?!" Paul gave a hearty laugh. "That wouldn't tip 'er off ta somethin' goin' on now, would it?" He continued to laugh as he started up the steps, which suited me as I was beginning to feel too exposed on the street. "Gimme a birdcall, or a cricket, or somethin' that don't sound like yer chippie voice 'ollerin' out me name!"

Charlie snapped about immediately, cap in hand, looking ever so like the forlorn ragamuffin he was. It would do, I decided, but we would have to work quickly. This was bound to be our only chance. With any luck Colin would come along shortly and we could have her arrested within the hour. But in the meantime I meant to discover whatever I could about her, just in case, I told myself, which only set my stomach aflutter.

Paul pushed inside the building ahead of me, and as the door swung wide I could see along its edges that it had once been painted canary yellow. The inside of the building looked very much better. It had a small entry, but the slate tile floor looked buffed and polished, and the walls looked freshly painted and free of the markings usually found in these types of buildings. A staircase rose directly in front of us, its balustrade a warm cherry-colored wood, and the burgundy-patterned runner wrapped around those steps was plush and well maintained.

"The building is deceiving," I muttered.

"Wot?" Paul mumbled, but I could tell he was hardly paying any attention as he studied the postal boxes imbedded under the staircase. I did not bother to repeat myself as I went over to him. "Are any a these 'er name?" he asked.

There were twenty slots with paper nameplates attached to seventeen of them: last names, first initials. It came as no surprise that none of them said *Hutton, C.* I scanned a second time looking for the name she had used when she'd made her way to the Continent, Mary Ellen Witten, but that name was not there, either. She was far too clever for such a witless mistake.

"No. None of these are right." I swiped a hand through my hair and wondered if it wouldn't be best to just leave and find Colin. What did I expect to accomplish here anyway? And was it worth the chance that she might return and discover me here? "I think . . ." I started to say with a glance back toward the front door, and for no particular reason suddenly changed my mind. "Let's check the flats with no name tags on them."

Paul looked at me and gave an easy shrug. "If ya want."

I barely knew what I should want but nodded my head anyway. "It looks like one of these is on the third floor and the other two are on the fourth."

"Yep." Paul gave a snicker and was halfway up the first staircase before I could even reach the initial riser.

As I rounded the second- and then third-floor landings, I made sure to notice the proximity of the fire escape. While I did not wish to make use of it after my acrobatics at Freddie Nettle's boardinghouse, neither did I intend to be caught here.

"3B," Paul announced as though I couldn't read it for myself. "Why don't you push off some and let me knock on the door. If someone answers I can handle it better if you ain't standin' right behind me."

"All right. Good thought," I said, stepping back to the top of the landing so that I was out of sight if not out of hearing.

" *'Ello* . . ." I heard him call out, pounding a fist on the door. He was met with silence, and in another moment he did it again to the same result. I was about to come back around the corner when I heard a knob rattle and a door swing open.

"Who is it?" an elderly-sounding man's voice demanded.

"Pardon, sir," Paul answered in a tone as sweet and polite as I had ever heard him use. "I'm lookin' for the bloke wot lives over 'ere. Gotta message I been asked ta give 'im."

"Well, you ain't givin' nothin' to anybody over there. The place is empty. Nobody lives there. You don't suppose maybe that message is meant for me, do ya?"

"Are you Mr. Pruitt, sir?"

I rolled my eyes even as I strained to hear the conversation.

"Pruitt? That ain't me. Wasn't a Pruitt lived there before, neither. I think you're lost, boy. I hope they didn't pay ya good money to deliver that message. Now feck off."

The door clicked shut again, and after another minute Paul came strolling back around the corner. "Place is empty," he said.

"So I heard."

"I stuck me 'ead inside after the old bastard shut 'is door. People lie all the time, ya know." And having made his pronouncement he catapulted himself up to the top floor, me trundling along behind him, unease slithering deeper into my chest with each step I took.

"Are you sure we'll hear your mates' signal if one of them spots Mrs. Hutton?"

"A course." Paul chuckled as though I were being absurd. "Now wait 'ere," he ordered with a stiff arm pointed at my belly before he headed for the flats at the front of the building again, and I, dutifully, did as instructed.

Knocking followed just as before: once, twice, three times, but with no one poking their nose out to see what the fuss was about. Because I had almost been fooled on the floor below, this time I waited until I heard Paul quietly call out, "It's locked."

A chill coursed up my spine with the speed of light. Why would an empty flat be locked? I came around the corner and found Paul bent over the doorknob with a hairpin in his hand, already working the lock. "If you don't know how to do that . . ." I started to say just as a soft *click* echoed in the small space and Paul stood back with a satisfied smile. Of course he knew how to do this.

"Keep watch on the staircase," I bid him. "You will be our last assurance that we don't get caught."

"Ay," he answered smoothly. "And you keep yer ears out fer birds and crickets wot sound like me lads."

"Yes . . ." I repeated, but I was already lost to the sight of the room that was slowly coming into view as I pushed the door wider.

It was tidy with dusky mauve walls and contained a small settee and a single high-backed chair, both covered in the same soft floral pattern. There was a half table tucked into the space between the two street-facing windows and there was a newspaper flung there, along with something else. Leaving the door slightly ajar to be sure I would hear if Paul called to me, I crept over to the table as though I might disturb someone sleeping in the next room. That thought made me abruptly turn in my tracks and move in the direction of the darkened bedroom.

White sheers were covering the one window in the room, leaving it to look muted and gray, though I could still see clearly enough that no one was there. A tiny water closet stood just beyond and I could tell that it too was empty. What did catch my attention, however, was the trunk lying open on the bed and the carpetbag next to it. The trunk was obviously in the midst of being packed since clothing, shoes, purses, and hats had been carefully placed inside, leaving the armoire on the farthest wall with its doors thrown wide and nearly empty.

I moved into the room and peered into the trunk without touching anything—not even allowing myself to brush against the bed lest I should leave any sign whatsoever that someone had been here. Nevertheless, I needed to see if these things truly belonged to Charlotte Hutton. I had to be sure since the multiple pairs of slim, black, leather laced boots and colorful garments could belong to any woman. What did I know of Charlotte Hutton's taste or style? I had only spoken with her a handful of times, and on two of those occasions she had been completely encased in a hooded black cloak.

When the trunk offered nothing personal, nothing that would allow me any certainty, I rushed over to the gaping armoire only to find it as useless as the trunk. It was left with nothing more than personal garments folded neatly across its bottom that could, once again, belong to almost any woman.

I turned back to the carpetbag, knowing that within it lay my best chance at discerning the identity of its owner, and though it was closed, I was relieved to see that it was not clasped. Without a second's thought, I withdrew a pen from my pocket and stabbed it into the jaws of the case, delicately prying them open. Almost at once one side of the soft, pliant bag gave way, sagging over and making it look as if it had been kicked. I cursed as I jammed the pen back into my pocket before impatiently pulling the ruddy thing open with my hands.

There was a folded black shawl inside keeping me from being able to see anything beneath, leaving me forced to plunge my hand within where I felt the laces and silks of underthings as well as the soft cotton of what was surely a nightdress. I was about to pull my hand free so I could reset the bag when my fingers brushed against something hard.

With a harsh intake of breath, my heart ratcheting in my chest, I took a second to see whether I could catch the sound of a bird's trilling in a young boy's falsetto. The rhythmic clip of horses' hooves and the clatter of carriage wheels on the cobbles below rose to my ears along with the murmur of a sea of people going about their business, but there were no birds or crickets.

With my breath held tight in my chest, I carefully removed the shawl and placed it on the bed, and then dug out the garments with as much care as I could, given that my hands had grown unsteady even as my heart continued to rage in my ears. Leaving the remaining few items where they were I reached back to the bottom of the bag and brought out a small wooden box that jingled metallically as I lifted it free. Even before I could make my fingers release the tabs on the ends of the box, I knew what I was going to find.

A dozen bright, shiny .41-caliber bullets slid out into my hand with a *clang*. I stared at them as if I had never seen a bullet before, unable to stir myself for what felt like the longest time. They winked with newness, their gently curved points rising above the casing, the round disk of their primer at the opposite end pristine and just waiting to be struck. The room around me seemed to fall back and then abruptly rush in on me again, leaving me light-headed and struggling to control my breath.

A shout from the street below startled me and I did not move until I realized it was a man cursing at a passing driver. But it was enough to finally compel me to action. I tipped the bullets back into the box and carefully placed them at the bottom of the carpetbag just as I had found them. I straightened the garments I had left inside before adding the ones I had removed, making certain to place them just as I remembered seeing them. Calm and steady, I told myself, but I knew I was anything but.

The shawl was the last thing. With the precision of a diamond cutter, I settled it back on top, taking care to arrange the side of the carpetbag so that it no longer looked deflated. I coaxed the lip of the bag closed and stood back, trying to study it for a minute. It looked good, I told myself. It looked right. At least that's what I wanted to believe.

With a sudden sense of urgency I could not explain, I moved back to the sitting room where the pieces of the newspaper once again caught my eye. I listened for a moment, waiting to hear anything that might alert me to flee, but no such sound came. Nevertheless, I could hardly walk a straight line as I hurried to the table with a stealth much less convincing than it had initially been and allowed myself to peek out the window to the street below. Almost at once I noticed the very thing Colin had supposed when we had first been brought to this street. The building we'd been taken to was across the street and two buildings over. This window revealed a perfect view of the Gothic stone-and-brick structure with its looming gargoyles. It was an ideal place to keep watch on the building's comings and goings, and there was every reason to believe she could have seen us.

A soft, high trill struck my ears from some distance, followed by another one much closer by. It was the signal. I glanced down and found the newspaper opened to the train timetable with the schedule for the Channel ferries beneath. There could be no doubt now, Charlotte Hutton was about to make her move.

I let my eyes quickly drift around the room, checking to see whether there was anything else I should notice or, worse, anything I needed to rearrange, but there was nothing. It looked as it had when I'd come in, and I felt certain she would be unaware that I had been here. Even so, my heart thudded in my chest as I told myself to hurry, rushing out into the hall and pulling the door closed. "Paul . . ." I hissed, pleased to see that he was still at his post looking down the stairs. "We've got to get the door locked. She's on her way."

"Wot?" he said with surprise as he moved to me at once. "I didn't 'ear nothin' from me boys."

"Just a moment ago," I insisted. "There were two trills, one right after the other. You didn't hear them?"

Paul immediately bent over the lock and set to work on it. "I 'eard that," he said with a frustrating casualness. "That weren't me boys. That were birds. Me boys ain't that good." He stood up and rattled the doorknob before tossing me a wink. "After you."

I stared at him a second, unsure whether he was being serious or not, before deciding that I didn't care. The sooner I was out of this place the better. "We'll need to know where she's been," I said to him again as I hurried back down the stairs, trying to move as naturally as I could, though quite certain that I was failing terribly.

"I'll get ya word soon's they come back."

"Thank you," I muttered with mounting distraction as we finally reached the ground floor. I attempted to glance out the sidelights for any sign of Charlotte Hutton's long black cloak, but they were so fouled it was more an exercise in futility.

Paul gave a laugh. "It weren't me boys, I tell ya," he said as he pushed past me and on outside. And even though I realized he was right, I still could not coax my heartbeat down to a saunter until sometime thereafter.

CHAPTER 28

—⟶•⟵—

The cab had me back at our flat with remarkable haste. That I had given the man his tip up front had proven to make all the difference.

With Paul and his lads left in place, I had every faith that we would hear from them again shortly. With a bit of luck I hoped the two of us would be back at Cumberland Terrace before Charlotte Hutton herself returned from wherever she'd set off so early. But I was mistaken.

No sooner did I push the front door open than Mrs. Behmoth appeared from out of the kitchen with her hands on her hips. "You got 'im all foul when 'e came back and you weren't 'ere," she announced with the sort of accusation that seemed to suggest I had been out doing something illicit. "And now 'e's gone again and wantin' ya ta catch up ta 'im in one bloody 'urry."

"Did you tell him where I was? Did you give him the note I left with you?" And now it was my turn to sound accusatory.

"The note . . ." she repeated, her arms springing free of her waist as though they had suddenly become terrifically heavy. "I can't 'member every damn cursed thing ya go and toss on me tray like rubbish. And 'e were all wound up the minute 'e walked in the door anyway. Wouldn't listen ta nothin' once 'e saw you were gone."

"Did you at least tell him I'd left with Charlie?"

"Charlie . . . ?!" She glared at me like I had lost my senses. "And just 'ow the ruddy 'ell am I s'pposed ta know that little shite's name is Charlie?"

I groaned even though what I really wanted to do was shriek. "You didn't even mention that I was with the boy?" I snarled. "He'd have known where I'd gone if you had said that."

" 'E didn't ask 'oo ya left with. 'E were downright daft when ya weren't 'ere, and when 'e flew outta 'ere after about one blasted minute, 'e said ta tell ya ta get yer skinny arse over ta the Endicotts' place before ya take another breath."

"Colin said that?!"

She tossed off a dismissive shrug. "Somethin' like that."

I scowled at her. "But we're not due there until tomorrow."

"I'm jest tellin' ya wot 'e said," she insisted.

"Nice to see that you can remember *his* messages so well," I grumbled, and did not wait for the retort I knew would be coming but instead turned and slammed out of the flat.

The sky was becoming dappled and a breeze was picking up, and I knew it was only a matter of time before more rain swept in. I cursed myself for forgetting my umbrella but started off the porch anyway, unwilling to confront Mrs. Behmoth again.

" *'Ey . . . !* " She abruptly yanked the door open and yelled louder than was necessary. " 'Ere." She thrust my umbrella out. "It's gonna rain, ya know."

"Thank you."

"There was one more thing." She spoke again, and I thought there was a note of chagrin in her voice. " 'E wants ya ta pick up that Stuart woman wot does the magic on yer way. Said 'e didn't 'ave time ta bring 'er 'imself." She thrust out a folded piece of paper. "Wanted me ta give ya this." With no small measure of surprise I took the paper from her. "Try not ta be late fer supper. I'm makin' a leg a lamb and ya know 'ow 'e loves me leg a lamb."

And before I could think what to say she stepped back and swung the door shut.

I took a quick glance at the note, which was really nothing more than a short list of items, before hurrying down to the corner and flagging a cab. I called out the address to Lady Stuart's Lancaster Gate home, and the man managed to wend our way there with great haste. To my surprise, Lady Stuart was not only expecting my arrival but had already assembled the items Colin had requested, all of them neatly tucked into a leather satchel. She informed me that Colin had sent a lad over to forewarn of his need of her and the things he wished her to bring, and it only reconfirmed what I had always suspected, that Mrs. Behmoth could not be trusted.

"I assume you know what Mr. Pendragon has up his sleeve?" Lady Stuart said with a sly smile as we headed off for Layton Manor.

"I believe it is what's up *your* sleeve that is propelling this current trip to see Eugenia Endicott. But otherwise, no. I have been quite preoccupied on another matter entirely."

"Another case?"

"Quite. This one rather personal, I'm afraid. It stands as a smudge against Colin's reputation and, as I am sure you can imagine, he does not bear it at all well."

"Nor, I am sure, does he deserve it," she said. "He is quite something."

"He is determined."

"I just hope I will not disappoint him. Whatever it is that he wants from me, I hope I can provide it." She flushed ever so slightly and wrung her hands. "I must confess to a case of butterflies."

"You mustn't worry." I tried to sound consoling, though in truth I had no idea what he was going to expect from either of us. "Colin has a way of ensuring that things turn out as he intends them to, one way or another. I am sure today shall be no different."

"You know him well."

I found it was my turn to avoid a flush to my cheeks as I

quickly turned and stared out at the passing scenery. "I suppose I do," I allowed after a moment.

The remainder of our trip was borne in silence as it seemed neither of us was particularly compelled to engage in idle chatter. It suited me well enough, as it felt like we had broached a tenuous boundary that I had no desire to breach. I decided it best to let her fret over Colin's intentions for her while I indulged in my own ponderings about where he had gone so early this morning and what he found there that had provoked him into summoning Lady Stuart and me so abruptly.

It wasn't until we had started up the great macadam driveway to Layton Manor that Lady Stuart spoke again. "I do hope Miss Eugenia will allow me entry to the house. Miss Adelaide let me know that her sister would not tolerate such an occurrence."

"Colin would not send for you if he did not have faith in his ability to accomplish what he seeks. There would be no use in having you come all this way only to be relegated to the back of the cab with your trappings. I must assume . . ." I was about to say, *He must have a plan*, but as I flicked my eyes back out the window I realized at once what was going on. "Oh . . ." I heard myself say, sounding rather foolish even to my own ears, ". . . Lord Endicott is here."

His horseless carriage, standing at the summit of the drive, was the first I had seen up close. It looked very much like an open two-seat carriage waiting patiently for a pair of horses to whisk it away, though, noticeably, the carriage contained no shafts from which to harness the horse nor a carriage tree to drape the reins through. That there was a large metal box jutting out from under the seat and fully into the area where a trunk might have been stowed did not become obvious until I had crossed behind it.

"I cannot decide whether these things are a marvel or a horror," Lady Stuart said as we swept past the conveyance.

I could not help but smile. "There is no stopping progress. Besides, imagine how much cleaner our streets will be if they are no longer clogged with the leavings of a thousand horses."

She gave a small nod. "I suppose you have a point."

Before we could reach the portico the front doors swung wide and Mr. Galloway stepped out with the stiff and polish he inevitably displayed. "They are waiting for you in the rear parlor," he said in his concise way, giving no hint of the sort of mood we might be walking into. "I will announce you, Mr. Pruitt, and Miss . . ."

"Lady Dahlia Stuart," I answered for her as we moved inside. He did not give the slightest reaction to her name, which made me wonder whether he was unfamiliar with who she was or if his deportment was truly that impeccable. "Do you know if they are awaiting anyone else?"

"I would be remiss in trying to answer that question," he said at once, his tone flat and smooth and without so much as a modicum of reproach. "You will need to make such enquiries for yourself." He gave a clipped nod of his head, all propriety and decorum, and then swung open the doors to the parlor, ushering us inside with the proclamation of our names.

My gaze fell at once on Eugenia Endicott, whose eyes looked about to bulge from their sockets. Colin, it seemed, had apparently not mentioned to her that Lady Stuart would be accompanying me.

"Genie . . ." Lord Endicott was the first to speak up. "We will have an end to this today, and Mr. Pendragon tells me he needs this woman to do so. Therefore, I will ask your indulgence and we shall see if Mr. Pendragon is a man worthy of his reputation." He flicked his eyes back to Colin. "I will remind you, Mr. Pendragon, that I will not suffer folly. You will see to the end of this and you will do so with haste and concision."

"Rest assured that I seek nothing more than the proper resolution to a murder that ended the life of a woman whose very depth of compassion would prove her undoing."

"And just why is that horrid woman here?" Eugenia Endicott demanded, her eyes boring into Colin even as she referred to Lady Stuart.

"Because she holds a key to this case," Colin answered at once, his tone coming out soothing and calm. "And yet . . ." Colin continued, shifting his gaze to Lord Endicott, "I do not believe Lady Stuart will prove to be the worst of the people I must request your tolerance of today."

I had thought Colin would explain himself, clarify whomever else he had summoned here, but he did not immediately do so, which left me with little other choice than to look around at the people he *had* already assembled. Lady Stuart and I sat down on a sofa next to Colin, facing an accompanying table upon which tea had already been laid between two silver candelabras that were ablaze in spite of the house's electrical lighting. Across from us, on a sofa identical to the one we were on, Miss Eugenia and Lord Endicott were seated, neither looking particularly content to be there, though I noticed they were the only ones having tea. A fireplace, nearly large enough for an adult woman to walk into, was on our right, and directly to my left was an empty chair. The only one in the room.

On the right side of Lord Endicott was Miss Adelaide's night nurse, Vivian Whit, and against the back wall to Miss Whit's right was a settee upon which Mr. Galloway had been relegated alongside the housekeeper, Clarice Somerall, and the lovely cook, Lucy Barber. The groundsman, Denny McPherson, and the coachman, Devlin Fischer, were looking ever so awkward on yet another settee behind me that had a muslin sheet thrown upon it in an obvious effort to protect it from the scruffy clothing both men wore.

The room's last settee was a curious piece that was constructed to sit in a corner, bent like the letter *L*, with two cushions on either side of its crook. Miss Adelaide's day nurse, Philippa Bromley, was perched on one cushion with the serving maid, Emily Wilton, and the upstairs maid, Winifred Britten, sharing the other. Who then, I asked myself, was missing?

The certainty of it struck me at the same moment it appeared to do so for Eugenia Endicott. I watched her spine stiffen and her eyes bloom once more, and I knew she had landed on the same realization that had just occurred to me. But before she could expel her horror in words, a great knocking came from the front of the home and Mr. Galloway slipped back out with the stealth of a lifetime's practice.

"You cannot mean to suggest . . ." Eugenia Endicott spoke up as he left, her frantic eyes turning on her brother, who nevertheless managed to look wholly unaware of what was about to happen. "I cannot have this," she said emphatically. "You cannot allow this, Thomas. I will *not* have that man in my home."

Her poor brother blinked his eyes twice, casting his gaze from his sister to Colin, his thick gray muttonchops covering the bulk of his face to keep his obliviousness mostly shrouded. "Mr. Pendragon . . . ?" Lord Endicott said, and I could tell by the quizzical tone in his voice that he had no real idea exactly what he was asking.

"You must either trust me completely," Colin answered simply, "or do not trust me at all."

Because I knew Lord Endicott had no real notion what his sister was reacting to, he could do little more than nod his head brusquely at Colin before turning a resolute eye back to his sister. "There, you see?" he said with the sort of bluster I was convinced he must use in the parliamentary chambers quite frequently. "We must follow this thing through with Mr. Pendragon, Genie. It is the very least we . . ." But it was too late for him to say anything else as Mr. Galloway appeared back in the doorway with Freddie Nettle on his heels. "Oh good Christ . . ." Lord Endicott choked, for there was little else he could say now.

Colin leapt to his feet and circled around behind the sofa, barreling over to the door with his hand extended and a welcoming smile set on his face. "Mr. Nettle. You have done us a great service in consenting to be here this morning."

"Your note said it was urgent. That it would be an opportunity to clear my name. . . ." he responded with notable hesitation, the look on his face as filled with resolve as it was with trepidation.

"And so it shall be," Colin reassured as he gestured him to the empty chair to my left. "Do sit down. I require only that you set yourself to the truth as you know it to be, Mr. Nettle, no matter the consequences or how you fear it may portray you."

Freddie Nettle dropped his eyes to his lap as he took the proffered seat, well aware of exactly what Colin was referring to.

"Yes, sir," he answered, though there was far less of the determination that had just been there a moment ago.

"Then . . ." Colin turned with a slight nod to Miss Eugenia, ". . . with your consent, Miss Endicott . . ." But she gave him nothing, her broad, lined face remaining as stoic and unmoving as if he had said nothing at all. ". . . We will begin with the night of Miss Adelaide's murder."

He came back around the far sofa, walking behind Vivian Whit and the Endicotts before planting himself in front of the fireplace, the only spot in the room from which he could address all of us properly. His eyes drifted from one person to the next, and I found myself wondering whether he was taking the measure of everyone or testing some theory he had cooked up on his early-morning errand. Whichever the case, it was Lord Endicott who interrupted Colin's muted survey.

"You were saying, Mr. Pendragon . . . ?" And I could not help but notice the warning in his voice.

"Yes." Colin tossed a tight look at Lord Endicott and I could see that he did not mean to be hurried. "I would see a show of hands for those of you who were here that night," he requested.

I heard Miss Eugenia *tsk* her disapproval and yet she raised her hand for the briefest instant, though she did not hold it aloft. Vivian Whit, Mr. Galloway, Clarice Somerall, and Freddie Nettle all held their arms up to varying degrees, and when I glanced behind myself I could see that only the serving maid, Emily Wilton, did as well.

"Is it your habit to stay the night?" Colin asked her, obviously struck, as I was, to learn that she would be required to do so.

"It was at my request." Miss Eugenia spoke up before Emily Wilton could. "I had kept her late into the evening because of an afternoon tea that Addie and I had hosted, and I did not want her walking home on her own at the dead of night. With Mr. Fischer having been released hours before, there was no one else who could drive her." Her tone was clipped and irritated, so I was not surprised when she swiftly turned on her brother and added,

"Really, Thomas, must I explain myself as though I am guilty of having done something wrong?"

Lord Endicott glanced at Colin. "Mr. Pendragon . . . ?"

Colin stopped him with an upturned palm. "You mustn't persist in interrupting me after every question. We have an agreement and I will abide by it if you and your sister will. Otherwise Mr. Pruitt and I will leave now and make a full report to the Yard exonerating Mr. Nettle here."

"Your cheek is impertinent," Eugenia Endicott fired back.

"We are talking about your sister's murder," Colin reminded her harshly. "I do not see how any greater offense can be taken or given." The frown on her face hardened, but she said nothing further as Colin turned his attentions away from her. "Can you tell me please, Nurse Bromley, how were Miss Adelaide's spirits that particular day?"

"No different than they had been lately."

"Meaning . . . ?"

I could sense Philippa Bromley hesitating from behind me and stole a peek over my left shoulder in time to see her eyes dart from Vivian Whit to Miss Eugenia. "I believe she had been suffering from bouts of hysteria over the last six months or so and the spells were getting worse."

"This is outrageous," Miss Eugenia started up again. "This woman is not a physician and has no right speaking of such things. Come now, Thomas, I must insist you stop this travesty this instant."

I was certain Colin had reached the end of the tether Lord Endicott was willing to give him, so I was surprised when the man reached over and patted the back of his sister's hand in an almost conciliatory way. "The young lady is speaking the truth. She is a nurse, Genie, and she knows well what she witnessed. If this helps us determine who harmed our Addie, then we will be thankful for it. Let us give Mr. Pendragon his moment and see what comes of it."

"Thank you," Colin said swiftly, though his voice sounded neither grateful nor contented. "Tell us, Miss Bromley, what sorts of spells had you been witness to?"

"Me . . . ?!" Her large round eyes looked ready to pop from her head as if Colin had accused her of some impropriety herself. "I never saw anything of the sort. What she suffered happened to her in the evenings or at night. I would hear about it the next day. She would tell me what she had seen or heard and I was left to try and calm her down. If she was agitated enough I was authorized to give her a tincture of laudanum."

"And what sorts of things did she tell you that she saw and heard?"

For the third time the young lady's gaze roamed around the room before she seemed willing to settle on her answer. "It was always the same thing," she said, her voice dropping to a delicate timbre and making it clear that the memory of it still caused her discomfort. "She said it was a little girl who was lost and crying. That she was looking for someone. I don't know who she was supposed to be. I never asked. It wasn't my place."

"Not your place," Eugenia Endicott repeated with a sneer. "Nothing that concerns this family is the business of any one of you. This is utterly unseemly. And it is *that* charlatan who is to blame for the ravages that cost my poor sister her faculties." Her arm shot out with one bony finger pointing squarely at Lady Stuart.

"Ah . . ." Colin's gaze followed that finger just as it was meant to do, yet the whisper of a smile on his face belied the outrage that Miss Eugenia had intended to impart. "And so, Lady Stuart, your reputation has been called into question. What say you in return?"

Since she was sitting beside me I did not want to simply turn and stare, though the rest of the room's occupants were free to do so, yet I could sense a wisp of amusement in her posture and took note that she seemed neither surprised nor taken aback by Colin's question. "It would seem I must tolerate the injury to my reputation for I fear I can take no umbrage. I mean only to soothe those whose lives are suffering from some manner of discontent and, while I will not deny that mine is a profession rife with fraud and deceit, I seek to practice neither."

"Then what of Miss Adelaide?" Colin pushed ahead, clearly

determined not to give Miss Eugenia any further opportunity to press her contention. "We all know that she came to see you regularly. What sort of discontent did you seek to alleviate for her?"

"*Thomas!*" Miss Eugenia demanded almost before Colin's question was fully formed. "You cannot mean to allow Addie's privacy to be disgorged in so public and humiliating a way. In front of the staff . . ."

"If I may . . . ?" Colin turned to Lord Endicott before he could respond. "I should like to remind you that Mr. Nettle here stands accused by you, Miss Eugenia, of your sister's murder. And while that has yet to be proven, it is the people in this room, the household staff, who must also stand accused. For there is no one else who had the means to harm Miss Adelaide that last night, save for the people in this room. So I should think it their right to hear the fragments that led one of them to hound Miss Adelaide to her death."

Lord Endicott remained quiet for a moment before reaching over and pressing a hand onto his sister's tightly clasped fingers again. "Let it be, Genie. I suspect everyone here already knows the fears that drove our Addie. Let us have this be done with."

"Lady Stuart . . ." Colin turned back to her with nary a breath taken at the end of His Lordship's decree. "Tell us what you spoke with Miss Adelaide about. What brought her to your parlor?"

Lady Stuart shifted slightly on the sofa, and I felt her body stiffen the tiniest bit, though it seemed out of sorrow or regret rather than any sort of fear. "She was a kind and sensitive woman who was much aggrieved by an event that happened when she was herself young. She spoke to me of it often, and I sought only to convince her that she had no reason to carry such guilt. That she was free of blame."

"And did this incident involve a young girl?"

"Not as such, but that seemed how it manifested for Miss Adelaide."

"Curious . . ." Colin said as his eyes drifted across the room, noting, I was certain, who was looking back at him and who was not. "Can you explain yourself?"

Lady Stuart released a silent sigh and I felt her body sag with the pressure of whatever words she was struggling to say. "There was a young unwed woman who worked for the Endicott family and became with child when Miss Adelaide was herself barely in her adult years. It threatened to cause a blight on the Endicott name, so both the woman and her unborn child were sent away, but not before the woman suffered a terrible beating that Miss Adelaide herself felt responsible for."

"However so?" Colin asked, and I noticed in the faces I could see that not one of the people was looking at Lady Stuart. All eyes seemed haphazardly arrayed about the room as though to make contact with another person might somehow sully the lot of them.

"She did not stop the beating against the young woman, and it cost the poor thing her life at the birth of her baby. A daughter. And it was that daughter who Miss Adelaide believed was seeking vengeance against her." Lady Stuart hesitated for a moment, and to my surprise Colin did not fill the silence with another peppered question, and that was when I realized that Lady Stuart knew more. "Miss Adelaide had tried to keep track of the little girl. . . ."

"She what . . . ?!" Lord Endicott sputtered, flicking a quick gaze at his sister as though trying to gauge whether she knew this to be true or not.

"That is preposterous," Eugenia Endicott howled, her scowl filled with malice and accusation. "My sister would never have done any such thing. It is simply too foolish to believe." Yet again she swung round on her brother and I almost felt sorry for him. "Really now, I insist you call an end to this."

"Margaret," Lady Stuart said in a voice so soft I almost did not catch it myself.

"What?" Eugenia Endicott turned her glare on Lady Stuart. "What did you say?"

"The child's name was Margaret Helen Hardiston," Lady Stuart answered. "She told me she had learned that much after the baby's birth but had been unable to find her thereafter and feared she had not lived past childhood."

Eugenia Endicott bolted to her feet and looked ready to strike

Lady Stuart. I thought that I should do something, say something, but found myself at a loss for words, and when I allowed a quick glance at Colin I saw that he had not even moved from his leisurely position in front of the fireplace.

"I suspect this is all nothing more than your mystical contrivance to lure my sister in," Eugenia Endicott sneered viciously. "To make her fear your trickery while you . . . what? . . . stole her inheritance? Forced her to pay to tame the nonsense you had created? I will not have these people in my home another minute, Thomas." She stared down at her brother. "You clear this lot out or I will."

"Now, now . . ." Colin started to say.

"No." Lord Endicott pushed himself off the sofa looking wearied and resigned. "Eugenia is right, Mr. Pendragon. You are sliding down a slope without a foothold, and I will not subject my sister or myself to it a moment longer. You promised to reveal our sister's killer and you have failed to do so. I can only presume you are grasping at straws, sir, and it is an affront." He started to walk around the sofa, though where he was headed or what he meant to do I could not say, but Colin stopped him, moving right up to the older man before he could make his way to either of the hall doors.

"You are mistaken, sir," Colin answered him back, staring directly into His Lordship's eyes in a fashion that broached insult. "I know precisely the two people responsible for driving your sister to her death. Or, if you wish to be more exacting, the five people. But I shall not proceed unless you and your sister sit back down and allow me to finish this my way, which is something I should think Miss Adelaide deserves." Colin took a step back and tipped the slightest shrug of one shoulder.

"Five people . . . ?!" Lord Endicott paled and stumbled back a step.

"How dare you," his sister snarled. "Mr. Nettle—"

"Is an innocent man," Colin cut her off. "I am quite tired of repeating that to you, madam, so if you will allow me, I shall explain how I know that to be true."

Lord Endicott shook his head as if he was about to refuse, but then fell back onto the sofa without a word, though I could see that he was quite unsettled. This was clearly true for his sister, who continued to glare at Colin with something edging toward revulsion before suddenly tossing her brother a look that I could not decipher, though it was far from warm. After a moment she too lowered herself back onto the sofa, her spine and demeanor remaining stiff and unyielding.

"Lady Stuart . . ." Colin stepped back to the fireplace and called over to her. "Did you tell Miss Adelaide the name of the child?"

"No. It was she who told it to me."

"Would you deny that there is chicanery used in your line of work?"

She allowed the ghost of a smile as she shook her head. "I cannot. As I said before, mine is a field filled with such wiles."

"Such as . . . ?" he prodded.

"Small scraps of wood bound to the knees of the medium to simulate knocking by the ethereal, although the Fox sisters have admitted to achieving this ruse by cracking the knuckles of their toes. Photographs from magazines and dolls have been hung in darkly lit rooms to symbolize a loved one, manipulated on a thin string by the medium from behind a gauze or other such fabric. And the supposedly paranormal substance left by the deceased, ectoplasm, is usually nothing more than butter, petroleum jelly, and cheesecloth." She heaved a sigh that assured me she found the whole of it embarrassing. "Tables can be manipulated, appearing to move or rise by simple mechanics placed at the medium's feet like the pedals on a piano—"

"And did you employ any of these deceits on Miss Adelaide?" Colin interrupted her.

"Never. I do not perform séances. I do not purport to be able to raise the dead to the earthly plane."

"Then what is it, exactly, that you do?"

Lady Stuart lifted her chin and her lovely face caught the electric lighting just so, accentuating both the warm-honey tone of her skin and the angular beauty of her Romanian features. And along with those attributes I could see a wellspring of honor and

pride. "I listen. People come to me for a reason. They have suffered a loss or grievance that they cannot rectify themselves, and
I try to give them the peace they seek by helping them unearth
the answers they have carried within them all along."

"You make it all sound so very noble," Colin remarked with
an arch of his brow. "As if you should be permitted to hang some
sort of license outside your door."

Lady Stuart gave a soft laugh that sounded almost jarring
in the harsh quiet of the room. "Would that it should be so. But
there is one deception I do often employ to ensure my clients
that I speak with authority on their travails."

"And what would that be?" Colin asked with the assurance of
one who knows precisely what is coming next.

Lady Stuart leaned down to the satchel she had brought and
pulled out a small bottle of oil and a little canister. "Phosphorous," she said. She unstoppered the bottle and sluiced some of
the oil onto the fingers of her left hand. "When used at just the
right time, as I profess to consult with their loved one or speak
about things I should have no right to know, it gives me credibil-
ity." And without a moment's hesitation she plunged her hand
into one of the candles and lit it up with flames of brightly colored hues that leapt over a foot in height. She moved her fiery
hand back in front of herself, her fingers clutched tightly together and pointed skyward, and then just as suddenly snuffed
out the flame with a cloth she pulled from the satchel with her
other hand. "The oil burns off long before the skin begins to
singe," she explained to the astonished faces of everyone around
her, including me.

"And the powder . . . ?" Colin prodded.

"I rarely use it," she said as she opened the little canister and
dipped one of the Endicotts' teaspoons into it. "It won't hurt the
spoon," she assured Eugenia Endicott, but the older woman had
paled slightly and looked unable to say anything. Lady Stuart
drew the spoon up to the same candle and tilted it ever so slightly.
As the contents began sputtering like miniature fireworks she
swung her arm wide, leaving a burning rainbow of color raining

through the air like an otherworldly trail. "It is much more effective with a greater volume," she added unnecessarily.

"And that, Mr. Nettle," Colin announced with noticeable satisfaction, "is what you witnessed on the night you raced into Adelaide Endicott's room."

"Oh . . . !" he murmured, and I could see that his face had gone a ghastly shade of white and his shoulders had crept up as though he was chilled or trying to sink into himself.

"You were no more out of your senses than Adelaide Endicott was," Colin continued. "Instead you were both the victims of parlor tricks, the tools of which came from the pantry of Lady Stuart."

"I did not know," Lady Stuart spoke up before Colin could continue, staring at Eugenia Endicott with a shame I knew she did not deserve. "You must believe me when I tell you that I had no idea."

Whether Miss Eugenia gave even the whisper of credence to what Lady Stuart was saying I could not tell. She had turned her gaze to her brother, and if I thought she had looked poorly a moment ago, she appeared even more so now. It occurred to me that she had almost assuredly been unkind to her sister, refusing her access to Lady Stuart in their own home and dismissing Miss Adelaide's haunted visions and disembodied voices as though they were the ravings of a lunatic. But here, now, for the first time, she was seeing that there was something sinister at work against her sister. That someone had indeed worked very hard to unhinge the poor woman's mind.

"How were these things brought to Layton Manor?" Lord Endicott asked, maintaining his decorum in spite of the fact that it was obvious he too had also lost much of his bluster.

"Ah!" Colin held one finger up as he paced around behind me and Lady Stuart. "Other than Miss Adelaide, the only other person who was a regular visitor to Lady Stuart's home was Mr. Nettle. We know that he was invited in and spent his time in the kitchen with Lady Stuart's houseman in the event that he was needed by Miss Adelaide."

"Then it seems we always come back to Mr. Nettle," Lord Endicott stated, but with far less determination than he had shown before Lady Stuart's demonstration.

"And so it would seem you are right." Colin nodded once, his blue eyes hard and dark. "But that would be to ignore both the key element of motive, Your Lordship, and the fact that there was also someone else who was regularly at Lady Stuart's home." He turned away from me and Lady Stuart and settled his eyes on Mr. McPherson and Mr. Fischer. "You drove Miss Adelaide and Mr. Nettle, did you not, Mr. Fischer?"

Mr. Fischer looked momentarily startled before a benign smile slowly edged onto his face. "Well, a course I did. But I don't get invited into houses like Mr. Nettle. I'm left ta tend ta the simpler creatures."

"Come, come, Mr. Fischer," Colin chided. "Did you never once need to avail yourself of the WC or perhaps request a touch of water to clear our insipid fog from your throat?"

"Such a thing would hardly be proper," he answered, his smile replaced with a staunch sort of distaste. "There are standards. . . ."

Colin turned back to Lady Stuart, blasting right over Mr. Fischer. "Would you mind if we ring up your Mr. Evers to see whether he might corroborate Mr. Fischer's contention that he never set foot inside your home?"

Lady Stuart hesitated no more than an instant, which was remarkable given that she had no telephone to ring, before answering, "Most definitely. I am certain he will be available. . . ."

"I never said I didn't go inside a time or two," Mr. Fischer interrupted, his spine stiff and his expression wary. "I prob'ly did. But I can hardly be accused of pilfering the lady's tonics."

"I have made no such accusation," Colin responded offhandedly. "I sought only to reveal opportunity. You mustn't perceive anything further," he hastened to add, though I well knew that was precisely what he wished Mr. Fischer to do. "Which brings us back to the night of Miss Adelaide's murder when Mr. Nettle admits to having seen what he ascribed as a spectral vision but which, in reality, we now know was phosphorus powder that had been set afire and blown in through the window."

"How could you know such a thing?" Lord Endicott interrupted with evident confusion.

"There were traces of unburnt powder on the floor and wall just beneath the window Miss Adelaide fell from. Nothing the least bit spectral about it and yet, as you have all seen, highly effective just the same. Beyond that, there are two worn divots in the sill just outside that same window, which precisely fit the vertical stiles of the ladder that Mr. McPherson keeps in the stable. Mr. McPherson helped me discover that." He glanced back at Mr. McPherson, who suddenly looked as uneasy as Mr. Fischer seated beside him.

"I don't understand. . . ." the older man said, his sun-mottled face knit with concern as he glanced about the room. "I didn't have nothin' ta do with Miss Adelaide . . ."

Colin quickly shook his head. "Opportunity, Mr. McPherson. I am only talking about opportunity here. And the only other person with access to the stable and all of its contents is, once again, our notable friend Mr. Fischer."

"Now just a ruddy minute . . ." Mr. Fischer blurted as he began to stand up before abruptly seeming to think better of it and sinking back into his seat. "Plenty of people have access to the stable. We don't lock it. It's never locked. Ain't that right, Denny?" He looked to Mr. McPherson for validation.

"You miss the point," Colin spoke up before Mr. McPherson could answer. "How many people have access to the stable *and* the pantry at Lady Stuart's home?"

Mr. Fischer sputtered for only an instant before flinging an arm out and pointing an accusatory finger. "Mr. Nettle!" he protested. "He had more opportunity than me. Why are you protectin' him?"

"He was in the room at the time of Miss Adelaide's death. He could not also have been standing at the top of a ladder blowing burning phosphorus powder in through the window." Colin turned his back on Mr. Fischer and strode past Mr. Nettle. "Why don't you tell us what else you witnessed that night?"

"There was a child's voice. . . ." Mr. Nettle's own voice was soft and hesitant, and I could sense his embarrassment as he started to confess the tale. "She was crying and calling out, and I thought surely I must be going mad. . . ."

Colin let the man's words hang in the air for a minute as he slowly made his way back to the fireplace, crossing behind Lord Endicott and his sister. "And so we return to the ghostly young girl. Is there anyone here who would deny any knowledge of the fact that Miss Adelaide had complained for some time of being plagued by this apparition?"

I let my gaze slide around the room before settling on Lord Endicott, the only person with an expression of confusion on his face.

"What is this . . . ?" He turned to his sister. "Why didn't I know about this?"

Eugenia Endicott looked pained as she avoided meeting her brother's eyes. "I assumed it a reflection of her increasingly addled state," she answered quietly. "I did not know that someone . . ." She did not bother to finish her sentence, and I felt her regret like it was a living thing.

"And I will tell you that the little girl who stalked Miss Adelaide is as real as the phosphorous powder and the divots in the windowsill," Colin said flatly. "Can you imagine who she is, Miss Bromley?" He shifted his eyes toward Miss Adelaide's day nurse sitting in the far corner of the room.

"Me?!" She looked aghast. "Why ever would you think I have any knowledge of such a thing?"

"Because, Miss Bromley, I do not believe you to be a frivolous woman."

And then she did exactly what I knew Colin had expected her to do: She flicked her gaze for the briefest instant to her former coworker, Vivian Whit, before snapping her eyes back to Colin. "I don't know what you mean."

"Now, Miss Bromley," Colin responded in a tone that was edged with condescension. "We are talking about access. Who might have access to such a child . . . ?" Miss Bromley did not answer, and her eyes quickly drifted to the floor by her feet. "Let me be more specific," Colin continued more ardently. "Who amongst our collective members here knows of such a child and would have had the access to bring her into Miss Adelaide's room the night of her death, secreting the child in a cubby near the window?"

"What?!" Miss Eugenia gasped. But she said nothing more and the room fell quiet, only the sound of the crackling fire filling in the awkward silence.

Colin slid his eyes over to Vivian Whit. "Perhaps you can assist Miss Bromley with her memory. . . ." he said.

Miss Whit frowned deeply with a look that seemed somehow heedless and disjointed. "Well, Mr. Nettle—" she began after a minute's consideration.

"Mr. Nettle," Colin cut her off, repeating his name with a quick, tight glance at the young man. "He did most certainly have access to bring a child into the room that night, but then so did you," he added as though it was no more than a passing idea. "Yet Mr. Nettle has no association with a child of any sort. And that"—he pursed his lips and tapped his chin with a finger as if deep in consideration—"that is where you and Mr. Nettle diverge. You have a young sister, do you not, Miss Whit?"

"What . . . ?" She sucked in a sudden breath as if Colin had just asked something confounding.

"A sister," Colin repeated with immense patience. "You have a young sister who is fond of ginger biscuits and doing her older sibling's bidding. You hid her in that cubby the night of Miss Adelaide's death and at a signal from you had her start crying and calling out. Mr. Nettle heard her but in all the confusion could not discern where the voice was coming from."

"That's absurd," she snapped. "Is Mr. Nettle paying you to concoct such things to protect him?"

Colin laughed, the sound coming out dry and mirthless. "Mr. Nettle can ill afford a decent place to live. Do you really believe my services can be so cheaply gained? And to what end?"

She looked around the room, her eyes imploring everyone but me and Lady Stuart. "It isn't true," she said emphatically. "It's simply not true!"

"Very well." Colin looked back at the other nurse, whose shoulders were now hunched toward the ground in concert with her eyes. "Then can you tell me of anyone else who had the sort of access that your friend here had?"

Miss Bromley did not utter a sound, but her head shifted subtly from side to side just once.

"You see." Colin flashed a tight smile. "It is all about access, Miss Whit," he repeated again to the former night nurse.

"But why . . . ?" Lord Endicott spoke up with a note of something in his voice that I could not place.

"Ah . . ." Colin stepped away from the fireplace again, passing behind Lord Endicott and his sister. "Do you have an answer for His Lordship, Miss Whit, or will you insist on continuing your charade?"

Colin was not far from Miss Whit as he posed his question, and while she did not respond to him neither did she meet his gaze. She looked unable to do so as she kept staring toward the fireplace with an almost desperate raptness that made her appear very much on the verge of shattering.

"Very well," Colin sighed, and I did not miss the tinge of disappointment in his response even though I could not imagine he had really supposed she might so easily abandon her resolve. "Perhaps you yourself do not know the answer. We shall know in due time." He let his voice fall silent, his unsubstantiated claim hanging in the air like some scurrilous indictment.

"Mr. Pendragon . . ." Lord Endicott warned, his lips pressed so thin they looked about to disappear. His great bushy eyebrows had collapsed forward, making a singular line across his forehead that accentuated his displeasure.

Colin held a hand up toward him without bothering to shift his gaze, which, I noticed, had shifted back to Philippa Bromley. "Your honesty is appreciated, Miss Bromley, but I must impose upon you for one more answer."

As before, she neither looked at Colin nor anyone else in the room, keeping her eyes locked on her fingers, which she had begun to fidget as though they were sore and troublesome.

"How is it that you and Miss Whit came to work for the Endicott sisters?"

"We were both studying nursing at Royal London and working part-time while trying to get into the Tredegar House nursing program. Mr. Fischer suffered an accident and was brought in for treatment, and Vivian . . . Miss Whit . . . assisted in attending him. He told us about Mrs. Denholm. She's the one who placed us with Miss Adelaide. . . ." She let her voice fade out, not finishing her thought as the pieces of what had ultimately transpired seemed to finally bring her up short.

"Did you believe Miss Whit had grown rather fond of Mr. Fischer by the time you both came to work here?"

"What does this have to do with anything?" Mr. Fischer asked, his tone respectful and yet somehow foreboding.

I thought Colin would be the one to answer the question, but it was Eugenia Endicott who spoke up first. "Carry on, Mr. Pendragon," she said concisely. "I should very much like to hear what it is you are poking at."

"Miss Bromley . . . ?" Colin pressed.

"They had been courting. . . ." the young nurse answered after a moment, and even though there was hesitation in her voice, there was also something else, something confused and questioning. "I knew that she had an interest in Mr. Fischer and he in her." She finally shifted her gaze directly over to Miss Whit and her forehead flinched with the slightest grimace. "Is that what you mean, Mr. Pendragon?"

"It is precisely what I mean. And tell me, Miss Bromley, are you familiar with Miss Whit's youngest sister?"

"Emmy . . . ?" she said at once. "Vivian, what is he talking about? Is any of this true?"

"Hush up, Philippa," Mr. Fischer growled, but it was far too late.

Colin stepped toward Mr. Fischer for the second time, placing himself between the coachman and Philippa Bromley. "Thank you, Miss Bromley. Your honesty has been refreshing amongst the layers of deception at work here. I had thought to find you innocent and I am pleased to see that you are."

"I don't understand. . . ." Miss Bromley mumbled, stabbing a sleeve at her eyes and I realized that she had begun crying. I gently moved off the sofa and handed her my handkerchief, and as I stepped back, I found Colin looking at me with the faintest hint of a smile.

"Mr. Pruitt . . ." he said, his tone all grim authority. "Will you be so kind as to open my valise and extract its contents."

Valise? I had not even noticed a valise when I'd come in and so was forced to move around to the front of the sofa before I caught sight of the small, black leather satchel tucked beneath. "Of course," I answered. I seized it from where he had placed it and flicked open the latch, stuffing my hand inside.

"The paper first, if you please," he said, and I could tell that he had come up behind me, his anticipation as keen as that of everyone else in the room.

I pulled out a thin piece of paper that was laid atop something small and hard wrapped inside tissue paper. With my heart beginning to gallop and my stomach lurching for reasons I could hardly fathom since I had no idea what I held in my hand, I carefully unfolded the paper and stared down at what was written there. After a minute I glanced back at Colin and was about to ask what he wanted me to do with it when he said. "Would you read it for us, please?"

My throat was already dry as I felt the eyes of everyone in the room fall upon me. "It is a certificate of live birth," I began, "for Devlin Fischer. The date is April twenty-fourth, 1865. The father is Bertram Fischer, listed here as deceased, and the mother . . ." My voice faltered as I quickly cleared it again. "The mother is Margaret Helen Fischer, nee Hardiston."

"And what else is in the valise, Mr. Pruitt . . . ?" Colin asked quickly before anyone could even react to the name.

I thrust my hand back inside and grasped the hard, pointed object wrapped within. Holding my hands as steady as possible I unwrapped the small object, revealing a woman's hairpin in the shape of a butterfly, covered with tiny diamond chips all along the delicate wings. I lifted it up for everyone to see, and as I did so, something on the back of it caught my eye.

"That's mine. . . ." Mr. Fischer protested, jumping to his feet. "That belonged to me mum."

"There are initials on the back," I continued as I suddenly realized what I was looking at. "A.E.," I read before letting my gaze slide over to Eugenia Endicott.

"I happened to find this in your flat this morning, Mr. Fischer," Colin spoke up into the abrupt silence. "Regrettably, you weren't there, so I had to let myself in. I'm afraid Miss Whit's grandmother does not regard you well and was only too pleased to tell me of this astonishing lady's pin she claimed you liked to show about that she was quite sure did not belong to you." He gave a small shrug. "You say this was your mother's and yet the name Margaret Hardiston does not carry the initials A. E."

Mr. Fischer's eyes narrowed and his face went rigid. "You lot are not fit to say me mum's name," he seethed, his face red and his demeanor menacing even though Colin had him shielded in the corner. "She was a kind woman, a good woman, who spent the whole a 'er life sickly and frail because she'd been cast out by the Endicott family before she were even born as a shame and an embarrassment. She 'eld on to that bloody pin as though it were a point a pride, but it weren't nothin' 'cause we had nothin' . . . nothin' . . . and none a you lot ever cared a shite. I tried ta get 'er ta sell it, we coulda lived off it fer a year, but she wouldn't do it. Made me swear not ta sell it after she were gone. Told me it were a reminder that we come from noble people even though she didn't even know 'oo the bloody 'ell A.E. was. But I found out after me mum died. I were only a lad, but I swore I'd spend the rest a me life findin' these people and makin' 'em pay fer wot they did ta 'er. *Ta me.*" His eyes were filled with hatred as he glared at Lord Endicott and his sister. "Every one of 'em."

"That's enough, Mr. Fischer," Colin warned. "You have had your say and I have heard quite enough of your murderous excuses." To punctuate his words he sucked in a breath that puffed out his chest in a display of the muscles he so carefully tended. It appeared to have the intended effect, as Mr. Fischer rocked on his heels a moment before dropping back onto the settee next to Mr. McPherson.

Colin turned his gaze to Miss Eugenia. "This pin once belonged to your sister, didn't it?" Colin pressed her. "Miss Adelaide could not bear the thought of that child being left to the world's caprices, even though you could."

"You will stop now, Mr. Pendragon," Lord Endicott snapped, shuffling in his seat, though he did not stand up.

Colin glanced back at Mr. Fischer, his eyes boring into the younger man's. "I'm afraid you made a terrible mistake, Mr. Fischer. You may have intended to make Adelaide Endicott pay for the ills of your birth and those of your mother, but Miss Adelaide was innocent. She was simply a woman with a kind heart who tried to assuage the grievances of her father"—he swung his eyes to Miss Eugenia, who looked sallow and near to fainting—"and her sister Eugenia, who is, in fact, your grandmother. Margaret Hardiston was your child, wasn't she, Miss Eugenia? There was no scullery maid. You are the one who nearly lost your life at the hands of your father. You were the one forced to give up a child you could never keep. That was why your sister could not let it be. She knew—"

"That is an abomination and a lie," Lord Endicott howled as he forced himself to his feet, his face fouled with anger.

"Then I invite you to prove me wrong," Colin tossed off in the simplest of tones. "Reveal your back to us, Miss Eugenia. Show me that it bears no scars from a beating that almost took your life and that of your unborn child sixty years ago."

If a group of people can hold their collective breath, then that is surely what happened before Lord Endicott seemed to recover himself and roar, "*She will do no such thing!*"

It hardly came as a surprise, given the unseemliness of Colin's suggestion, and yet I was startled when the grimmest sort of smirk bolted across his face as he stared back at Lord Endicott. "I presumed you would object to such a display." He turned to Emily Wilton, still seated next to Philippa Bromley, taking a single step to the side so that the young woman could no longer see her mistress. "Miss Wilton," he said, "I know you attend to Miss Eugenia and must now ask you to divulge whether you have observed these egregious scars that are upon your mistress's back?"

Emily Wilton looked horrified as she stared back at Colin, and it was all the answer that was needed.

"Enough," Eugenia Endicott demanded as she stood up and rounded on Mr. Fischer, who looked as though he had been punched square in the face. "You are a wretched man. You thought to exact revenge and succeeded in nothing more than stealing the life of the only person who ever gave a damn about you. About any of you. A woman whose kindness was far greater than my own. And if you believe I have not paid for my transgression every day of my life since the birth of your accursed mother, then you are indeed the hollowest of men. I wish we *had* died that day. At least that would have spared Addie from the scourge of my recklessness. But now I shall see you hang for what you have done, Mr. Fischer, and perhaps you as well, Miss Whit. For that is all I have left." She seized her gown and swept from the room without a glance back at any of us.

"No . . . !" Miss Whit cried out. "It wasn't my fault. *It was him . . . it wasn't me . . . !*" but Miss Eugenia was already gone.

"Vivian . . ." Miss Bromley groaned as she started to move to her friend before pulling up short and sagging impotently.

"You will ring Scotland Yard, Mr. Galloway," Colin ordered, "and tell them they are urgently needed by me. Ask for Acting Inspector Maurice Evans, if you please."

"As you wish," the man said in little more than a whisper as he headed out of the room.

No one else moved except Colin, who went to the door and leaned against it with a casualness that belied what had occurred. "If you wish to attend to your sister . . ." he suggested to Lord Endicott after a moment.

"I fear I have contributed enough to her undoing and shall wait here for the Yard to sort these villains out." He looked over at Emily Wilton, and as his gaze rose I could see that his eyes were rimmed in red with a grief that felt almost palpable. "Would you mind tending to her, Miss Wilton . . . ?"

The young woman rose at once and left the room, leaving the rest of us to linger in the awkward silence with nary another word spoken between us.

CHAPTER 29

We waited at Layton Manor just long enough for Maurice Evans and a contingency of his men to arrive from the Yard, and with little more than a hurried explanation and a promise to stop by his office within a couple hours, we hastened away with Lady Stuart. I had finally managed to alert Colin to Paul's success in finding Charlotte Hutton's rooms, which made a marked change in his demeanor. There was little time for celebration with Mrs. Hutton so close at hand.

"However did you happen upon Devlin Fischer's birth certificate?" Lady Stuart asked Colin the minute the three of us were headed back to her house.

"There is a studious young man in the General Register Office who thinks me fascinating and colorful, and I have done nothing to dissuade him," Colin answered absently, his eyes focused on the road ahead, and I knew he was desperate for the driver to move faster.

"But how did you make the correlation between Mr. Fischer and Miss Eugenia in the first place?" she continued to pry, clearly unaware of Colin's distraction.

"Mr. Fischer had the means to have committed the murder every bit as much as the nurse, Miss Whit and, of course, Mr.

Nettle. But given the association between Mr. Fischer and Miss Whit, the fact that it preceded the start of Adelaide Endicott's hauntings, it seemed to me that one of them had to be leading the other. In this case I suspected it most likely to be Mr. Fischer, since Miss Whit's family resides in the Highbury ward of Islington and has for some generations without incident. But Mr. Fischer's upbringing quickly proved a far sight murkier. . . ." His voice trailed off as his attentions went back to the road.

"And . . . ?" Lady Stuart pressed.

Colin glanced back at her as though she had not been paying the least bit of attention. "I knew a motive was almost certain to be found there. What else could it have been? Mr. Nettle was far too convenient a scapegoat. Even a fool could concoct a better defense for himself than what Mr. Nettle was left with. So once I knew that Miss Adelaide had not taken her own life, I had only to review the remaining possibilities to see who was left." He turned his face back to the window. "It was always about access, motive, and reason," he muttered, squinting into the distance ahead of us. "Just as it ever is." Without warning he abruptly whipped around and stared at me. "Did you tell Paul we would be at Lady Stuart's?"

"Mrs. Behmoth knew where I . . ." But my response instantly became irrelevant before it was roundly overwhelmed by a great *whoop* and the unmistakable sound of Paul's young voice hollering.

"*MR. P.!*"

And that was all it took for Colin to fling the carriage door open and leap down, which was also well before the driver had any inkling that he was about to do so. Lady Stuart let out a gasp, but not before the driver, having doubtless felt the shift in weight beneath him, sharply reined in the horses, sending the two of us jerking forward like a couple of raggedy dolls.

"Wot's 'appened?" the man called out in alarm as he brought the cab up short.

"We need to get out here," I answered even as Lady Stuart was climbing down from the cab with me on her heels. I reached into my pocket to settle his fare when I heard Colin.

"Don't let him go, Ethan," he said, signaling back to me from where he was standing, huddled with Paul. "We'll not be staying. Fetch Lady Stuart another cab."

He didn't bother to finish his sentence, nor did he need to. It was evident by Paul's presence and the animated way in which the young lad was conferring with Colin that Charlotte Hutton had reappeared.

"You must forgive our hurried retreat," I said to Lady Stuart as I waved another carriage down for her, "but I suspect our other case is coming to its own culmination." At least I hoped that to be the case.

"You needn't explain." She turned and offered me her beautiful smile, making it clear that she had already guessed and understood.

"We mustn't delay...." Colin announced as he hurried back over to us. "Pardon our haste...." he flung back over his shoulder as he and Paul climbed into the carriage. "Your assistance was crucial this morning, and we shall be back to pay you our highest regards as soon as possible," he mumbled as he took a seat before turning back and staring out at me. "*Are you coming?!*"

"Go," she insisted with that smile as another cab pulled in beside her, and I did not have to be prodded twice.

"To Victoria Station," Colin hollered up to the driver the moment my foot struck the running board. "And twice your fee if you get us there with ungodly speed."

Our driver also did not need to be prodded twice as the coach whip cracked and the carriage lurched forward before I had even made it fully inside. With the door wagging behind me, I threw myself sideways into the seat across from Colin and Paul, leaving Paul to lean out with a snicker and snatch the door shut with a resounding *bang*.

"Charlotte Hutton returned to her rooms some time ago," Colin explained in a rush as though I might not have already figured that out for myself. "Paul sent one of his boys back to our flat but you'd already left, so they followed her down to Victoria Station."

"She's 'eadin' fer Dover and then goin' to the Continent," Paul piped up, which I had also surmised.

"How long ago did she arrive at Victoria?" I asked.

Paul gave a shrug. " 'Bout an 'our."

I was about to ask when the train was scheduled to leave but instead was forced to seize the nearest handhold to keep myself from flying across the carriage's interior as we heaved around a corner, and given that action I assumed I already had my answer.

"Tip this driver extra," Colin mumbled under his breath, although I noticed that he was holding on every bit as hard as I was. "Unless he sends us onto our side," he added.

There was a sudden slew of curses hurled from our driver as we lurched first one way and then another, and I was certain I felt one of the back wheels raise up before slamming back down, sending us in a paroxysm of rocking that tossed my stomach unrelentingly. I glanced toward the window but did not see what had caused our trouble, and was grateful when I spotted the station drawing closer. The tall redbrick structure with its slate mansard roof and cream-colored chimneys rising high above felt like a beacon as, inconceivably, I felt the coach gain speed.

"We're almost there," I said, more for my own edification than anyone else's, which became even clearer when Paul gave a roar of delight as though he would be sorry to see the ride end.

"Which platform is her train leaving from?" Colin asked as a flurry of shouting and wrath could be heard pelting us.

"Number seven," he answered, and as before I could not help but be impressed by this young lad. "I left two a me boys behind ta keep an eye on things. They'll know where she's sittin' and if she's moved around any."

"Outstanding," Colin said under his breath, having been forced to brace himself as the carriage jerked to so abrupt a stop I feared the horses must have suffered some injury. "Be quick, Ethan," Colin prodded unnecessarily as I shoved a handful of change up to the driver before adding an extra half crown.

I leapt to the ground and my legs felt wobbly for an instant as they gauged whether the earth beneath them would now hold steady. The driver beamed down at me and shouted something I did not catch as I was already sprinting toward where I had seen Colin and Paul fade into the crowd. I bolted through the entrance, my eyes raking back and forth in search of Colin, while making great haste toward platform seven. It did occur to me that I might need to be somewhat inconspicuous lest Charlotte Hutton might still be wandering around to ensure her own successful departure, and yet as I drew nearer to the platform there were so many people running one way or another that I realized I looked no more or less obvious than anyone else trying to make a connection.

"'Ey . . ."

The voice startled me until I realized it was Paul's. I had flown right past him and Colin, and another, smaller boy, all of whom were huddled right at the entrance to the platform. "She got on 'bout twenty minutes ago and ain't left since," the smaller lad was saying, a skinny little redhead with an angular face and a nose like a hawk's beak. "I got Ernie 'alfway down the tracks keepin' an eye on things. I ain't moved from 'ere. She ain't gone nowhere. You can pick 'er off like a boil."

Colin's brow furrowed as he stared down the platform, the diffuse lighting giving it an ethereal, almost mythic radiance. "You had best stay here," he said to the redhead, "but you must holler if we flush her out this way." He looked back at Paul. "Get us to your boy Ernie and then I want the two of you to come back here with this tyke and wait. If she does come back this way, you lot should follow her, but do not, *do not,* try to engage her in any way. I will have your word on it, Paul. For you and both of your mates."

Paul made a face as his eyes rolled skyward. "A'right . . ." he conceded. "But ya ain't gotta worry 'bout us."

"I shan't worry about you," Colin shot right back, "because you will not be involved." He started for the platform, keeping to the side farthest from the train itself. "Now where is your friend?"

Paul gave the sigh of a man many times his age and struck out down the length of the train, carefully following Colin's initiative by staying to the far side of the platform. We had passed no more than four or five cars before Paul waved us to halt. Colin and I sidled up to the nearest pillar and waited as Paul let out a *coo* that sounded more like a real pigeon than any of the innumerable birds that were loitering and rummaging on the rafters above. A response was immediate and not an instant later a pint-sized boy with a floppy cap tugged low on his head and brown eyes the size of saucers was next to us.

"She ain't moved," he said with such rigid seriousness that it would have made me laugh had the circumstances not been so grave. "She's two cars up in the second room from the back. I followed 'er in before the buggered conductor threw me arse off 'is ruddy train."

"Well done," Colin said, his eyes already set on the train car young Ernie had referenced. "Now you two get back to where I've instructed and wait, and keep your eyes open. We will be needing a bobby shortly, and there will almost certainly be a reward for your help once this wretched woman has been turned over to the Yard."

"I'll take a piece a that!" Ernie grinned.

"You'll take wot I give ya," Paul quickly corrected. "Now scoot, ya little pox." The young lad, still grinning like a fool, did precisely as ordered even though Paul hung back, turning his gaze back to Colin. "Ya sure ya don't need me ta 'elp out . . . ?" he asked again.

"You will get back to where I have indicated or you will find yourself decidedly out of work as far as we are concerned."

"A'right . . ." Paul groaned, his voice thick with disappointment.

The train's whistle suddenly screeched its warning, alerting those of us thronging the platform that the time was nigh to climb aboard or move away. A great gust of steam was expelled from beneath the sides of the engine, setting Colin to motion in an instant.

"Go in through the front of the car," he instructed as we both crossed the platform's width, "and work your way back to me. With any luck she is seated in her compartment and will be none the wiser until we are at her door. But if you do come upon her, you must do your best to flush her back to me."

I nodded before splitting off from his side and making my

way to the front of the car. It was fortunate that the train was parked to the left of the platform so that the compartment windows faced out onto the tracks beyond rather than toward the platform itself. Unless she was traversing the hallway at this precise moment, there was no way she would spot me.

I seized the handrail and swung aboard, entering a small lounge area that served the compartments stacked behind it. Two men were seated at a table conversing over drinks, paying me no mind whatsoever, and this continued good fortune was enough to set my pulse quickening. A lady would never sit here on her own, and for that I felt great relief. We would catch Charlotte Hutton unawares and, for reasons I could not exactly put my finger on, I knew the outcome would be better for it.

With a quick intake of breath I made my way over to the side of the car where the narrow hallway stretched out from the lounge, and immediately spied Colin already planted just outside the door that young Ernie had indicated. He was standing stock-still in front of it, staring directly at it, and I could not help but wonder what thoughts must be racing through his mind.

His eyes shifted to me as I approached him, and he moved a single finger to his lips before, to my surprise, a tight smile broke out behind it. He said nothing, for there was nothing to say, but reached out and twisted the knob, pushing the door open with the simplicity of a man merely searching for his seat. I caught my breath, as though the very act of inhaling or exhaling might cause Charlotte Hutton to disappear or reappear, and whether there is any truth to such a notion, it was only after I saw the woman sitting by herself at the window, her gaze just beginning to swivel around, that I was finally able to expel the air I had been hoarding.

For an instant I thought we had failed as the woman before us had a hat pulled low over her head and what fragments of hair I could see looked to be a coppery color, and yet when those icy-blue eyes slid over me, I knew it was she. I cannot say what I had expected would happen when she saw us, but it was not the sight of the serene smile that slowly played at her lips. "You know," she said after what felt like an interminable amount of time, "I was beginning to think you actually weren't going to make it. How disappointing it would have been to make such a pedestrian retreat. Well beneath you, Mr. Pendragon."

The train's whistle gave another resounding blast as the two of us hovered in the doorway, Colin filling its slender frame while I loomed just behind him. If Charlotte Hutton intended to make some last-minute bid for freedom, she did not seem the least anxious about doing so, though neither did she stand up. She was wearing the same black cloak that she had worn on both of our previous encounters. It was clasped at her throat but had otherwise fallen open to reveal an emerald-colored dress beneath that made a striking contrast to her newly auburn hair. The whole of it made her look different enough, yet even so, there was no denying that familiar beauty and those cold, remote eyes.

"I am glad we have not disappointed you then," Colin said, his voice as calm and steady as ever, though I could feel the tension rolling off him. "Perhaps you would not mind joining Mr. Pruitt and myself on the platform so we may finally settle on the proper resolution to the many murders you left scattered about in your wake."

"You already have Wynn Tessler convicted and awaiting the gallows. Is that not enough? Whatever is it you want from me? I have already confided to your Mr. Pruitt that I was every bit the victim of those who actually lost their lives to Mr. Tessler."

I could feel Colin stiffen as he stared back at her. "You extorted an inordinate amount of money from innocent people and left without any regard to the murders of seven people including your own husband and young son. If you were really so tortured by your fear of Mr. Tessler, then I fail to see how, in the months since his arrest, you never came forward to assist in his conviction."

"If you needed me to seal the fate of that monster, Mr. Pendragon, then I am afraid I must believe your reputation to be more fiction than fact." She continued to stare at Colin, not even blinking, her voice coming as smoothly and easily as if we were conversing on the state of the weather. "I was terrified of Mr.

Tessler, which is why I stole away with my daughter and whatever money I could get my hands on. You were certainly of no use in protecting my family. I had already lost my husband and son; did you want me to stay there until my daughter was taken from me too? Or perhaps you wanted me to wait there until I could be dispatched as well? Would that have consoled your vitriol against me?"

"Let me see the wounds on your chest that Mr. Tessler caused," Colin asked, his tone dropping in timbre.

"What?!" she said at once, her tone abruptly inflamed with offense, but not before I noticed the flicker of something startled and off guard stirring behind her eyes. "What sort of effrontery is this? Do you intend to demean me even further?"

"Come now," he pressed quietly, yet with an underlying force that was diamond hard. "You were keen to share them with Mr. Pruitt when you thought to convince him of your innocence several nights ago. Surely you would not begrudge me the same evidence."

Her face slowly curled with distaste. Whatever game she had been playing at had evidently reached its zenith, as I realized the wounds she had shown me had indeed been fake.

She stood up slowly and, though she was not tall, there was something almost regal in her manner as she shrugged her shoulders back, her eyes still pinned solely on Colin. "I believe you are correct, Mr. Pendragon," she said after a moment just before the train's whistle let out its third shriek. "It would seem we will indeed need to settle this elsewhere, for I will put myself in the hands of a Scotland Yard matron before I will ever allow you such a glimpse."

Colin's head snapped back as though she had struck him, and then he took a single step out into the narrow hallway. "As you please," he said.

She reached into the space above her seat and pulled down a large bag and a small valise, turning to me. "If it would not be too much trouble . . . ?" she asked, even as I took it from her. "Ever the kind one. That's why I made sure to speak with you alone. I'll bet you even believed me when I told you I'd meant to find the two of you together that first night." She let out a low, soft chuckle. "So uncomplicated."

She slid her purse onto her wrist and took Colin's arm with her other hand, allowing him to escort her toward the exit just as the train let out a last peal and belch of steam. I felt the car beneath our feet jerk brusquely and then begin to move with the slow ponderousness of a tortoise upon waking. Colin quickened his pace, pushing out into the open space where the door that led back down to the platform still stood agape. "Give me your hand," Colin instructed to her as he moved down to the step floating just above the platform. We had hardly gained the slightest speed, and I realized I would be able to easily toss her bags out and collect them once I had made my own escape.

"As you wish," Charlotte Hutton answered, a curious answer, I thought.

She quickly slid her purse from one arm to the other, and that's when I saw that there was a palm-sized derringer in her hand that had not been there only an instant before. The train screeched once more, warning all the stragglers still rushing to get aboard that their last opportunity was rapidly closing, which effectively covered the sound of the twin pops. Had it not been for the immediate sulfuric smell of spent powder, it would have taken me another moment or two before I realized that Colin had sagged back in the open doorway. Before I could move, or think, or comprehend, Charlotte Hutton raised her left foot and kicked Colin squarely in the chest.

His arms pinwheeled backward as I saw the two small red blotches beginning to blossom on the chest of his white shirt. I fumbled Charlotte Hutton's bags in an effort to lose them and lurch forward to grab Colin, but I was too late. He tumbled backward onto the platform like a discarded puppet, and I felt certain my heart had stopped even as the train began to pick up a modicum of speed.

"What will it be, Mr. Pruitt?" I heard the low, malicious voice purr into my ear, her lips so close I could feel her breath rake across my neck. "Will you stay here and detain me or will you leap down to save that scourge?"

She had not gotten the words fully out of her mouth before I flung myself down onto the platform, slamming onto the wooden planks hard enough to steal my breath, as we had gained far more speed than I had realized. I scrabbled to right myself and regain my feet, my mind an echo of terrified silence, and that was when I heard it. A sound that chilled me to the bone. She was laughing. Charlotte Hutton was laughing.

CHAPTER 30

———◆◇◆———

Patience is a trait upon which the cases that Colin and I persevere are inherently constructed. They resist being hastened and will only reveal themselves once the layers that inevitably comprise each one are meticulously peeled away. So a person could not be faulted for supposing that a man with such a learned gift for patience might well be able to apply the very same principle to himself. But that would be wrong.

I had bellowed like a madman the moment I managed to shove myself back to my feet on that godforsaken train platform, and had done so with such frantic desperation that I'd not even realized I had twisted my ankle, which would be the size of a melon within an hour's time. All I knew in that instant was that I needed to get to Colin, and there was nothing in the whole of the world that was going to stop me in my pursuit. I had ceased being aware of the departing train, though I sensed its accelerating movement off to my right. My sole concern was Colin, laid out on the platform, arms and legs akimbo, two spots of burgeoning redness on his chest, one of them a clustering mass of frothy bubbles forewarning that at least one of his lungs had been punctured. But before I could fully register that fact, I was horrified to see a larger pool of blood oozing from behind his head.

I'm not sure when I became aware of the fact that Paul and his mates had come skidding over to me, but I started barking directions at them as though I had some control of the situation, which I most assuredly did not. I sent Paul's lads to fetch a bobby, or a whole phalanx of bobbies, whatever it was going to take to ensure that we got Colin to a hospital with the greatest of haste. Paul stayed at my side and I told him to compress the two wounds on Colin's chest to stop them from seeping, and felt my throat instantly catch when, without a word, he flung himself across Colin's torso, using his small body to apply the necessary pressure that his scrawny arms would likely have been ill-suited to achieve.

"Don't hurt him. . . ." I heard myself start to say before clamping my foolish mouth shut.

I turned my attention to the wound at the back of his skull. His cranium bled profusely, as was the case with the head, I knew that, but it was still terrifying to see the puddle slowly pooling there. He was unconscious, and when I pried one of his eyelids apart it was to find his pupil so blown open that there was only the thinnest ring of blue visible. I shed my coat and draped it over both Colin and Paul, hoping the heat from the boy's body would help keep Colin warm. And only then did I finally become aware of the passage of time. If I have ever been a man of patience it deserted me in that second, and I thought surely I would fly apart in a million fractured pieces if help did not arrive at once.

And so it finally did.

The two boys came skittering back with two bobbies, a doctor one of them had found on another platform, and an elderly health care worker who worked at the station treating motion sickness and other mild discomforts. An ambulance was summoned, and even when the doctor tried to shoo me away after peeling Paul off Colin's chest, I would not move. I prayed for the learned man to announce that everything was going to be all right, but he said nothing as he hastily fussed over Colin. Even after his prostrate form was loaded into the back of the ambulance, I was offered no encouragement or consolation. It made me feel that I might truly burst from the dread. In that moment, patience was as foreign a concept as I could have conceived.

None of that compared, however, to the unrestrained rashness that occurred later in the day.

While a group of doctors at St. Thomas's Hospital worked on Colin in one of the surgical rooms, I was exiled to a hallway two floors below with explicit instructions not to pester the staff. My presence, I was curtly informed, was superfluous, as I was not family and could therefore make no decisions on Colin's behalf. So I sent Paul and his mates in opposing directions to collect Sir Atherton and Mrs. Behmoth. There was no doubt that Sir Atherton's presence would be critical, but I cannot precisely say why it had suddenly felt so important to have Mrs. Behmoth with me as well.

Only after Sir Atherton had arrived were we finally able to learn that Colin was a very lucky man. While one bullet had indeed punctured his chest and collapsed a lung, the other had entered at so steep an angle that it had been diverted by a rib before exiting at the midpoint of his underarm. The wound to his head was nothing more than a gash of several inches and there was no underlying damage to his skull. It all amounted to a great deal of discomfort ahead, but Colin was expected to make a full recovery as long as infections were kept at bay.

The news brought such an embarrassment of relief to me that I found myself struggling to maintain my decorum. I had to excuse myself and go for a walk to steel my heart and head; and upon returning some thirty minutes later was met by an agitated Sir Atherton, who hurried over to me.

"He's awake." He said it as though it were a single word, ensuring that I had the good news at once. "He's awake and he's . . ." Sir Atherton waved his arms and stepped back. "Go to him. It's you he needs."

I dashed down to the room where Colin was, a sense of defiance in my stride as I felt the eyes of the staff, who could no longer keep me from seeing him, follow me as I pushed my way inside. And there was Colin: lying on his side on a wheeled table with a pile of sheets beneath him, his face so sallow and drawn that he looked almost monochromatic. My breath caught in spite of my best efforts and I had to blink several times to assure my composure. It took another moment before Colin finally looked up and spotted me, his eyes once more a brilliant blue, if shot through with cracks of red, and there was a great deal of fire there. Indeed. A *great* deal of fire.

"*Where the hell have you been?!*" His voice came out breathless and slurry. "These people are cretins. How could you leave me with them? Get me the bloody hell *out of here!*"

And so it went for the entirety of a full week until he was finally released, against the doctor's orders, but with Mrs. Behmoth's assurance that she would see to it that he convalesced as directed. I cannot say whether Mrs. Behmoth actually believed her pledge, but only two days after coming home he began to complain of boredom, even though he was shuffling around the flat like a wizened old man, flinching and wincing with nearly every move he made. Had I ever truly believed that Colin could harness himself to exhibit the level of patience he could so readily bring to bear on a case? I decided I had not.

Which was why, a mere week after Colin's homecoming, I begrudgingly agreed to allow Maurice Evans to come for a visit. I also could not deny the feeling that we owed him something after our deception around Charlotte Hutton. What I refused to do, however, was allow myself to imagine how differently the case might have turned out had Mr. Evans been at Victoria Station with a battalion of his men.

". . . And it is without any thanks to either of you," Mr. Evans was explaining with a touch of mockery in his tone, even as I continued to study Colin's pallor so as to ensure a quick end to this conversation when his strength inevitably waned. "Nevertheless, I am pleased to inform you both that I have finally been granted the title of Inspector. I am no longer simply *acting* like one." He chuckled.

"Well, it's about bloody time," Colin said. "I was beginning to think your Yard incapable of making even the most banal of decisions."

"Banal, is it?"

Colin winced as he shifted in his chair. I knew better than to fuss over him with company on hand, so I took the opportunity to refresh our tea, making a show of reaching the bottom of the pot without calling for a refill in hopes of subtly encouraging the inspector to bring his visit to a close.

"You are about the only man among that whole lot who is worth a damn," Colin continued as he appeared to settle in again. "It is nice to hear they have likely figured that out for themselves as well."

"Even your compliments have teeth." The inspector laughed before his face slowly drew into something more thoughtful, and I feared I knew what was coming. "I do wish you had included me at Victoria Station when you went after Mrs. Hutton. I might have been able to help, you know. I could have made a difference."

Colin's face paled as he stared down at his tea still sitting on the table in front of him. It hurt my heart to see him looking weak and contrite, and I had even less of a stomach for anyone else to see it. "Come now—" I started to say.

"The regret is mine," Colin cut me off. "And you may be assured that I am unable to forget our folly with Mrs. Hutton for even an instant while I am awake. She has even begun to haunt my dreams." His expression darkened. "I tell you I will not cease until I have captured that woman and made her pay for everything she has wrought. She is the devil himself."

If Inspector Evans had intended to chide Colin further, it dissipated as he pushed himself to his feet. "Then I hope you will allow me and my men to work with the two of you to finally bring this woman to justice. I'm talking a real partnership. I'll not need anyone's approval anymore."

Colin flicked his eyes to the inspector as a warm smile brushed past his lips. "That would please me. I shall not lose this woman a third time."

A sudden pounding at our door startled all three of us before I managed to jump to my feet and hurry to the landing. "We'll have no more company," I called down to Mrs. Behmoth.

"And I had best be getting back to the Yard before they come looking for me," the inspector said, taking my hint.

Colin pushed himself to his feet in spite of the incessant discomfort I could see he was suffering and shook the inspector's hand. "You have been a worthy ally, Inspector, and I shall not allow Ethan to treat you with such disregard again," he announced impishly.

"Consider me admonished," I said with a chuckle of my own, only to have it quickly die on my lips as I heard the sound of twin footfalls thudding up the stairs. My brow furrowed as I turned to find Mrs. Behmoth trudging up with Superintendent Tottenshire close on her heels. Was the whole of Scotland Yard intent on coming over to disturb us?!

"Now don't ya be givin' me one a yer looks." Mrs. Behmoth scowled at me as she ushered the superintendent into the room. "You want 'im out, you'll 'ave ta do it yerselves."

"I thought I was jesting when I said they would come looking for me. . . ." Inspector Evans spoke up with a wry snort.

"Settle yourselves," Superintendent Tottenshire demanded of all of us. "Mr. Pendragon . . . Mr. Pruitt . . ." he continued as he pulled his hat from his head and sat down on the settee as though he had been invited to do so.

"I suppose I'll fetch some fresh tea, but I ain't got any biscuits."

"Tea is fine," the superintendent answered before either Colin or I could. "We won't be staying long enough for biscuits, though Inspector Evans tells me you're quite the baker." He tossed a quick smile to Mrs. Behmoth that looked more pained than pleased as his eyes drifted over to his inspector, who had remained standing beside me on the landing. "Get in here and sit down, Evans. Why are you hanging by the stairs like that?"

Inspector Evans did as instructed while Mrs. Behmoth headed back downstairs. I moved around to sit next to Colin again, determined to give this man five minutes to have his say before I tossed the two of them out like yesterday's paper.

"What a pleasant surprise," Colin said archly. "So very unexpected that you would come to check on me."

"Yes . . . well . . ." The superintendent's eyes snapped from Colin to Inspector Evans and then back to Colin again. "How are you then?"

"I have been better," Colin answered, and even through his glibness I was struck that he had told these men the truth.

"You know we could have helped if you had taken us into your confidence. . . ."

"Inspector Evans has already made that very point," I said, wishing Mrs. Behmoth would hurry back so I could end this strained conversation.

"It remains to be seen." Colin shrugged noncommittally.

I waited impatiently for the superintendent to counter Colin's rebuff, all the while trying to decide how I could bring this conversation to its most expedient conclusion, and was surprised when he said nothing. Instead, the four of us sat there in awkward silence, listening to the sounds of Mrs. Behmoth as she finally plodded back up the stairs. We all remained just so as she came back into the room with a tray filled with tea things, including some of yesterday's gingersnaps, which she had clearly unearthed from somewhere. She set the whole of it on the low table between us and I gave her a rudimentary thank-you. Colin poured the tea and passed our cups around, his ministrations the only noise impeding the otherwise churchlike hush.

"So tell me, Superintendent . . ." It was Colin who finally broke the silence as he sat back, cradling his teacup almost lovingly. "Beyond your obvious concern for my well-being, whatever is it that has brought you to our door in the wake of your newly christened inspector?"

To my surprise the man heaved a burdensome sigh before sagging back on the settee, his eyes raking past Inspector Evans before finally settling on Colin. "I see you remain astute, Mr. Pendragon. It is good to know that your wounds have not diminished you."

Colin flashed a tight smile. "I am not so easily undone. Now out with it."

"There was a murder just over a week ago," he began, sipping at his tea as though he were discussing the most ordinary thing. "You'll not have heard about it as it took place in Whitechapel, just off Framingham Lane, and we have worked exceedingly hard to keep it quiet."

Colin frowned and I could tell he was already intrigued. "Keep it quiet? Why ever would you do that?"

"You will understand precisely why when I explain to you the circumstances around it," he answered grimly.

"Was it a woman?" Colin asked, though I wasn't at all sure why he would have arrived at that conclusion.

The superintendent's face darkened, standing in stark contrast to the grayness of his oversized sideburns, as he stared back at Colin, his eyes veiled by something I could not yet place. "Not diminished at all. . . ." he mumbled again as he set his teacup down. "Yes, Mr. Pendragon, it was a woman. A prostitute. An addict. It was a brutal killing. Evans here saw it. . . ." He nodded toward the inspector, who took the acknowledgment as consent to have his say since Superintendent Tottenshire evidently had reservations about continuing himself.

"Perhaps you're not up to hearing this. . . ." he began to say.

"Nonsense," the superintendent fired back at once. "Of course he wants to hear it."

Colin gave the merest of nods, though he couldn't have hidden the interest shuffling around behind his eyes if he had tried to.

"It was indeed a horrible thing," Inspector Evans finally reiterated. "She was found in her room, her chest cleaved open from her neck to her nether regions. But the worst of it was that her organs had been removed and lined up on the floor alongside where she lay as though they were on display. The coroner says there's an ovary missing and a goodly portion of her bowels, but everything else was there."

Colin set his tea down and leaned in. "How have you managed to keep this quiet?"

"It's been damn well nearly impossible," the superintendent spoke up again. "We've kept the woman who discovered the body in custody." He slid his eyes sideways. "For her own protection," he added without conviction. "And we haven't released a word of it to the press as of yet. But the victim's neighbors are getting suspicious having the Yard crawling all over their building, asking questions, poking about. I'm afraid they're not going to believe the story we've been peddling—that she's gone missing—for very much longer." He heaved another sigh and ran a nervous hand through one of his sideburns.

"There's more," Colin stated with extraordinary surety.

Superintendent Tottenshire nodded his head dismally. "It happened again sometime late last night. Another prostitute. Not a half dozen blocks away. Same sort of vicious thing. Carved her up . . . laid her out . . . It's barbarous."

Colin stood up and went over to the fireplace, and I wondered if they noticed how gingerly he moved. "You're afraid it's your Ripper again, aren't you?" he said as he leaned against the mantel and stared at the flames. "What's it been . . . seven years since he last struck?"

I thought surely my heart had ceased to beat as I watched the superintendent grit his teeth with an expression that bordered on agony. "Seven years exactly," he confirmed. "The Yard would value your assistance, Mr. Pendragon. We simply cannot be swallowed up by that terror again. It will be the undoing of us all."

I stared at Colin's back, slightly bent with the pain and exhaustion I knew he continued to suffer, and willed him to refuse the case. I knew it was a terrible thing I wished for . . . selfish . . . but I could not help it. So I waited for him to turn around, holding my breath as if my bidding could be assured through the silence of my very being, but when he did finally turn I understood at once what his response would be.

"I will not answer to the Yard," he said.

"We work together," the superintendent parried back at once.

"I shall take the lead."

"We work together."

"I shall take the lead and allow Inspector Evans to work with us at all times. He can keep you and yours informed as he sees fit."

The superintendent gritted his teeth again and ran a hand down a massive sideburn for the second time. "Very well, but you will report to me on a twice-weekly basis."

"Mr. Pruitt will do that," Colin answered blithely, and I was not in the least surprised that he would agree to nothing more. "And while I am working on this case for you, I shall expect you to use your vast resources to find Charlotte Hutton in Switzerland or wherever the hell else it is that she's gone. That woman will *not* be allowed to escape. And I shall have your word on that or you may leave this flat at once."

I could see that both Superintendent Tottenshire and Inspector Evans were taken aback, nevertheless it took no more than a moment before the superintendent nodded his assent. "You have my word, Mr. Pendragon."

Colin pushed himself off the mantel and forced himself fully upright, his tenacity marred by the briefest of flinches. "Then let us begin at once," he said, his voice strong and assured. "And woe be unto this Whitechapel fiend and the abhorrent Charlotte Hutton."

ACKNOWLEDGMENTS

Having a novel published is an exciting and remarkable event. Having a series released is an utter thrill. None of it would be possible without you—the loyal and curious reader. It is to you that I owe the humblest thanks. You took a chance on me, whether with this book or one before it, and I hope I did not let you down. If you will stick with me I promise to do my utmost to keep you entertained whenever you crack open a Colin Pendragon tale.

There are many other people who are critical to the process that propels a story from my laptop to your hands, and I would be remiss if I did not mention some of them here. The folks at Kensington, especially John Scognamiglio; one of the first to take a chance on me. Paula Reedy and her team keep me honest—any mistakes or historical errors you may find are mine and mine alone. Kristine Mills, Vida Engstrand, and Morgan Elwell all do tremendous work on my behalf.

Huge thanks to Diane Salzberg, Karen Clemens, and Melissa Gelineau, who push me in the best possible ways.

Kathy Green, who was the first person to decide that Colin and Ethan were worth her time, and I am grateful to her for that.

I must give a special shout-out to Mysterious Galaxy, in San Diego, California; Anne Saller of Book Carnival, in Tustin, California, and Barbara Peters at Poisoned Pen, in Scottsdale, Arizona, all of whom have been wonderful to me. Please frequent their independent stores!

My family and friends are endlessly supportive, and I am honored.

Last of all I must thank Tresa Hoffman: Forever in my heart.

Connect with Us

Visit us online at
KensingtonBooks.com
to read more from your favorite authors, see books
by series, view reading group guides, and more.

for sneak peeks, chances to win books and prize packs,
and to share your thoughts with other readers.

facebook.com/kensingtonpublishing
twitter.com/kensingtonbooks

Tell us what you think!

To share your thoughts, submit a review,
or sign up for our eNewsletters, please visit:
KensingtonBooks.com/TellUs.